Also by Amy Poeppel

Limelight
Small Admissions

MUSICAL

CHAIRS

A Novel

AMY POEPPEL

EMILY BESTLER BOOKS
—
ATRIA

New York   London   Toronto   Sydney   New Delhi

EMILY BESTLER BOOKS

ATRIA

An Imprint of Simon & Schuster, Inc.
1230 Avenue of the Americas
New York, NY 10020

First Emily Bestler Books/Atria Paperback edition April 2021

EMILY BESTLER BOOKS/ATRIA PAPERBACK and colophon are trademarks of Simon & Schuster, Inc.

For information about special discounts for bulk purchases, please contact Simon & Schuster Special Sales at 1-866-506-1949 or business@simonandschuster.com.

The Simon & Schuster Speakers Bureau can bring authors to your live event. For more information or to book an event, contact the Simon & Schuster Speakers Bureau at 1-866-248-3049 or visit our website at www.simonspeakers.com.

Interior design by Wendy Blum

Manufactured in the United States of America

3   5   7   9   10   8   6   4   2

Library of Congress Cataloging-in-Publication Data has been applied for.

ISBN 978-1-5011-7641-8
ISBN 978-1-5011-7642-5 (pbk)
ISBN 978-1-5011-7643-2 (ebook)

For my perfectly imperfect family

Things can fall apart, or threaten to, for many reasons, and then there's got to be a leap of faith.
Ultimately, when you're at the edge, you have to go forward or backward;
if you go forward, you have to jump together.

—*Yo-Yo Ma*

I take a very practical view of raising children. I put a sign in each of their rooms: "Checkout Time is 18 years."

—*Erma Bombeck*

PRELUDE

Twenty-Seven Years Ago

For the fourth time in less than twelve hours, Bridget was doing something that could get her pregnant. Staring up at the acoustic-tile ceiling, she sincerely hoped the doctor (an older gentleman who had an air of celibacy about him) wouldn't be able to tell that she'd already been pretty spectacularly inseminated three times since midnight. And she had to remind herself—on the off chance that the doctor *could* detect the cost-free sperm occupying the territory where he was currently placing very expensive Ivy League sperm—that she shouldn't feel guilty about the situation she found herself in. She'd made a clearheaded, deliberate, positive decision to have this procedure done, regardless of what had happened last night, which was why she'd shown up after almost canceling the appointment earlier that morning. She'd settled on one point: she wanted a baby. So all she had done, really, was up the chances. What difference did it make from whom the sperm came, as long as it came from a well-chosen, clever, handsome donor? The donations in Bridget's uterus, whether freely given or contractually obtained, were specimens of the finest order.

With her feet in the stirrups, memories of the previous night ran through her mind, and she smiled.

"And that's all there is to it," the doctor said, snapping off a surgical glove. "Not so romantic, but it may do the trick."

"Super," Bridget said. "I guess we'll have to wait and see."

After lying flat on her back for the requisite period, she left the office, hungover but glowing. She found a pay phone and called Will, who picked up on the first ring.

"I was about to call the police to report you missing," he said.

"Are you hungry? Meet me at that place."

"I was worried! The egg place or the croissant place?"

"Egg," she said. "Half an hour. Love you."

She got on the crosstown bus and took a window seat, deciding she would enjoy this little moment of not knowing one way or the other, of standing on a threshold. She was at the edge of something new, in that space before you begin.

On your mark, get set . . .

JUNE

1

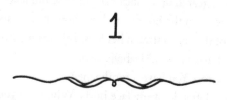

Halfway up the leafy, winding driveway, past the grove of ferns that were beginning to unfurl along the rubbly wall, Bridget's station wagon hit a pothole. The grocery bags on the passenger seat tipped over, sending lemons and onions rolling around on the floor of the car, while one of the suitcases slid from the top of the pile and smacked against the back hatch, upsetting the cats in their carriers. Bridget slowed down. Next to one of the granite boulders was a downed tree, directly under the electrical lines, that had left a debris field all the way to the spot where the driveway forked, the woodsier side leading to the guesthouse, a small Hansel-and-Gretel cottage with gingerbread trim and peeling white shutters. Bridget took the slightly more manicured route, startling a bunch of turkeys by the edge of the forest as she approached, making them scatter like teenagers busted at a keg party. She turned off the car in front of her clapboard weekend house, grateful to stop the sound from both the engine and the radio, which was playing a version of Beethoven's Fifth that was so bad she hadn't been able to stop listening to it. Bridget opened the car door to a preferable sound:

the chirping and croaking of every horny amphibian in and around the pond.

She looked into the backseat, where her cello was securely wedged in, and geared up to start carrying the full load she'd packed for the summer into the house, but her phone rang before she could even get out of the car to stretch her legs. The cats meowed in protest.

"I think I have a cavity," Isabelle said.

"Hi to you, too. You have a toothache?"

"The whole left side of my face hurts. Where are you?"

"I just got to the house and spooked a gaggle of turkeys," Bridget said. "The weather's looking a little iffy—"

"A *rafter* of turkeys. Don't even tell me; I'm so jealous. So, I woke up with this throbbing pain, and I have to go to work. What do I do?"

"Compresses," Bridget told her grown daughter, who was over six thousand miles away. "Gargle with warm water and salt and take Tylenol. Can you make an appointment to see a dentist during your lunch break?"

"I want to go to Dr. Herndon, not some random—"

"You can't wait a year to fill a cavity."

"You think I should come home?" Isabelle asked, as if that were a completely reasonable question.

"There are excellent dentists there. Did you eat breakfast?" It always amazed Bridget to think that in Hong Kong, Isabelle was already experiencing tomorrow.

"I can't chew."

"Have a yogurt."

"I wonder if it's my wisdom teeth; I should have gotten them out in college like everyone else." Isabelle's voice came into focus, and Bridget could tell she'd been taken off speakerphone: "Have you talked to Oscar, like in the past couple of days?"

"I've texted him." Bridget was having a tough time negotiating a pattern of communication with her newlywed son. She didn't want to be overbearing, but she certainly didn't want to seem uninterested in the details of his life. She *was* interested, very much so, in fact. Were weekly calls acceptable? And should she try calling Matt also? Or was it okay that she usually reached out to Oscar, leaving messages since her calls often went to voicemail? They both worked all the time.

"You should call him," said Isabelle. "Cold compresses or hot?"

"Is your face swollen?"

There was a pause as Isabelle, presumably, consulted a mirror. "Not really."

"Hot then," said Bridget. She got out of the car, noticing how damp and warm the air was, how good it smelled, and opened the door to the backseat. "Trust your instincts; they've always been excellent."

"I'm fine, don't worry." And then she added, "It's just that, I some-times wonder what I'm even doing here. I feel like I'm not living my best life, or maybe I mean the *right* life." Isabelle sighed. "I miss you."

That last sentiment made Bridget feel even worse than the thought of her daughter suffering a toothache. "I miss you, too, but this all seems perfectly normal. You're adjusting to a new place. You'll be great as soon as you settle in and make some friends."

"Are you coming to visit?"

The cats were scratching at the bars of their carriers.

"I don't have our fall schedule yet. It depends on our new violinist, who—"

"Oops, crud, it's almost seven. I gotta go to work."

"See a dentist," Bridget said. "Love you."

She got her cello case out of the backseat and put the straps over her shoulders, reaching back into the car awkwardly to get the cats. She carried them to the front door, looking out across the field to the barn in the distance. It was surprisingly dusky, the evening providing a dim filter that flattered her well-worn home.

There was a low rumble overhead, and the sky darkened.

———◇———

First nights in the country by herself were always spooky, and this one was no exception. Bridget's heart raced with every creak and rattle, and the noises were constant, thanks to the torrential rain and terrified cats. She kept wishing her kids were sleeping upstairs, that Will was reading in the loft, or—even better—that Sterling was in her bed, telling her how overjoyed he was to be there, even in a typhoon.

In the middle of the night, during the worst of the storm, the lightning split a big branch off the willow tree and left it for dead in the pond. Heavy winds pressed on the backside of the tennis court fence until the rotted cedar posts fell over, taking the chain link with them. When Bridget woke up the next morning, having barely slept all night, the temperature had dropped fifteen degrees, and there were deer grazing on the weeds that grew between the deep cracks in the asphalt court. With three sides of the fence still up, it looked like she'd opened a petting zoo.

It was early, and Bridget had over four hours before she had to look presentable, so she threw on sweatpants and sneakers with the T-shirt she'd slept in. Before brushing her teeth or her hair, she went to the kitchen, where the old Sub-Zero was buzzing loudly in the background. She made small talk with the cats, Eliza (as in Doolittle) and Henry (as in Higgins). While the coffee brewed, she turned on NPR to drown out the racket coming from the fridge and texted her boyfriend in New York, knowing how much better she would sleep once he was under the same roof:

Beautiful, sunny morning! Can't wait for you to get here :)

She added a heart emoji.

Sterling answered right away:

Read your email.

And then:

Please.

His clipped, businesslike tone grated, but he was right to be annoyed. Sterling was a novelist, and he'd asked her to proofread the foreword he'd written for a Cambridge University Press book on literary symbolism. She was certainly no expert on the topic, but she was a good and careful reader. Unfortunately, she'd let that task, along with a slew of other pressing matters, go undone that week while she was preparing her Upper West Side apartment for summer subletters. They were acquaintances of Sterling, his Dutch publisher, her husband, and their sixteen-year-old daughter. The family had arrived safely the night before—notifying her with a text that her place was smaller than they'd expected—at the same time that Bridget was discovering that an industrious mouse had spent the winter nesting in her underwear drawer.

Bridget pulled on a sweater she found draped over a chair, fed the cats, and ate a handful of stale granola. Alone in the Connecticut house, she wouldn't have to think about feeding anyone other than herself and the cats. That would all change when Sterling arrived, but for the next two weeks, she could eat whatever she wanted at whatever time she chose without sitting down or even using a plate if she didn't feel like it. In the early evening she could stand at the kitchen counter—in the same spot where she'd dutifully cut up watermelon and poured glasses of milk for her kids when they were young—drinking wine and scooping pub cheese onto crackers and calling it dinner.

She decided to go outside to assess the storm damage, and on her way to the front door, she noticed a puddle directly under the skylight. That was unfortunate. Looking up to see where the water was coming from, she saw a brown stain on the lower left corner, nothing too serious. She got a beach towel and dropped it on the floor.

Opening the door, she let her city cats run out after her. They dropped to the ground like a rookie SWAT team as they took in the scent of bears and bobcats in the woods and hawks overhead. Dozens of downed branches, still holding on to their tiny green leaves, were discarded all over the lawn. On the tree limb that was now floating in the middle of the pond, four turtles were sunbathing. The grass was soaked, the pond was full, and the wind was cool. The storm might have wreaked havoc, but it had left everything gloriously clean.

The peace was disrupted by the sound of a pickup truck coming up the long, wet driveway and making a sharp turn in front of the garage. The driver turned off the engine and opened his door. Her caretaker, Walter, stepped out slowly, reaching back to the passenger seat for a carton of eggs before walking over to her in the yard. "Thought I'd come see how you made out last night," he said.

Bridget had never quite adjusted to the idea of unannounced visitors, but she'd learned long ago that locals had a different code of conduct from weekenders.

Walter stopped to peer up at her roof, putting an arthritic hand up to shade his eyes. He was tall and skinny, wearing jean shorts hiked up with a belt and a red T-shirt tucked in, giving him the look of a knobby-kneed, overgrown toddler.

As caretaker of the property for the past fifteen years, Walter had repeatedly alerted Bridget to problems with her house. He would call her in New York—in the middle of a meeting, a rehearsal, a concert—to report bad news: *You got ice dams on the roof. There's a litter of baby squirrels in the attic. The heat's out in the guest cottage.* It was up to Bridget to do something about these problems, and she tended to postpone repairs. She had, of course, addressed the direst issues, but she'd allowed all cosmetic or even mildly structural problems to fall by the wayside. The result was a wonderfully lived-in, cozy, but shabby home that could use a fresh coat of paint, a new hot water heater, and an exterminator.

He showed her the egg carton. "From our chickens."

"Thanks."

But instead of handing the carton over, he held on to it, pointing his finger at the bushes. "Be careful with those cats. We don't let ours out. They kill the birds. It's a big year for bears, you know."

"Is that right."

"And foxes and coyotes'll kill cats, too. Seen any herons?" he asked.

"Not yet," she said.

"They'll eat your fish."

It was hard to know in Walter's worldview which predators were bad and which were good. One minute he was cursing the herons for eating the smallmouth bass in his pond, but the next he was cheering the bobcat for catching a rabbit. Bridget tried to avoid such topics since they rarely saw eye to eye: she felt happy for the heron and bad for the bunny, for example.

"Your kids coming to visit?"

"Too busy," Bridget said. "Isabelle moved to Hong Kong and works sixty hours a week, and Oscar rarely leaves DC."

"How's that friend of his?"

"Husband," Bridget corrected. Bridget was humble by nature, but she couldn't help but speak well of her twins and son-in-law. "Matt's working for a congressman now, as his chief of staff."

"A Democrat?" Walter said, frowning.

"Jackson Oakley. The young star of the party."

Politics, also a world of fighting animals, was another topic Bridget knew better than to discuss with Walter.

"When's Bill coming? Haven't seen him in a while."

No one, but no one, called Will, her oldest friend and music colleague, "Bill" other than Walter, and he had insisted on using the nickname for years in spite of frequent attempts to retrain him. "I'm not sure. *Will's* pretty busy this summer in New York, and our trio's on a break until our new violinist starts—"

"Uh-oh," Walter said slowly, catching sight of the tennis court. "Oh, boy, would you look at that." He shook his head. "You gotta fix that in a hurry, or the rest of the fence is coming down with it."

"Yeah, well," Bridget said, "we don't play much tennis anyway."

"You want Kevin to come take a look?" He seemed fixated on the fence, while Bridget was certain that the big rocks protruding through the asphalt all over the court were a much bigger impediment to the game.

"I thought he moved to Maine."

"He came back home," Walter said, pointing vaguely to the north. "He's living with his mom just up the road."

Bridget shuddered; Walter's grandson Kevin was a few years older than the twins. Was it possible he was already thirty?

"Kevin can come by," he said, "give you a quote for some new cedar posts. And then maybe . . ." He glanced across the overgrown field at the old board-and-batten barn. ("Bird-and-bat barn" was the misnomer Isabelle had used as a child, and then more recently "Batshit Barn" was the nickname Oscar had given it, an appropriate moniker given the neglected structure's broken windows, rickety stairs, and shitting bat squatters.) ". . . Maybe it's time you take on that big project?" Walter said.

Bridget adored the barn, the steep roof, the silo, the muted gray paint. "Grand" and "historic" were the words the Realtor had used to describe the eighteenth-century building when she'd bought the property, but after another two decades of decay, even Bridget had taken to saying things like *Batshit Barn lost a lot of shingles this winter.* The truth was, Bridget hadn't dared look inside in a decade. It looked like it needed a demolition team rather than a renovation expert, but Bridget couldn't even imagine. Who was she to tear down a barn that had made it through over 220 Connecticut winters?

"Maybe someday I'll restore it," she said.

"Kevin's got time to help you out this summer. He's working

part-time for the park and rec commission. Trail maintenance and the like."

Bridget figured outdoor work might suit Kevin well. Lacking muscle tone and snappy synapses, he looked like he belonged in the woods, carrying an axe over his shoulder, bootlaces untied. Bridget had often worried about him when he was a young, chubby-handed, nearsighted, excessively drooly child; he'd believed in Santa Claus until he was twelve.

"I'll think about it," she said, hoping Walter didn't plan on chit-chatting much longer. She wanted to put clean sheets on her bed, arrange flowers in a vase on the kitchen counter, clear off the desk in Will's loft to give Sterling a proper writing space, and buy a case of wine.

As if he were reading her mind, Walter said, "So you don't need me stopping by? You'll be around?"

"With my boyfriend," said Bridget. "He's never been here before, and I think he's going to fall in love with the place."

She didn't mention that she was hoping to see if her relationship with Sterling might get bumped to the next level. Sterling had an eleven-year-old daughter who was heading off to sleepaway camp for eight weeks, and they were going to spend all that time together, a summer of romance, quiet, and privacy. So, no, she didn't want anyone stopping by.

"I hope your new guy's handier than Bill—"

"*Will*."

"—because you need to clean out your flues."

Bridget couldn't quite picture Sterling as a chimney sweep. "I sort of doubt it."

"Well, enjoy the summer." He walked back to his truck, saying, "They say we'll be getting a lot of rain."

"Thanks for the eggs," she called after him.

She turned to go back in the house, standing in the doorway while the cats made up their minds whether they wanted to come in or stay out. Eliza Doolittle decided to come in, while Henry Higgins stayed out.

Bridget walked under the leaky skylight in the entry, through the living room, and into the kitchen. She needed to shower and get dressed in decent clothes before she went to her lunch, but her laptop was sitting in the center of the table in the breakfast room, as if to say, *Pssst, remember me?* She sat down and opened her email; right at the top, above a message from her sister, Gwen, was a new email from Sterling, with the subject line *Airflow?* She started reading, something about allergens and his need for a fan that made a nice breeze but wasn't too loud, but before she could get any further, the battery gave out and her computer went dead. She got up and found her power cord, leaned over, and reached for the outlet under the window. A flash of heat rushed up the length of her arm, all the way to her heart, and—just as the wind had shoved the tennis court fence onto the ground—an electric shock knocked her flat onto the floor.

After driving to the Sharon Hospital, Bridget found herself lying on a gurney, hooked up to an EKG, with a red streak running from her hand to her elbow.

"We'll get you out of here," the nurse said. "Just taking precautions."

Bridget closed her eyes and pretended she was getting a facial.

"What's your name, hon," the nurse said, verifying that the person in front of her matched the chart on her laptop. She was wearing eggplant-colored scrubs with bright pink Crocs, an outfit that clashed with itself and the peach-colored walls. She was a cheerful creature, making Bridget feel as though her electrocution had absolutely made her day.

"Bridget Stratton."

"Date of birth?"

"June third, 19—"

A quick inhale. "I don't suppose you're related to *Edward* Stratton?" The nurse was looking down at her with excitement.

"No."

"He's from England, they say, but he's got a house around here."

"No kidding."

"Our local celebrity."

Bridget pointed and flexed, pointed and flexed her feet.

"Even at his age," the nurse said, happily nodding her head, "they say he's got that . . . appeal, you know. He's still got it."

Staring at the ceiling, Bridget listened to the EKG machine as it beeped an A, at the same pulse of that Pachelbel piece she'd always hated.

"Your blood pressure's high," the nurse said, sounding pleased.

"Thanks," said Bridget.

"No, I mean you should keep an eye on it, watch your diet. Are you exercising?"

The doctor came in past the pastel room divider, saving Bridget from having to answer. He studied her results, took off his glasses, and told Bridget she could go home. She sat up and turned so she was facing him, ready to get the stickers off her chest. The nurse began detaching the wires.

"This happened at work?" the doctor asked.

"She was at *home*," said the nurse.

The doctor looked at her like he felt sorry for her. "You should have an electrician check out your wiring." Lifting her arm, he turned her wrist over and examined the streak. "A shock like that can kill you."

He got his prescription pad and scribbled on it as Bridget wondered what painkillers or relaxants he was giving her. She didn't feel like she needed anything but had no intention of turning down meds.

"Braxton & Sons," he said, handing her the prescription with the name of a local electrician. "They did my outside lighting, and the whole entry is much more inviting." He looked down at the e-chart again. "Stratton? Say, are you—"

"No relation," the nurse said, sounding disappointed.

"Too bad," said the doctor. "What a guy; I'll never forget hearing him conduct Gershwin in Central Park. Did you know the queen's a big fan? They say he has a standing invitation to Buckingham Palace."

Release papers in hand, Bridget walked out to her car and sent a quick text to Will:

Got electrocuted in the breakfast room :)

He answered immediately:

Jeeesh!! That house!!!!!! You okay????

His excessive use of punctuation amused her; for someone so reserved, his text messages were highly expressive.

She drove to the main intersection in the town of Sharon and sat at the stop sign, admiring the old stone clock tower with its pointy red roof. She wished the clock said it was eight in the morning so she could start the day over again. She wished she'd at least taken a shower. The car behind her honked. She waved in apology, made a left turn, and drove to her father's house.

2

I f a pigeon were to perch on the rusty air-conditioning unit in the window of 66 Barrow Street and look into the fourth-story living room, it might be under the false impression that Will was taking a nap. It was ten in the morning, and he was lying on the couch with his feet up, planning out his summer schedule and estimating his potential earnings. He wouldn't make as much as, say, people with normal jobs, but with the trio on hiatus, he'd found opportunities to make some extra money doing commercial work, like recording a jingle for a low-testosterone ad at a studio in New Jersey. He'd performed at a B-list celebrity wedding the night before with a terrific ensemble—a last-minute invitation after their pianist called in sick—and it was a windfall.

Gounod's *Faust* was playing on his iPad, and he was cross-checking a series of emails with the lessons and gigs he kept track of in his calendar, an old-fashioned, spiral-bound throwback he carried in the pocket of his button-down shirts. When he was certain everything was entered (in pencil so adjustments could be made), he moved on to the next business: scheduling a three-way phone conference around the insanely busy schedule of their new violinist, Caroline Lee, so that he and Bridget could welcome her into the trio and discuss logistics. She was out of the country for most of June, but when Will requested a few dates in July, she had never gotten back to him. Will hoped this wasn't an indication of her level of commitment. He tried calling her manager, Randall Bennett, but the call went first to Randall's assistant and then to voicemail. Instead of leaving a message, he sent an email to Caroline, copying Bridget and Randall to keep them in the loop.

Randall was obsessed with what he called their "platform," so Will picked up his iPad and took a look at their website. It hadn't been updated in years. It didn't list upcoming performances and certainly didn't invite visitors to purchase downloads with a click; neither Bridget nor Will knew the first thing about how to manage it. There were good pictures of them on the home page, but it was the wrong trio; Jacques appeared beside them, posing with his violin, not Caroline with hers.

Will had been sorry to see Jacques go last month. He and Bridget had become good friends with him over the past decade, but after Jacques and his wife had a baby, they moved back to Europe. He and Bridget had tried to change Jacques's mind, making the case that Bridget had managed to raise two children in New York City, and they had turned out quite well, thank you very much, but Jacques had already decided: "Everybody knows France is ze best place on earth to raise a child." Will didn't know if this was true or not, but he thought the trio should have meant more to Jacques than a random opinion.

———◇———

Will lived in the West Village with his yellow Lab, Hudson, in a very small one-bedroom apartment with high ceilings and a playground out his bedroom window. For almost twenty years, he'd been living in the walk-up, a building owned by an invisible landlord who never bothered to make any improvements or repairs but, in exchange for his negligence, had only raised the rent a handful of times. The apartment was a bargain, possibly the last one in all of Manhattan.

Will's style, if he were pressed to name it, was minimalist '50s hip: he had an expensive tailored couch and a knockoff Eames lounge chair and ottoman, a Danish bar cart in one corner and a dumbbell set in the other, and his upright Baldwin in between, a piano he'd bought for fifty dollars from his friend Mitzy, who lived next door. He loved his home and everything in it.

Will taught piano lessons all over Manhattan but mostly on the Upper West Side, in the same neighborhood where he and Bridget had met and founded the Forsyth Trio. They'd replaced the violinist several times over the years, but he and Bridget had kept the ensemble together, carrying on the group's name and identity. (They had called themselves Threesome their freshman year and changed it to Three Strikes as sophomores in an attempt to sound less risqué. After they graduated, they went with something more professional and dignified, borrowing the name of the Lower East Side street where they rented a rehearsal studio.) Pretty much every violinist they'd ever rotated in had assumed he and Bridget were together, or had been at one time, or would be eventually. They bickered like a couple and finished each other's sentences. They irritated people with their inside jokes. "I wish my marriage was half as good as what you two have," Bridget's sister, Gwen, had once confessed before divorcing her rotten husband. "You look so good together," Jacques always told them. Bridget had high cheekbones and long legs; he was broad-shouldered and square-jawed. Some went so far as to ask if he was Oscar and Isabelle's father. "Can't take credit for them," Will would say.

Will got up off the couch and stretched, turning off the music in mid-aria and wiggling his fingers.

Hudson looked up to see if they were taking a walk. But when Will didn't make a move for the leash and instead sat down at his Baldwin piano, Hudson wagged his tail and went back to sleep.

Most of the time, Will practiced on the pianos at the music schools where he taught, but there were days when he preferred to play at home, even though his piano was significantly worse in tone and action (as in it was tinny and sluggish) than those at Juilliard and Mannes, where he taught in their precollege programs. No amount of tuning could fix the flat sound of his Baldwin. He checked his posture and played through a Mozart Sonata in F Major and the first movement of Schumann's *Faschingsschwank aus Wien*, focusing on his left hand for the latter. After an hour, he put his iPad on the stand and opened the music for one of his upcoming commercial gigs, and yes, it could be argued that playing this jingle was somewhat beneath him artistically, but Will took jobs like these all the time; this was how a professional pianist survived. He'd studied piano and tinkered in composition. He'd even entertained the idea of becoming a composer, but his strength, as it turned out, was in arranging, a skill that had become a hobby, not a profession.

Next Will opened the music for the country ballad he'd been hired to play in a video, a song called "About You and I," and he gave it a whirl. It was terrible. Putting aside the corny and grammatically incorrect lyrics, the music was repetitive and stupid. According to the producer's notes, the musicians would be filmed pretending to play first in a field and then, inexplicably, underwater while the female vocalist (who was apparently famous, though Will had never heard of her) sang in the background, riding a bucking seahorse. As he continued to play the song, Hudson looked up and cocked his head, as if to say, *What* is *this shit?*

"A ditty," Will told him. "It's garbage. Cover your ears."

He played through it again and found it was decidedly *not* the kind of song that grew on you through repetition. Finally, he checked his watch and got up to walk Hudson. At three, he had a lesson with Jisoo, a rising high school senior who was preparing her auditions for Peabody and the New England Conservatory. He'd been teaching her since she was in middle school. She was good, really good, much better than he was at that age. What, he wondered, would Jisoo think to see him on YouTube playing bad country music underwater with air bubbles coming out of his nose? What kind of example would that set? A good one—that musicians can and should seek innovative ways of supporting their careers? Or a bad one—that a sellout is a sellout, and no one should ever lower himself to such (watery) depths?

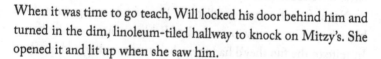

When it was time to go teach, Will locked his door behind him and turned in the dim, linoleum-tiled hallway to knock on Mitzy's. She opened it and lit up when she saw him.

"Hello, neighbor," she said. "Look at you."

He smiled back. Like many New Yorkers, Will had assembled a faux family for himself. He had Bridget, he had her children, he had Hudson, and he had Mitzy, his Manhattan grandmother. She was cartoonishly short and wore big, round black glasses that didn't seem to do much to help her failing vision. She reached out and gave the tips of his fingers a squeeze.

"I heard you playing something very catchy on the piano," she said. "You sounded marvelous."

"Country music," he said. "I'm branching out. I hope I didn't disturb you."

"*Disturb* me? I stood outside your door so I could hear you better. Are you heading out?"

"I'm going to work, but I'll stop by the grocery store on my way home."

She reached in her dress pocket and handed him a list and a ten-dollar bill. "Thank you, love. My left hip has gone wonky, and I'd like a grilled cheese."

"Do you need an Advil?"

She waved him off. "How's Bridget?"

"She's away for the summer with her boyfriend."

"Isn't that nice," said Mitzy.

Will wasn't so sure. He was having a hard time imagining Sterling happily ensconced at Bridget's country house. Sterling was one of those New Yorkers who didn't know how to drive a car. And he seemed pretty pleased with his life in Park Slope. He had a young kid, a job teaching in the MFA program at NYU, and bookstores all over New York that clamored to host him whenever he read from his latest novel. How exactly would Connecticut fit into all that?

Not a fan of nature, small-town life, or unnerving quiet, Will himself was in no way enamored of Bridget's large, cranky house. In spite of the fun they'd had there, he'd never understood her deep attachment to the place. Who could love something so needy and broken? He regularly stubbed his toes on the warped floorboards and got a wave of panic every time he flushed the toilet, and, as if to show it was capable of doing real harm, the house had now electrocuted Bridget in the breakfast room. What Bridget saw as charming, Will saw as burdensome and mean. He had always resented the house's insistence on punishing Bridget for not paying enough attention to it. It reminded him of his ex-wife.

"No concerts this summer?" Mitzy asked.

"No, but I hope you'll come hear us play in the fall." He held up the shopping list. "I'll see you tonight."

"Bring Hudson. I'll have the gin out."

Will waved and went down the stairs, the song "About You and I" stuck firmly in his head.

———◆◇◆———

Even though conservatory auditions were a few months away, Will decided to set up a mock audition, asking Jisoo to enter the practice room and introduce herself as though they didn't know each other.

"Seriously?" she said. "That's so embarrassing."

"Every second you're in the room with the faculty is an opportunity to make a good impression. I don't want you to waste any chance to connect. Look alert. And remember, they'll likely stop you right before you get to the development section, so don't let that throw you. They're often short on time. Ready?"

Jisoo walked out in the hallway, closed the door behind her, and then entered. "Hello," she said.

"Eye contact," said Will. "Don't be slouchy."

She went out and came in again. "Hello," she said, looking at him this time.

"Hello."

"I'm Jisoo, and I'll be starting today with the first movement of Beethoven's *Waldstein* Sonata." She sat down and launched right in.

"Wait, wait, wait," he said. "Take a beat to focus. Let the room go quiet, just like you would for a concert."

Jisoo took a moment and began playing again. As he listened, he wished he could take credit for her performance. She played so accurately, with a lovely touch and a good deal of joy. Like any serious musician, she never went a day without practicing, and unlike a lot of students, she practiced efficiently and always had.

Teaching Jisoo was the opposite of his experience trying to teach Bridget's twins to play when they were young. They all gave up soon after he gave them Bach's Minuet in G; Oscar never even opened it.

"I don't want to play piano." He had dropped the thin score on the floor, an act of defiance. "I hate practicing."

"I don't understand," said Will. "What does that even mean?"

"It's *boring*."

This attitude was incomprehensible to Will, who had practiced every day since he was six. And to Bridget, who'd been handed a quarter-size cello at the age of seven and never put it down again except to go up a size every time she grew.

Bridget was an excellent musician, while Will would describe himself as a highly competent one. He was dedicated, precise, careful. "Robotic" was the word Edward had once used when he'd heard the original Forsyth Trio play, doing a number on Will's self-esteem. Will admittedly was at his best with Bach, where the beauty is in the music itself. He was worse with contemporary composers. Schoenberg made him want to stab someone. And musicians like Lang Lang—or the insufferable, pompous Gavin Glantz, their very first violinist, with all his drama and flair—nauseated him. *Enough with the histrionics*, Will wanted to yell. *Just play the music*. Gavin would whip his hair around in a ridiculous arc whenever the trio finished a piece. "He's an outstanding player," Bridget would remind him. "What difference does it make what he does with his hair?"

She was right. But, of course, Bridget was more forgiving of flair. She was Edward Stratton's daughter after all. And Edward's flair was his signature. For conductors, a little drama was part of the job description. Unlike for an instrumentalist, the conductor's job was all about interpretation, of infusing oneself into the music. If the conductor was lacking in personality, then a piece lacking personality was what the audience would get. Edward Stratton was brimming with personality. He was scintillating, informed, gregarious, and the most popular guest at any party. He was also one of the most narcissistic people Will had ever known.

Gavin was the other. At the very first opportunity, just when the Forsyth Trio was getting recognition and high praise, Gavin left them to take a seat with the orchestra of the Sydney Opera House.

It was rotten timing when he left. They'd gotten a great review in the *New York Times* from Alex Ross, who noted their "distinct sound" and "unparalleled vigor," saying they were this generation's Beaux Arts Trio and calling Gavin an artist "of precision and exuberance." But in spite of the accolades, Gavin would insist on fishing for compliments from Will, even though reviewers usually highlighted him as the star of the trio. Gavin put on an act of being insecure even though he knew perfectly well he had no reason to be, and Will found the charade wearing and pointless. *Good riddance*, Will had thought when Gavin announced he was leaving.

Their new violinist was a star; Will hoped Caroline's personality was nothing like Gavin's.

———◆———

Jisoo had reached the end of the piece.

"Well done," he said. "Really, really nice. Remember: don't accent the grace note, but rather the quarter note that follows." He gave her homework for the following week.

"Is the room free for the next hour?" she asked.

"Keep on playing until somebody kicks you out," said Will. "Hey, we should put that on a bumper sticker." He turned to leave. "Jisoo," he said, stepping back in the room, "are you good with computers?"

She looked up. "Sure, I guess."

"Do you know anything about doing websites?"

"Oh," she said, "no, I'm not good like that."

"Yeah, me neither," he said.

"But I'm friends with a guy who's super smart. You want me to text him?"

"Who is he?"

"A sophomore in the engineering school at NYU. He's very techy."

College kids were usually cheap and brilliant. "Interesting," said Will.

She was already texting at lightning speed. "I shared your number."

"My trio has this website, but it's a little—"

"Brendan answered," she said. "He says do you need a new website or an update?"

"I need it updated. Or improved. I don't know exactly." The whole transaction was moving a little faster than Will was ready for. "Wouldn't hurt to talk to him, I guess, right?"

She was still texting. "Brendan says he'll do it. He's at work right now, but he'll contact you later."

"Thanks," he said, feeling excited about taking a positive step and advancing the trio's next chapter. "A new website would be terrific."

He left to the sound of Jisoo practicing scales.

After a quick trip to pick up Mitzy's groceries and a few things for himself, he walked down his beautiful tree-lined street toward home, stopping dead in his tracks when he looked up: there beside the cracked sidewalk—directly in front of his beloved building—was a large sign with the words *For Sale*.

3

G avin was somehow lost.

It was hard to get turned around in New York City, what with the grid and all, but there was an area around Astor Place, where Lafayette turned into Fourth and Bowery turned into Third and then Third and Fourth went off in different directions instead of staying parallel like all the other avenues in the city, where he always got confused.

Getting lost in Manhattan reminded him of the joke the seniors told him when he first got to Juilliard from a middle-class suburb in Maryland: A lost tourist asks a New Yorker, "How do you get to Carnegie Hall?" The New Yorker says, "Practice!"

Gavin would not ask for directions. Tourists ask for directions, and he was not a tourist. New York had once been his home.

He kept walking south, knowing he could take a right on Great Jones (or what might be called 3rd Street, depending on where he was) and end up at Washington Square Park.

Returning to New York City was a mixed bag every time. Gavin rarely had the time to visit his favorite old haunts (the deli on 93rd above which he'd lived or the café on Columbus where he'd learned to like coffee), but he also managed to stumble across places that held not-so-great memories. Even today, he happened to pass a street corner where he'd tried to make out with a girl who'd turned him down with the old *I just want to be friends* line; he'd pretended like he didn't care. And now he spotted a club where he'd been the only one in a group of guys to get carded, and the bouncer had made him leave. Standing on the sidewalk outside that very place, which was now a pop-up clothing and jewelry market, he could still feel the bitterness and embarrass-ment. Gavin had been only sixteen when he'd started conservatory, and he'd frequently felt like he was playing catch-up to the other students. He had been inexperienced and naive but tried to play it cool. Kind of like he was doing now, pretending he knew where he was going when he didn't, acting like his shoelace hadn't untied when it had.

On this trip Gavin made an intentional decision to have lunch at a pizza dive in the Village. A college student he once knew—an attrac-tive soprano who was kind enough to let him lose his virginity to her the summer *after* he graduated from college—had worked there, back in the day when it was called Rico's, and she gave him a free slice when-ever he came by to say hello. The place had changed since then, unsur-prisingly, and Gavin had to decide if he wanted to eat there now that the space housed a Sweetgreen, a restaurant he could go to anytime in LA. Disappointed, he went in anyway and ordered the kale Caesar and a chai tea and took his lunch outside to a table on the sidewalk.

He liked New York, but he wasn't sorry that he'd left. His life in LA suited him better in every way. Still, this was the place where he'd grown up, where he'd begun the long, painful process of figuring out who he was and who he wasn't.

A woman walked by his table and then stopped abruptly, slowly turning around. "Gavin? Gavin Glantz."

He looked up from his salad, his other hand on the brim of his plain, navy blue baseball cap. "Miriam," he said, putting down his fork and getting to his feet. He kissed her cheek. "Good to see you. What are you doing here?"

"Having a ball," she said. "I'm an empty nester now, so my life is my own again. I came to see a show, do a little shopping. And now I've had my first celebrity sighting of the day. Are you performing?"

"Tonight, yes." He didn't want to show off, but she was waiting for details. "It's just a thing at Lincoln Center. Is Nicholas here with you?"

"God, no," she said, giving her hair a shake and lifting her shoulders so that her shopping bags were raised in the air. "Haven't you heard? We called it a day."

"What, really? I'm sorry to hear that." He motioned for her to sit. "After how many years?"

"Twenty-nine." Miriam put her bags on one chair and sat across from him. "I finally got the hell out of England and bought a small house in Westchester. I can't tell you what a relief it is to be living back in the States."

"Well," he said, unsure of the best response, "you look great." She did actually. Miriam had always been pretty.

"That's because *I* am not the injured party," she said. "Nicholas is faring less well, from what I hear."

Nicholas Donahue was a professor at Oxford and a well-known theoretician, his research focusing primarily on contemporary British composers. He was one of the few musicologists who truly understood the mechanics of being a musician, perhaps because he was, in fact, a decent pianist in his own right. Gavin had gotten to know him over the years and liked him. Nicholas knew an endless number of funny and often scandalous facts about dead musicians, making him great fun to have a glass of whiskey with.

"I'll give him a call," Gavin said.

"As long as you don't tell him you saw me. He'll put two and two together and know I wasn't here alone, and I don't want to cause additional pain."

"Ah," said Gavin, "I see."

She looked off to the side, somewhat shamed. "Nicholas found out I was having an affair, and that was that. I should have been honest about it from the start, but I was too much of a coward. The truth is I didn't want my children thinking poorly of me."

Surprised she would share something so personal, Gavin made a conscious effort to be nonjudgmental. "You and Nicholas seemed happy."

"We weren't well suited at all," she said. "He's so academic, and I never understood his humor. I was too dumb for him."

"No, I'm sure he didn't think that."

"But I did."

Gavin felt a pang of guilt, knowing that he, too, had had that thought: that Nicholas was brilliant and fascinating, while Miriam was not a particularly deep thinker. There was probably sexism at work in that opinion.

"The man I'm with now is an obscenely rich New Yorker, and the only thing he reads is *Businessweek*, and everything feels very right. What about you? Are you still with that young thing we met when we saw you out in California? A life coach, wasn't she?"

Gavin was glad to set Miriam straight: "That 'thing' is a well-respected psychologist who turned thirty-eight last week, published a successful self-help book, and yes, Juliette and I are very much together." He held up his left hand and showed her his wedding band.

Miriam's mouth dropped open. "Gavin," she said, "I didn't think you were the marrying type."

"Why is that?" he asked, half hoping she would accuse him of being a playboy when, in fact, he'd had very few meaningless affairs. Just as well since they'd always left him feeling unsettled.

"I didn't think you were one to make sacrifices for someone else."

"We have a four-year-old."

Miriam's eyes opened wide. "I'm shocked."

"Do you want to see a picture?" He clicked on his home screen where a photo of his darling, curly-headed child appeared.

Miriam took the phone and smiled. "Cute," she said. "Name?"

"Daniel. Danny, actually."

"It must be tough keeping up with him," she said, and then she smiled, adding, "at *our age*."

"Juliette's an incredible woman and an amazing mother," he said. "We're a good team." Miriam was right, though; Danny was exhausting. Juliette often used the word *discovery* when explaining his behavior. "He's in a period of *discovery* regarding temporal restrictions," she would say when he fought bedtime. "He's *discovering* his voice," she would say when he screamed. "He's *discovering* his power," she would say when he hit another child at preschool.

Miriam returned his phone and showed her own home screen: a picture of three good-looking twenty-somethings, smiling on a beach. "The most noble thing Nicholas ever did," she said, "was *not* to tell our kids why we split up. They found out anyway, of course. It's impossible to keep anything a secret this day and age."

Gavin didn't like the sound of that. "It is?"

"Technology," she said with a look of warning. "I was careless with my text messages." She took the sunglasses perched on the top of her head and tossed them in her bag. "The timing was probably for the best, though, since Nicholas just started working on a new book. He's spending the whole summer at a house in the Berkshires, doing research for his next tome. I'm glad I don't have to be by his side through that nightmare."

"I don't follow—"

"Watching him write a book was torture. He talks to himself and gets obsessed with the subject matter, working day and night, and— worst of all—he used to ask me to read his chapters, and honestly, I wanted to light myself on fire the whole time I was pretending to read."

Gavin was about to laugh, given that Nicholas would probably win a Pulitzer someday, but he could see by her expression that she was completely serious.

"What's his new book about?" he asked.

"Some kind of biography. Oh," she said, sitting up. "Wait, who was that woman you played music with after college—what was her name? Brenda? Britney? You were in that trio together."

"Bridget," Gavin said. He sipped his iced tea, trying to mask his discomfort at hearing that particular name. "Why . . . why would Nicholas write a book about Bridget?"

"No, not about Bridget, silly. He's writing a book about her father."

After Miriam left, Gavin picked at his salad. He had a concert that night; he couldn't afford to get distracted by thoughts of Bridget Stratton. He finished his tea and decided to take an Uber back to his hotel to do some of the mindfulness exercises Juliette recommended.

Sitting in the backseat as the SUV headed up Sixth Avenue, passing the red brick Jefferson Market Library, he saw him. Older, yes, but there was no mistaking his friend, who was walking right by the car. Astonished, Gavin rolled down the window. "Will," he shouted. He turned to the driver. "Could you stop the car for a second?"

The driver turned down the music. "Sorry?"

"Could you pull over? To the left?"

Gavin leaned out the window. "Will," he called again. Will was headed in the opposite direction of the traffic with a big dog on a leash, headphones over his ears. Gavin tried not to resent his full head of hair. Will was moving quickly and suddenly disappeared in the crowd.

Gavin felt like he'd been rejected, which might or might not have been paranoia. It was possible Will despised him, but he tried to dismiss that idea. Besides, if he wanted to see Will so badly, he could text him the next time he was coming to town, not accost him on a sidewalk. But he never had texted him, in all the times he'd come to the city. Will had never texted him either.

He rolled the window back up, wondering if he'd ever be as comfortable in his own skin as Will had always seemed in his.

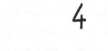

riving into the courtyard of Edward's estate, Bridget saw that Edward's grass was freshly cut, as usual, in a manicured crosshatch pattern and the indigenous landscaping was impeccably groomed. There was no trace of the storm that had blown through the night before other than a slight dampness to the steep slate roof and the copper flashing. The house had the look of a fortress. Will called it "the Castle," and for good reason. Mother Nature didn't stand a chance here.

There were four cars parked side by side, and she considered leaving; the last thing Bridget wanted was to have lunch with actual people. It was bad enough having to face her sister and father in sweatpants. A quick look at the cars, however, convinced her that she wasn't getting pulled into a photo op: a beat-up pickup truck, Gwen's Range Rover, a minivan, and, on the far side, a Subaru with a half-ripped-off *I Brake for Chipm*— sticker.

In an effort to primp, she tilted the rearview mirror down, checking her face and trying to run her fingers through her unbrushed hair; it was a lost cause. She got her purse and phone from the passenger seat, and walked across the cobblestone courtyard to ring the bell. It made a deep, soft gonging sound. Bridget had never had a key to the Castle; there was always someone manning the door.

The door opened silently, and her sister, Gwen, appeared on the other side. Gwen smiled, put her finger to her lips, and pointed down the hall to the living room, where Mahler's Fifth was playing on Edward's fancy sound system. Bridget stepped out of her shoes and left them in the row next to all the others, as Gwen took her hand and led her barefoot into the kitchen. Not until the heavy swinging door closed behind them did Gwen say, "You're here!" giving Bridget a hug with her perfectly toned arms. "Welcome to another summer in crazy town."

Bridget, assuming Gwen had been stuck in the living room for one of Edward's famous listening session slash musicianship lectures, said, "Did I just rescue you?"

"No, he's wrapped up with some musicologist from, I don't know, Yale or Harvard probably," Gwen said. "Nicholas somebody. They were talking for at least an hour when I heard this nightmare start playing."

Bridget laughed. "*Nightmare?*"

"I hate Mahler, always have. And don't try to shame me. Do you think they're going to listen to the whole godawful thing? It's making my teeth itch."

"At least it's not as long as the Second Symphony, so be grateful."

Checking the time on her phone, Gwen said, "I wish I'd known you were coming. I made plans."

Bridget began to realize that she'd missed something. Gwen was not dressed for lunch, and what they were hearing from the speakers was only the first movement of the symphony. Edward wouldn't be coming out of the living room anytime soon.

"Our lunch was moved to tomorrow," Gwen said. "You should check your email more often."

"My computer blew up, and I—" Bridget had to think before she could remember her very reasonable excuse. "I got electrocuted."

Gwen tilted her head, looking concerned. "Sweetie. Is that what happened to your hair?"

Bridget ignored her.

"Whoever the guy is in there, he's clearly more important than us," said Gwen.

"That's okay. Tomorrow's better for me anyway," Bridget said, relieved she could go home.

Gwen picked up a turquoise Nalgene bottle and filled it with water. "Did you hear Dad hired a new assistant?"

Edward's assistants rarely stuck around. He hired smart, young people, usually with degrees in arts administration, and expected them to anticipate his every need, understand his every thought, and be quick about it. They needed a musical background, administrative smarts, and thick skin, an elusive combination.

"Jacob," Bridget said. "I met him already."

"Jacob's gone. It's Jackie now."

Bridget wasn't surprised. "At least their names are similar," she said.

"I talked to her for a few minutes on the phone this morning, and she seemed nervous."

"About what?"

"I don't know," Gwen said. "I said something about what it's like here, bear sightings, lightning storms, psychotic composers, and she got very quiet."

"You scared her on purpose." Bridget started to ask Gwen how she was doing, but the answer was as clear as the sparkle in Gwen's eyes and the flex of muscle showing through her expensive patterned yoga pants. She'd never had kids, and Bridget wondered if that was why she looked so damn young and perky. Once a week she interviewed visual and performing artists, writers, and thinkers, on camera from her living room on Fifth Avenue; she made introverted men and women feel comfortable and extroverts feel deep. She brought out the most interesting parts of people and sometimes got them to divulge secrets.

Her interviews were run in a segment each week as part of a popular program on Netflix called *Influence*. Everything she'd ever gotten from Edward—her contacts, her conversational skills, her ability to hold people's attention, and her money—she'd put to excellent use.

Bridget picked up her keys.

"Don't go yet," Gwen said.

"I have to take a shower," said Bridget, feeling sorry for herself. "I slept terribly, and my morning got off to a rotten start."

"Same," Gwen said. "I'm a mess."

Gwen was not a mess. Gwen was never a mess, not as a child, not throughout her bad marriage, and not since her divorce. Even now, she looked like she was auditioning for the part of a celebrity fitness trainer with her hair pulled back into a slick ponytail and her zip-up, fitted, white Nike sweatshirt. Bridget's top was a stretched-out knit sweater she was pretty sure had once belonged to her son, and her mismatched socks had bright yellow stars on the left one and black and green stripes on the right.

"But I'll be better once my masseur arrives," Gwen said.

"How did you find a masseur around here?"

"I asked Meryl Streep."

Bridget flashed a look: *Are you kidding me?* Gwen had a way of dropping names effortlessly into conversations in a way that made her life seem ideal and glamorous, which it hadn't always been. Bridget liked to keep her circle small, whereas Gwen's grew and grew over time, and she loved the idea, not of showing this fact off, but of introducing all of her favorite people to each other.

"I injured my left shoulder yesterday," Gwen said, "and since I promised I'd come this weekend, I asked Meryl for the name of someone local. I'm hoping I'll be okay to go riding later. Are you hungry?" Gwen said with a quick lift of her eyebrows.

Not only was Bridget hungry; she also knew exactly what she was hungry for. Gwen went to the fridge for skim milk, while Bridget got glasses and pulled two big chocolate chip oatmeal cookies from a jar on the counter. They sat on stools at the island, and Bridget pushed up her sleeves.

"I can't wait for you to meet Sterling."

"I've met him before, around five years ago at the *New Yorker* Festival."

"I mean get to know him. He'll be here for eight weeks, and we've never spent this much consecutive time together." The idea was both thrilling and mildly terrifying. Bridget got her phone and showed Gwen a bad selfie: Sterling's face was too close for comfort, and her eyes were closed.

"Adorable," said Gwen flatly. "How old is he?"

"Fifty-six." Bridget took a bite of her cookie and swiveled on her stool. "But," she said with her mouth full, "he looks like he's in his forties."

"My producer sent me his new novel."

"Are you inviting him on your show?" Bridget asked, excited about the possibility. Sterling and her sister collaborating, becoming friends.

Gwen made a gesture with her hands that said, *Not so fast*. "I don't know yet," she said. "It's not up to me."

Bridget was pretty sure that wasn't true.

"Wait, fifty-six?" Gwen asked. "Didn't you say he has a little kid?"

Bridget could feel Gwen slipping into interview mode, and she didn't mind one bit; she was happy to share the details of her new relationship, the first serious one she'd had in years. "He has an eleven-year-old named Madison. And he gets along fantastically well with his ex-wife. They could write the book on co-parenting for divorced couples."

"The ex must be young."

"Thirty-something."

"What's Madison like?"

"I haven't met her. Mallory thinks we should wait until the fall."

"Mallory's the ex?" Gwen made a face. "Is she controlling? Because that sounds a little controlling."

She was controlling; there was no question about it. But she was also treating Bridget as though she were part of the patchwork family picture and, therefore, as someone who needed to be looped into plans, and Bridget appreciated that. "I like to think she sees me as . . ." She was going to say *an experienced ally*, but Gwen cut in.

"Are those pajama bottoms?"

Bridget looked down and patted herself on her thighs. "They're sweatpants. I wouldn't normally wear them out of the house, but I got zapped when I plugged my computer in an outlet today. I went to the ER to make sure I wasn't dying."

Gwen said, "I would have to be dead already before anyone could make me put on those pants. I would retire them before Sterling gets here."

"But I love them," Bridget said. She tended to get sentimental about her favorite things; the longer she had something, the longer she wanted to keep it.

Gwen took Bridget's hand, pulled her up, and turned her around. "They make your butt look saggy."

"I've had these since the kids were born."

"I can tell," she said. She took a sip of her milk. "I talked to Isabelle last week. I got confused about the time change, and I called her at three in the morning. You think she's doing okay?"

"She's adjusting," said Bridget.

"Because she sounded exhausted."

"At three in the morning?"

"Apart from that. She sounded . . . unwell."

"She's homesick," Bridget said. "And she has a toothache."

"What do you think's going on with Dad?" Gwen said, lowering her voice. "Something's up with him."

"I had lunch with him a few weeks ago, and he seemed fine.

He was talking about the controversy over the costume budget at the Metropolitan Opera and that embezzlement scandal with the orchestra in Santa Fe." In fact, he'd been especially engaged throughout their tasting menu at Jean-Georges, asking Bridget personal questions about everything from her trio's future with Caroline Lee to her relationship with Sterling. His interest had surprised Bridget.

"Did I tell you," Gwen said, standing up and tying her sweatshirt loosely around her waist, "that I'm interviewing Mikhail Baryshnikov next week for the eightieth anniversary of the American Ballet Theatre."

"Can you get Will an autograph?" Bridget said.

"I'll see if I can introduce them," Gwen said, sitting back down. "I had no idea Will liked the ballet."

"He doesn't especially," said Bridget, "but after he got divorced, he found out that Baryshnikov didn't believe in traditional marriage, and he joined the club."

Gwen looked confused. "But Baryshnikov *is* married."

"He betrayed the cause; Will has been disappointed in him ever since. You'll have to tell us what he's really like."

"I've met him before," said Gwen. "I don't mean, like, I *know* him or anything. I only met him once when I was maybe fourteen or something. Dad had a performance, and Baryshnikov came backstage."

"Big deal," Bridget teased. "*I* was there when Elton John came backstage."

"Braggart," Gwen said, pushing her shoulder. "We should plan something sensational for Dad's ninetieth."

"I need to wait until I've seen our concert schedule," Bridget said. "His birthday's months away."

"I can't believe you got Caroline Lee to join your trio. I've tried to get her to come on my show, but she's very hard to pin down."

Bridget wouldn't exactly say they'd "got" Caroline, since having her in the trio was on a trial basis, but she didn't feel like explaining that Caroline was, in a sense, auditioning them. "Do you think Will and I are insane to have our whole future riding on the whims of a twenty-six-year-old?"

"I heard her interviewed on Terry Gross, and she sounded very mature. How does Sterling feel about you traveling so much?"

Bridget had to think. Travel was simply part of her job, so what could he have to say about it?

Before she could respond, the door to the kitchen swung open, and Marge, their nanny of two generations, housekeeper, and all-around fixer of forty years, came in with a Greek god of a man who was holding a portable massage table as easily as if it were a tote bag. He'd been instructed to remove his shoes, and Bridget admired his tanned, muscular feet. Edward's homes, wherever they were, were shoes-off; he couldn't abide the idea of the outside making its way in. When she was young, Bridget would wear her Stan Smiths in her bedroom of the family's Park Avenue apartment as an act of rebellion.

Gwen greeted her masseur as Marge came over to ruffle Bridget's already messy hair and give her a hug. She was a plump, short, direct woman who wasn't into small talk. She was also the closest thing Bridget had to a mother since her own had died when she was a girl.

"How many people for dinner tonight?" Marge asked.

"Not me," Bridget said.

Marge looked doubtful, saying, "You got a better offer?"

Gwen was openly disappointed. "Why can't you have dinner with us?" she asked.

"Too much to do." Bridget clapped her hands together. "I'm turning the loft in my house into a quiet, peaceful writing retreat."

"Are you working on your memoir?" asked Marge wryly. "Am I in it?"

"Her boyfriend's a novelist," said Gwen.

"Marge met him already," Bridget said.

"Oh, him," said Marge with a shrug. "I forgot."

"Oh, please," said Bridget, thinking of Sterling's piercing blue eyes and gruff voice. "Sterling is not forgettable."

"Why's he taking over Will's loft?" said Marge. "What's wrong with the desk in the living room?"

"The loft has a better view, more privacy, and its own bathroom," she said. "Will won't mind." She took the last bite of her oatmeal cookie and swept up the crumbs. "Outstanding cookie."

"You're welcome," said Marge.

Gwen turned to her masseur—"Do you have time to do us all?"—and gestured toward Bridget and Marge. "My treat."

"Hell, no," said Marge, as if Gwen had suggested something lewd.

Bridget stood up. "Me neither."

"Tony, this is my big sister." And Gwen came over to put her arm across Bridget's shoulders. Gwen always, *always* had to mention that she was younger.

"Cool," he said. "So where do I set up?"

"Sunroom?" Gwen asked.

"Fine," said Marge.

Tony backed out of the door, bumping the table into the door-jamb, and before following him, Marge pulled a cloth from her apron pocket and leaned over to inspect the damage. She rubbed the spot vigorously.

Just as she straightened up, the door swung open again, narrowly missing her head. Edward, his wild gray hair standing out in cheeky contrast to his dignified cardigan sweater and slacks, entered the room in search of Marge.

He acknowledged Bridget's greeting, giving her a quick kiss on her cheek, but then turned to Marge, saying, "You didn't hear me."

"I didn't hear you what?" she asked.

"You didn't hear me . . . *madam*." He smiled at his own humor.

"Funny," said Marge without expression.

"I was calling for you," he said.

Marge sighed. "What can't you find now?"

"A photo album." He had an elegant scarf draped around his

39

neck and his old pair of worn embroidered house shoes on his feet, the overall effect being elegant, aristocratic even. Bridget felt proud of him and simultaneously grateful that he was too preoccupied to notice how slovenly she looked in comparison.

"Narrow it down," Marge said.

"Circa 1972."

"I'll bring it to you," said Marge.

He bowed in mock seriousness, straightened his glasses, and said, "I just saw a man wandering about who appears to be a stripper."

"He's a masseur," said Gwen.

"Well, he's loose in the house, in case anyone's looking for him." He then turned to Bridget. "Are you ill?"

"No, I—"

"You have the look of Mimì in *La Bohème* right before she dies of consumption."

He didn't wait for an answer, and instead pushed open the door and exited before Bridget could ask who he was with in the living room.

Marge started to follow him out but turned back, pointing at each of the girls in turn. "I like having my girls under the same roof." She winked and left them alone.

Gwen put the glasses in the dishwasher. "When's Will coming?"

"I'm not sure." Bridget was sort of hoping Will would wait a few weeks before coming so she and Sterling could establish a routine together and have a chance to be alone. For the first time ever, Will would be staying in the guesthouse.

"Does he like Sterling?"

"Of course." Will hadn't said much about him, but they seemed to enjoy their man-banter when they saw each other. "How often are you coming up this summer?"

"I'll get here when I can. My job is crazy right now."

The music coming from the living room got louder for a moment, and over the orchestra, they could hear the intensity of their dad's voice. "He's on overdrive," said Gwen, "and I'm finding it unnerving."

Bridget thought of the reaction she'd gotten in the emergency room at the mere mention of her father's name. "If we're half as popular and youthful as he is at that age, I'll throw us a party."

"Liar," said Gwen. "You never have parties." Smiling, she went off to the sunroom for her massage.

———◇———

Before leaving, Bridget's curiosity got the best of her, and she decided to find out who was visiting her father. She went to the library and leaned into the adjacent living room, catching sight of the back of her dad's wing chair. His foot was tapping the floor like a metronome. Sitting beside him was a dignified-looking man whose head was tilted upward in profile, eyes closed, fingers laced together over a Moleskine notebook, lips in a smile, one gray-socked foot resting on the opposite knee. Bridget recognized him right away: Nicholas Donahue, a musicologist from Oxford. They'd met a couple of times over the years, at parties and events, but one time stood out in particular when she, Jacques, and Will were at a music festival in Salzburg. They went to a cocktail reception and were getting a lot of praise for the Brahms piano trio they'd performed earlier in the day when Nicholas and his wife, Miriam, approached them. Nicholas seemed interested in only one thing: what it was like to be the daughter of the great Edward Stratton. Bridget, wanting to celebrate her trio's performance rather than her dad's accomplishments, had excused herself as soon as she could do so politely, taking Will's hand and fleeing to the bar.

It seemed now from the blissful look she saw on Nicholas's face that there was no place on earth he would rather be. She could imagine what he was thinking: *Someone take a picture! I'm at Edward*

Stratton's country estate, listening to Mahler with the master. He opened his eyes suddenly, and Bridget quickly stepped out of his sight line.

Behind where Nicholas was sitting and in front of the bay window was her father's seven-foot Bösendorfer piano, moved to this spot thirty years earlier after Edward sold their beautiful tenth-floor home on Park Avenue and bought a smaller apartment on Central Park West, where he'd lived ever since with a baby grand. But in the prewar apartment Bridget grew up in, her mother, Sophia Stratton, and her father hosted an annual winter party, during which she and Gwen would slip away from Marge so they could get a better view of Edward when he made his annual toast, a presentation really, from his seat at that piano. Past the Christmas tree and the roaring fire, Gwen and Bridget would sneak through the crowd to watch their father improvise off Christmas songs as their mother, dressed in dark green or burgundy velvet, stood nearby, smiling when he asked their guests to raise their glasses to her. Then he would tell stories (as his rapt audience listened, forgetting even to sip their champagne) about his celebrity encounters, his travels, or, Bridget's favorite, about the origin of the piano itself. He'd bought it at auction in London from the great-grandson of a wealthy socialite, pianist, and singer named Elizabeth Vogel, who had shocked British society when she took off with a Venezuelan businessman, leaving her husband and four children behind. Months later, she'd written her husband, telling him he could keep the kids but asking him to send the piano to her in Caracas. It had been his wedding gift to her, after all. Her husband agreed, a shocking concession given the circumstances, but when the time came for the instrument to be sent across the ocean on a Blohm und Voss ship, the movers found letters from past lovers stashed in the body. One of the letters detailed an encounter that happened on the very instrument itself. The piano never made it onto the boat. Edward would end the story by saying it was no wonder the keyboard had such excellent "action." Bridget hadn't understood the joke until many years later, but that line always went over well with the audience, including with her mom, who would laugh as if she were trying not to, shaking her head at him in a way that said, *You're incorrigible, but go on.*

In the library, she picked up Edward's new Golden Globe statue, won for Best Original Score, and held it in her hand, feeling the cool weight of it. She put it down next to the Tony he'd gotten in the '70s for his hit musical based on Colley Cibber's play *The Careless Husband.* On the desk, there was music for a piece he was currently working on, and she studied it while listening to the third movement of Mahler through the open door.

When they were young, she and Gwen would sit with their father for hours to hear recordings, while he pointed out tempo shifts or unusual interpretations of a certain movement and judged the excellent or heinous results for which the conductor (usually Karajan or Seiji Ozawa and later Edward himself) was wholly responsible. He would replay the same measure over and over again until they could distinguish subtle differences between two different recordings of it. Then he would test the girls to prove they could hear it. Gwen, at six or so, was good at it, better than Bridget, although sometimes Bridget suspected she was simply a better guesser.

One day, Edward took the testing in a different direction, declaring proudly, "What fun—Bridget has perfect pitch."

Gwen had tapped her father on the arm. "Do I? Do I have perfect pitch?"

No, he told her. She didn't.

Bridget was proud, thinking this actually meant something, that she had an innate skill that would propel her to mastery of the cello. "Don't get too excited," said her father when he heard her boasting about it. "It might help with ear training, but otherwise it's nothing but a party trick. The only thing that matters is practice. Perfect pitch won't get you anywhere." So instead of relying on her aptitude, Bridget put in her twenty-five thousand hours.

———◇———

Picking up a catalog of the collection from the Victoria and Albert, Bridget sat down on the leather chesterfield sofa and leafed through it. Right down the hall in Edward's first-floor master suite, there was an early Turner over the headboard and a late Gainsborough over the dresser, dreamy British landscapes that had belonged to her mother. Bridget would stare at them and feel transported. The Turner, depicting a sky that looked like it was either about to storm or had just stopped—Bridget could never quite decide—showed an eerie light reflecting off a pond, and it seemed to change every time Bridget studied it. The Gainsborough was similar in that the field was lit in the background, while dark clouds formed over shadowy trees in the foreground, leaving her unsure if trouble was coming or going.

"I like his face," a voice whispered in her ear.

Startled, Bridget turned to see Marge, holding a photo album under her arm and a duster in her hand, looking over her shoulder at Nicholas.

"Sorry to disappoint you," Bridget whispered back, "but he's taken. He has a very attractive wife."

"He's fancy-pants, like your father."

Nicholas was not, Bridget noticed, wearing fancy pants. He had on jeans with a linen blazer, giving him the look of a much younger professor.

Marge looked down at Bridget. "I don't want to hurt your feelings, poodle, but you look like you spent last night on a park bench."

Marge had worked for the Stratton family ever since the day Bridget got her first Chapin School uniform. Bridget tried it on and said she looked stupid in it, and Marge had agreed with her. "Stupid indeed. So wear it ironically," she suggested. Marge lived with her son in Yonkers now, but Edward still asked her to spend the summers at his country house. Edward used the title "Housekeeper Emeritus" and paid her a good salary to call the right person when anything needed attention, to order fresh flowers, dust the antiques, and write shopping lists. She cooked for Edward, but if there were more than three guests, she called the caterer.

"It's not my fault," Bridget whispered, showing Marge her arm. "I got electrocuted this morning."

Marge examined the red mark, looking horrified. "Hire an electrician. *Today*. Do you need the name of ours?"

"Is it Baxter and something?"

"Braxton and Sons."

Bridget liked to have more than one problem before she dragged any workers to the house. "Maybe I'll get some new fixtures put in while I'm at it. Sterling prefers lights with dimmer switches."

Marge straightened up. "I get the feeling your beau is sort of difficult."

"Not at all."

"Persnickety."

"He's not persnickety; he's brilliant and thoughtful. A few weeks ago, he recorded me playing a piece, and now he listens to it while he takes walks. Isn't that sweet?"

Marge pursed her lips together disapprovingly and then said, "I'll let you know when I make up my mind about him."

Bridget wasn't worried. By the end of the summer, Marge would like Sterling just fine.

She was looking into the living room now with a puzzled expression. "He's got something cooking, and I don't know what it is."

"Dad?" Bridget asked. "What's he got cooking?"

Marge shrugged. "I thought maybe you knew."

"Do you think he's retiring?"

Marge shook her head. "The opposite. I think he's got a new passion project."

"Gwen said he's in overdrive," Bridget said, giving his state of mind more attention now that Marge was backing up Gwen's opinion.

"He talks about you girls a lot lately."

"Is he going soft in his old age?"

"Aren't we all?" Marge asked, patting her hip. She offered the photo album to Bridget. "Would you like to take this in and say hello?"

"Absolutely not."

Bridget craned her head to the side so she could watch as Marge walked into the living room. Her father took the leather album, delighted to see it, while giving Marge a clear smile of appreciation. Marge went out the far door, waving her duster at the furniture like a wand.

All around this massive house were old-world antiques, the seventeenth-century armoire, the Empire rolltop desk, carved headboards in the bedrooms and medieval-looking wooden candelabras in the dining room. On the table next to Bridget, in an antique silver frame, was a picture of Edward conducting the Munich Philharmonic. She recognized the concert hall by the details of the ceiling (which led to controversy about the hall's acoustics), and her father by the familiar view of his back. Munich was home to Edward's oldest friend, Johannes, a man he'd known for sixty years until he'd died about a year ago. *Sixty* years! A friendship lasting that long was something to be treasured.

Bridget's phone pinged, and she quickly silenced it.

Will had texted to check on her: *Are you recovered from your electric shock???*

Bridget responded with a string of emojis (lightning bolt, surprised face, thumbs-up). Then she wrote: *All okay. Hanging out at my dad's.*

There was a pause. And then: *Didst thou receive an audience with his Majesty?*

Ha and no, Bridget texted. *He's holding court with a loyal subject.*

Will was the only person Bridget knew who didn't hero-worship her father, mostly because he resented Edward for the insecurity Bridget had when she started conservatory. This was not irrational; Edward had told her bluntly when she was young that, in spite of her dedication, he didn't think she was good enough to become a professional cellist. When she turned sixteen, he admitted she had become a decent player, but said it was unlikely she would ever become an exceptional one. It would not be a constructive use of her time, said Edward, to go to conservatory, and she probably wouldn't finish anyway once she met the competition: prodigies who were far superior. She insisted on going anyway, so he suggested she spend a summer in London, living with her grandmother while attending an intensive program (that culminated in a master class she'd barely survived) so that she could work on her "wholly inadequate" technique (poor thumb position and bow balance, to name a few issues). He was less critical of her after she returned, but Will spent a lot of his time in college convincing Bridget that she deserved to be at Juilliard, that she could succeed as a professional musician, no matter what Edward had told her when she was a kid. Will finally met Edward the day he and Bridget graduated. Will threatened to say something snarky to him, but he didn't, of course. It would have been rude, and Will was unfailingly polite. Besides, Edward was intimidating. He was a genius. He had charmed the pope. He'd delighted dictators. Everyone loved Edward.

The sound of men's laughter came from the next room, just as the fifth movement was ending. Bridget opened her eyes, realizing she had no memory of hearing the fourth movement at all and that she'd drooled a bit on her sleeve. She stretched her neck, stood up, and saw her father and Nicholas shaking hands, Nicholas thanking him in a deep voice. Bridget slipped out of the room and hurried down the hall, past the grandfather clock that struck twelve as she went by. Picking up her shoes by the door, she quickly left the house and drove home in her mismatched socks.

That afternoon she practiced for over an hour, going through the Schubert with a metronome. Seeing Edward always compelled her to work hard, but there was something about the sight of him today (or his feet, anyway, from the back of his wing chair), adjacent to Nicholas, the two of them listening so intently to every note, intention, and manifestation, that motivated her. She wanted to be on top of her game to impress Caroline when they started playing together in the fall.

Once again, they were starting over. It was hard to fold in a new violinist, to work out the group chemistry and make sure that she and Will were allowing a new personality to help shape the group dynamics. This time the experience would likely feel different: Caroline Lee was out of their league and the answer to their prayers; Bridget was grateful to her.

The Forsyth Trio had seen better days. It was getting harder and harder to book concerts, their fees were stagnant, and their manager of twenty years seemed completely uninterested in helping them turn things around. Meanwhile new, younger groups were popping up all the time. These kids might not have the experience, connections, and professionalism of Forsyth, but they knew how to use social media and build a brand. Forsyth didn't have a SoundCloud account or a YouTube channel or an Instagram page. They had nothing but an old website and their reputation.

Through a friend (and likely with a little help from the cachet of Bridget's last name), they scored a meeting with Randall Bennett, a manager who handled the careers of the world's top classical musicians. Randall, a slightly balding, fast-talking, intimidating alpha man, had heard them play at Alice Tully Hall once, and he told

Bridget and Will that he thought they were impressive; nevertheless, he turned them down, with a clear and absolute shake of his head. "I'm sorry, guys, but I can't sign a two-person trio," he'd said. And, amused by the absurdity, he laughed. Bridget and Will didn't think it was funny at all. "But I'll tell you what," he added. "If you can find a soloist, a Hilary Hahn or an Anne-Sophie Mutter, a Christian Tetzlaff, someone of that caliber, then get back in touch, and we'll talk."

A few days later Randall contacted them with a proposition: His client, the exceptionally talented, well-known violinist Caroline Lee (graduate of Curtis, winner of the Martin E. Segal Award, named on several fabulous-people-under-thirty lists), wanted to expand her repertoire with ensemble music. She'd heard Forsyth play in New York a few years before. Would they consider working with her, on a trial basis, of course, for one year?

Bridget and Will discussed the proposal.

"If it doesn't work out," Will said, "we'll have no manager, and we'll be in worse shape than we're in now. It's a huge risk."

"*But* if it goes well," Bridget reminded him, "Randall will represent us."

They decided to take the risk.

Randall began booking concerts for the fall, starting with the Frick in mid-September. However, he had explained to them, he was not representing them *yet*, so everything else involved in getting Forsyth back on track was Bridget and Will's responsibility. He told them to "up their game" in order to deserve Caroline. He recommended a PR firm that would launch a publicity campaign, and a company that would revamp their brand and their whole look as an ensemble.

Will was nervous about the plan, but Bridget was thrilled.

———◇———

Bridget put her cello back in its case just as a loud screeching came from the other side of the field, making her wonder who was eating whom in her backyard. Every year, ice storms chewed up the cedar shingles, and the summer heat warped the doors in their frames, making them creak when they opened. The seasons had given her house a lot of its character. She poured herself a glass of rosé and went out to the porch to look at the mountain, the trees, and the outline of Batshit Barn. It was so beautiful, and it made her all the more excited to share it with someone. She couldn't wait for Sterling to get there and picked up her phone to tell him so.

"Here's the plan," she said, as soon as he answered. "We're going to sleep in as late as we want, work as much as we need to, and have sex anytime we like, day or night. Happy hour begins at seven p.m. sharp."

"Hold on," he said.

Bridget heard voices, a woman's and then a child's. Something crackly like an intercom.

"Where are you?" she asked.

"The hospital."

"No way," said Bridget, "I was at the hospital today, too." He didn't say anything. "Are you okay?"

"I had a twinge in my back."

"A *twinge*. What's a twinge?"

There was a rustling and then the woman's voice again. "Bridget? It's Mallory."

"Hi," she said. "Is Sterling all right?"

"He's not taking care of himself," Mallory said. "He sat writing for so long today, he's pinched a nerve in his lower back."

"Oh, shit," said Bridget. "I'll have to make sure he takes a lot of breaks this summer."

"You should get him up from the desk every two to three hours," she said. "And he should do some core-strengthening."

Was sex core-strengthening? Bridget had the good taste not to ask. "There couldn't be a better place to take walks."

"I was thinking," said Mallory, "since he'll be there for so many weeks, why don't you guys go on a health kick together? You should do the Whole30."

A bullfrog croaked in the pond, and Bridget took a sip of her wine.

"I'm sending you a book about it," said Mallory. "Sterling's blood pressure's high, and the doctor thinks a high-fiber, low-carb diet would be good for him. I'd rather you follow Juliette Stark's program, but I think it's too rigid for Sterling. Have you heard about Juliette's book? Gwyneth Paltrow swears by her."

Bridget put her glass of wine down, feeling defensive. "I eat fairly well here." She didn't mention the scolding she'd gotten about her own blood pressure that very morning.

"You guys should cut carbs and all processed foods."

"Who needs fun, right?" Bridget joked.

"No one over fifty," said Mallory sternly.

Bitch. "Lucky you then."

"No dairy, no sugar. And no alcohol."

Bridget saw her wine-and-cheese hour under assault. "Did Sterling agree to this?"

"Hang on," she said.

There was more rustling, and Sterling got on the phone. "Hi, hon. Not to worry, I'm taking ibuprofen and feeling better already."

"Whole30?" she asked. "Really?"

"Fantastic! So, you're on board? And Bridget, I was wondering: You said the study, the loft or whatever, it has a bed in it, right?"

Will's bed. "Of course. And a desk and—"

"How's the mattress?"

"In the loft? It's fine, why?"

"Is it firm?"

"Posturepedic," said Mallory in the background.

"Is it Posturepedic?" repeated Sterling.

"You mean mine? Not really. It's a little squishy."

"No, the mattress in the loft."

Bridget had no idea. "But I don't want you to sleep in the loft," she said, hating the whininess of her voice. "I want you to sleep with me."

"Just in case I have a flare-up."

"Did she bring the cats?" she heard Mallory ask.

"You brought the cats, right?"

"Yes," Bridget said.

"She brought the cats."

Bridget heard the mumblings of a conversation.

"I'll need a hypoallergenic pillow," he said.

"Is Madison excited about camp?" Bridget asked, trying to shift the focus away from allergies and back pain.

"She sure is. Aren't you, Madison? Madison? My friend Bridget wants to— *Madison?*— She wants to know if you're looking forward to camp." More mumbling. ". . . if you're *excited* about *camp?*" Sterling said.

"I loved camp," said Bridget, not sure if he was even listening. "And the twins loved it as well." This was not exactly true, but Bridget was certain several weeks in a cabin on a lake would be good for Madison, not that she knew her or her personality, but Bridget's instinct told her it was the right thing.

"She's nervous," Sterling whispered.

"Totally normal," said Bridget confidently. "She'll get over that as soon as she arrives and makes new friends."

"She's homesick."

"She hasn't left yet."

"I mean," he said, "she's *anticipating* being homesick."

"Just stay positive about it," Bridget said, "and she'll follow your lead."

"You think?"

"Can we cheat on the Whole30?" The thought of eliminating rosé in the summer sounded horrendous. "Can we at least do the Dirty30?"

"*Oh, hell*, now Madison's crying, I gotta run, Bridget. I'll call you later," he said and hung up.

Bridget thought Sterling hovered too much over Madison, paying way too much attention to her every feeling, complaint, and anxiety, but she would never say so. She had conscientiously tried to get the balance right with her own kids, giving them time and attention while allowing them room to feel sad sometimes, to work out their own problems.

Her own father had been so hands-off that Bridget figured she wasn't the best at knowing what good fatherhood looked like. After Sophia died, Edward threw himself into work, leaving it up to Marge to keep the girls from feeling adrift.

Young Bridget did not accept being ignored by her dad, no matter how focused he was on work; she would follow him around the apartment from room to room when he was around, call him at his hotels when he wasn't, practice the cello right next to wherever he was sitting, and show up at his concerts in the city.

"You're a nudge," he said to her one night before heading out to conduct the New York Philharmonic. He was tying his bow tie at the marble sink, while Bridget was sitting cross-legged on his bathroom counter, asking him question after question about his life and childhood; she had learned to stick to his favorite subjects.

"Thank you," she said. "A nudge is good, right?"

He admired his face in the mirror, the left profile and then the right. He ran his hands through his thick hair. "You'll probably nudge your way right into Juilliard."

Bridget was only in middle school at the time, but she made up her mind right then and there that that was exactly what she would do. Edward had gone to Juilliard; she would nudge her way into Juilliard.

She followed him into a career in music.

Later she followed him to Connecticut.

She imagined Sterling sitting on the porch beside her. What would he think of the house? From her spot in a wicker chair, she could see that, yes, the screens were rotting out of their frames, leaving gaps that let in moths and mosquitoes. She glanced up at the fan over her head, the warped blades drooping down like dead flower petals. And she looked out at the grass and weeds in the field that were so overgrown that no normal mower could forge through now. She checked the red mark on her skin, now a faint line running up her forearm like an old scar. Much like the scar Isabelle got on her elbow when she fell off her scooter, flying down the long driveway that sloped to the main road. Her house was fine; it was just scarred in the same way, bumps and bruises that represented a full, well-lived life.

Bridget went inside and made an appointment with the electrician her ER doctor and Marge had recommended. She couldn't have Sterling's computer getting zapped mid-novel. Next, she called Kevin, who promised to stop by to help with a few odds and ends, although he was irritatingly vague about when that might happen.

Finally, she Googled "Whole30" on her phone and made a shopping list. She wanted to have a good attitude about the program—they would get healthy and in shape!—but all she kept thinking was: *What a drag.* Knowing Sterling as she did, she was pretty sure that he, too, would find it a drag, and one night, maybe a week after he arrived, they would quit the Whole30, break out the wine, and let the fun begin.

Her phone rang. "Isabelle!" Bridget said. "How's your tooth?"

"My tooth?"

"You had a toothache."

"Oh, *that*," she said. "No, I've got much bigger issues than a toothache."

An inkling of something bad filled the silence. "Everything okay?"

"Yes, great actually, I haven't felt this good in a long time."

Bridget was relieved. She got up and found her purse and car keys, deciding she would go buy the portable fan Sterling had requested and some sheets with a high thread count. "Wonderful," she said. "Glad to hear it."

"I'm at Heathrow."

"*Heathrow?*" Bridget said, stopping at the kitchen counter. "In London? Why?"

"I couldn't take it anymore, Mom. It's like, I've been racing around my whole life, blindly going along, never stopping to reflect or assess my well-being, and for what? I'm not *happy*, and I need a break, you know?"

Bridget did not know. "You're vacationing in London?"

"I left my job! I walked in my boss's office, I quit, and I got the next flight out."

"But, Isabelle!" Bridget didn't know where to start. "You didn't give notice? You can't just *quit*—"

"I had this sliding-door moment, an epiphany actually: I'm going to die someday! And I haven't even really *lived*. I had to escape the drudgery before my life passes me by. I'm so glad I found the courage to do the right thing. I feel really proud of myself right now."

Millennials. "Courage" and "pride" seemed like a pretty self-congratulatory interpretation of what sounded to Bridget like downright irresponsibility. "What are you . . . ? I mean, where are you . . . ?"

"I've decided to spend the whole summer with you. Catch my breath and figure out what I want to do with my life. And I'll get to know Sterling! It'll be so nice."

No, no, no, no, no, no, thought Bridget.

"And don't worry," she went on, "I'll stay in the guesthouse so I won't be in your way. But we can spend time together, and you can help me figure out who I am and what I really want for my future."

Bridget did something she'd never done to her children before in her entire life: she hung up the phone. She looked at the screen and touched the red button, like a reflex. She needed to think for a second because . . . what was she supposed to say? *Good for you?* This wasn't *good.* This simply would not do. Bridget ran through the options in her head. She couldn't send Isabelle to the New York apartment since Sterling's Dutch friends were living in it. Maybe Isabelle could spend the summer with Oscar and Matt? Or maybe Bridget should try to make her see how impulsive and crazy this was. She thought of a few talking points about burned bridges and lifelong consequences. Then she took a breath and called Isabelle back. "I don't know what happened," she said. "I must have lost signal."

Isabelle was talking as though there hadn't been any break. ". . . because I have no long-term plan whatsoever—*that's* the coolest part! I'll stay here with a grad school friend for a few days, because *London.* Why not? You've always told me how much you love it here. And then I'll fly to JFK and take the train up to the house. Can I use your car while I'm there?"

Hell no, Bridget wanted to say. *No, you absolutely cannot use my car.* "I don't think—"

"Jumping in a cab now. I love you, Mommy. I'll see you soon."

She couldn't stop her. She would never close the door on her own daughter. "Be safe," she said, but Isabelle had already hung up.

This was not—in any way, shape, or form—the summer she'd been imagining. She had pictured lazy mornings in bed with Sterling. Quiet dinners for two. Long walks and deep conversations.

She would have to make it work, that's all there was to it. The property was obviously big enough for the three of them. She would soldier on. She would buy pillows for Sterling. She would buy a coffee maker for the guesthouse so Isabelle wouldn't come over first thing in the morning. She could establish some house rules. Meanwhile, she would have to call Sterling to explain this new development to him, but she had no idea what to say or how to say it.

She picked up her phone and called Will instead.

5

Will walked Hudson down the tree-lined streets of the West Village, listening to Debussy on his headphones. He bought a newspaper and a coffee at his regular café and then sat on the steps of his brownstone, in the shadow of the Sotheby's *For Sale* sign. He scooted to the left railing to be in the sun and to give himself some distance from the garbage cans that sat below him on the right. He usually loved a morning like this, a summer day in the city, especially before it got uncomfortably hot, but with the worry that he might lose his home, Will was having a hard time enjoying anything.

He patted Hudson on his big head and was opening the newspaper when his music was interrupted by a *ping*, and he saw that Bridget, whom he hadn't seen in almost two weeks—possibly a record for them—had texted:

Well, fuck. Did you see the email?

He hadn't, and his first thought was that Caroline was ditching them.

He checked and saw that Bridget had forwarded an email from Sterling:

Dear Bridget,

Mallory and I have given it a lot of thought, and we have come to the decision that Madison isn't ready for camp this year. She doesn't want to go. I told Mallory that you said a little pushback was normal, but pushback turned into an outright refusal, and we decided it would not be right to force her. We feel she should want to go. Instead she gets triggered every time the word "camp" is uttered. It isn't healthy, so we're letting her off the hook, which means I'll need to spend my summer in Brooklyn.

I was up for hours last night, knowing this would come as a great disappointment to you given the plans we've made. And then I had a disturbing, profound realization: none of this is fair to you. You're in such a different phase of life. Your children are adults and off living their lives. You're on your own and free in a way that I'm not . . . and won't be for many, many years to come. I had a hard but good conversation about this with Mallory, and she agrees that it would be best if you and I take a break. I will focus on parenting and writing, while you can focus on your trio, your house, and . . . well, whatever you like!

I wish you well, Bridget. Please accept my sincere apology and know how much I've enjoyed our time together.

Your friend,
Sterling

Bridget picked up on the first ring.

"Wow," he said. "Are you okay?"

"No! No, I'm not okay. Why did he say 'take a break' when his sign-off sounds so final? Should I call him? Can't we talk about it?"

Will reread the email; Sterling really hadn't left any wiggle room.

"What the hell?" she said. "Do you know how I spent my time

this past week? I converted the loft into a lovely, tranquil writing space—"

"My loft?"

"—and I made a list of food we needed to do the Whole30. Have you heard of the Whole30? It's like an eating cult."

There was a pause, and he could hear her sniffling. "I bought an air purifier and hypoallergenic pillows," she said, clearly in tears now, "and a really good fan. He's very persnickety about airflow."

"Oh, Bridget," he said, wishing he could help, "can you return it all?"

"And I have no wine in the house because Mallory said it's not allowed."

"You got dumped, and you can't even get drunk tonight? Good God, Bridget, come home."

"I can't," she said, crying. "*I have Dutch subletters.*"

"Oh, right." Sterling had talked her into that dumb arrangement. "Come back anyway."

"I'm too old to sleep on your couch."

"I never said you could sleep on my couch."

He heard her stifle a laugh.

Someone was coming up the steps, and Will got Hudson up and pulled him closer to make room. Two men in suits, one with a clipboard, the other with a briefcase, went past him and into the building; they had the word "Realtor" written all over them. Will had to stop himself from tripping them.

Bridget had gone quiet.

"You still there?" he said.

"I never saw this coming," she said. "I feel so stupid."

"No, *he's* stupid. This isn't about you at all." Will couldn't believe Sterling was such a jackass. To act as if he were performing some kind public service by setting Bridget free was just so . . . Sterling. Will wanted to take the subway out to Park Slope and let him have it. "Was he mad that Isabelle decided to come?"

"I never even got up the nerve to tell him," she said, "so that wasn't it. Don't you think he could have had the decency to come up here and break up with me in person?"

"Would that have been better?"

She didn't answer.

"Well, shit," he said. "Sterling is a total idiot. He'll regret this." He put Bridget on speaker and reread the email on his phone. "And that Mallory woman is a piece of work. She's horrible."

"You think? Their relationship seemed so healthy."

"No," said Will. "It's weird. Why's he talking to her about his relationship with you? You dodged a bullet having his ex in your life."

"I can't believe this," she said and blew her nose. "This is *so* not the summer I had in mind."

"When's Isabelle getting there?"

"I don't even know. She's so busy living her 'best life' in London, she's stopped updating me."

"Why don't you go there to visit her? You love London."

"I'm too depressed."

Will did not want to leave New York for the wilds of Connecticut. He had students to teach and a gig to play. He had a blind date. He had Netflix and a bottle of chardonnay in the fridge. "Tell you what," he said, "I'll be there tonight."

"Really?"

"Of course. After my last lesson."

"I'll put your room back like it was before," she said sadly. "I don't suppose you'll let me meet your train?"

He didn't bother answering, saying instead, "Flanders Tavern, seven o'clock."

"Will?"

"Yes?" He prepared himself for her usual *What would I do without you?*

"Can you go to the Apple store and get me a new laptop? Mine never came back to life after we got electrocuted."

"Sure," he said, smiling and folding his newspaper. He and Hudson stood up on the brownstone steps, looking out over their street. "How many gigawhatevers?" He had two private lessons to teach at Lucy Moses on 67th that afternoon, and the Apple store was literally at the corner of Broadway. He hoped his credit card could handle it.

<hr />

Late that afternoon, Will and Hudson took the subway to Grand Central and caught the Metro North train two minutes before the conductor closed the doors. Relieved to have made it, he settled in for the two-hour trip with Hudson at his feet, a computer in a box on the seat next to him, and his backpack overhead.

He looked out the window, watching Harlem go by, glad to be spending a weekend with Bridget, now that he'd rearranged his schedule. They would take a walk along the Housatonic, cook tomorrow night, and drink the chardonnay he'd brought along. He always brought her some kind of offering (cheese from Murray's, coffee from Joe's) as his way of being a considerate houseguest. He also insisted on taking a cab to and from the train station so that Bridget didn't have to pick him up. And he would spend some time this weekend keeping Bridget's antique upright Steinway from falling into complete disrepair, unlike everything else in the house. As the only person who played, he did his best to keep it tuned. He wasn't especially good at it and often told Bridget that she needed to hire Edward's tuner to install a Dampp-Chaser and address the sticky keys, but Bridget never got around to it, leaving it to Will to adjust the flatness and sharpness caused by humid summers and dry winters.

In some respects, he missed the old days when Oscar and Isabelle were small and wild and running all over the house, wearing ski clothes, or *Star Wars* costumes, or nothing at all. But if he was being honest, he much preferred not being constrained by the needs of children. Little kids were too much for him.

Ages ago, long before she got pregnant, Bridget asked Will if he wanted to father a kid with her, "no strings attached." But as soon as the words came out—impulsively and after several glasses of wine— she gasped, clapped her hand over her mouth, and then insisted on taking them back. They were sitting in her first studio apartment, he on the couch and she on the foot of her bed, Chinese takeout containers on the coffee table in between them. She had a lime-green rug and a view of the Hudson River out the window.

Will had put down his chopsticks and laughed uncomfortably. "No strings attached? We see each other every single day—"

"Never mind!" she'd said. "Forget I said it. That would be incredibly weird. It would mess up what we have." And she gestured to the egg rolls and to the space between the two of them. "I'll get a stranger or—what do you call it? A *donor*. I was just thinking that the process is so complicated and impersonal, with sperm banks and legal contracts and what? A turkey baster? I was thinking it would be so nice to *know* the man. But it's fine. I can do it. Pretend I never said anything."

"Said what?"

She'd smiled. "Exactly."

He could imagine it, of course. All he would have to do is take a step across the lime-green rug to her side of the coffee table. He even loved her. But it would have been, as she said, "incredibly weird," discombobulating, and way too risky. Even then, she was the closest thing he had to family.

They never discussed the possibility of his involvement again.

Will, who was already divorced at that point, had been wrestling with so much regret, wishing he had slowed down and thought things through before making promises he couldn't keep. He hated to see Bridget make a similar mistake by becoming a mom before she was ready or for the wrong reason or because of some societal expectation.

But a few months later she brought it up again.

"I want a baby," she said, "and I don't want to feel pressured to find the right guy at exactly the right time, like *now*, or, even worse, nudge the wrong guy into having a kid just because he's around when I'm ovulating. I'd rather have a child on my own terms."

"They're a lot of trouble, aren't they?" He wasn't keen to have kids himself, so it was hard for him to understand this urge. "Why don't you start with a cat?"

She looked like he'd hurt her feelings.

"You'd be a great mom," he added quickly, "that's obvious, but what's the rush?"

"My mother was thirty when she had me, but she'd been married since she was twenty-four. Six years?"

"So?"

"So, I think she had a hard time getting pregnant. And then it was five more years before she had Gwen. I don't want to wait and then find out it's too late."

Bridget started researching insemination, making appointments, and visiting clinics. She told Will she was still thinking things over, but then—without even telling him—she went ahead with it, having the twins in her very first round. And even though Will wasn't the biological father, he quickly discovered that there were strings, strong ones, attaching him to her children. He was in the hospital when they were born, and they were the first infants he ever held and hummed to, the only ones who had fallen asleep on his stomach, fingers wrapped around his thumb.

He was right about one thing: kids were a hell of a lot of trouble. Isabelle and Oscar were screamy babies and klutzy toddlers. Even with Marge in the picture, Will couldn't believe how much time went into picking them up off the floor, feeding them, and putting their spit-up-soaked clothes in the laundry. Oscar would climb up on his lap and pat Will's face with his sticky hands, while Isabelle would bring him a revolting, damp lump of Play-Doh as a gift. One or both of them would always cry whenever he left Bridget's new three-bedroom apartment to go home.

When the kids were about five, they all drove around Litchfield County to find a house that had a big yard, a place to ride bikes, and trees to climb. Will was in dire financial straits at the time, trying to manage about $42,000 of debt. That Bridget had money was blatantly obvious. She never worked in college. He, like most of the students he knew, had held countless jobs: he'd bused tables, played Christmas songs in department stores in New Jersey, busked in Manhattan subway stations, and made sandwiches with names like "The Spicy Bird" and "Hog Wild" at a deli. He'd even apprenticed for a seventy-year-old Japanese piano technician in Brooklyn one summer to learn the basics of tuning. Bridget played cello; that was her work. Bridget and Will were WASPy enough that they never discussed money in detail, unless it directly involved their business, and her circumstances didn't entirely make sense to him. On the one hand, she complained about New York expenses like everyone else he knew, and she made good use of the New York City public school system instead of putting her kids in a private school like the one she'd attended. She didn't spoil the twins with excessive toys or fancy clothes. On the other hand, she'd bought a country house and put her kids through college while still living in a nice uptown apartment. How, he'd often wondered, had she managed it all? How could one explain Bridget's consistent lack of urgency and panic in the face of an artist's poverty? And then he would remember: *family money.*

He didn't hold their financial disparity against her; it wasn't her fault that she was born into wealth. It wasn't her fault that her mother died when she was eleven, leaving her and Gwen with an inheritance stemming from their great-grandfather's business, a company that had made, among other things, gold and mother-of-pearl opera glasses, accessories that helped the wealthy see better. The great-grandfather invested the company's profits well. Nor was it her fault that her father had—with pomp and circumstance and revolting narcissism—given her a graduation check made out for a huge sum of money, along with a drawn-out, self-indulgent toast in which he quoted everyone from Derrida to Winston Churchill to Samuel Clemens. *Good for her*, Will had thought. "Holy shit," Gavin had whispered. *Bitch!* a few had probably said behind her back, although no one would gossip about Bridget in front of Will.

When the train pulled into the station, Will stepped out into the sunshine and waved to the car waiting for him in the parking lot. The driver, Frank, waved back. With his backpack over one shoulder and the Mac box under his arm, Will walked Hudson over to the field to let him sniff around and pee. One other passenger, a college girl by the looks of her, walked by them and got into the backseat of an Audi sedan that was waiting with the engine running. Will walked over to Frank's car, put Hudson in the backseat, and got into the front, saying hello and asking to be dropped in front of Flanders Tavern. Frank, a straight-talking man who drove a Honda Accord and wore flannel shirts year-round, had been picking him up in the same spot for years and had the utmost pity for Will and anyone else who had to live in New York City.

"How's that awful place you call home?" Frank said, as if he were asking Will about a dying relative.

Will rolled the window down and watched a chipmunk scamper over a stone wall. "Pretty much the same."

"I don't know how you stand it," Frank said for the thousandth time. Will had learned it was best not to argue. "It's too big, that's all there is to it. How can you stand living with nine million hostile people?"

How to explain? *They aren't* all *hostile*, Will wanted to say, although there was a child living in the apartment directly upstairs who liked to drop marbles on the hardwood floor right over Will's bed on Sunday mornings, which sometimes felt hostile.

The *For Sale* sign in front of his building felt hostile as well.

"It works for me, what can I say," said Will. "And besides, Manhattan has less than two million people."

Frank whistled. "Sounds lonely to me. That's no way to live."

"I love it there," Will said sincerely. "There're people in the streets night and day, at all hours, so it's certainly not lonely, and there's always something to do. Although the building next to mine has been under construction for ages, and the noise can get pretty annoying," he added.

"It's quiet here," Frank said. And then he stopped talking for a moment as if to demonstrate. "And people know you. Like they really *know* you. Life is all about the steady folks and places in your community."

No, thought Will, considering the shops that closed down, restaurants that went under, the piano students who left for college, and neighbors who moved to less expensive places. *That's not quite it.*

How could he explain to Frank what it felt like to drink coffee on his stoop in the morning or gin on the roof at night. To walk through Washington Square Park in the spring and along the Hudson in the winter. To teach a good lesson on the Upper West Side and rehearse a good piece on the Lower East. To be part of Forsyth through it all. Will was content, and New York had everything to do with it.

It had occurred to him, ever since that *For Sale* sign went up, how easily it could all be taken away.

The restaurant owner (Anne? Anna?) was wiping down the bar where two men, locals by the look of them, were already having drinks.

She waved to him. "Your wife's not here yet."

Will didn't bother correcting her. "I'm early. Can I leave my stuff while I walk the dog?"

She pointed toward the coatroom. Will left his backpack and the new laptop, an unthinkable act in New York, and went back to the dining room.

"You'll want a table on the porch," she said, patting Hudson on the head.

Will smiled. "Perfect. I'll be back at seven."

The town attracted an odd mix of visitors, from leather-clad motorcycle enthusiasts who cruised the scenic routes of Litchfield County, to bandana-wearing hikers in need of a shower who were taking a break from the Appalachian Trail, to rich New Yorkers dressed in black in search of all things quaint. Will was in a different category: he was a nonrich New Yorker with a wealthy friend who was a weekender. Without Bridget, he would never have found his way here.

Will wandered the full length of the main street (the only street), past antique stores, an upscale coffee shop, and the brick library. In the bookstore, he bought a thriller and Anne Tyler's latest. He would let Bridget choose which one she wanted to read first.

Back on the sidewalk, Hudson trotted along next to Will, stopping to sniff the grass every few feet. When they reached the Civil War obelisk at the town's center, Will checked the time on his phone and then kept going. A store caught his attention. Inside were large-scale armoires and antique mirrors. Old, ornate chandeliers and reclaimed-barn-wood furniture, distressed and full of character. Not Will's taste, but cool nevertheless. Out back, there were large sculptures of stags, verdigris urns, and a stone cherub spitting water into a massive fountain. He found an unusual folk art weathervane in the shape of a bat in flight that Will thought would look perfect on the top of Bridget's barn. The price tag said $1200. Will kept walking.

He soon came to the very last stop, where the sidewalk ended at a large nursery. As a man who had absolutely no interest in gardening,

Will turned around. But then someone caught his eye. A stunning woman, in her forties maybe, was pulling a red wagon full of plants through the gravel parking lot. She had a heart-shaped ivy wreath hanging off the crook of her elbow, and a most appealing laugh that he could hear all the way from the sidewalk. She was wearing a tight tank top and loose overalls, and she made the whole rig look ridiculously sexy. He stopped and watched her load the plants (or shrubs?—some kind of leafy creatures) into the trunk of a sedan. Will watched as she stepped back with her empty wagon and waved while the customer drove away.

She glanced up in his direction, and Will pretended to be looking elsewhere, focusing on the flats of pink and yellow flowers behind her rather than on the shape of her hips, the curl of her hair, the smear of dirt on her cheek, and the flower tattooed on her arm.

"Cute," she called out.

Will looked behind him, seeing there was no one else she could be addressing, and said hopefully, "Sorry?"

"Your dog. He's cute."

That was an invitation if ever there was one. Will looked at Hudson, patted his side in gratitude, and brought him over to say hello.

Thirty minutes later, he was sitting on the porch of Flanders Tavern with a gin and tonic in his hand, Hudson under the table, and a robust, potted rhododendron taking up the whole seat next to him.

"I would apologize for being late, but you're in good company," Bridget said, taking a seat across from him and the plant. Hudson got up, happy to see Bridget, knocking into the table legs to get to her. Bridget greeted him and then shook hands with one of the plant's leaves.

Reaching in her purse, she pulled out a check and handed it to

Will, saying, "Thanks for the laptop. Mine literally had smoke coming out of the keyboard."

He folded the check without looking at it and put it in his wallet; knowing Bridget, she had probably rounded up considerably. "Show me your burns."

She turned her right arm over, palm side up. "I'm healed," she said.

"And your heart?"

She squeezed his hand. "I keep checking my phone, expecting him to call and say he's made a big mistake."

"He did. He made a colossal mistake," Will said with certainty.

Bridget took a tissue from her pocket and wiped under her eyes. She attempted a smile, and he noticed that her eyelids were lined with smudgy black makeup and were shadowed up to her brows. "That's a lot of makeup for a day where the chances of tears are a hundred percent," he said.

She looked up at him. "Do I look silly?"

She didn't; she looked beautiful. "I'm not used to seeing you so done up."

"You see me done up all the time."

"This is different. You're all . . . shimmery. Like you're heading to Studio 54 in 1980."

Bridget touched her tissue lightly to her thickened ink-black lashes. "This is Gwen's handiwork. I went to my dad's house this afternoon in search of a shoulder to cry on, and Gwen's solution to my heartbreak was to give me a makeover."

"Are you okay?" he asked, watching her struggle to put on a brave face.

"No. And Gwen threw away my favorite sweatpants while I was in the shower. I loved those sweatpants."

"*The* sweatpants?"

She started to tear up again.

Will stood halfway, leaned across the table, and kissed the top of her head. "I'm so sorry." Will decided if he ever saw Sterling again, he would . . . he would . . . he would have *very* strong words to say. It wasn't necessarily a good idea to criticize an ex-boyfriend, but Will couldn't help himself from making one jab as he sat down again: "Sterling did have a stick up his ass."

"Marge said the same thing," Bridget said, "using different words."

Knowing Marge was an ally gave Will the courage to say something more. "Sterling's suffering from the bitter taste of his first novel's success. He's threatened by his younger self who won the National Book Award."

"His most recent book did well."

Will had seen it on the front table of a bookstore in Grand Central that afternoon, with its dull graphic design on the gray cover that screamed, *I am a book to be taken seriously!* Will hid it under a bright yellow pop-health and diet book, a small act of revenge that made him feel good. "It's not doing that well. And anyway, no matter what he writes, he'll never again be the young genius bursting onto the literary scene." Will had given this phenomenon a lot of thought and was convinced, based on cases he'd seen, that too much success in one's twenties was a terrible thing. In Sterling's case, it had given him the belief that he was precious.

"Are you asking me to feel sorry for him?"

"Not at all," Will said. "I'm just armchair-analyzing his terrible personality."

"You think he's terrible?" she said. She unrolled her napkin and put it in her lap, lining up the silverware on her placemat. "I sort of thought he was perfect, or very close to it."

"His relationship with his ex is bizarre." Will had had zero contact with his ex since the divorce, which, he knew, was extreme as well. Something in between would be healthy. "I don't get why she has such a leading role in his life. You would have been fighting for that position before long."

"I thought I was getting my own role," said Bridget sadly, "but Sterling obviously didn't like me that much since he threw me away so easily. I bet I'm more upset about losing my sweatpants than he is about losing me."

"Maybe, but to be fair, those sweatpants were in your life a lot longer."

Bridget attempted a smile.

"And if he didn't appreciate *you*," Will went on, "he's not very smart."

"That's what my dad said."

Will set his drink down. "Since when do you confide in Edward about matters of the heart?"

"He asked what was wrong, I answered, and then he delivered a verdict: 'He must be stupid.' It was touching."

"Edward Stratton? Asked a question about somebody else's well-being?"

Bridget smiled. "He put his *hand* on my *shoulder*. I was so shocked I invited the whole family for dinner tomorrow night."

Will turned around and called the waitress over. "Another gin and tonic, please. And, Bridget? Rosé?"

"Yes, please," she said and ran her fingers through her hair. It looked silky, and he could smell something vaguely almond. "Sorry about the impromptu party," she said. "Gwen caught me in a weakened condition, and the next thing I knew, I was issuing an invitation."

"I can't wait to spend an evening listening to Gwen name-drop while Edward broods about something but won't tell us what it is. Promise me Marge will be there to fill the awkward silences."

"I wouldn't expect silence. My dad's becoming downright chatty. When I was leaving, he said to tell you hello."

Will allowed his mouth to drop open. "Why would he do that?"

"I don't know. 'Send my regards to Will,' he said. I couldn't believe it."

"Is he all right?"

71

"He's exuberant. Gwen finds it alarming, Marge thinks it's curious."

"And you?"

"Haven't decided," she said, crossing her arms and considering the question. "He's focused on work, as always. Do you remember Nicholas Donahue?"

"No. Should I?"

"He's that good-looking, talkative professor from Oxford—you've met him and his wife a few times. He dresses nicely and speaks upper-class Queen's English in a very low register."

"Sounds pretentious. Musician?" he asked.

"Historian slash musicologist. He's written a few books. He was visiting with Edward last week and seemed enthralled." Bridget was looking at the potted plant seated across the table. "Are you taking this back to New York on the train?"

"Of course not," Will said as he imagined maneuvering through the crowds in Grand Central, hugging the plant to his chest. He was dying to tell Bridget about the woman he'd just met, but given what she was going through, it seemed completely inappropriate, bordering on mean. Better, he thought, would be to share his worry about his apartment, to tell her he was scared he was about to get priced out of his building and out of Manhattan itself. But he couldn't bring himself to admit that, at his age, he was in a situation that could lead to a real financial crisis. It was humiliating. Instead, he put out his hands to signify an offering. "The plant is a breakup present," he said. "I'm contributing to your garden."

Bridget looked at him skeptically. "Planting things involves digging in actual dirt. The dirty kind. Your fingernails will never recover."

It was true that Will was compulsive about his nails, but given the amount of time he spent looking at them, he thought it was reasonable. "I'll get old man Walter to plant it as soon as he comes."

"I'm done with Walter. But I'm sure Kevin can do it."

"Ah, Kevin," Will said, leaning back in his chair, remembering the absurdly wide-legged, husky-size cargo pants that Kevin wore with pride through his unbearably dorky preteen years. "Diamond in the rough. Salt of the earth. Ferdinand under the cork tree."

Bridget shushed him.

"What?"

"Everyone in this town knows everyone," she said. "I don't want it to get back to Walter that we were bad-mouthing his grandson."

"Those were compliments. Anyway, I thought the lumpy boy had moved away."

"He's back, so I'm hiring him to do some odd, outdoorsy jobs."

"Perfect. Kevin was born to dig holes. And if he's around, you won't make *me* haul firewood or, God forbid, check the chimney for raccoons. I was covered in soot for days."

"Poor you." Then she sighed sadly. "Poor me. Thank you for rushing up to see me, and I can't believe I'm saying this, but I'm so glad Isabelle's coming. I don't know what I would have done here all by myself."

Will didn't believe Isabelle would actually stay the whole summer and worried how Bridget would feel after she left.

"I have an idea," she said, "but you'll probably think I'm nuts. I was thinking maybe this is all a sign. Maybe I should take the next couple of months to clean the place up, get rid of some things, and put the house on the market."

Will was quite sure this was the sadness of a breakup talking. "You told me you wanted to retire and die here."

"Connecticut winters are too cold for old age," she said. "I would only retire if you came with me, and *you* always say you want us to grow old and die together in Santa Barbara."

"Well, sure," he said. "They don't call it the American Riviera for nothing."

"Forest fires are getting worse, and earthquakes can strike at any moment."

"That's why we're going there to die." Will looked up at the porch ceiling. "I don't think earthquakes 'strike.' Lightning strikes."

"What do earthquakes do?"

"They hit."

"Either way," she said, "earthquakes are better than blizzards, icy roads, and power outages."

"You don't want to sell your house," he said. Were it not for the serious look on her face, he would have assumed she was joking.

"It's a thought. It would be sensible," she said plainly.

"The kids will want to bring their families here someday—"

"We can go to Edward's instead, take advantage of Marge's TLC and the pool. Every time we get a break, I come here. But what about all the other places to see and things to do? What if I want to take up . . . sailing or something?"

"Sailing?"

"What if I want to go on an adventure at the Great Barrier Reef? Or to Antarctica?"

"You want to go to Antarctica?"

"It would be nice to have the freedom to do something different."

"You can," he said. "Why don't you do this country music video with me? Or the low-testosterone commercial? It would be so much more pleasant to do odd jobs together."

"You're doing a commercial for low testosterone?"

"It's *against* low testosterone, not for it. I'm helping cure sad men of their flaccidity, giving them a new lease on life. Join me!" he said, with as much enthusiasm as he could muster. Hudson thumped his tail in response.

"I can't. I'm stuck here. Maybe this summer is a chance for us all to enjoy the house and then say good-bye to it. Start a brand-new chapter in the fall."

"But isn't this"—and he waved his arm to indicate the whole town—"I don't know, our special place."

"Our rehearsal studio on Forsyth is our special place. We've spent a lot more time there."

He couldn't argue with that. And he'd always thought the house was more trouble than it was worth. Walter would call Bridget about the leaky roof, or a power outage during a nor'easter, or her hypersensitive alarm system. "Are you being serious?"

"I think so."

"Because it's not the worst idea you've ever had."

"It isn't?"

"A new chapter, I'm all for it." He imagined her regretting such a big decision, and added, "But there's no reason to rush into it. What're the kids going to say?"

"I'm not sure about Isabelle," she said. "But Oscar won't care. He and Matt are always too busy to come visit."

Will reached his arm down to pat Hudson on the head when he realized, too late, that he was accidentally smiling. Bridget had already noticed. She squinted her eyes at him.

"Nothing," he said before she had even posed a question.

"What's nothing?"

Will shrugged nonchalantly. "I'm happy to see you. Hudson and I took a nice walk through town." Will picked up his menu and looked at it. "I saw a bat weathervane at an antique store. You should buy it for the barn."

"And?"

"And I got us books."

She pushed the menu away from his face. They stared at each other. "What?" he said.

She was still watching him as he took a last, big sip of his drink and placed the empty glass on the table. "Fine," he said, and he licked his lips, "and I'm sorry if this is bad timing, but I met a really nice woman." He rubbed his jaw and looked to Bridget for a reaction. "I think I like her."

Bridget dropped her menu. "Will! That's great."

"I don't know her or anything about her, but she's . . . First impressions? . . . She's beautiful and funny and sexy. I felt this intense attraction, so strong I found it almost impossible to string a sentence together."

"Wow," she said.

"I don't want to gloat, given what's happened with Sterling—"

"No, it's fine, gloat away. Tell me about her."

The topic was uncomfortable under the circumstances, but maybe he could take her mind off Sterling. "I don't have much to tell. Her name's Emma."

"Where'd you meet her?" Bridget said.

"Here," said Will. "She works right down the street—"

"Wait, *here*?" Bridget said. "You met her here? In town?"

"—at the plant store."

"Ah, I see." She reached behind her and began looking through her handbag.

"What? What do you see?"

She pulled out her reading glasses and began perusing the menu. "Have we had the duck before?"

"Bridget. What?"

Bridget shook her head.

"Say it."

She took off her readers and set them on the table. "You live in Manhattan. In the Village."

"Yeah?"

"And you *love* it there."

"I know." He did love it. He loved it, and he needed to find out what he and Mitzi could do proactively in order to stay where they were.

"And you don't love the country," Bridget was saying, "and you sure don't have an interest in *plants*."

"So?" he asked. They'd discussed his dating life many times, and

Bridget often came up with new explanations for why his relationships ended. She always made sense, and he wondered what her theory would be this time.

"I just wonder if you're not starting out with the odds against you. You do this. You pick women who come with built-in deal-breakers, starting with your ex-wife."

"That's not true. I have . . . bad luck. I can't help who I like."

The waitress came and took Will's empty glass, and set down their drinks. "Are you ready to order?" she asked.

"No," they said.

The waitress walked away.

"You pick the wrong women," Bridget said, "every time. Remember Amanda? You fell for her even though you knew when you met her that she was moving out of the country."

"So?" he asked again.

"I'm saying, maybe you picked her *because* she was moving out of the country."

"You're overthinking things," Will said.

"In the last five years you've dated a lesbian—"

"She was bisexual."

"—and a woman who completely *despised* classical music. And let's not forget Evelyn—"

"What? I really liked Evelyn."

"—who told you the day you met her that she had a paralyzing fear of big dogs."

"I thought she'd warm up to Hudson once she got to know him, and you know what I think?" he said. "I think you're feeling grouchy because of Sterling—which is completely understandable—so you're raining on my parade."

"Not at all. Nothing would make me happier than to see you attached."

They were quiet, Bridget studying her menu and Will pretending to.

Bridget broke the silence. "Sorry, I don't mean to be grumpy."

"You're allowed to be grumpy."

"I'm just thinking, what if we're too old to find the right people? What if Sterling was *it* for me, my last chance?"

"We're not old," Will said, trying not to feel offended. "We don't act old. You don't look a day over thirty, and when you *were* thirty, you didn't look a day over twenty. I remember, when we were in Texas one time, we got invited to a party after we played a concert at Rice, and everyone mistook you for a college student." They'd played badly, he recalled. Gavin had left them already, and their new violinist, an older woman named Martina, simply wasn't that good. Bridget was distracted, calling Marge from the hotel to check on the twins, who were sick. "A freshman tried to get you to go back to his dorm room."

"I have no memory of this."

"You were sleep-deprived. The point is we're still young. You can find someone new, when you're ready."

"Maybe we shouldn't bother. We have each other. And maybe we should just put the trio first and focus on our relationship with Caroline."

"I wish Caroline were a better communicator," said Will, knowing he sounded like a needy boyfriend. "I don't feel like we're a priority."

"She'll prioritize us once we get started. She's our partner now. She's hooked her cart to our ass."

"I'd say she hooked her ass to our cart. We've placed our fate in the hands of a twelve-year-old."

"She's twenty-six. And she's excellent—"

"I know, I know," he said wearily. "She's very hot."

Bridget looked up at him. "*Hot?* Really?"

"I mean *in demand*," he said. "And it isn't very generous or feminist of you to misunderstand me on purpose. Give me some credit. She's a child."

Caroline Lee was, in fact, strikingly beautiful. Her website featured her posing with her violin on a beach in front of the Golden Gate Bridge, staring intensely into the camera, as if challenging the listener to find fault in her playing; they would be hard-pressed to do so.

"Please be optimistic about her," Bridget said. "She's all I've got right now, and I'm trying to keep in mind that my dream in life has always been to play music at St. Luke's in London, not to get married there."

"Married?" said Will with horror. "Who's talking about marriage?"

But from the look on Bridget's face, he could tell that marriage had been exactly what she'd been thinking about: an end-of-summer engagement to Sterling and a spring wedding on Edward's lawn. Will was glad she'd dodged that bullet; marriage was a hideous institution.

The waitress came back and took their order. Will, feeling motivated to stay trim, ordered fillet of sole, while Bridget, bless her, ordered pasta with gorgonzola sauce.

After dinner they drove up to the house, listening to Stravinsky's *The Rite of Spring* on the radio, arguing over which recording it was. They had to sit in the driveway to hear the opening of the "Sacrificial Dance" to find out who was right (Bridget), but also because it was too good to turn off until it was over.

When they opened the car doors, Hudson jumped out and ran happily in circles around Bridget.

"I'll be in after I walk him," Will said.

"Need a hand?" she asked, as he lifted the rhododendron out of the backseat.

"Nope, I got it."

He set the plant on the steps and went back for his backpack and Bridget's laptop.

Hudson ran out into the field, and Will walked with him in a big circle around the yard, stepping through the tall grass with his hands in his pockets, sucking on a butterscotch candy. The moon was full, and it was hard not to be impressed by the ruckus coming from the thicket near the pond, cicadas or peepers or crickets or whatever critters carried on like this at night. And then there was the business with the stars overhead, scattered across the sky.

He felt a lightness, an excitement for the night to pass and the morning to come. How soon could he go back to see Emma, he wondered, and what excuse could he come up with? A need for fertilizer? A garden gnome? Vegetable seeds?

While they'd listened to Stravinsky, Will had been thinking about Bridget's words and decided that although she knew him better than anyone, she was wrong about his feelings in this case. He wasn't trying to sabotage anything; he was only hoping to get to know this woman, find out who she was and whether she'd felt the charge between them. He liked the way her eyes watered when she laughed, explaining that the plant had to be taken *out* of the plastic pot before being planted in the ground. And the way she'd thanked him as he was leaving, handing him his receipt and pressing a butterscotch candy into the palm of his hand.

It was then that he noticed a light was on in the guesthouse, and he saw a shadowy movement inside. Hudson put his head up and growled, low and deep. There was definitely someone in there. The lock on the guesthouse door hadn't worked for the past ten years or so, but it had never occurred to him anyone would ever break in. And then he saw her in the living room: Isabelle. Through the big window, he could see her as she pulled clothes out of her suitcase and tossed them in a pile. He felt like he was watching a flashback, a glimpse of carefree, ten-year-old Isabelle rather than the serious, business-minded woman she'd become. She looked happy, which was good, but Will had a feeling the summer was about to get much more complicated.

He whistled to Hudson and hurried back to the main house to get Bridget so they could go welcome Isabelle together.

6

No one, not her son or her grandchildren, not her friends, and none of the Strattons, seemed to fully appreciate that Marge had developed a superpower. It was a gift that had emerged after years and years of taking care of people. It had intensified recently, until one day, she realized: all she had to do was tune in, and she could figure out how or what the people closest to her were doing, feeling, and thinking. The laundry held secrets, as did the mail, as did hushed conversations, bedroom trash cans, and open laptops, but Marge had no need for snooping. Nor would she describe herself as psychic. Rather, the knowledge came to her. As for the Strattons, she had known before anyone else, for example, that Gwen would be a much happier, more satisfied person once she got rid of her jack-ass ex-husband, Charles, and started focusing on her career. She'd known Isabelle would never last the year in Hong Kong. Just like she knew that Edward was up to something very, very big because there was an energy radiating off of him she had never felt before. And that Bridget was grasping at straws to give her midlife meaning, unaware that what she needed was change.

Marge was only a part-time employee now, a temp, and barely one at that. Her son dropped her off every year at the end of May, and picked her up after Labor Day weekend, and all she did throughout the summer was tell other people what to do. She had a list of numbers at the ready (from a landscaper and an appliance repairman to a window washer and even a tapestry-restoration expert), and she made appointments, opening the door whenever the bell rang, and watching workers while they did their thing. She was an overseer.

One of these days, Bridget would ask for help. Marge hadn't been to Bridget's house since the previous summer, and she could only imagine the state it was in after another year of neglect. Her apartment in New York wasn't much better. Bridget was not a messy person by nature. She was clean, and she had good taste. But she had a blind spot when it came to seeing when change was needed. When a lightbulb burned out, it stayed burned out. When a window latch broke, it stayed broken. Screens stayed torn; floors stayed damaged. She was sentimental, keeping T-shirts for decades, regardless of their condition, and driving the same car she'd gotten when the kids were born, convinced it would have its feelings hurt if she sold it.

Marge was no therapist, but it was clear that losing a mother to cancer at only eleven, the greatest, most difficult loss imaginable, had left Bridget wanting to keep everything in her life *steady*. The same house, the same job, the same music partner.

Marge also knew that Bridget was ready for so much more.

Edward, who had been up since six that morning, was composing in the living room. Marge would hear him every so often, vocalizing a line with a "pa-pa-pa" or playing the same notes over and over on the piano. He was quiet now, and Marge wondered if he was pacing, as he sometimes did when he was writing music, or if he was sitting at the desk, pencil in hand.

At ten in the morning, Gwen still hadn't come downstairs.

While Marge waited for Edward's new assistant to arrive from New York, she baked two desserts to bring to Bridget's house that night, a blueberry crisp, a family favorite, and a pie for Bridget, tripling the amount of Irish cream the recipe called for. It would be a small consolation for the cowardice of that dumb Sterling. Marge was not surprised he'd blown up the relationship; Sterling was a weasel. He was one of those stupid men who thought he was smart. A weak man who thought he was tough. He had a fragile ego, and what he wanted was a mother, not an equal. His ex-wife, as far as Marge was concerned, could keep him.

The doorbell rang, and Marge walked to the entry, wiping her hands on a dishcloth. Opening the door, she pulled twenty dollars out of her pocket and handed the money to Frank, who was standing next to a young woman under the portico.

"Hello, Frank," Marge said.

Frank carried the woman's suitcase inside the doorway, saying, "Hiya, Marge."

He walked back to the woman, who had not yet taken a step toward the house, and said to her with a laugh, "I gotta say, that's the first time anyone's ever asked to see my driver's license before. You New Yorkers sure aren't very trusting." He turned and walked out to his car, waving at Marge before he drove off.

Marge introduced herself. "Welcome, Jackie," she said. "Come on in. Shoes off, please."

Jackie walked in stiffly, posed like a Christmas caroler with her hands clasped in front of her, a small handbag hanging off the crook of her arm.

"Excuse me?"

"Your shoes? Mr. Stratton doesn't allow them in the house."

83

Jackie looked flustered as she stepped out of her black patent leather pumps, and Marge, looking down, could see why. Jackie's toenails were painted a nice shade of pink, but they were chipped and peeling. "I didn't get a chance to—"

"No worries," said Marge. "What size shoe do you wear?"

"Seven?" Jackie said.

Marge went to the closet and found a pair of small-size, close-toed, terry cloth slippers.

"Thank you," Jackie said. She took the slippers, noticing the *S* stitched in green, pulled them out of the plastic sleeve, and stepped into them. "I didn't know. I'll get my own."

"You can have those," Marge said. "Consider them a gift, a perk of the job."

Jackie, who looked to be about the same age as the twins, had long, straight hair with bangs and a fitted buttoned-up blouse.

"How long have you been working for Mr. Stratton?" Marge asked.

"Only a week. I'm mostly helping him with . . . technology."

As Jackie leaned over to pick up her pumps, Gwen flounced down the staircase in bare feet, wearing a tennis dress and carrying a racquet over her shoulder. "Good morning!" She walked up to Jackie and introduced herself. "We talked on the phone the other day. I'm Edward's daughter, the younger one. Did you take the train up?"

Jackie nodded.

"And you're here most of the summer?"

"I'll be here this week," Jackie said formally, "and we'll discuss future visits before I leave."

"I come and go, come and go," said Gwen, "depending on my work schedule, but I stay away as much as possible after the dreaded composers arrive."

Marge saw a look of fear cross the new assistant's face.

"Mr. Stratton told me," Jackie said, "that I'm supposed to be here in August while the composers are in residence."

"Well," Gwen said, clearly amused, "better you than me."

"Now, Gwen—" said Marge, wishing she wouldn't scare the poor girl to death.

But Gwen was already doing her falsetto impression of a guest composer: "*Oh, help, I need Faber-Castell pencils or I can't write a single note! . . . Can someone silence the crows outside? They're cawing off-pitch . . . I must have Darjeeling tea, and only Darjeeling tea, if I'm going to finish my composition to the Maestro's liking.*"

"Don't generalize." Marge turned to Jackie. "Most of them are perfectly nice, actually, if a tad needy."

"They're eccentric, almost always," said Gwen. "You were saying on the phone you haven't been in the area before, right? Let me know if you want some tips, places to see or things to do."

Marge appreciated Gwen's easy way with people, how quickly she befriended them, but some people, Jackie appearing to be one of them, needed more time to warm up, more space in order to feel comfortable. Gwen could come on a bit strong. "Don't you have a tennis lesson?" Marge asked her.

"I'm off to use the ball machine." She turned to Jackie. "It's a great workout. Thirty minutes of randomized shots is about as much as I can manage. Do you play? Because I need a partner. Nothing competitive, just hitting the ball around."

"Don't fib," said Marge. "You play to win, and you should say so. She has a right to know what she's getting into."

"Fine," said Gwen. "Well?" she asked Jackie. "What do you say? I'm not very good."

"Gwen!" said Marge sternly.

"Fine, I'm good. I'm very good. I'll probably demolish you."

Jackie looked flustered. The bottoms of her cuffed slacks were pooling on the floor, too long now that she'd swapped her heels for slippers, and her upper lip was getting sweaty.

"You can think it over," said Gwen. "I'm in desperate need of coffee."

85

Gwen walked away as Marge turned to consider the suitcase. It looked heavy. "You can leave your bag, and I'll find someone to carry it up. I don't do luggage anymore; I'm ancient."

Jackie looked flummoxed. "I can carry it myself."

"I don't want scuffed walls," Marge said as a warning. Jackie didn't look like she could lift a toaster.

"If you don't mind," Jackie said, "I'd be more comfortable carrying it myself."

It's your back, thought Marge. She led Jackie up the stairwell, through the billiards room, and down the hall toward one of the guest rooms, the farthest from Gwen's so they wouldn't be bumping into each other.

"I thought it would be prudent," Jackie said, giving her suitcase a tug to get it rolling on the Persian rug.

"What's that, dear?"

"I thought it made sense to ask for the driver's ID. His cab was unmarked, and I had no way of knowing who he was."

"Of course," said Marge. Jackie was new to rural life—that much was clear.

"He said he was 'Frank,' but," she said, shaking her head, "he could have been anyone."

"That's true."

"I could have gotten in the car and—"

"You've got street smarts," said Marge.

"I didn't mean to offend him."

"Don't give it another thought."

They went into the bedroom, and Marge pulled open the drapes. "Here we are," she said. "You have extra pillows and plenty of hangers in the armoire. Towels are in the linen closet in the bathroom. If you have clothes you need to have washed, put them in the hamper, and the ladies will take care of it. There're towels down in the pool house, so you don't need to bring one with you when you go. There's sunblock down there and drinks, too, so you can pretty much show up empty-handed."

"I won't be swimming or playing tennis," Jackie said. "I'm here to work."

"True," said Marge. "But he can't work you twenty-four hours a day, can he? Do you have a suit?"

"Of course," she said, somewhat indignant. "I have several."

Marge noted that Jackie was wearing a blazer that matched her slacks. "I mean a swimsuit. We can find one for you if you want. Just let me know."

"That won't be necessary," said Jackie.

"I hope you'll take some time to enjoy yourself while you're here. Do you ride?"

"Ride what?"

"Horses," said Marge.

Jackie didn't say anything. Her eyes were wide open and her mouth shut tightly as she shook her head no, definitively.

Fish out of water, thought Marge, resisting the urge to pat her on the shoulder; Jackie wouldn't like to be touched, Marge could tell.

"But I run," said Jackie.

"There are plenty of places to do that, too, about three hundred acres, in fact," said Marge, trying to sound cheerful. "We have trails, or if you don't mind a hill, you can stay on the driveway, which will take you all the way down to Hardscrabble Road. There's very little traffic on it. Either way, check for ticks at night."

"Ticks?"

"I can offer tweezers if you find one. Don't wait; the sooner you remove it, the better."

Jackie flinched, like she could feel a tick crawling up her leg just from thinking about it.

"Or you could use the gym if you prefer the indoors," Marge said. "It's in the basement and has weights and all that other equipment you girls use. I can show you when you come downstairs. Would you like some coffee?"

"Yes," she said, "thank you. I'll settle in first. May I have the Wi-Fi password?"

"The network is called Stratton," said Marge, "and the password is 'Stratton,' uppercase *S*."

"That's not very secure," said Jackie.

Marge had no opinion on the topic. "There's a printer in the office off the kitchen."

"Great," said Jackie, "I'd like to know where that is."

It struck Marge as very telling that Jackie showed more interest in the printer than the pool. "I'll see you downstairs."

She didn't want to underestimate this young woman, but she couldn't help but notice that Jackie did something peculiar right then, bending her knees primly, in a manner that brought to mind a curtsy. Marge suppressed a smile and left the room, hoping Jackie would change into something more casual, like pedal pushers or Bermuda shorts, before she came down. Gabardine pantsuits weren't really the right costume for the country.

She walked back down the hall, hearing a ruckus coming from downstairs, followed by Gwen's voice, sounding alarmed: "Marge!"

Getting from point A to point B in a big hurry was not something Marge enjoyed doing anymore. She felt off balance and her knees hurt, especially going downstairs. By the time she made her way to the library and took in the scene—Edward in his bathrobe sprawled on the floor, unable, apparently, to get up—Gwen was already on the phone, calling 9-1-1.

7

Bridget woke up, saw the sun shining out her window, and did a gut check: she was sad, yes, but she had to admit she'd slept well. Having both Will and Isabelle with her certainly took the sting out of Sterling's rejection.

Will and Bridget had brought a bottle of wine over to the guesthouse, where Isabelle was settling in by piling up her dirty laundry on the living room floor. She thanked them for the wine but made herbal tea instead; her throat was sore. "I think I have some kind of growth," she told them. "I can feel it whenever I swallow."

"You don't have a growth. Strep maybe." Bridget wondered if the doctor she'd taken her kids to for ringworm when they were ten was still around.

"I'm so glad I got out of that toxic workplace," Isabelle said, as though she deserved a trophy. With Hudson beside her on the couch, his head on her leg, she spoke as though coming to terms with some newfound wisdom: "I'm going to start appreciating my life more, spending my time in a way that has value, cherishing the people I love. I don't want to be part of a massive corporate machine anymore. Small, local businesses, *that's* what I want to explore."

Bridget glanced over at Will to see if he was similarly baffled by Isabelle's new personality, but he was listening to her politely, paying attention, nodding his head.

"How did you get here?" Bridget asked. "We would have picked you up."

"Frank drove me," she said. "I didn't want to disturb you and—" Isabelle, looking first at Will and then at Bridget, suddenly realized that something was wrong. "Where's Sterling?"

Will put his arm over Bridget's shoulders and said, "You won't be meeting him after all. He's . . ." Bridget could tell Will wanted to say something hostile. ". . . had a change of plans."

A change of heart was more accurate.

Isabelle took the news of the breakup with righteous outrage: "What is wrong with him?" "You're such a catch, Mom!" "He's an idiot!"

Her indignation soothed Bridget's wounded feelings, although her use of the words "toxic," "toxin," and "toxicity" was over-the-top: "You know, if you'd stayed with him, his narcissism would have become a toxin in your life."

Will changed the subject, telling Isabelle about the woman he'd just met, and she gave her enthusiastic support: "Good for you!" "Go for it, Will!" "Look at you, you're blushing!"

And it was true, Bridget noticed. He was blushing.

———◆———

Isabelle had called her a "catch." Lying in bed in her sunny bedroom that morning, Bridget lifted her T-shirt and patted her stomach; she could use a few sit-ups, and tagliatelle with gorgonzola cream sauce was probably not the sort of thing she should be eating. But she felt she'd earned it. Getting dumped was certainly justification for a high-calorie, comforting dinner.

Bridget was usually the one who did the breaking up. Seth was the first man she dated and dumped after having the twins. He was a urologist with an attractive smile; reliable, respectable, and energetic. He loved reading about well-reviewed cultural happenings in the *New York Times* and *Time Out* and making plans, whether it was going to movies, museums, or plays. Lectures or poetry readings. It was fun to attend so many interesting, talk-of-the-town events, but Bridget decided she needed more than a seat in the audience, and Seth's own performance was not deserving of a five-star review in any paper; Bridget wasn't willing to settle for mediocre sex.

There were others she broke up with: A choral director she met in New Hampshire one summer whose veganism became a source of constant conflict. A high school teacher who she had reason to suspect liked Will more than he liked her. A couple of men Gwen fixed her up with, an immigration lawyer and a restaurant owner, neither of whom fit the bill for one reason (too much chest hair) or another (not enough confidence).

There was one notable exception when Bridget was the one who got dumped. After the kids went to college, she met Benjamin, a tattooed percussionist who had a gorgeous smile and a very cool, steady job playing in a '50s rock musical off-off-Broadway. He was funny, sexy, and edgy, and Bridget was crazy about him. Six months after they started dating, he got cast in the international touring production of *Stomp* and had no plans to return to New York. She missed him, longed for him, in fact, and was ready to hop on a plane to visit, but when she called to plan a trip, he said she was only postponing the inevitable, and he didn't see any point in pretending they had a future together. Bridget was blindsided. She tried to change his mind. That was when he told her he was already hooking up with a girl in the cast, stomping on her heart.

Bridget liked being in a relationship. She just hadn't managed to find the right guy. Will, on the other hand, didn't actually want his relationships to work out, not after his failed marriage to Molly, his Holy Roller, high school sweetheart from Louisiana. He'd married her right after his Juilliard graduation, in spite of the fact that he'd become a die-hard New Yorker in four short years and Molly had never been farther north than Memphis.

Bridget went to the wedding, a *praise Jesus*, Bible-thumping day-time ceremony in an ugly church in Shreveport, and she tried not to be a snob. She met Will's dour, tacky mother and gum-chewing, humorless father in the church parking lot before the service. She said hello at the church door to the effeminate Baptist pastor, who wore cowboy boots with his robe, and she took her seat in the church, looking around her. She simply couldn't believe that Will—*Will!*—was actually going through with this, that he came from this place where he didn't belong, was connected to these people he had nothing in common with. It actually crossed her mind to kidnap him, to grab him by the hand and run. Instead she sat there with a fake smile on her face, trying to feel enthusiastic when she heard her twenty-two-year-old friend say "I do," knowing his marriage would never last. After the ceremony there was a reception in the neon-lit, multipurpose room in the church basement. Bridget almost died from culture shock—*What, no candles? No champagne? No sexual innuendo in the best man's toast?*—but she nibbled her sugar cookie, sipped her lemonade, and watched in horror as Will and Molly danced to a country song called "I Cross My Heart," played on a Sony cassette deck. No one else might have noticed, but Bridget knew Will's face so well, having studied it hour after hour while they played music, and she could tell he was miserable.

After their Hampton Inn honeymoon, the newlyweds moved to New York and became spectacularly miserable together. Molly hated their studio apartment, hated that Will was out teaching lessons during the day and performing at night, hated everything about New York City.

Bridget tried to bond with the bride, assuring her that the city was more welcoming and charming than it appeared. As a native New Yorker, Bridget felt a responsibility to highlight the city's best attractions, but Molly was a tough audience: Central Park was too dangerous, MoMA was too crowded, and tea at the Plaza was a total scam. She was probably right about all three, but Bridget felt she could have at least tried to enjoy it.

And then, one night, Bridget was in her studio watching TV when Will buzzed up, saying through the intercom, "Buy me a drink?" Bridget put on her coat and met him downstairs.

He had come home from teaching to find Molly gone and a note that said, *I'll pray for you.*

They sat side by side on bar stools, Bridget's arm over his shoulders, while Will explained what had happened.

"Did you have to tell her you slept around?" Bridget asked. "You were still in college and she was . . . five thousand miles away; of course you cheated."

"Fifteen hundred," Will said. "And I broke our pledge."

"I don't understand," Bridget said. "What pledge?"

Will drank half his martini in one sip. "It was a long time ago. We were young."

"So, wait," Bridget said, incredulous, "you and Molly hadn't . . . ? You were a *virgin* when you got to college?"

"Until I met that girl at the ballet school during orientation."

Bridget remembered her, a dark-haired dancer with a mousy squeak of a voice. "You had sex with her?"

"It was clumsy," Will said, shrugging, "but yes."

"And this whole time, Molly thought—? I mean, what did you say on your wedding night?"

"I pretended," Will said, head down, trying not to smile.

"To be a virgin?" Bridget couldn't help laughing. She signaled to the bartender for another round. "What happens now?"

"All hell breaks loose. We'll get a divorce. She called my parents."

Bridget gasped. "Oh God."

"I'll never be able to show my face in Shreveport again."

"That's okay," Bridget said, remembering the bridesmaids' bouquets of pink carnations and baby's breath. "You belong here now."

"I'm a bad person," he said.

Bridget was feeling the martinis at this point and wanted Will to know he was loved. "You're a *good* person," she said. "That's why you married her. And Molly will be fine. She has her family and church and friends."

"I have nothing."

"You have me." She squeezed his shoulder. "Molly wasn't right for you anyway," she scoffed. "She couldn't tell Telemann from Stockhausen."

Will laughed. "Most people can't. Most people don't even know who they are."

Bridget tried to think of a better example. "She couldn't tell Mozart from Messiaen."

Will dropped his head. "I've known her longer than anybody."

For some reason, that hurt Bridget's feelings. She was jealous. He and Molly might have known each other longer, but she and Will knew each other better, had more in common, were more honest with each other.

"I lied and cheated," he said, "and I broke our promise by sleeping with, like, ten women before we got married, and I feel like a real piece of shit."

"Don't beat yourself up," Bridget said, patting him on the back. Ten was at least six more than she'd known about. She wasn't sure if that omission counted as deception or not, but she made note of it. And she wondered: Did it follow that she didn't have to tell him everything either?

"No more," he said.

"No more what? Sleeping with women?"

He looked appalled. "I'm not dead, Bridget," he said. "No, no more marriage."

That was a pledge he'd kept.

Since Gwen had confiscated her sweatpants, Bridget put on jeans and went to see if Isabelle and Will were up. The coffee was already made and still hot, and her new laptop was on the island, but the kitchen was empty. There was a note:

> *Gone shopping! Back soon.*
> *—Will*

She could hear Hudson barking from up in Will's loft and was sorry she hadn't stocked up on everyone's favorites before they'd arrived. And then she remembered that the whole family was coming over later, and she hadn't planned a menu. She texted Will: *Forgot that we'll be six for dinner tonight!*

I'm on it, he answered.

Bridget hoped he wouldn't get pulled over, a concern when Will took her car because his Louisiana driver's license had expired over thirty years ago, and he'd never bothered getting a new one after he moved to New York.

Bridget slid on flip-flops and went outside, stepping into the overgrown, dewy grass to go find out if Isabelle was in need of a strep test. "It's like swallowing glass shards," she'd said the night before, which sounded overly dramatic but worrisome.

There was Kevin. He was sitting comfortably in an Adirondack chair in Bridget's yard, admiring the view, it seemed.

He stood up when he saw her coming. "Morning," he said. "I

rang, but no one heard me." He'd changed quite a bit since she'd last seen him; he'd thinned down, muscled up, and had a nicely groomed beard. He wasn't wearing the thick glasses of his childhood, and without them, his eyes were bright and greenish. But that he hadn't bothered to pick up the phone to let her know he was coming was annoying. She hadn't even showered yet and wasn't ready for a conversation about the house.

"The bell's broken."

"Yeah," he said, "I figured. My granddad mentioned—"

"Sorry, Kevin, can this wait? Isabelle got in last night, and . . ." She pointed a thumb over her shoulder.

"I just wanted to know what you need me to do." He looked past her out to the field. "You want me to tackle that?" he asked. "Get the grass and weeds under control?"

"Sure. That would be great."

"You've got some pretty bad invasives out there," he said. "I was sitting here and thinking I could maybe—"

"Yeah—"

"Because in the end—"

She wanted Kevin to get things done, but she really didn't care how he did them. "Absolutely, whatever you think is best. Thank you so much!"

"Okay, then," he said happily.

Bridget turned and walked along what used to be the path to the guesthouse and turned the doorknob, thinking maybe she should start a to-do list. *Busted guesthouse lock* and *broken doorbell* could go at the top. Isabelle had a big duffel bag open on the couch, and a bottle of Cetaphil cleanser, a pair of sandals, a tube of Bobbi Brown cover-up, a box of tampons, and a Jennifer Weiner novel on the floor beside it. On the coffee table, there were tissues, a glass of water, and a tangled knot of chargers.

Bridget knocked and then opened the door to the small bedroom, assuming she would find her daughter asleep. The bed had been tossed and turned in, but it was empty.

She stood in the middle of the bedroom, taking in the underwear, pair of jeans, sweater, and socks scattered at her feet. There was a wet towel on the bedspread and a half-eaten package of Ritz crackers on the night table, crumbs on the carpet below.

She went back to the living room just as Isabelle came in the house in running shorts and a tank top. "Amazing," she said, panting and wiping the sweat from her face on her shirt. "I can't remember the last time I went running when I didn't spend the whole time obsessing about work, or feeling stressed about being late to work, or worrying about some problem at work. I feel so free."

"You're okay?"

"I'm great. Why?"

"How's your throat?"

Isabelle looked confused and then put her fingers on her neck, swallowing hard. "It's all better," she said. "Yay!"

"No shards of glass?"

"I just needed a good night's sleep and a run. I'm cured."

"Your grandfather, Marge, and Aunt Gwen are coming for dinner. Will took the car to get groceries."

"Fun," she said happily. "How's the Maestro?" Edward Stratton was not the kind of man to whom you could give a cute nickname, like "Gramps" or "Grandpa."

"He's fine. You're really all right?"

"I woke up feeling so happy, like I'm exactly where I'm supposed to be for the first time in years."

Bridget looked around the house. "This place, it's a lot to deal with, you know?"

"I'll clean it up. I'm still unpacking."

"No, I mean the whole property. Kevin's here doing some yard work."

"Kevin?" said Isabelle. "Ugh, he's such a lump."

"I just saw him, and he's looking a lot less lumpy. I've got an electrician coming tomorrow, too, but in the meantime, be really careful if you use any plugs in the main house, like wear rubber-soled shoes. Don't charge your computer over there." The floors under her feet were badly stained from a pipe that burst last winter. "You know you can move over to the main house, if you want. This place is pretty shabby."

"I figure we could both use a little space, no?" Isabelle seemed to remember the new circumstances, and added, "Unless you want my company."

Bridget was fine with a little space as well and said so. She walked into the outdated kitchen and opened the pantry. It was full of old cereal, tea, cans of soup, and mouse poop. The refrigerator didn't seem to be working, and the house's hot water heater, long left alone, was making angry noises from the utility closet.

Isabelle got a glass from the cabinet and filled it with tap water, waiting out the initial brownish sputter and letting it run until it came out clear.

"Maybe it's time to say good-bye to all this," Bridget said, surprised to have shared the thought out loud.

"What do you mean?" Isabelle said. "Sell the house?"

Bridget hadn't meant to start Isabelle's day by dropping a bomb. She wished she could take it back. "Just thinking about it."

"Wow."

"You're upset."

"No, surprised," she said, sitting at the round table, one of the first pieces of furniture Bridget had bought after college for her studio apartment. "It's not a crazy idea."

Bridget felt a need to clarify. "I'm only *considering*—"

"I get it," Isabelle said, sounding positive. She finished her glass of water and got back up to fill it up again. "You need to do what's right for you and your life."

"I'm not rushing into anything," Bridget said. "It was just a thought."

Isabelle was nodding encouragingly. "You should talk to a Realtor."

Bridget thought she might cry. She'd anticipated pushback. Didn't all kids hate the idea of losing their childhood home?

Somehow, being told by Isabelle that she *could* sell made Bridget not want to, and she wondered if that had been the strategy. "I'm going to go take a shower," Bridget said. "Want to help me cook later, after Will gets back?"

"Sure," Isabelle said. She was looking at her intensely and said, "Let's have the best, brightest, most awesome summer ever."

Bridget liked her attitude but thought she'd need a bit more time before she could embrace the awesomeness of being without Sterling, especially since Sterling's Dutch publisher and her family had usurped her condo. She was on a detour now that didn't seem to have a clear direction, and how "awesome" it would be was not immediately obvious.

Walking back to the main house, Bridget focused on the literal brightness of the day, hoping it would catch on, hoping she could enjoy being with her family tonight.

She noticed, as she walked the path, that neither Kevin nor his truck were anywhere to be seen.

She went back to her room, took off her clothes, and stepped into the shower. The shower head, encrusted with whitish lime deposits, caused the water to shoot out in all different directions; Bridget held up her hand to find the most concentrated spot. The second the hard water soaked through her hair, she heard loud knocking on the bathroom door and Isabelle calling her name.

"Be right out," she called back.

"Hurry," said Isabelle. "It's important."

What now? thought Bridget. Was it her throat again? Her tooth? In a matter of minutes, she washed her hair, dried off, and threw on the same jeans and a sweater. With wet hair, she opened the door to find Isabelle standing right on the other side of it. She was dressed now, too, with her phone in her hand, waiting impatiently.

"What?" Bridget asked.

"We have to go. Edward fell."

Bridget had six missed calls, four from Gwen, one from Isabelle, and even one from Oscar. It was like being transported back to those busier, noisier days when her kids would call from school, sounding desperate: *Mom, I left my homework on the kitchen counter. I forgot money for lunch. I lost my MetroCard!*

Although maybe not all that much had changed after all: *I think I have a cavity. Hot compresses or cold? I feel like I swallowed glass.*

Will had the car and wasn't answering his phone for some reason, so she called Frank to come and get them. As they headed quickly down the long driveway in the backseat of his car, they saw Kevin coming up in the other direction. Frank had to do a complicated maneuver to get by Kevin's pickup, which was filled with wooden posts and was towing a trailer of some kind. He had two guys in the cab of the truck with him.

"What the hell is he planning to do with all that?" Bridget said. "Start a bonfire?"

Kevin smiled and waved as they passed each other. They all waved back.

"I agree," Isabelle said. "Kevin looks a lot less lumpy."

Bridget couldn't believe she was back in the Sharon Hospital so soon, standing next to the same pastel room divider and the same peach walls.

Even the same nurse who had taken care of Bridget before was there, now attending to Edward while she and Gwen stood nearby. With the help of an orderly, the nurse wheeled Edward in from radiology and positioned his bed in the room. She took his vital signs, while Edward, his eyes closed and his glasses folded in his left hand, did not stir.

"How's he doing?" Bridget asked quietly. The nurse didn't seem to recognize her. She bustled around, arranging Edward's bedding.

"No concussion, no broken bones," she said. "Does he live alone?"

"Sort of," said Bridget. "He has Marge."

"And that would be his caretaker or . . . ?"

"The nanny," Bridget said. "I mean, she was *our* nanny. And then she was my children's nanny. And now she's his summer housekeeper."

The nurse did not seem interested in the details. "If you want the names of services that provide home help aides, let me know."

"He has plenty of help," said Gwen. "And he has us." Gwen was dressed like she'd just stepped off the court at Wimbledon.

The nurse turned back to Bridget. "The doctor will be in soon," she said. "Does your dad want a snack? Some crackers maybe?"

"For the record," said Edward, blinking his eyes open, "I'm conscious. I'm alive and of sound mind, so if you have any further questions, you can direct them to me."

"I thought you were sleeping," said the nurse, turning to him. "Are you hungry? I can have something brought up. A cup of Jell-O?"

"Jell-O? Well," said Edward, shifting to make himself more comfortable, "that is a lovely offer. May I ask your name?"

Here we go, thought Bridget.

"I'm Stella."

"Stella. *Stella?* Ah, like the nurse from *Rear Window*. Lovely. I'm in very good hands then. Thelma Ritter not only played the role of Stella in that well-loved Hitchcock film, but she was nominated many times over for her various roles as a supporting actress. And here you are, Stella, supporting me. Thank you. You are doing the hardest work there is.

"Now, I'd like to respond in the negative to your kind offer," he went on, "but I'd hate to think that by saying 'no' I'd be indicating a lack of appetite, making you suspect I'm overcome by some sort of plague. So, I'll state for the record that although my appetite is perfectly healthy, I'm simply not interested in hospital cuisine at this point in time."

Bridget noticed that Gwen, who had taken a seat in the room's only chair, was smiling, fist covering her mouth.

"No Jell-O," said the nurse. "Got it." She began hooking up an IV. "We're gonna give you some fluids, though, all right, hon? What's your name?" she said, double-checking his identity with the order for the IV bag.

He cleared his throat. "Sir. Edward. Stratton."

Stella snapped to attention. She looked at Edward, then at Bridget. At Edward and then back at Bridget again. She raised her eyebrows and wagged her finger, saying, "No relation, huh?"

Bridget shrugged. "I was going incognito."

"How're you doing?" Stella asked her, looking concerned. "Did you hire an electrician?"

"I made an appointment for—"

"Excuse me," said Edward, "but am I not today's featured guest at this fine institution?"

The front of Edward's hospital gown was exposing too much of his chest for Bridget's comfort, and she wanted to pull it up to his throat or wrap a scarf around him. His bluish, skinny ankles were sticking out from the white blanket, and his veiny wrist was sporting a plastic hospital bracelet. Bridget didn't like seeing him diminished like this. It was such a departure from how he usually appeared: standing tall and strong, in black tie.

"Oh, yeah. Sorry," said the nurse, focusing her attention back on him. "Date of birth?"

"Date of birth. Let's see. March thirty-first. Seventeen thirty-two."
The nurse looked up.

"You didn't specify whose date of birth. That was Franz Joseph Haydn's. Bach was also born on March thirty-first, but in the year 1685. And the birthdate of yours truly, me, that is, Maestro Stratton to some—but you, Stella, can call me Edward—was also March thirty-first, but if you make me state the year in which I was born, I'll report you to the local authorities for impertinence. Suffice to say, it was eons ago."

He used the bed adjuster to bring himself to a seated position and then put on his glasses. "You know, you remind me of someone," he said, studying her face. "A young Maria Callas."

"Who?" said the nurse, as she connected the IV.

"Maria Callas. You're the spitting image. She was a highly distinctive soprano with extraordinary eyes. Look her up when you get home, and you'll see the likeness."

"Thanks," said the nurse, sounding delighted.

Edward used this line often, varying the musician depending on whose face he beheld.

"I can only hope you have a more satisfactory relationship with your mother," he said.

Bridget reached for the bottom of the blanket and covered her dad's feet.

"You're feeling okay?" said Gwen. "Because for a while there, you weren't yourself."

"I'm not teetering off my perch just yet, as I tried to tell you before you insisted on dragging me here. No bones are broken. I'll likely have a small bruise on my hip. There was no cause to waste the hospital's scarce resources." He turned to the nurse. "I apologize for my daughters," he said. "They convinced themselves I was only moments from taking my last breath. They were so confident I was expiring, they began surveying my property for the perfect site for a funeral pyre."

Both Bridget and Gwen began to protest as the nurse said, "You're lucky you fell in a good way. You coulda hit your head or broken a hip."

"I'm fond of my head, so I protect it at all costs," he said. "Head and hands. The rest I could do without."

"You're a hoot," said the nurse. She presented him with a cup of water, pointing the straw at his mouth.

He sipped. "Very refreshing. Thank you."

"Do you remember what happened," Bridget asked, "as in why you fell?"

"How on earth should I know?" Edward said. His tone suggested that Bridget had asked him something ridiculously hard, like the square root of a square root of a decimal. "But I do recall a tufted ottoman playing the hero; it broke my fall."

"I just thought you might be able to remember," Bridget said. "Did you trip on something? Or did you get dizzy?"

"What a useless line of inquiry," he said. "Why are you so focused on events of the past?"

"Are you dizzy now?" the nurse asked.

"Not in the least," Edward said. "I feel perfectly fit." He turned to Bridget and Gwen. "This tireless nurse, Stella, a.k.a. Thelma, a.k.a. Florence Nightingale, who should be sitting with her feet up under the bright, fluorescent lighting of the staff break room, is working herself to the bone over my frivolous case, while I, who should be sitting at my desk working on an exciting project, which I'll share with you if I'm ever released from this asylum, am lying here like a ne'er-do-well manatee." He turned back to Stella. "May I go home?"

"Soon," she said. "The doctor'll be in to release you when she can." She checked the IV to make sure it was dripping, and then said, "It was nice to meet you."

Edward nodded his head solemnly at her as she left the room and closed the curtain behind her.

"We were worried," Bridget said, feeling defensive, "because you couldn't seem to get up off the floor."

"Like a turtle on its back," said Gwen.

"I could get up," he said. "I just couldn't organize my legs to do as they were told. Now, as to your obsession over *why* I fell, I will speculate that Lady Marge left a dustpan in the middle of the room."

Gwen was leafing through a *People* magazine. "I was there," she said, "and *I* didn't see any dustpan."

"That's probably because Marge hid it during the melee that followed. Now listen up, daughters, in spite of your complete lack of faith in my organ systems and brain function, I have no intention of dying today, or tomorrow either. In fact, I may live to be a hundred and twenty-six years old. Conductors' longevity is scientifically proven. All that waving our arms around and working up a sweat, it's very aerobic. There's not a thing in the world wrong with me."

Bridget sat on the edge of the bed. "I'm sorry you're spending your day here," she said, "but we had to be sure you were okay. What can we get you? Tea? Juice? A magazine?"

"Nothing," he said. "Stop nudging me."

Bridget felt the old pang of hurt feelings and stood up.

Edward patted the side of the bed. "I didn't say you had to go anywhere."

She sat back down.

He used the remote to sit himself up even straighter. "It occurs to me that I have you as a captive audience," he said.

"I think *you're* the captive audience," Gwen said.

"We're stuck here together, though, aren't we?" he asked. "And I have a matter of importance to discuss. In spite of appearances"—and he used his arms to indicate his current state of affairs—"I'm about to launch into something very invigorating."

"Are you starting a new composition?" Bridget asked, remembering the score she'd seen on his desk.

"No."

"Are you writing your autobiography?" Gwen asked.

"Good grief, no. Mine is a more meaningful endeavor than a self-indulgent rehashing of my life story. And besides *that* venture has already been undertaken by a Dr. Nicholas Donahue."

Bridget thought of Nicholas's content face, deep voice, and gray socks from her dad's library. "He's writing a book about you?"

"Don't get me off topic." He took a deep breath. "When I was a young man," he said, "as you may know, I was invited to a retreat."

Bridget and Gwen looked at each other. "A yoga retreat?" Gwen asked him with a serious expression.

"A Buddhist retreat?" asked Bridget.

"A nudist retreat," said Gwen.

"Are these attempts at humor?" asked Edward, growing impatient, "because I'm telling you something significant that will impact us all, and you're making jokes."

"Sorry, Dad," said Bridget, dropping her smile.

"You were saying?" said Gwen. "A retreat?"

He smoothed the hospital blanket over his legs. "It was a summer residency program, highly selective. I sailed from England, my first trip to America, and made my way to a secluded boarding school campus in upstate New York. When I arrived, I quickly ascertained that there would be no distractions; we lived like monks. The dorms were bleak and simple, the schedule was grueling, the town had nothing of interest. Each day began with a swim in a cold lake at six in the morning, lights were out at ten p.m. The food was bland and meager. They served watery oatmeal for breakfast and watery soup for dinner. I've never been so homesick in my life."

Bridget had heard this story many times before. The food got worse with every retelling.

"But we were productive. We were a small group, all composition students, and we were accountable to each other. That's where I met Johannes Lang, along with six other composers I've stayed in touch with my whole life. We had two professors, both dead now, of course, who taught theory and reviewed our work. I wrote *Synchronicity* that summer, the first truly ambitious piece of my career, a nod to Henry Purcell and my love of baroque music written for English country dance. That retreat was so meaningful to me that once I reached a certain level of achievement as a musician, I made my commitment to mentor composers every August, this summer being no exception."

The image that came into Bridget's mind whenever she heard the word "synchronicity" was of synchronized swimming, women with nose plugs and caps on their heads pulling together in a circle, pushing apart simultaneously.

"Didn't you meet Mom there?" Gwen asked. She had closed the magazine.

He held up a finger. "I'm getting there. At the end of the summer, they bused us all to New York City, hired professional musicians to play our work, and invited important people who were in positions to commission pieces."

"At Carnegie Hall," said Bridget. She loved this part. "Mom was sitting with a group of her friends from Barnard, and she spotted you through her opera glasses."

"You're ruining my story," he said, and then raised his eyebrows at her in mock warning. "There was a terrible storm that day with wind and torrential rains, and our bus nearly skidded off the road. It continued raining well into the evening, so many people decided not to come to the concert at all."

"There was a storm?" said Bridget. She didn't remember anything about bad weather.

"Our pieces were being performed in the small recital hall at Carnegie," her dad said, "which is now Weill Hall, and your mother came in spite of the storm and even though there were plenty of seats closer to the stage, she chose to sit in the back. She didn't need opera glasses because it's an intimate space, but she was using them anyway, and while my piece was being played, she trained her lorgnette on me and watched as I watched the musicians." He closed his eyes for a brief moment, as if he were picturing the scene. "I met her after the program, and she said, 'Well?' 'Well what?' I asked. 'Were you satisfied with how the musicians played your piece?' I was not, not at all actually, but I smiled and said I thought they did a fine job. She leaned over and whispered, 'I don't believe you.' 'Why is that?' I asked, thinking she was being presumptuous. 'I could tell by your expression that it was all you could do not to jump out of your seat and play all the parts yourself.' She was right, of course. That was precisely what I had wanted to do."

"And you took her out for ice cream," said Gwen with a sigh.

"Coffee," said Edward.

They sat quietly, as Bridget remembered sitting with her mother eating raspberry sorbet. Pink lipstick. A '70s key chain with a bright yellow smiley face.

"Now," said Edward, "why am I telling you this story when you've likely heard it countless times before?"

"Because it's meaningful," said Bridget, wistfully, "and you want us to remember it."

"Because Mom always knew what you were thinking," said Gwen, "just by looking at you."

"Because that summer was life-changing. That retreat turned out to be the most pivotal experience I ever had, professionally and personally, setting off a series of events that shaped the course of my life, brought me to my wonderful wife, and eventually led to you girls. Consider that I wrote a piece called *Synchronicity*, and your mother and I, as if in sync, appeared at the same concert, on the same night, in spite of a storm. Which is all to say—and I know this may come as a surprise—I'm getting married."

The clock on the wall ticked the seconds along as if nothing unusual had been said. Bridget was stunned, noticing all at once the healthy pink of her father's cheeks, the brightness of his eyes, the happy thrumming of his fingers on the white waffle-knit hospital blanket.

"Married?" said Gwen. The magazine slid off her lap and onto the floor. "You're getting *married*?"

"Who is she?" Bridget asked.

"She is, in fact, someone you know quite well. She's smart, entertaining. Fabulous company. We have everything in the world in common."

"Who?" said Gwen.

He paused, smiled, and said proudly, "Lottie."

"Lottie?" Bridget asked, startled. "As in Charlotte? Johannes's *wife*?"

"Widow," he corrected.

"Right, widow," said Bridget, getting up from the hospital bed. Bridget had last seen Lottie and Johannes in Munich at a winter chamber music festival, but she couldn't remember how long ago. Ten years maybe? They'd invited her, Jacques, and Will to their house for an overly formal dinner of venison stew and a lot of red wine. Bridget was touched at the end of the evening when they'd stood on the doorstep together, waving good-bye in matching fur hats, holding gloved hands.

"Doesn't she live in Germany?" Gwen asked. "How did you . . . reconnect?"

"I saw her at Johannes's funeral last fall, and we've been emailing ever since."

"Emailing?" asked Gwen. "Just emailing?"

"And texting. Jackie set me up on something called WhatsApp, and it's marvelous. Did you know you can make an overseas call and pay nothing for it?"

"But you've visited in person," said Gwen, flashing Bridget a *WTF?* look. "You've seen her?"

"Her lovely face lighting up my iPad, yes. The wedding will be at my house at the end of summer, and we'll all toast to our happiness."

"That's so *soon*, Dad," said Gwen. "Shouldn't you give it some more time? Take it from me, you should do a *lot* of thinking before you decide to tie the knot."

"I'm almost ninety years old," said Edward. "Why in God's name would I wait another minute?"

"When is she coming?" Bridget asked, shocked her father hadn't shared his feelings along the way before coming to such a momentous decision. "And where will you live? Is she moving to New York?"

"In the words of Tennyson, ''Tis not too late to seek a newer world.'"

"Huh?" asked Gwen.

"Meaning . . . ?" Bridget said.

The doctor came in, and Edward abruptly shifted gears, turning his full attention to the visitor in the white coat. She was the spitting image, he said, of Jessye Norman.

8

Will pushed his shopping cart out into the bright parking lot and was loading his paper bags of groceries into the back of Bridget's Volvo when his phone rang. He glanced at the screen and answered right away with an overly enthusiastic "Hello, Caroline!"

"Will Harris?"

"Speaking."

"It's Caroline Lee."

Yes, I know. "I'm so glad you called." He leaned on the car and put a hand over his ear so he could hear her better.

"I'm looking forward to our collaboration," she said formally.

"So are we. We're thrilled to have you join the trio."

There was an uncomfortable pause.

"Is everything okay?" he said.

"Yes, but I'm calling to let you know," she said, "the dates you proposed for rehearsals aren't going to work. I'm incredibly busy."

Will's heart sank. "All right, of course. I'll check with Bridget, and I'll get back to you with some other options. Could we try for August? We won't have much time before the Frick."

"It's just that I'm so busy," she said again.

"I know," Will said. "We're quite tied up as well, but I'm sure we can find—"

"And we need to resolve a few matters first," she said. "Have you agreed to everything?"

"What's everything?"

"Randy talked to you?"

Randy? She called Randall "Randy"?

"Like, on all the advertisements, posters, emails? My name should appear first. And in a larger font, okay?—so that my name stands out."

Will cringed. This was exactly the kind of diva bullshit he hated. The sort of Gavin Glantz–style egotism that made his blood boil. "Well, Caroline, maybe Randall should—"

"And we need professional photographs taken of the three of us for promotional materials—"

"Okay, but—"

"—with me standing in the front."

"*Seriously?*" He realized he'd accidentally said that out loud, so he quickly added, "We're only three people. How far in front of me and Bridget do you need to be?" He wanted to embarrass her by posing a specific question (*one foot? two feet?*), but he stopped himself.

"I'm bringing something important to the trio," she said with an edge to her voice, "so it's reasonable to expect that fact to be acknowledged."

There might have been some truth to that, but it was in terrible taste for her to spell it out. Her youth and her success were not a good combination, and Will did not like the implication that he and Bridget were somehow riding on this child's coattails.

"I have a photographer I want to use," she said. "I'll send you her information?"

The expenses were stacking up, and although he wanted to divide everything evenly with Bridget, he simply couldn't afford to.

"We should set up a photo shoot for July. He'll need a deposit to hold a date."

"I thought you said you're busy," Will said.

"I can make time for that," she said as though it were obvious.

"Anything else?" Will tried to keep the annoyance out of his voice.

"No. Yes, actually—I know you guys are good, okay? And it would be nice to join an ensemble."

Why was she using conditional tense? "But . . . ?"

"Well," she said, "when I searched 'Forsyth' on the internet, I had a hard time even finding you." She pronounced their name *foresight*, which Will found annoying. "The Forsyth Grill in . . . Where was it? Kansas City or something comes up first, and then Forsyth Lighting Warehouse. You have, like, no web presence at all. You need a platform. We're not amateurs, right? You'll deal with it?"

Will felt an urge to throw his phone across the parking lot and into the brick wall of the grocery store. Instead he said, "We're hiring a publicity firm Randall recommended, and we're redoing our website, and soon we'll be on all the . . . Across the social media landscape. Twitter, Instagram, and all that. We're going to get a whole new . . ." He struggled to find a word that was fitting. ". . . to-do."

"Good," Caroline said. "Otherwise, it's just embarrassing."

Asshole.

"We have to be much more visible. So how soon?" she asked.

The contract for the PR firm was sitting unsigned in Will's backpack in the loft. They were requesting a payment of $32,000, money he certainly didn't have. He had hoped to be able to pay some of his share before giving Bridget the bill.

"Soon," Will said.

"I hope so," Caroline said. "Did Randy discuss my travel?"

"No."

"Nothing unusual, just what I need when we're on tour. The kind of hotel rooms I require, although I'm sure you stay at nice places. And I obviously don't fly economy," she added, "ever."

Fuck this, thought Will. He wanted out. He wanted to replace this brat with someone nice, a team player.

"Okay, Will? Are we cool?"

"Yeah," said Will flatly. And then, "Actually no. We're not 'cool' at all. I need to talk to Bridget." But as he ran that conversation through his mind, he already knew exactly what Bridget would say *(We need her! She's the answer to our prayers!)*, so he swallowed hard and said, "Never mind, yes, it's fine. We're cool."

"You aren't sure," she said. It wasn't a question.

"I'm entirely sure. One hundred percent."

"Hmm. Good-bye, Will." And she hung up in such an abrupt way that it reminded Will of the olden days when one could still slam a phone down onto a receiver.

What the hell, he wondered, was her problem? And why hadn't she had Randall call to discuss these logistical matters? The only thing he wanted to talk to her about was what music they wanted to play together and what times were good to rehearse. Now it was awkward, and Will didn't even know what she'd meant by "Hmm."

He pushed his empty cart back to the store and then went back to the car, sitting in the driver's seat while the ice cream went soft in its tub.

There was a time when musicians would have given their left nut to play with them, but here was this inexperienced girl acting as though she was doing them a huge favor.

The fact that they were finally working on their "brand" was a good thing, no matter who was in the trio, and for that Will was grateful. They'd gotten the kick in the pants they'd needed. Bridget had already paid a brand/logo lady, and Will had met with Jisoo's friend Brendan from NYU's engineering school. He asked all sorts of questions Will didn't know the answers to, using normal words Will didn't understand in this context ("platform," "domain," "content," "host," "conversion"). In any case, though he might not have grasped the details, Forsyth was getting a whole new website, and Brendan only charged him $300.

"Just Venmo me, dude, and I'll get started."

Then he had to explain what Venmo was.

Obviously, Caroline would be good for them. She would generate a new, possibly younger audience and the press attention they sorely needed. They would be playing better festivals and better venues because they had Randall doing their booking.

But chemistry mattered, too, and the chemistry with Caroline was clearly going to be lousy.

The chemistry was bad with Gavin, but as a trio, they'd been successful in spite of that. The three of them would rehearse diligently in their studio, Gavin watching Bridget, Bridget watching Will, and Will watching Gavin watch Bridget. Gavin was at least a little in love with her—that was obvious from their first days together at Juilliard. Of the three of them, Bridget was the native New Yorker, the one who could take them fun places on the subway, from clubs in Harlem to the boardwalk on Coney Island, without ever getting lost. She might have been insecure as a cellist, but she was confident in every other respect, not to mention beautiful and interesting, the daughter of a famous father. To Will and Gavin, although they never discussed it, she was perfect. On more than one occasion, Will saw Gavin ogling her, trying to flirt in his cocky, childish way, but Bridget never gave him the slightest encouragement. She was too cool for him.

Sure, the three of them had some beers and laughs together as well. Given the conversation they'd just had, it was hard for Will to imagine having a laugh or a beer with Caroline, but maybe that was okay. They would have a professional relationship, but likely not a personal friendship, and that would have to be enough.

Isabelle had told Will to "go for it," so in spite of the melting ice cream in the backseat, he took a left out of the parking lot and drove to the nursery. Emma wasn't in front by the parking lot where he'd seen her the day before, nor was she in the pavilion that was filled with flowering plants hanging on hooks. She wasn't in the store either, and he nodded his head at the young guy in a Pink Floyd T-shirt standing at the cash register.

"Can I help you find anything?" he asked.

"Just looking," said Will casually as he wandered into the greenhouse, which was damp and warm. It smelled like a tropical swamp, earth full of minerals and decay, and Will felt like he was breathing underwater. There were citrus trees, ferns, and orchids, all of which he could identify but only because of the signs. Was that her loopy, carefree handwriting?

If he played piano for her, would she be impressed by his fast, expert fingering, his precision, his concentration? Would she smile at the end of the piece—something by Rachmaninoff maybe—if he found her in the audience? He would smile back and wink.

Then again, maybe she hates classical music. Maybe she hates men. Maybe she's happily married. He didn't know anything except that he felt a longing, an urge to know her. Experiencing such a strong attraction was not new to him, but something about this woman made him feel they'd seen something in each other, felt something reciprocal. Will touched his finger to a cactus needle.

"Hello, again." Emma was wearing a long-tiered skirt, a tight white T-shirt, and beaded chandelier earrings. Her leather bracelets made her wrists look small. She was leaning on a shovel and smiling at him. Her mouth was perfect. "Forget something?"

Will swallowed and felt dizzy.

Emma tilted her head. "I'm surprised to see you again," she said. She took one of his hands and examined it, the clean nails, the smooth skin. Will's stomach did a little flip as she ran her thumb over his knuckles. "You don't seem to be much of a gardener."

When he got back to Bridget's house, Will opened the back hatch of the car to retrieve a forty-pound bag of topsoil, which he deposited next to the rhododendron. He then returned to the car to get the groceries he'd bought for dinner. A sound made him stop in his tracks, and he looked out in the field, spotting something that confounded him: there was a pack of dogs— No, there were *sheep* all over the place, some standing together in a huddle like they were gossiping, heads down and bleating, some off on their own. He thought he was hallucinating. He blinked and used his hand to block the sun. A fence had been erected, starting at the shed door of Batshit Barn and circling around the field, and inside the new enclosure was a flock of sheep. Will tried counting them.

Hudson was barking inside the house, but before letting him out, Will carried the groceries to the kitchen and threw the melted ice cream in the trash. Dinner was still happening in spite of Edward's fall. He felt guilty that he'd missed Bridget's call saying she needed the car; he'd been chatting with Emma and ignored his ringing phone. Good thing Frank had been able to drive them. Gwen had texted later from the hospital: *We've got BIG news. There better be a whole lot of wine.* He'd taken that hint and stopped at the liquor store, leaving his checking account with about ninety dollars in it. Although the ice cream was a loss, he had everything he needed to prepare a dinner of grilled chicken, scalloped potatoes, corn on the cob, and a salad.

From the breakfast room, he looked out into the field and saw a man outside working to secure the new fencing to the side of the shed. It took a moment before he could convince himself that this broad-shouldered, rugged dude was, in fact, Kevin.

Will went upstairs to the loft to let Hudson outside, and they walked together to get a closer look at the field that had somehow been turned into a corral. The sun was high. Will felt the warmth on his back and rolled up his sleeves as he walked across the field to the barn. "Hey, Kevin, what's all this?"

Kevin, sweaty and out of breath, grinned, and took off his baseball cap. His hands were filthy, and Will was glad he didn't offer one in greeting.

"Borrowed these fellas from my buddy," he said, nodding his chin in the direction of the sheep and putting his cap on backward.

This response in no way helped Will understand what was going on. "Why?"

"Ms. Stratton said she wanted her lawn cut."

"Uh-huh."

"So . . . sheep," Kevin said as if that explained everything. "Since you're here," he added, and he pointed to the barn, "can you give me a quick hand? The guys had to leave before we got finished."

Will shuddered. *Oh, hell no.* But Kevin was looking at him as though he were issuing a generous invitation.

"Sure," Will said. They went into the filthy barn, and following Kevin's directions, he helped move a pile of hay from one part of the barn to another (without knowing why) using a pitchfork. *An actual pitchfork!* He'd never held one before. While Hudson watched, he then used a shovel to spread pine shavings in the shed stalls. When he was done, Kevin handed him two empty buckets he found in a pile of crap that included a pair of petrified boots, some empty paint cans, random pieces of lumber, and a stack of old tiles. Will ran water from the spigot by the damaged tennis court. He lugged the buckets back across the lawn, water slopping onto his shoes, and emptied them into an old galvanized metal trough. And then Kevin sent him to do it again, three more times. He showed Will how to fill a mineral feeder and asked him to check the fencing on each post to make sure it was secure. When they were done, Kevin clapped him hard on the back.

"Thanks, man, I didn't want to do all that by myself. Teamwork, right?"

Will was itching from head to toe, convinced some kind of sheep lice had invaded his scalp. His left knee hurt, and his socks were damp. He needed a shower.

"Can I ask a question?" Will said and pointed in the direction of the rhododendron. "Could you help me put that somewhere?"

Kevin looked across the lawn where the potted plant sat by the front door. "It'll bloom in late summer or early fall," he said. "How about by the breakfast room?" He took a big shovel off a hook in the barn and started walking.

Kevin was such a good sport, and Will thought he could learn a lesson or two from him. He decided he would—starting right then—be a better sport about Caroline.

He grabbed another shovel and caught up to him. "Hey, Kevin," he said. "What are you doing for dinner tonight?"

By four in the afternoon there was so much dirt packed under Will's nails, he wondered if he would ever get them clean again. He and Hudson walked around the house and up to his room where he took a shower, followed by a bath, followed by a final rinse, and then he dried himself vigorously before putting on clean clothes.

His phone dinged, and he saw that Bridget had texted: *My dad's ok, but staying home w Marge. Gwen and I will be there by around 7. Wait til I tell you Edward's news . . .*

Will was curious to know what kind of news Edward could possibly have that would generate so much surprise. Selling his house, maybe. That would make sense at his age and would certainly cause Bridget to rethink selling her own. But would it make her more inclined to sell or less? He picked up a book, went out onto the splintery-wood deck off his room, and settled in a plastic lounge chair. Below him the peepers were croaking in the pond and the sheep were bleating by the barn, and Will found it all very pleasantly pastoral. He couldn't remember ever feeling so wonderful in his entire life. Outdoor labor—so *that's* what it feels like. He raised his shoulders, rolled them back, and stretched his neck, wondering if he was going to be sore the next day. Those buckets had been heavy. He examined a small, tight blister on his right palm, from the pitchfork, and felt a sharp, lovely pain in his heart, for Emma.

He wondered if Bridget knew about the sheep who'd made themselves perfectly at home on her property. And that's when he heard what sounded like the engine of a race car.

Hudson began to bark loudly as a silver Porsche convertible, revving angrily, came to a jerky stop in front of the house. Will watched in complete surprise as the soft top of the car raised and folded back, revealing the brown-haired driver and his two enormous dogs. The motor went silent.

"*Oscar?*" Will said, stunned to see him there.

Oscar got out of the car, followed by his yellow Labrador, Hadley, Hudson's littermate, and his black Newfoundland, Bear, both of whom ran around, joyful to have arrived. They caught sight of the livestock and began barking as they headed across the lawn. Matt, Will noticed, was glaringly absent from the scene.

"Oscar," Will said again, louder this time, leaning over the rail from his perch on the upper deck.

Oscar looked up and waved limply.

"Hi," Will said, smiling at the sight of him. "What are you doing here?"

"I could really use a drink," he called.

"That can be arranged." He decided not to ask after Matt yet.

"What's with . . . all that?" Oscar said, pointing to the sheep.

"Lawn mowers," Will said.

"What?"

Will pointed down to the door. "Meet me in the kitchen," he said. "Need a hand?"

Oscar shook his head and then turned back to the Porsche. Will watched him pull out a duffel bag that had been wedged onto the floor of the passenger seat. Oscar then popped the tiny trunk and grabbed two stuffed-full, heavy-duty trash bags. Not the kind of packing one does for a weekend jaunt in the country. He clearly intended to stay a while. *What on earth?* Will thought. Isabelle had done the exact same thing: made a hasty departure, bringing everything she owned.

Before heading downstairs, Will got his phone and sent emails to the schools where he taught, telling the administrators that he had a family emergency and would be out for the entire week.

Will followed the deck around the house and took the stairs down to the back door, whistling Wagner's "Ride of the Valkyries." In the kitchen, he rinsed the martini shaker, iced the glasses, and pulled out the new bottle of gin he'd bought.

Oscar slouched in, looking dejected, as the dogs ran after him, bumping into each other and knocking into the legs of the breakfast room table, making the candlestick holders rattle. The cats jumped onto the kitchen counters and hissed.

"So," Will said.

"So." Oscar shrugged and held out his hands, helpless. Will put down the shaker, crossed the room, and hugged him.

9

Jackie was in the backseat of a car she'd never been in, with two women she didn't know, going to a house she'd never seen, with a group of people she'd never met. In what felt like the longest damn day of her life, she'd been on the subway, on a train, in a so-called cab, in a seriously big-ass mansion, and now she was being driven down a deserted country road past barns and cows and fields to who knows where, and Jackie just wanted to go home.

Or at the very least she wanted to be working, and so far, she hadn't exchanged a single word with her new boss. Did Mr. Stratton even know she'd arrived? No one had bothered to fill her in about what was going on, so when she'd left her five-star room and gone downstairs for coffee, all she could think of, when she caught sight of his crumpled body being tended to by paramedics, was every *Law & Order* episode she'd ever watched. Stupidly—and she really wished she could take it back—she'd asked Marge if he was dead. Even now, she couldn't shake the feeling that there was a murderer on the prowl somewhere in her midst.

"Estate"—the word itself was absurd. Who were these people?

"I'll find someone to carry your bag," Marge had said. *What?* Like, there's a bellhop on hand? And had she let Marge call for someone, was Jackie expected to tip that person? If there was a rule book for this "estate" somewhere (in the night table drawer, on the desk, under a magnet on the fridge), she wanted to get her hands on it. It was like she'd ended up in an episode of *Downton* fucking *Abbey*. And— *oh my God*—she'd *curtsied* when Marge left her in her bedroom. It was some reflex, a stupid little involuntary bend of her knees. She'd actually curtsied. Her face burned with the memory of it. She hoped Marge hadn't noticed.

She was now in the backseat of a white Range Rover with two foil-covered pans Marge had put on her lap. The Stratton sisters, women twice her age with whom she had absolutely nothing in common, had insisted she come along for dinner, even though she'd been very clear about wanting to stay put. Gwen said she was going to change out of the ridiculous tennis getup she was in all day, so Jackie went to dress for dinner as well. She decided to go a step up in formality, so she changed into a pencil skirt and a blazer, carrying her heels down the stairs because of the no-shoes policy. And there was Gwen, wearing super cute torn jeans, a white T-shirt, a diaphanous pink scarf, and a linen jacket. *Fuck*, thought Jackie.

Marge got to stay home with Mr. Stratton. "You go on, dear," she'd said, giving Jackie a little push out the door, "and have fun."

They got in Bridget's car, and for the first few minutes, Bridget, the older of the two, was on the phone, freaking out about something but using one of those fake-calm mom voices she recognized. When Bridget hung up, she said with a tone that was half overjoyed but half furious, "Well, guess what? Oscar's at the house."

"Yay!" said Gwen, sounding genuinely happy.

"No, not *yay*," said Bridget.

Jackie didn't know who the hell Oscar was, other than another new person to contend with.

"Apparently, Oscar brought both dogs and a ton of stuff with him," Bridget said, "so this can't be good."

Jackie did not like dogs.

"And the cats are going completely crazy," Bridget went on.

Jackie hated cats.

"You didn't know he was coming?"

"No," said Bridget. "And he's *alone*. Something's definitely wrong."

"He never mentioned any problems or fights or anything?" Gwen asked.

"Oscar doesn't open up to me like that."

"I hope they aren't splitting up," Gwen said, "but if they are, I have a very good divorce lawyer."

"Good God, Gwen!" Bridget said. "That's a leap."

Gwen—as if to say, *Is it?*—took both hands off the steering wheel and put her hands out, palms facing up. Jackie gripped the pies in her lap.

"Did Isabelle know he was coming?" Gwen asked.

Jackie had met Isabelle briefly when she'd come to the house with Bridget, just as the paramedics were wheeling Mr. Stratton out to the ambulance. Jackie didn't want to like her, but she sort of did, and she was glad she'd be at the dinner so that at least there would be someone her own age to talk to.

"No. I don't think she knew," Bridget was saying. "Or if she did, she didn't tell me."

"Holy shit," Gwen said, cracking herself up, "you've got both your kids living back at home, and we've got a surprise wedding at the end of the summer."

Whose wedding? Jackie wondered, because if it was Isabelle, that bitch seriously had *everything*. Jackie could imagine the kind of Brooks Brothers–wearing, polo-playing, money-making frat boy she'd be marrying.

"It's *not* funny," Bridget said, but she started laughing, too. "God, what's happening to my life? Can you imagine Sterling in this mix? How would I explain this?"

"So maybe it worked out for the best, in a way, with your kids here and no Sterling."

What the hell was a sterling?

"No," said Bridget. "My kids should be off living their lives, and I'm supposed to be living mine and having sex all summer."

Jackie was pretty sure they'd forgotten she was there.

"I actually thought," Bridget said, sounding super bitter, "that *I* might be the one getting engaged because it's *my* turn. *That's* what was supposed to happen."

"I'm sorry," Gwen said, and she patted Bridget on the knee. "I know this is tough."

Bridget made a subtle move that Jackie caught: she touched at the corner of her right eye, very quickly and with a shake of her head, and then wiped her fingers on the leg of her jeans.

Gwen, meanwhile, sighed dramatically. "God, I feel like I aged today, don't you?" she said. "Seeing Dad there, on the floor like that? So pitiful and old in that hospital gown? And then, *boom*. That was some news."

"I can't believe it."

"I guess it's time to go dress shopping," said Gwen.

What her boss's falling on the floor and buying dresses had in common was a mystery, unless Gwen was predicting a need for funeral attire. Was her entire job coming to an end? Maybe Mr. Stratton was too old to finish what he started. When her own grandfather fell down in the bathroom a few years earlier, he had one problem (immobility) after another (bedsores) after another (pneumonia) until he died. That was that.

"Lottie!" said Bridget. "Wow. What would Johannes think about this? And what is Hans going to say?"

Apparently, the cast of characters from a World War II movie was part of the story.

"Hans, oh my God, I remember Hans," Gwen said. "He was awful."

"You hated him so much, and he was only, like, ten when we met him."

Gwen scoffed. "He was a little shit at ten."

"I think I'm having an anxiety attack. Do you have a Xanax?"

Ugh, thought Jackie, *rich people are the worst*.

"Breathe," said Gwen, rolling down the window and taking a left so hard that Jackie's shoulder knocked into the door of the car.

Gwen started driving up a bumpy, long driveway, and Jackie had to hold on tight to the desserts to keep them from flying off her lap. She looked out the window and saw the house. It was pretty, but not nearly as elegant as Mr. Stratton's. Less intimidating, less like some kind of grand hotel. And, *holy shit*, there were real, live barnyard animals out in the yard. God, these people were weird.

"What the fuck?" Bridget said, her hands on the dashboard as she leaned forward to look out the windshield. "Kevin must be out of his mind."

They hadn't even come to a stop when not one but two totally freaking hot guys approached the car. Wait, make that three, although the third was handsome in an older Clooney kind of way. It was like she'd stumbled onto the set of an Abercrombie commercial. They were all, every last one of them, wearing jeans and T-shirts, and Jackie had never felt such regret for her choice of clothing in her life. She could not possibly have gotten it more wrong, wearing shoes she could barely walk in, looking like she was heading to work at an insurance firm.

And why was she tasked with holding the stupid pies? She wished she had something more dignified, like a bouquet of flowers or a box of Russell Stover.

The older hot guy opened the door for her, and as she got out, he offered his hand as though she were stepping out of a carriage. He saw the desserts, and said, "Oh, thank goodness, because I had to throw out the ice cream. I'm Will, family friend."

"Jackie," she said and tried to duck as a Frisbee grazed her head and sailed on into a huge field. "I work for—"

"What's with the sheep?" Bridget was asking, but she got distracted before anyone could answer, and started hugging one of the two cute guys, hard. "What are you doing here?" she shrieked at him, sounding excited and happy but also kind of like he was yet another uninvited farm animal hanging out on her property. The guy didn't, Jackie noticed, answer her question.

Isabelle introduced Jackie to him, saying he was her twin, and then to Kevin, not saying who he was, and then they all walked inside the house together, making their way into a big, noisy kitchen, where bad singer-songwriter bullshit was playing off a laptop and martinis were being made. There was a cat *on the counter*, right where the food was being prepared, and no one seemed at all grossed out or even bothered by it. Jackie watched as the cat rubbed its neck and face on the sink faucet. Bridget turned the water on, and the cat started drinking out of it, its tongue actually touching the place where the water came out. No fucking way would Jackie drink tap water tonight.

Something smelled really good, like cooked onions and grilled meat, and she realized she was absolutely starving, having eaten nothing other than half a stale muffin at Grand Central early that morning.

Without even asking her what she wanted, Gwen stuck a big glass of pink wine in her hand, took her out to the porch, and left her there alone, saying, "Make yourself comfortable, back in a jiffy."

Jackie looked around the porch and saw a tray full of cheese on a low table, but she was too uncomfortable to help herself. Instead she pulled out her phone to check her email. She had a hideously long row of unopened messages, all having to do with Mr. Stratton's travel. When she'd taken the job, she thought it was going to be a challenging, interesting position, assisting one of the world's most influential musicians. But soon after she started, she found out that the work was easy stuff pretty much anyone could do, booking flights mostly. But a job was a job. Unfortunately, this one meant spending much of the summer, and in fact all of August, up here in the middle of nowhere, at a place that didn't even have a public transit system.

She felt something massive brush up against her ass and jumped as an enormous, shaggy black dog, drooling and clumsy, galumphed up to her, stuck his head in her crotch, leaving slime all over her skirt, and then promptly began eating all of the cheese off the platter. "No, no, no," Jackie said, backing away from the beast and into the house. "Umm, there's a dog eating the cheese . . ." she said to anyone who would listen.

"No!" yelled Bridget from the kitchen. "Oscar, get Bear off the porch."

"Got him," he said. Smiling broadly, Oscar came out and pulled the dog away, putting the platter up onto the table that was nicely set for dinner. Jackie did a quick count and saw that there were only six place settings. She knew instantly that of the seven in attendance, she was the one who wasn't supposed to be there.

Oscar took the dog, who was the size of a love seat, by the collar and back into the house, saying, "Sorry about that."

"Oh, I don't mind," Jackie called after him. She did mind, and no way was she going to eat that cheese now; she could see a long black dog hair stuck to the perfectly gooey brie. Her stomach growled.

She was alone again. She took a napkin from the table and wiped the dog drool off her skirt and knees. She then folded the napkin neatly and put it back under the fork.

The other young guy, Kevin, came out on the porch with a bottle of beer and sat down, taking in the view. "Gorgeous evening."

Jackie sipped her wine and smiled.

"You're up from the city, right?" said Kevin. He was stocky and strong-looking, the picture of health with his ruddy cheeks and thick forearms.

"I arrived this morning," she said. "I've never been here before."

"Ahhh, welcome to Litchfield County," he said. "Incredible wildlife. Bears, bobcats, deer, turkeys."

Jackie sat down, crossing her legs. She looked at her shoes and felt ridiculous. This guy was wearing lumberjack boots. "I've never even seen a turkey that wasn't on a Thanksgiving plate."

"Turkeys are very intelligent," said Kevin in all seriousness. "Ben Franklin thought they should be the country's national bird, but the bald eagle won out."

"They're not my cup of tea," Gwen said, coming out to join them and refilling Jackie's almost-empty wineglass. "I'm not a fan of anything going droopy under the chin."

Isabelle and Oscar came out then, too, sitting on the wicker furniture, and Jackie felt very popular. She was filling the room. She looked at Kevin and Oscar, sitting side by side. How had she managed to find the two cutest guys in the whole state of Connecticut, and possibly New England?

"I hope whoever buys this place keeps the barn," Isabelle said, looking across the field.

"Excuse me?" said Oscar, leaning forward. "What?"

"Buys the place?" said Gwen. "What are you talking about?"

Isabelle seemed to like that all eyes were on her now. "Mom's thinking about selling," she said.

Oscar looked upset, and Jackie felt an urge to sit on his lap and comfort him. The wine was going to her head.

"She's not selling," said Oscar, waving his sister off. "I don't believe that for one second."

Isabelle shrugged like it was no big deal, and suddenly Jackie wasn't so sure she liked her after all. Jackie couldn't imagine being the owner of a property like this, and she certainly couldn't imagine letting it go so nonchalantly.

"Did you guys know," said Kevin, "you've got one of the oldest barns in the county. It just needs a little love."

Bridget appeared out of nowhere with yet another wine bottle. "Love and a whole lot of money," she said. She, too, topped off Jackie's glass.

"Is it landmarked?" Kevin asked.

Isabelle pointed at him and then turned to her mother. "It should be. Can we do that?"

"I can look into it for you," Kevin said. "I can ask at the town hall."

"Here's a better question," Bridget said, sitting across from him. "What's with the sheep?"

It was clear Bridget wasn't thrilled about the animals. What kind of life path does one have to be on, Jackie wondered, to end up with a flock of sheep you didn't ask for?

Kevin sat up straight like he was at a job interview. "Well, you said you wanted the field out there under control, and sheep are terrific lawn mowers."

"What about coyotes?" Bridget asked.

Kevin didn't answer for a second. "Coyotes don't eat grass."

"I know *that*," said Bridget. "No, I mean, am I going to have a massacre on my hands tonight?"

Jackie shuddered. The country seemed full of dangers, from ticks to coyotes to murderers breaking into the house. She wondered how she would sleep tonight and felt homesick for her safe little apartment in Queens with its one door and four locks.

"I'll round the sheep up into the barn before it gets dark," Kevin said. "And if you don't like them, I can return them to their farm. You can do the job with machines instead. I know a guy—"

"No!" said Isabelle. "We're keeping them. They're so cute. And so are alpacas; they have loads of personality."

Oscar gave his sister a push on the shoulder, a fairly hard one. "I'm surprised you haven't invited them all in for drinks," he said.

Kevin considered that. "Sheep are very social, so they'd do well at a party, as long as you invite the whole flock. They panic when they're alone. Same with alpacas."

Jackie felt like she was an extra on a movie set. She was watching the ones with speaking roles and trying to figure out the plot. Isabelle, she decided, was a brat but not a bitch. Kevin was not exactly one of them, but not out of place either. He was very literal but seemed to enjoy the banter. "Beautiful" was the wrong word to describe Oscar, although it would not be incorrect because his face was perfect. She remembered the conversation in the car and put it together that he was the one maybe getting divorced. He didn't look old enough to be married in the first place; maybe that was the problem. *Whatever*, she thought, he was unbelievably cute.

He turned to her, as though he could tell she was thinking about him, and she blushed. "How do you like working for my grand-father?" he asked. He reached in his martini glass, picked out a fat olive between his fingers, and popped it in his mouth.

Jackie took a sip of her wine, giving herself a second to think. She hated to be put on the spot in front of everyone. "I like it." If there was a prize being given tonight for lamest answer to a question, Jackie decided she'd just won it.

"It's cool he's still accomplishing so much," Isabelle said. "I wish I could find a job I love as much as he loves his."

"Your grandfather has some rather unexpected news," Bridget said and then paused. "He's getting married at the end of the sum-mer."

The perfectly perfect twins went berserk, asking a million ques-tions, while Jackie managed to keep her face completely still so no one would know this was the first she'd heard of it. It did explain, however, who Charlotte was, something Jackie had been wondering about every time she booked another hotel reservation. Her boss was, like, seriously ancient. Why would someone that old be getting married?

"I love that!" said Isabelle. "Good for him."

"Are you on the wedding-planning committee?" Oscar asked. Jackie realized he was talking to her.

"No," she said. Weddings were in no way her area of expertise. "That's outside my job description."

"What's he got on your agenda this summer?"

Something about the way he posed the question made Jackie want to impress him, prove that she wasn't some girl fetching coffee. She took another sip of wine; it was so tasty. "I'm helping Mr. Stratton with everything he needs to be able to do his work efficiently." It would be indiscreet to go into detail, so she decided to share something noncontroversial. "For example, I recently set up an electronic music library for him, catalogued by composer, year, conductor, and genre, with all of the music he wanted. He can access the recordings and the accompanying scores on an iPad that connects to a speaker system." She wished she'd chosen a different task to describe; this one sounded like something any high school kid could do. "Also, I'll be helping run his retreat in August when the composition students come." That task sounded a bit more impressive.

"Ah, the composers," said Oscar.

"What happened to him today?" Isabelle said, clearly uninterested in Jackie's job. "I can't get over seeing him lying on a stretcher like that."

Jackie wished she could unsee that disturbing image; she couldn't unhear the sound he'd been making either, an angry sort of moaning. She took another sip of wine, shaking off the memory.

"He lost his balance," said Bridget.

"I can't believe he's getting married," said Oscar. "I'm more mystified by Edward getting it up than Edward falling down."

Gross, thought Jackie. That was not an image she wanted in her head either.

"*Ewww*, stop," said Isabelle.

"Oh, please, Oscar," said Bridget. "Let's keep it clean, shall we?"

"Are you selling the house," Oscar asked her bluntly, "without even talking to us about it?"

"Probably not," said Bridget casually. "But I'm at a stage where I need to think about my options and make some rational decisions about my life."

"*Exciting* decisions," said Isabelle, encouraging her. "You're at a stage where you should do all the things you'll regret not doing."

Jackie liked Isabelle's attitude, though it was privileged as fuck. Bridget was the most down-to-earth of the whole group, but she seemed sad. Where, Jackie wondered, was Mr. Bridget, father of these preppy, polished children?

"I know whatcha mean," Oscar said. He got up. "And my first exciting decision is: I'm going to go smoke a joint. Who wants to join me?"

"Oh, come on," Bridget said. "We're about to eat."

"A little weed will spark our appetite," said Isabelle, getting up as well and putting her arm over her brother's shoulder. "And look at Oscar: he's clearly experiencing anxiety of some kind."

Jackie felt for him. *You and me both, dude*, she wanted to say.

Bridget leaned forward as if she were about to ask Oscar a question when Kevin raised his left hand high in the air, waiting to be called on.

"Yes, Kevin," said Isabelle.

"I'd like to join you," he said.

"Excellent."

"Gwen," asked Oscar, "are you coming?"

"No, thanks, kiddos," Gwen said.

Isabelle looked at Jackie.

"No, thank you," Jackie said. "I'll stick to wine." She did not understand these people. Bridget was allowing her kids to smoke pot? In her own backyard? Jackie's mother would . . . Jackie's mother . . . well, it was so inconceivable, she couldn't even finish the thought.

Oscar held the door open for Kevin and Isabelle, and as they started to leave, Jackie felt left out. She belonged outside with the cool, fun young people, not on the porch with the two boring old ladies, drinking rosé that wasn't as sweet as pink wine should be but was yummy nevertheless.

"But I wouldn't mind coming along," she said. She felt like she was applying for membership to a private club. Oscar was squinting at her stilettos, and she knew she was about to be rejected for a dress code violation.

"Outstanding," he said warmly, "but we need to find you some more suitable shoes."

The next thing Jackie knew, she was walking a mile in somebody else's Uggs, wandering through a field with grass up to her knees, and getting stoned with some rich kids and their slobbery dogs. She'd somehow landed a role in this strange movie, with a cast of characters and a setting completely foreign to her.

10

Bridget did not want to get high with her children. She never had, never would. Still, her feelings were hurt that they hadn't even invited her to join them. They asked Gwen. They asked Jackie. Bridget would have said no, anyway, but they could have at least included her, just to be nice. When they came back to the porch, talking loudly and laughing uncontrollably, she left them out there and went into the kitchen, where all three dogs, who were soggy from having waded into the pond twice, were underfoot and pacing, in search of dropped food.

She'd lost control of the evening. She didn't know where Will was hiding, Jackie was drunk, Kevin was so stoned he was almost comatose, and she had no idea what Oscar was even doing here.

Henry was on the counter, licking a stick of butter, while Eliza, terrified of the dogs, had apparently gone into hiding.

Bridget shooed the cat off the counter, got the lettuce from the fridge, and started making a salad, wondering what this evening would be like if Sterling were here. *Better*, she decided. She wanted him with her in the kitchen, laughing at the chaos, reaching for her hand to give her palm a kiss. But then she remembered he was on a deadline. He likely would have excused himself to go up and work in Will's loft. And where would Will have stayed? In the guesthouse. Then where would Isabelle have stayed? Upstairs in her room, right next to Oscar and his 215 pounds' worth of Hadley and Bear. It certainly would have been more crowded, but crowded-good or crowded-bad?

Bridget squeezed a lemon, a drop of which flew into her right eye.

Her father was getting hitched, and she had been dumped. What a turn of events. She vaguely remembered the first time she met Lottie, recalled going on a picnic with the Langs when she was six or maybe seven years old. But where were they? Central Park? The English Garden in Munich? Or was it Regent's Park in London? Her mom and Lottie were standing together, both wearing knee-length dresses and flats. Johannes and Lottie's son, who was about her age, was lying down on a blanket staring at the clouds, and she remembered thinking he was no fun whatsoever. He had a stomachache or some ailment that day and refused to play. Bridget was running in circles around the blanket, where Gwen, who was only a baby, was sleeping. When Bridget stopped running, she reached out, dizzy, and wrapped her arms around her mother's legs, but when she looked up it wasn't her mother at all. Bridget recalled feeling mortified, but Lottie looked down at her, thrilled, it seemed, by this (accidental) show of affection, and she patted Bridget on the head. "Sophia," she said, with a bright smile, "I've always vanted a girl. May I keep her?" For a moment, Bridget worried that her mistake had cost her her family, and she wanted nothing more than her mother.

Why on earth had Oscar come home without Matt? Without any warning whatsoever? And with all these people here, when would she get a chance to talk to him about it?

She worried that whatever had happened, she was partly to blame. Maybe she'd jinxed Oscar and Matt by not giving them the wedding they'd asked for last year: a ceremony at her house out on the lawn under a tent. Bridget wanted to host it for them, but they'd picked a date only six months away and she wondered how she would manage to get her house ready. When Walter called after a storm to say that a pipe had burst in the guesthouse, a big tree was down, blocking the driveway, and her garage door was broken again, Bridget knew that there wasn't nearly enough time to repair all the damage, get the field mown, and hire a florist, a band, a caterer, and a company that would deliver tables, chairs, tents, and porta-potties. Above all that, she was afraid the event would be a disappointment or, even worse, an embarrassment. What would they do if the power went out, as it so often did, in the middle of the party? So she apologized to Matt and Oscar and went to Edward, who said they could have the party at his estate. Thanks to Marge, it was a beautiful wedding, much better than anything Bridget could have pulled together, but she felt sorry she hadn't hosted it herself. Matt and Oscar had wanted a fun, casual affair, grilled steaks and a bluegrass band. Instead they got black tie and a string quartet.

Oscar complained to Bridget afterward that it was all a bit too precious, but Matt was grateful. "I loved every part of it," he told Bridget, sounding almost convincing.

"Come on, you hate caviar," Oscar said. "And you're certainly not a fan of waltzing."

"I waltz just fine," said Matt with a laugh. In his typically goofy way, he counted out loud and demonstrated: "One-two-three, one-two-three . . ."

Imagining Matt in their DC apartment, sitting alone at the Restoration Hardware dining table she'd given them, made Bridget upset, wondering what had gone wrong between them. She let out an exaggerated, heavy sigh.

"Don't feel too sorry for me," Oscar said, coming into the kitchen.

"I'm worried," said Bridget. "Why isn't Matt with you?"

"Because I don't want to be anywhere near him."

"But, Oscar—"

"And he certainly doesn't want to be anywhere near me."

"What on earth happened?"

Oscar's jaw was clenched. "Matt wrecked everything, and then I overreacted and made it even worse."

This statement did not surprise Bridget as much as she wanted it to. Oscar had always tended to jump headfirst without checking the water.

"Wrecked everything how?" she asked.

But Oscar was on the floor now, playing with Hudson and Hadley, while Bear came over and tried to sit on his lap. Bridget watched while he wrestled with the dogs, looking like he did in high school.

He got back on his feet, brushed off his shirt, and reached for the martini shaker. "I feel ridiculous coming home like this, but I need some time to reboot, figure out what to do next. I'm not staying long," he said, "just for the summer, if that's okay. I can work from here and take some time to sort my life out."

The whole summer? Oscar worked at a political think tank promoting renewable energy and green initiatives. Bridget wasn't so sure it was the kind of work one could do remotely. "Of course," she said. "Whatever you need."

"Thanks, Ma."

Bridget went back to whisking the vinaigrette. "Have you seen Will?" she asked, wondering if it was too early to dress the salad.

"Not since my last martini." He was pouring himself a new one from the sweaty shaker, and then he got a bottle of wine and a beer from the fridge.

"Easy does it," Bridget said, knowing booze wasn't going to help anything, especially since Oscar got hit with the worst hangovers.

"It's not *all* for me," he said, laughing. "It's for everyone."

Gwen came inside with her phone pressed to her ear. She held up a finger, pointed in the direction of Bridget's bedroom, and then went in, closing the door behind her. Bridget figured she was either getting an update from Marge or talking to the producer on her show.

"Isabelle told me you and your boyfriend called it quits," said Oscar. "Sorry to hear it."

"I wish I could say Sterling and I came to a mutual decision," Bridget admitted, "but I was blindsided. He dumped me."

"I guess we're a couple of sad sacks then, aren't we?"

"Are we?"

"For different reasons maybe, but yes." He had a look of defiance rather than one of sadness as he said, "Matt's with someone else."

Bridget dropped the oily whisk on the counter. "No, he's not," she said. "*What?* No, I can't—"

"It's been going on for a while," said Oscar. "He's completely fallen for the guy, and I can't even blame him."

"Who? How could he—"

"Doesn't matter. I told him to fuck off, and I left him."

Bridget started to ask for an explanation, but Oscar cut her off.

"Not tonight, okay? I don't want to get into it." With the wine under his arm, the bottle opener sticking out of his shirt pocket, a beer in one hand and his martini in the other, Oscar walked carefully back out to the porch, where Isabelle and Jackie greeted him with a high-pitched "Whoop!" These people needed food and fast.

The side door opened, filling the kitchen with the smell of charcoal-grilled chicken, and Will came in with a platter that he quickly covered with foil.

"So *that's* where you were hiding," she said. "Do we have enough food?"

"Not really," he said. He put down the chicken and started arranging thin slices of cooked potatoes in the oval Le Creuset baker.

"We'll make it work." He pointed to the empty ice cube trays. "Could you refill those? The ice maker isn't working." He seemed nervous.

"Are you okay?" she asked, taking the plastic trays to the sink and then carefully placing them in the freezer, water lapping over the edges and onto the floor.

"You need a plumber, too," he said, clearly preoccupied. "The powder room toilet isn't flushing."

"Oops," Bridget said. "I knew the sink wasn't draining." She went to the breakfront, and as she opened the lower cabinet, Eliza leapt out and ran away. "I have to squeeze in one more place setting on the table," she said.

"Two more," Will said.

Bridget counted again. "We're seven," she said.

"We're eight."

"Wait," said Bridget, turning to face him. "You invited a date?"

"Emma." He was flushed. "I really want you to meet her."

"Tonight? You're sure you want to expose her to this level of craziness?"

"I invited her before I knew Oscar was in a crisis," Will said. From the porch came the sound of uproarious laughter. "Am I going to regret it?"

There was a loud knock on the front door. Ears up and fur flying, all three dogs started running, barking, and knocking into each other on their way to the entry. The cats ran up the stairs to hide.

"Another adult is welcome," said Bridget. "The drunk twenty-somethings are outnumbering us. Want me to—?"

"That's okay. I've got it." Will wiped his hands on a dish towel, tucked in his shirt, and turned back to Bridget. "Remind me to tell you later: Caroline called earlier to talk about . . . some things."

"Oh, good!" Bridget said, delighted. "I *told* you she's committed to us."

"She was prickly," he said, backing away. "I'll fill you in later."

As soon as he turned his back to walk to the front door, Bridget dropped the smile and took a moment to close her eyes and breathe. She cursed Sterling in her mind, wishing upon him a severe migraine, the kind he often got that hurt so much he would have to sit in a darkened room for several hours. She was instantly sorry for having such an evil thought and took it back, hoping instead that he was at the very least suffering from the pain of missing her as much as she was missing him. She heard Will coming back, the sound of laughter between him and Emma, and steeled herself to get through the evening.

Carrying the two extra place settings out to the porch, she took one look at the table and realized how tight it was going to be.

Isabelle had a cordless speaker on the low table beside the couches, and the music had gone from mellow indie rock to the Grateful Dead, a band her kids had always loved for reasons Bridget couldn't understand. Kevin, who seemed to be rousing from his coma-like state, and Oscar were cracking up about something.

Jackie seemed bewildered by their conversation. "Wait," she slurred, "I 'on't get it. Cars are stolen around here, but iss because people don't bother to lock them?"

"We leave our keys in the visor," Kevin said. "Or we used to. Now it's like . . ." He raised his hands and then dropped them. Bridget didn't know what that gesture signified other than that he was too stoned to hold up his arms.

"Does anyone hear that?" Isabelle asked, looking up at the porch ceiling.

"Hear what?" asked Bridget.

"I think I have tinnitus," she said, sticking a finger in her ear. She turned to Kevin. "Do you say *tin-i-tis* or *tin-EYE-tis*? Wait, where were you?"

"Sitting here, I think," said Kevin, as though doubting his very existence.

"No, I mean, I thought you moved away somewhere."

"I was in Maine," said Kevin, "until the construction company laid me off. So now I'm living with my mother for a while."

"So, you guys all live with your *moms*?" Jackie asked. She didn't sound judgmental; she sounded dumbfounded.

"It's cheap," said Kevin.

"It's a choice," said Isabelle.

"It's temporary," said Oscar.

Isabelle grabbed on to Bridget's hand. "Kevin says if I buy stuff like paint and smackle and wood stain—"

"Sparkle," said Oscar.

"Spackle," said Kevin.

"—I can fix up the guesthouse."

"My apartmen' 's a dump," said Jackie, "but you do *not* move back in with *my* mother." Jackie had had way too much wine. Bridget picked up the bottle and moved it over to the dining table. Then she offered the basket of crackers to the kids, leaving it right in front of Jackie. "I have to ask, wha's it like?" Jackie said. "You guys have so much . . . everything."

"We do?" asked Isabelle, scrolling through her iTunes playlist to change the song.

Look around you, Bridget wanted to say.

"Horses and Porsches and sheeps, oh my," Jackie said. "Mr. Stratton is the richest, youngest old person I ever met. Who likes their life as much as that? Iss not even normal." Jackie was pulling off the Ugg boots, and Bridget noticed she was wearing a pair of fleece Christmas socks Will had given her. "I mean," said Jackie, "the trip he's taking iss the craziest shit I ever heard of."

"What trip?" asked Isabelle.

"Is he planning his honeymoon?" Bridget asked, realizing that his marriage to Lottie would extend past the ceremony itself, which was about as far as Bridget's mind had gone.

"Honeymoon?" Jackie said. "*Pffffft.*"

"What?" Bridget asked. "It's *not* a honeymoon?"

Before Jackie could answer, Gwen came back out and sat down. "Marge says Dad's fine. They're having croque monsieur for dinner."

"*Oooh la la*," said Jackie, laughing hard. "Let me tell you peoples something: words like 'Cock Mister' and 'bon voyage' were not bandied about in my household growing up."

"Did I miss something?" said Gwen.

"The trip, the trip," Jackie said, trying, it seemed, to be helpful. "He's spending hella cash on this whole shebang."

"What trip?" asked Gwen.

"How much money?" Bridget said.

Jackie stretched her arms out to indicate the extent of his spending.

"I don't understand," said Bridget. "Where's he going?"

"Where *isn't* he going?" She was cracking herself up. "*Jackie,*" she said, mimicking Edward's deep voice and British accent, "*fetch me two fuhhst clahhss tickets on SpaceX.*"

"No way!" said Oscar, and the kids all started arguing about the desirability of vacationing on Mars.

Bridget wanted to get back to the point. "Where exactly are they going?" she asked.

Gwen leaned in and whispered, "Forget it. She's pickled."

"He hasn't said anything about a trip," Bridget whispered back.

"He hadn't said anything about getting married either," said Gwen, "and that's happening, so . . ."

"Are you talking about me?" said Jackie.

Bridget looked up. "We were talking about Edward."

"Nahhh." Jackie's mood seemed to swing wildly from giddy to paranoid. "I kinda feel like everybody here hates me."

"Oh, no one hates you!" said Oscar.

"Hate," Kevin said, "is a waste of human energy."

"It's my left ear," said Isabelle, covering it with her hand. "It's definitely ringing. Nobody hears that?"

Jackie started putting her high heels back on but was having a hard time because of Bridget's thick socks on her feet. She was mumbling to herself, heading, it seemed, toward some kind of meltdown.

"We're all having a fine time, and no one hates anyone," Bridget said. "Where are you going, Jackie?"

"To Queens. I don't like it here."

Bridget tried to steer Jackie toward the table. "Let's eat some dinner, and then we'll drive you to Edward's for a good night's sleep. Gwen? A little help?"

And there was Emma, looking lovely at first glance, in a long tiered skirt and a tank top, floating out on the porch, giving everyone a timid wave. "Will asked me to tell you all the dogs got out, and they're swimming in the pond, so he's—"

"I'll get 'em," Oscar said, hauling himself up and going out the porch door to the yard.

Emma introduced herself to Bridget and then to Gwen, while Bridget told Kevin where to sit. "And Jackie, why don't you sit between Kevin and Oscar, who will be right here, and Isabelle can sit on Kevin's left." Jackie took a wobbly step, just as Oscar's soaking-wet dogs came bounding in, dripping water all over the floor. They stopped right next to Jackie. Everyone froze. And then the big dogs shook.

Jackie, dripping water from her eyebrows to her knees, sat down hard in her chair at the table, dropped her head down, and threw up in her own lap.

Half an hour later, Bridget and Gwen were standing over poor Jackie, having maneuvered her up the stairs, dressed her in pajamas, and tucked her into Isabelle's bed. Gwen got a glass of water for the night table, while Bridget put a plastic bucket next to the bed.

"Well, that was fun," Gwen said quietly. "I think puking might be my favorite emotion. There's nothing quite like . . . letting it all out."

The smell of vomit on the porch had been so off-putting that Oscar, Isabelle, and Kevin had taken their dinner plates and another bottle of wine to the guesthouse. Meanwhile, Emma and Will were in the living room, having what must have been the most unusual first date ever.

Jackie let out a noisy snore.

"What a beautiful ending to a truly exquisite day," Bridget said, stifling a laugh. Gwen couldn't stifle it, and Bridget shushed her.

They started to leave the room.

"What if she throws up again?" Bridget said. "She could choke."

"We'll babysit from the hallway." Gwen took Bridget's hand and pulled her away from the bed, leaving the door cracked open. They sat down side by side, leaning against the wall.

"Do we still have to whisper?" Gwen asked in a normal voice.

"No, but we'll have to rock-paper-scissors for who goes in if she barfs again," said Bridget.

"I'm an optimist. I think she's done for the night."

Bridget started laughing, thinking of Sterling, of her father's fall, of this chaotic dinner party. "Best-laid plans gone awry," she said.

"You need some new plans," said Gwen. "You've got almost three months before your trio starts up again. I can think of a million ways you can spend the summer."

"Like what? Should I enroll my kids in day camp? Teach cello lessons to the sheep?"

"Meet some new people," Gwen said. "You're so antisocial when you're here. Look at Will: he comes to town for one day and meets a woman."

"That was an anomaly," said Bridget. "He's normally just as anti-social as I am."

"Do you think we made a good impression on Emma?" Gwen joked.

"Did you see her tattoo? Is it a bougainvillea?"

"I don't know, some kind of vine. Wisteria? They look cute together."

Bridget shook her head, trying to understand why, with all the women in Manhattan, Emma had stood out to Will as a good choice. "I can't imagine what those two have in common," she said.

"What do I know? I'm no expert on relationships," said Gwen. "And I'm nominating you to talk to Dad about this shotgun wedding and trip. One of us should make sure he's not completely losing it."

"*I'm* an expert on relationships?"

"You're the family matriarch."

Bridget did not feel old enough for that title. Marge was more fitting for such a senior role; she was certainly more commanding. "Apparently, Lottie's the family matriarch."

"Why did he tell us that story today about the retreat and meeting Mom? You and Dad are sentimental in the weirdest way," said Gwen. "I didn't inherit that trait."

"I think it's cool that he still cherishes something from so long ago and replicates it every summer, mentoring prodigies."

"The August composers," said Gwen, "always messing up my summer plans."

"I wonder how Lottie will like having three houseguests, strangers really, taking up so much of Dad's time."

There was the sound of retching, and Bridget and Gwen did rock-paper-scissors. Gwen lost. "Shit," she said and got up to go hold Jackie's hair.

Bridget considered her situation: A whole summer with her two grown children living at home; she'd never thought *that* would happen again. A summer with her father; who knew how many more of those she would have left? She should try to enjoy this peculiar blip rather than fight it. It might not be the summer of romance she'd planned, but maybe it could be memorable in some way. Weird but wonderful.

Bridget heard the sink turn on and off in Isabelle's bathroom, and then Gwen came out looking ill. "The fun never stops."

As Gwen sat down beside her again, Bridget said, "I'll call Lottie tomorrow and welcome her to the family."

Gwen looked annoyed. "I'm not even sure I approve. Why's he doing this? And why her?"

"It could be so much worse. At least she's age-appropriate," said Bridget. "And they have history together. It makes sense."

"How can it make sense when they're living on two separate continents, wooing each other on WhatsApp? His best friend's wife? Isn't there something creepy about that?"

Bridget worried that it was somewhat creepy. Awkward at best. "I wonder what her son thinks. Hans."

"I get a bad, yucky feeling every time you say his name. He was such a little shit, wasn't he? God, I hated him."

"You remember Lottie pleasantly enough, don't you? She wore bright lipstick and hats, remember? And she always had chocolate in her purse." Bridget was about ten when Lottie visited New York and gave both girls German dresses, dirndls, with little aprons. Bridget said thank you and folded hers back in the box, when Lottie insisted she and Gwen put them on, right then and there. She vaguely remembered her dress being a size too big and Lottie making her pose for a picture.

Maybe bossy was what her father needed.

"Dad's getting a second act," Bridget said, liking the idea of a new chapter, something exciting to embark on. Her father loved marking momentous occasions, graduations and funerals, birthdays and even housewarmings. "I'm sure he'll want the wedding to be special."

"He loves toasts," said Gwen, "so at least there'll be a lot of champagne."

"Noooo," groaned Jackie from the other room.

"Fine, no champagne for Jackie," said Gwen.

As Bridget considered her father's plans, a notion began to form: the new Forsyth Trio could play at the wedding. That idea excited her; it felt meaningful and personal. This would be their debut concert, playing in front of a warm, receptive crowd. What a nice way to start their journey together, with a positive, feel-good concert, erasing any negativity Will was harboring about their collaboration with Caroline.

Will would know the right piece to play, but as she started to get up to go talk to him about it, she remembered: Will was busy with Emma at the moment. She didn't want to intrude.

"Tomorrow," she said.

"Tomorrow what?" said Gwen.

"Tomorrow I'm starting my summer over again."

11

Will tried his best not to move a muscle or open his eyes. He was sitting on the couch in the middle of the night (he couldn't check the time since his phone was in his back pocket), while Emma slept soundly, her head on his right shoulder, her shirt gaping open ever so slightly, showing a hint of white lace. He wouldn't peek.

They'd had an oddly domestic evening for a first date. While Gwen and Bridget were tending to Jackie, he and Emma had dinner in the kitchen, washed the dishes, and dozed off watching a cooking show on TV. However, the evening was far from boring. He'd watched when Emma took the leftover chicken and divided it into three equal pieces for the dogs, talking to them earnestly: "Now if Jackie comes downstairs hungry, asking for her dinner, let's not tell her you ate it. I'm not saying you should lie, I'm just asking for your silence." The dogs wagged their tails.

And then they fell asleep together (for an hour? two hours?) on the couch. Will woke up briefly to the sound of Bridget and Gwen whispering as they walked to the front door. Now he'd woken up again to the sound of a car pulling out of the driveway. Hudson heard it, too, and started growling.

Emma sat up and rubbed her eyes. "What time is it?"

Will shifted to reach his phone. "One thirty. Sorry, this evening wasn't exactly . . . romantic."

She made a face like he'd said something crazy. "Cleaning up vomit off a porch? Drying three big, wet dogs *and* doing the dishes? This was a dream date."

Will smiled. "Any chance I could try again? Maybe take you out next time?"

"Not sure you can top this, but . . ." She sighed and said, "I guess you could try." She stood up, pulled on her sweater, and got her purse.

"Are you okay to drive? You can take my room, and I'll sleep here on the couch."

"No, thanks," she said. "I'd hate to upset Ronaldo."

Emma hadn't mentioned a man in her life. Will didn't want to pry, but he took a guess. "Do you need to . . . let him out?"

"No," she said. "But he misses me terribly when I'm gone too long. And he gets very jealous."

Emma got her phone and showed Will a picture of a large blue parrot.

"Ronaldo," he said. "I like him already." He looked at the photo more closely. Ronaldo had a fierce glint in his eye, daring Will to try anything.

Will ignored the warning and asked Emma if he could kiss her good night.

Early the next morning, before anyone else was up, Will took Bridget's car and went to get hangover supplies for whoever needed them: Gatorade, ginger tea, saltines, eggs and bacon, Tylenol,

Pepto-Bismol, Alka-Seltzer, and the *New York Times*. His mission was so obvious that even the middle-aged guy behind him in the checkout line took a look in Will's basket and said, "Rough night?"

Will wasn't in the mood for a conversation this early in the day. "Yep."

"Big party, huh?"

"Something like that."

"Cool, man, I get it. You're hard-core."

"Ha," Will said. He felt a need to defend himself, but he kept his explanation simple: "We've got the grown kids back home, sort of indefinitely, and they got a little out of control last night."

"Yeah, when the empty nest doesn't stay empty, I know all about that, the ol' boomerang effect. My daughter's living with me, and I've got a friend whose thirty-year-old son came back home and moved right into his old room." The man put out his hand and shook Will's. This was precisely why Will didn't like small-town life.

"Mark Thomas," the man said.

"Will."

"You live around here?" Mark was wearing a blazer and khakis, making Will feel like a bum in his shorts and flip-flops.

"New Yorker," Will said. "I mostly come up on weekends."

"A city guy," the cashier chimed in. "Hey, Mark. How's it going?"

"Hey, Mary," Mark said. "Do you know Will?"

This, thought Will, *is a fucking nightmare.*

"How's it going?" Mary asked as she scanned Will's items. "I heard the fitness studio is getting sold."

Will seriously didn't care. He just wanted to pay and get back before someone else needed the car.

"That's right," said Mark. "It's gonna be a new bakery."

"A bakery? Replacing a fitness studio?" said Mary. "That's gonna do wonders for my waistline."

They both laughed.

Will handed his credit card to the cashier, while Mark handed his business card to Will. "If you're thinking of downsizing, give me a call," he said. "I'm pretty much *the guy* around here."

"He is," said Mary.

Will started to object, but Mark stopped him, putting his hand on his shoulder and leaning in. "Let me tell you something, Will: if you move into a smaller place, the kids aren't so keen to live with you anymore." He raised his eyebrows like he'd just revealed the top secret location of a military black site.

Will studied the card. He hated Realtors; Realtors and greedy landlords were the reason his building was going on the market. "It's not actually my place. It's my friend Bridget Stratton's house."

"Stratton?" Mark might or might not have gotten a hard-on. "How about I swing by sometime?" he asked eagerly, sticking a piece of gum in his mouth and offering one to Will. "Let me take a look at the place, give you my two cents?"

Will said no, both to the offer of gum and the visit. "She hasn't decided. She just happened to mention it the other day, thinking it's too much house given how little time she spends up here."

"I totally get it," said Mark. "Totally. The weekend places get tough to manage."

"I'll give Bridget your card," Will said.

"Please do. Hope the kids feel better," Mark called after him.

———◆———

The house was still quiet when Will got back. He made coffee, poured himself a cup, and went outside with Hudson and the newspaper. After perusing the front page, he skipped to the Arts section, where he read a worrisome and thoroughly bizarre story: Caroline

Lee had left the stage in the middle of a Tchaikovsky violin concerto with the Dallas Symphony, saying she felt woozy due to the heat. She'd taken allergy medicine and reacted poorly. She might have gotten food poisoning. Also, she was overtired. The excess of excuses made Will doubt the entire claim. And even if her health *were* to blame, he simply couldn't imagine how she could walk offstage mid-concert. Stopping a performance in the middle of a piece? Abandoning an audience? It was unthinkable. Through the years, he and Bridget had played tired, hungover, congested, and jet-lagged. With stomach bugs, fevers, and broken hearts. What kind of musician walks offstage before the end?

Will was so disturbed, he got his phone and called her manager. And for the first time ever, Randall took his call.

"Well, we're in a big fat mess now, aren't we?" Randall said.

"What happened? Is Caroline okay?"

"Fuck no, she's not okay, but that's hardly the point. She's out. She won't work with you."

Will was baffled. "*Me?*" he said. "What do I have to do with her walking offstage?"

"No, that was a stomach virus or something. She says she talked to you, and you were rude and insulting. She wants nothing to do with Forsyth."

"*What?*" Will tried to replay the phone conversation they'd had from the parking lot. "I wasn't rude to her," he said. "She was being *very* demanding, and I listened, and then I agreed to everything she wanted."

"That's not what she said."

"I may have hesitated for a brief moment, literally, like for a second, and then I said, 'Fine, we'll fly you first class and whatever else bullshit you want.'"

"No wonder she didn't like your tone."

"I didn't like *her* tone!"

"Well, good for you," said Randall, clearly furious, "because now we're fucked. She's dropped out, which puts me in a hell of a position. I've already scheduled concerts for you guys, and I'm gonna get my ass kicked when I have to cancel."

"Wait, come on. I'll call her back, I'll straighten it out."

"Do *not* call her. I mean it, Will. She specifically said she doesn't want to talk to you, and she's on shaky ground as it is. She's a serious musician."

That comment struck Will as a jab. "And we're not?"

Randall paused for a second and let out a big sigh. "I'm having a real shit day because of you two."

Will didn't know if by "you two" he meant him and Bridget or him and Caroline. Either way, Bridget was going to flat out kill him for this. He wasn't too pleased with himself either. One of the goals of this collaboration had been to end up with Randall managing them, and the prospects of that happening had just taken a serious dive. He hadn't even had a chance to tell Bridget the details about the phone call. What would he tell her now?

"It's a real shame," Randall said. "You would have liked Caroline if you'd gotten to know her."

Will doubted that very much.

"But it doesn't matter now," Randall said. "It's over."

"What if," said Will, running the names of violinists he knew through his head. "What if . . . we could replace her and still do the concerts?"

Randall coughed out a *ha!* sound. "Who are you gonna replace her with?"

"Someone with name recognition and serious talent. A famous soloist." As Will considered what he was saying, it occurred to him that he was "friends" with only one such person, and he couldn't stand the idea of asking him.

"Give me a name, Will," Randall said impatiently.

Will rubbed his forehead, wishing he could think of anyone else. "What if . . . What if I could get . . . Gavin Glantz to join us? At least for the concerts you already scheduled?"

There was a pregnant pause, and Will waited. If Gavin agreed to do even one of the concerts, it would be better than zero.

Randall finally spoke up. "How long was he with Forsyth?"

Will didn't have to think. He and Bridget marked time by who their violinist was at any given period. Gavin was from college until five years after Will's divorce. Martina was from Bridget's pregnancy to Oscar and Isabelle's toddler years. There was the Julian era, a brief period marked by great camaraderie, Will moving into his current apartment, and Bridget buying her Connecticut house. "Gavin was the original," said Will. "Bringing him back would be a reunion of sorts. We were together for over five years, nine if you count our time at Juilliard."

"I'll email the dates to you. If you can get Gavin, I can make the argument for the switch."

"Good," Will said, feeling his stomach start to hurt. "Hey, do me a favor, Randall. Don't tell Bridget about any of this just yet. Let me sort it out first, and I'll tell her."

Randall exhaled in irritation. "Your relationship issues are not my problem—"

"No, no, I only—"

"Call Gavin, and let me know when you've got him."

———◇———

After hanging up, Will went in the house and dropped two Alka-Seltzer tablets into a glass of water for himself. *Shit.* How could he reach out to Gavin after all this time? And how could he possibly persuade him to join them, given what a big deal Gavin had become, how busy he was, how little he cared about them.

His thoughts were interrupted by the pitiful sight of Jackie limping into the kitchen, looking pale, wobbly, and miserably uncomfortable in someone else's pajamas.

"Hi there," he said. "What can I get you?" She squinted at him and tried to put on a good face.

"I want to apologize for my behavior last night," she said. "I never drink to excess, *ever*, and—"

"It's fine," said Will, getting a pan from the rack over his head, the butter from the fridge. "We've all had nights like that."

"Not me," Jackie said. "I do not have nights like that, ever. I can't imagine what Bridget must think. Or you. Or Isabelle—"

"Don't worry about it. How are you feeling? Can I get you anything?"

"Do you know where my clothes are?"

"Oh, I don't think you'll be putting those back on. You kind of . . . destroyed them. But I'm sure we can find you some jeans or something."

"Oh my God," she said, getting teary, holding her head in her hands. "I feel just . . . I'm so embarrassed—"

"No need for that," said Will, coming over to her and guiding her to a stool at the island. "Let me ask you, Jackie. Other than the last part of the evening, did you have a good time?"

Jackie had to think for a moment. "I guess so, everyone was nice—"

"That's all that matters. We're not judging you. So you drank too much. And now you feel wretched, which is punishment enough, don't you think? Are you hungry?"

Jackie looked like she honestly didn't know.

"I'm going to cook some eggs and bacon, and you can decide when you see it."

"I need to go to work," she said, trying to stand back up again. "Mr. Stratton's expecting me, unless I've been fired for bad behavior."

"No one's firing you, and how would Edward even know?"

Jackie had to think for a moment. "Someone might tell him."

"Who?" Will asked. "Why would anyone do that? Besides, he needs to rest today. As do you. Doctor's orders. Coffee?" he asked.

She nodded weakly and sat back down on the stool.

Will poured her a cup and gave her a small glass of Gatorade. "Electrolytes," he said and went about the business of cooking bacon and eggs, hoping the smells wouldn't make her feel worse.

"Do you know if I can call that cabdriver from here? Frank?"

"Ah, good old Frank," said Will. "He despises New York. Did he tell you that?"

Jackie couldn't seem to wrap her head around that concept. "But why—?"

"Whatever you do," Will said, "don't ask him about it. You'll get an earful."

Jackie stared into her coffee cup and said sadly, "I love New York." Then she looked at Will. "I'll need to get to Mr. Stratton's, eventually."

"Not to worry. One of us will drive you."

There was the sound of the dogs thundering down the stairs, and then Oscar came in, darling Oscar, trudging after them. He moaned as he sat down next to Jackie. "Help me," he said. He was wearing a ratty Rolling Stones T-shirt and jeans, and his hair was in need of shampoo.

Will gave him a cup of coffee, a glass of Gatorade, two Tylenols, and a pat on the back. Jackie's shoulders dropped at the sight of him in such a sorry state.

Oscar turned to her. "You must feel even worse than I do," he said.

Jackie didn't answer. She looked like she wanted to disappear under the floorboards.

"Or maybe you feel better than me. Throwing up might have been the smartest thing you ever did."

From the pained expression on Jackie's face, Will thought it would be best if they dropped the whole topic. "After breakfast and a shower, maybe you could drive Jackie to Edward's? Or are you still drunk?"

"I can drive," said Oscar. "I was thinking later we could take the dogs to the river."

Will liked that idea, but he had problems that needed to be addressed before he could do anything fun. He scrambled the eggs, toasted and buttered slices of bread, and set the cooked bacon on paper towels, while Oscar and Jackie drank their coffee in silence.

When he put breakfast in front of them, Oscar dove right in, while Jackie approached the food cautiously, like she couldn't tell if this meal would save her life or end it.

Will cleaned up, tossing the eggshells down the disposal, which he soon discovered wouldn't turn on. He cursed under his breath. "It's one broken thing after another with this damn house," he grumbled. He turned to the kids, who hadn't seemed to hear him. "I've got some work I need to deal with, so I'll leave you guys to it. There's juice in the fridge. I recommend lying down on the porch under the fans. It's very soothing."

As he walked out of the room, he heard Jackie say, "Is your grandfather getting married, or did I dream that?"

Will couldn't be bothered with talk of weddings. He went upstairs to the loft, preparing to write the most sycophantic, desperate email of his life. Even if it killed him, he would make his letter warm and personal, in hopes of making a reunion sound appealing. He would be cool and confident, to make the proposition sound worthy. He never thought he'd have to rely on Gavin Glantz to save his ass.

JULY

JULY

12

Gavin's wife wrote in chapter seven of her book that the truth should always come out, regardless of the cost. "Lies lead to psychological disorders," Juliette said. "Secrets damage the soul." If that were true, his soul would be in intensive care.

Gavin was in Munich, drinking tea in the upstairs of Spatenhaus and watching people walk around in front of the opera. But as soon as he remembered the email he'd gotten from Will Harris, he felt a need to get out of the dark, wood-paneled restaurant and take a walk in the sun. Flagging his waitress, who was wearing a traditional German dress revealing a decent amount of cleavage, he paid his bill and headed out into the heat of the afternoon. He had plenty of time before he needed to be at the Philharmonic, so he walked toward the English Garden. It was too warm for the expensive Panama hat he was wearing to keep the sun off his face and hide his receding hairline, but he kept it on anyway because his hat was not the cause of his uneasiness. Walking past shops and cafés, dabbing at the sweat under the brim, Gavin thought of Bridget and felt a spasm of tension running across his shoulders.

Why had Will invited him to play with Forsyth, as if he were still a member of the trio, as if no time had passed? Will, whom he hadn't seen in years, other than the one accidental sighting last month on the street in Greenwich Village. It was a bizarre proposition anyway, even if they'd stayed in touch, which they hadn't. Bridget still owed him a phone call from over twenty-five years ago.

Gavin had been smitten the instant they met. How could he not? Bridget was two years older than him, pretty and confident. Not the best cellist in their class maybe, but still, she was the daughter of Edward Stratton, which was incredibly cool. Plus, she was funny and nice and laid-back, while also being serious about music. And she was sexy: long hair, gorgeous legs, and perfect lips. Gavin, young and virginal, wanted to make out with her so bad it hurt.

And then Will had called him out on it.

"I see how you look at her," he once said. It was near the end of senior year, and they'd just committed to spending the next three years playing together in the trio.

Gavin hated Will for seeing right through him. And, of course, he denied it. "What? Not at all, man," Gavin said. "I'm not even attracted to her." He did a move that was a casual shrug combined with a sneer, a look that he hoped said, *I could do way better.*

Will acted as though Gavin hadn't said a word. "I'm telling you, it's for the best, she's not interested in you. A relationship would mess up our group chemistry."

Gavin disagreed. He didn't think being with Bridget would mess up anything. He got it now, of course, all these years later, but he'd been immature then and unable to anticipate consequences like hurt feelings or awkward breakups.

But no, Gavin never made a move on Bridget because—and this was a fact, plain and simple—he didn't stand a chance with her. Will knew it, and he knew it, so he kept his horny thoughts to himself. Gavin was used to getting rebuffed by girls. As the youngest in their

164

class, he was treated by the other students like a kid brother. Will teased him for being underage. The girls told him he was "cute" and "sweet." They used the term "child prodigy," which had the word "child" right in it, making him feel unmanly. They never took his attempts at flirtation seriously, and his response to this was to become an unbearable, callous show-off. Juliette made him see how his insecurity caused him to put on the persona of a cocky, overconfident little prick, and it had taken years of retraining to be able to see himself as others saw him, and several more to become truly self-aware and humble.

His success in the dating arena improved after graduation. He finally got some facial hair that made him look older than a high school student, and he bought a leather jacket and Levi's that fit him the right way, T-shirts that showed off his chest muscles, the kind of stuff his parents had dismissed as frivolous but that Gavin found made him feel good about himself. He got a girlfriend, broke up with her, and then got another, normal for most people but a whole new world for Gavin. Women started to notice him when he performed with Bridget and Will, and he loved the attention, even mugged a bit onstage to attract a little more.

The trio was doing well, and after their first three years together, they committed to another five, shaking hands on it over drinks. Then, a couple of years into that period, he was invited to audition for an orchestra. It was a great opportunity, and Gavin jumped at it. *Who wouldn't?* As he prepared, he knew he should tell Bridget and Will what he was doing, but he justified keeping it secret: he wasn't going to get it anyway, he told himself.

One night he and Bridget went out for drinks together after a rehearsal in their studio on Forsyth Street. He felt guilty; auditioning behind their backs had been a rotten thing to do, so after they'd had a few cocktails, he and Bridget walked out of the bar, and he thought, *I have to tell her.* Chest pounding, he turned to her and held her hands, trying to think of how best to confess. Bridget, apparently misunderstanding the look of desperation in his eyes, held his face in her hands in a way that was sexy and surprising, and she started kissing him. His heart slowed, he focused on her mouth, and he breathed in deeply.

"Whoops," she'd said, pulling away.

"Sorry." Gavin wasn't sorry; he was elated.

"No, I'm sorry." An ambulance went by, and she covered her ears. After it quieted, she said, "God, now I made it awkward—"

"What? Nothing's awkward. See?" He was incredibly turned on but thought the best strategy would be to act like this situation was no big deal. He gestured to the normal world around them, the cabs, the people, the storefronts. "We're just a couple of friends, hanging out."

"I don't know what came over me," she said, her hands on her neck. "A couple martinis, and I suddenly wanted— I really shouldn't have done that."

"We'll pretend it never happened," he said, hoping, in fact, that it would happen again, and as soon as possible.

"Are you sure?" She looked worried. "Should we talk about it?"

"It was only a kiss, Bridget," he said with a laugh. "Don't make a whole thing out of it." Yeah, like he didn't care that he'd just *made out* with Bridget Stratton. His heart was beating so hard, he covered it with his hand. "Wanna go back to my place?"

Bridget hesitated.

"I mean as friends," he said. "I have a bottle of wine."

"Sure," she said, "but we're not—"

"No," he said, waving her off, "no, of course not. *Gross.*"

He loved making her laugh.

As they walked a few blocks to his crappy Lower East Side studio, he resisted the urge to reach for her hand, to put an arm over her lovely, bare shoulders. They went inside to the sound of a ringing phone, and he answered it. A voice on the other end told him he was being offered a position in the orchestra of the Sydney Opera House. The voice congratulated him, sharing details about salary and benefits. It asked him if he would accept. "Wow, yes," he said, looking over at Bridget's puzzled expression. "That's amazing. Yes," he said again more quietly and hung up the phone.

"What was that about?" she asked. She was standing in front of the one tiny window, looking, if possible, more beautiful than he'd ever seen her. He would lose her now, he thought, before he'd even had a chance with her. He got the bottle of wine from the counter and found the corkscrew. "I just . . . well, okay. I just got offered a job," he said, "in Australia."

She cracked up. "Australia," she repeated, like it was a bad joke.

He put the bottle down. "The Sydney Opera House." At that her expression changed completely. "I guess with the time difference it's the afternoon there," he said, focusing on the most irrelevant detail.

She was staring at him, expressionless. "You've been auditioning?"

"Not in general, no, of course not."

"Because we said five years," she said. "Five more years, we said, and that was only like two years ago."

"Two and a half," said Gavin.

"You *auditioned*? And you didn't think that was something you should tell us?" Her arms were crossed, her purse still on her shoulder. He hoped she wouldn't leave.

"I'm sorry," he said. "They heard us at Tanglewood and then— Look, I'm as surprised as you are, Bridget." God, he loved the sound of her name. He'd never even known a Bridget before her. "They want me to start right away." The reality of that fact was sinking in and making him feel homesick.

"You're *taking* it?"

Gavin considered her question: A young trio whose future was entirely uncertain versus a premier orchestra offering a steady salary and a path to greater things? This wasn't even a choice. "I'm sorry," he said, "but yes." The worst part, he realized, wasn't even that she wouldn't sleep with him now; it was that she would hate him.

"It's a big decision," she said. "Aren't you going to think it over? What about Will and me?"

He felt he was having the most adult moment of his life. And while he thought he might like to turn the job down and stay right where he was, he said what he *knew* was right: "I'm sorry, but I have to consider my own career."

"Nice," Bridget said sarcastically, dropping her purse on the floor. "Why didn't you tell us you were looking for a way out?"

"They contacted *me*," he said, walking over to her. "I didn't go looking for this."

She didn't say anything for a moment, and then she shrugged, dismissing him. "Whatever. We'll replace you in, like, a day."

He winced. He'd never seen Bridget be mean before.

Right away, she seemed contrite. "Look, I'm happy for you," she said. "I could kill you, but I'm really happy for you." She leaned toward him and gave him a fast hug, like he was her little brother. Then she stepped away. "You're a better musician than either of us, and it's not like we don't know it."

"Oh, stop." Gavin was pretty sure that was true, but he sometimes wondered if he wasn't *as* good as people said he was. Then again, he'd just been offered a position in a major orchestra. *Principal second violin.* At barely twenty-five years old! Of course, he was good. "Will doesn't think I'm better than him," he said.

Bridget smiled sadly. "Oh, he does. He just doesn't like to talk about it."

She leaned over abruptly and picked up her purse.

"Wait, where are you going?" He held up the bottle of wine.

"Home," she said. "I've got a doctor's appointment in the morning."

He didn't want her to leave. He thought about how far away

168

Sydney was, the other side of the world, and he felt ill. He wouldn't know anyone there. *Sydney?* How did this even happen?

"I'll see you tomorrow," she said, sighing. "Will is *not* going to like this."

Although he dreaded facing Will, Gavin was focused solely on Bridget. "Hey, since I'm leaving anyway," he said, stepping closer to her, "couldn't we end things between us . . . on a better note?"

"What do you mean?"

"All this time we've been working together, so it would have been inappropriate for us to, you know. But now if we're *not* in a trio together . . ." He guided her hands back to the sides of his face, positioning them the same way she'd had them before when she kissed him on the street. "I was just thinking maybe we could—"

"I'm mad at you."

"Are you?" he said, running his hands through her hair and holding the back of her head. "I bet you've always known how much I like you." He leaned in and kissed her.

She kissed him back, hesitantly at first. And then, as if to shock him, she dropped her purse and took off her shirt and jeans. She kissed him again, and he walked her backward across the room to his bed, his arm around her waist. He wished Will could see him now.

She stayed with him all night, but when he woke up late the next morning, she was gone.

Sydney was lonely, and the job was all-consuming. Often, Gavin wanted nothing more than to jump on a plane and go home. The transition from playing in an ensemble to playing in an orchestra did not go smoothly for him; he was told by the concertmaster that he needed to keep his head still, that his hair moved around too much and his face was too emotive. It was humiliating, especially when he found out that his swaying movements and ecstatic facial expressions had been the talk of the violin section behind his back.

And then, a few months later, Bridget called him. He was dressing for a concert in his one-bedroom, high-rise apartment, and he dropped his tie and sat down at the sound of her voice.

"Bridget," he'd said, surprised and delighted to hear from her. It was amazing how clear the call was, as though he were right back in New York with her. It made him want to cry.

"I know we've been out of touch," she said, sounding rather businesslike, "but I wanted to say hello."

"How are you? How's Will? I miss you guys."

"We're doing well, thanks. How are *you*?" she asked.

He lied and told her he was happy. "Everything's great. What's going on with you?"

"Well, I'm pregnant," she said.

"Hey, cool." He wasn't entirely shocked; Bridget had talked often about wanting kids. "Good for you."

"I'm really happy about it, and I'm—"

"That's great—"

"This is . . . *ugh*. Look, I've been using the term 'donor' because it was . . . It's truthful. That's what I did, I got a donor from a sperm bank. And it worked."

"Fantastic," he said, checking his watch. "That's really great. I can't tell you how nice it is to hear your—"

"But the truth is that it's possible, *highly* unlikely, but it's possible, I guess, that *you* were the donor. But probably not. It was more likely the guy from the sperm bank. But it's vaguely, remotely possible it was you. But probably not." She paused so long Gavin wondered if they'd been disconnected. "I don't know, that's the thing."

He laughed, sort of. What was she even talking about?

"I read up on it. *Science*," she said, as if she were ending with *good grief.* "In any case, I want nothing from you," she said. "I'm just relaying information."

"Science?"

"I wasn't going to say anything at all, but my sister told me I was being . . . what did she say? . . . an unethical asshole not to let you know it's a remote possibility."

He said nothing, thinking she would start laughing and say, *April Fools!* He picked up his tie.

"Look, I'm fine sticking with the anonymous-donor line," she said. "It's easier for me, frankly. But if you prefer, only if you want to, of course, we could find out for sure. The twins are due in four months."

"*Twins?* We only had sex once."

"That's all it takes," she said with a short laugh. "And it was three times actually, in one night." And then, in a more serious tone, she said, "We can forget I called if you want."

He was feeling dizzy, and he pulled his blazer off.

"You can think it over," she was saying, "decide if you want a paternity test to find out for sure."

"You actually think that *I* could be . . ." He didn't see how any of what she was saying right now would fit into the life he was living. He was dating an oboist. They had dinner plans that night.

"I really don't think so. You and I just casually, you know. Whereas when I got inseminated, the doctor wasn't kidding around, like he knew what he was doing. Not that you didn't know what you were doing, and I acknowledge that it is possible that—"

"*Bridget,*" he said, pacing to the end of the phone cord and running his hand through his hair, "this is a lot to take in, and I have a concert starting in—"

"I get it. It's just that I didn't think it would work on the first try, and by the time I found out that it did, you'd already left for Sydney. So how are you, anyway?"

"Dumbfounded."

"Look, I'm ninety-nine-point nine . . . nine percent sure it was the donor. So, what are the chances it was you instead?"

"I hope *zero*." It came out sounding harsh.

"Got it," she said. "Well, okay then. Let's keep this between us." She paused, and then said, "This call is probably costing a fortune. Love you, Gavin. Be well."

And she'd hung up. Gavin was convinced that this was the moment his hair started falling out.

The "love you" at the end had completely thrown him; it sounded sincere. It didn't strike him as a romantic declaration; rather, it was the "love you" of a dear old friend. It made him even more homesick. It made him want to start the conversation all over again. Instead he put on his tie and left his apartment.

A few weeks later, after he'd had time to process what she'd told him, he called Bridget back.

Gavin had walked all the way to the foot of the Monopteros, a round Greek-style temple in the middle of the park, and he checked his watch. Sitting down on a bench, he searched his mail to find the message he'd gotten from Will two weeks earlier and finally hit reply: *Nice to hear from you, Will, and sorry for the delay in responding. Thank you for thinking of me, but unfortunately, my schedule is booked this fall.* He looked across the park where he could see blue-and-white Bavarian flags in the distance and picnickers and sunbathers, some nude, in the field in front of him. He had everything he needed in life; why complicate things? He looked at his phone again and added, *My warmest greetings and heartfelt apologies,* and he signed his name.

But he didn't hit send. Instead he put his phone away, leaned back on the bench, and closed his eyes, trying to hear the music in his head that he would be playing that evening.

The Munich Philharmonic concert that night was in honor of the life of Johannes Lang, a man who had been the executive director of the concert hall for thirty-five years. Gavin was told by the event organizer that Mr. Lang's widow, Charlotte, who had once hosted a popular Sunday program on a Bavarian classical radio station, and her son would be in attendance, along with much of Munich's most cultured society.

At seven that evening in the Gasteig, Gavin played the Fauré Requiem, a piece with a beautiful violin part and a most surprising, rousing moment in the Sanctus movement, which enlivened the audience. The orchestra was outstanding and the conductor was a friend, and Gavin was able to push all of the memories of Will and Bridget out of his mind.

After the concert, he was invited to a private reception with the family and friends of the late Herr Lang in a gallery not far from the Gasteig. As he browsed the art, spooky paintings depicting misty, mythological forest scenes, he felt a tap on his shoulder.

"I see your glass is empty."

Gavin turned around to find a man in an expensive-looking dark suit offering a bottle of champagne. "Hans Lang," the man said, extending his other hand. "The concert was very good tonight. Not the program I would have selected, personally, but it was well done."

Uhh, thanks? thought Gavin. As Hans filled his glass, Gavin realized that he was the son of the man being honored. He considered saying something obvious, like *Sorry for your loss*, but he couldn't muster enough sincerity to make it believable. It wasn't like he'd known the guy. "Wonderful party," he said instead.

Hans shook his head sadly. "My father was a kind and loving man. He lived ninety-four wonderful years. I would have liked to have five more with him." Hans handed the bottle of champagne to a woman passing by in an apron, holding a tray of appetizers.

"*Häppchen?*" Hans asked. "Or as you Americans call it . . . 'finger food'?"

Gavin took one of the little bites, a miniature ham quiche, off the tray, and popped it in his mouth. Hans waved the server away before he could take another.

"My mother is doing well," Hans said.

Gavin hadn't asked about her and felt almost as though he were being reprimanded.

"She has never been one to wallow in sadness. She loved my father, but I suppose she has too much respect for life to waste a single day feeling sorry for herself."

This statement had a familiar ring to it. "My wife's a big believer in living every day well and gratefully," Gavin said. "She wrote the book on it. Literally." He wished she were with him. She was a better conversationalist, and people always liked her right away.

"Marriage," said Hans bitterly. "It is a tragic day when a man finds out he is disposable."

Even in trying to process this disagreeable proclamation, Gavin noted what impeccable English Hans spoke.

"How long have you been married?" Hans asked.

"Quite happily for seven years," said Gavin. "We had a beautiful wedding in Napa Valley."

Hans raised his eyebrows. "Vineyards, yes?"

"That's right," said Gavin enthusiastically. "California makes some of the best wine in the world."

Hans made a doubtful face and looked away. "You see," he said, pointing to his mother. "She's in good spirits. Perhaps your music was invigorating. Or maybe not." He shrugged. "Maybe it is something else entirely bringing her joy."

The widow was standing with a circle of lively people around her. She was dressed elegantly, her bright red lipstick and silver hair making her stand out from across the room. Juliette would call her a knockout.

Gavin thought this exchange had gone on long enough that he could make a graceful exit. "It was a pleasure to meet—"

"Lottie has reconnected with a lot of old friends recently. I think that's quite nice for her. She loves to be part of things, circulating."

"Lottie?" Gavin asked, trying to keep up.

"Charlotte, my mother."

Charlotte must have said something funny then, as the group around her erupted in delighted laughter. She sipped her champagne and took in the admiration of the room. She caught Gavin's eye and waved at him gracefully, like a queen.

"She's planning to visit someone in New England soon, a man," said Hans. "I remember the family vaguely from childhood. I'm worried about my mother traveling on her own, but I can't accompany her at the moment."

Gavin felt the jet lag kicking in now and suppressed a yawn. He wanted to go back to his hotel. "She seems to be doing very well."

"Oh, yes, she certainly is. May I ask you something, Mr. Glantz?" Hans said.

"Of course."

"It seems my mother is remarrying. The news has come as quite a shock, as perhaps you can imagine."

Gavin looked at Charlotte Lang again and didn't find it especially shocking. She was sparkling and lovely. Gavin wasn't sure what to say. "Congratulations?"

Hans took a step closer. "I'd like to get your opinion of Mr. Edward Stratton and his family. I understand you used to be in a trio with his daughter some years ago, yes? How well do you know her? This *Bridget*?"

———◇———

Gavin took a cab across the Isar to his hotel. As he walked into his room at the Bayerischer Hof, he placed his violin case on the desk and sat on the foot of his bed.

There was something at work here, or, to use Juliette's vocabulary, there was something the universe was trying to tell him. Miriam had dropped Bridget's name. Then Will, after appearing on the street in New York as Gavin's Uber drove by, had reached out, inviting him back into their lives. And now along came Hans, bringing up Bridget, along with some very odd questions about Edward, to be sure.

One thing he was certain of was that these points of contact could not go unanswered.

He got his phone out and opened Will's email again, deleting the draft he'd written.

"Secrets," Juliette always said, "damage the soul." In that case, he decided, as soon as he got home, he would tell her absolutely everything.

13

Bridget could swear there was heat emanating from the fireplace, even though it had been out of use for six months. Sitting with a book in front of the gray ash heap, she remembered now why she avoided coming to the house when the temperature hit ninety. The back of her neck and her face were sweaty, and she was missing the air-conditioning of her city apartment. It was early Saturday morning, and although she had fans whirring in every room, all they were doing was moving the hot, heavy air around.

Will, Isabelle, and Oscar had yet to make an appearance, so she started reading again, when Sterling's Dutch publisher interrupted with a text:

After one month residing here, we find the situations not good. Problems are 1. Sound of rapid stomping (bam bam bam - maybe a child?) coming from the apartment above, sometimes as late as 22:00. 2. Unappealing smell of cooked onions in the hallway at all hours. 3. A cockroach remains dead on the trash room floor this morning. Given the high rent, we need you to provide for solutions.

This list of grievances made Bridget slightly less homesick for

New York, but also angry at the gall of these people. "High rent"? She'd charged them next to nothing as a favor to Sterling. If they only knew how much Manhattan apartments actually cost, they'd be thanking her instead of bitching. The apartment was in a prewar doorman building, small, yes, but quintessentially New York. They were lucky to be there.

Onions and footsteps were not problems she could fix, so she texted back:

I'm sorry to hear you are disturbed by the sounds and smells of New York City. Please understand that in our building, we do not tell each other what to cook, nor do we dictate how late people can walk around in their own apartments. Furthermore, thank god the dead cockroach "remains dead" in the trash room, the alternative (zombie cockroaches) being too horrific to even contemplate. That being said, if you want to find other accommodations, feel free, and we can terminate our arrangement.

The upstairs neighbors were, in fact, annoying, as were the occasional cockroaches, dead or alive, but what could one do?

Connecticut was too hot, and New York was smelly and loud. Where, given a choice, would she escape? Resting the book on her face, she closed her eyes and imagined standing in an airport, scanning the screen of departures, flights heading to Berlin, Chicago, Dubai, Honolulu, Lima, Paris, Reykjavik, Tel Aviv, or Tokyo. London would be her pick, easy. It would be cloudy and cool, with architecture that complemented gray skies. She often fantasized about renting a small flat, going to the London Philharmonic, taking a guided tour at the Tate, attending a sherry concert at Wigmore Hall. She would walk around Regent's Park, past Buckingham Palace, and through Covent Garden, and travel by train to all the beautiful places her parents had taken her as a child: Stonehenge, Canterbury, Bath, and Brighton. She hoped it would be rainy; she would wander the Cotswolds, wearing a belted Burberry.

———◇———

Unable to focus on her book, she calculated the time difference between Connecticut and Germany and tried calling Lottie again.

"*Endlich*, Bridget!" Lottie said. "At long last!"

Bridget congratulated her on the engagement.

"Your warm wishes mean more to me than I can say. Edward says Marge is organizing the wedding plans. Do you sink she's up to zis challenge, to do what I am imagining for the flowers and food? I remember meeting her many years ago . . ."

Bridget wondered how Marge was going to feel about taking directions from this woman she barely knew. "Is the wedding going to be just family or—"

"*Ach, nein*, Edward's guest list vill be even longer than mine," Lottie said with a laugh, "knowing your father."

Yes, she did know him, but did Lottie?

"I'll be inviting perhaps . . . seventy or seventy-five friends from all over the world," she said.

That number was about four times what Bridget was expecting her to say.

"Edward sent pictures of the house," she went on, "and I'm glad to know we can accommodate such a large number. Ozzerwise, I would have suggested having it here in München. We're celebrating and want to include everyone, Bridget, *ja?*"

"*Ja*," said Bridget, wrapping her head around the scale of the party. With Johannes so recently deceased, Bridget couldn't help but wonder if a big bash was in poor taste.

"And here is somesing else, actually: I vant you, Gwen, and your children to be in my vedding party, and I'm sending somesing special, just for the occasion."

"Oh, that's unneces—"

"I need your sizes."

Sizes? "When are you coming here?" Bridget asked, wishing she could say that having bridesmaids seemed way over the top.

"I've had to put my trip off again," she said, "*leider*. I have too much to do here, many sings to prepare and less than two months before the vedding."

How much did an octogenarian have to do to get married? Was she shopping for her trousseau?

"How is Hans?" said Bridget. "Gwen and I were remembering the times we spent together as kids."

"So sweet of you to ask, dear. He's, what can I say?" said Lottie. "He will come, *natürlich*. But I don't sink Hans understands. Bridget, I vant to say sank you."

"What for?" Bridget asked.

Lottie didn't answer right away. "You are so kind to support Edward and me. Hans, *eigentlich*, he finds our relationship . . . He's not so happy about the plans."

Bridget wasn't completely surprised. She didn't mention that Gwen wasn't exactly thrilled either. "Well, I'm sure he'll come around—"

"Anyway," Lottie added with a sigh, "Marlene Dietrich once said, 'I do not sink we have a *right* to happiness. If happiness happens, say sanks.' So sank you, Bridget."

Bridget felt emboldened. "I, my trio that is, we'd love to play something for you and my father at the wedding. Would that be all right with you?"

"*Wunderschön!*" Lottie said. "What a lovely idea."

———◆———

After hanging up, Bridget took advantage of the quiet and got her cello out of its case. She'd bought the honey-colored instrument on a post-Juilliard trip to visit her father's family in London, using a good portion of the graduation check he'd given her to pay for it. She went from shop to shop, landing at Tom Woods (her father's recommendation) and decided on a Thomas Kennedy, made in the 1820s. Will never asked her what it cost; she would have lied if he had.

Her cello wasn't appreciating the weather either. It was grumpy about the humidity and oppressive heat, and it took Bridget over five minutes to tune it properly. Practicing had become a challenge here. It was hard to concentrate with Oscar's Skype meetings in the mornings, three-to-four-hour sessions where he would sit at the dining room table with his laptop, wearing a dress shirt, tie, and blazer on top, nothing but boxers underneath, and talk loudly about energy policy and legislation. When he was done, he would change into shorts and a T-shirt, pop open a beer, and lie down on the couch to watch Netflix. Or he would sit in the kitchen eating a bowl of cereal, leaving the milk out on the counter. She couldn't figure out how much she should parent him. He was too old to be assigned chores, and too young, apparently, to do them properly. Having him as a roommate was both a joy and a nuisance. Just that morning, when she'd gone to the laundry room to hang up her favorite clothes to dry, she found that Oscar had put a load in the washing machine and thrown her wet things in the dryer, shrinking her favorite shirts to toddler size.

She found her score for a Rachmaninoff piece and put it on the stand, thinking it might be a good choice for the trio to play at the wedding. She hadn't talked to Will yet about her vision for Forsyth's debut concert with Caroline, but as soon as he came downstairs, she would tell him. She felt like he'd been avoiding her the last two weeks. Every time she called him in New York, he made excuses to hang up, saying he was running late to a lesson, hopping on the subway, getting poor reception.

Bridget had only begun to play the piece when she heard an aggressive knocking on the front door. She set the cello down on its side and went to open it.

"Hi there," said the stranger on the doorstep. "Are you Bridget?" He stuck his hand out. "Mark Thomas, Realtor. I met Will in the grocery store a couple weeks back, and he said you were thinking about selling the house. Thought I'd stop by and introduce myself." He handed her his business card. "Is Will here?"

Bridget looked at the card. "I think there's been a misunderstanding," she said. "I'm not selling. It was just a passing thought I had after I got brutally dumped by my boyfriend."

"*You* got dumped?" Mark looked her up and down. Why, she couldn't imagine; she was wearing running shorts and an old, oversize T-shirt. "I find that hard to believe," he said.

Bridget couldn't tell if this comment was a terrible attempt at flirting or if he was buttering her up so she would give him a listing. "Anyway," she said, "it's just something I was considering."

"Well, I'm here anyway," he said, waiting for her to invite him in.

"Yes, and on a Saturday."

"Will said you guys are weekenders, so I figured you'd be up for the holiday. Want to take a look around outside? I have a couple ideas about the exterior already, some things you might want to address anyway, whether you sell or not. And then if someday, down the road, you decide you're ready, you'll know who to call."

It didn't sound like a bad idea to get an expert to tell her what needed to be done to the house. Seeing what needed fixing had never been her strength.

Rather than let Mark in, she walked outside with him. Blocking the sun with her hand, she stood with him in the heat of the yard, looking out at the damaged tennis court, the neglected barn, the flock of sheep and guinea hens milling about.

"So?" she asked. "What do you think?"

Mark's hair was parted far on the right, and his brass-buttoned navy blazer did not hide his slightly squishy midsection and sloping shoulders. He was wearing tired brown tassel loafers. Putting his hands on his hips, he turned slowly in a circle, making a rapid sound as he looked around, "Bah bah bah bahhh," like he was riffing off the sheep. He was sucking in his stomach, so Bridget involuntarily sucked in her own and stood up straighter.

"I can show you the inside, too," she said, "but I'll need to wake everyone up."

"Teenagers?" he asked.

"Not exactly."

"Oh, right," he said. "Will mentioned that the kids moved back home."

"I don't know about 'moved,' but they're here—"

"I know all about it," Mark said. "My daughter's living with me since she stopped going to college. She's only twenty-two, but we're gonna have to have a serious talk pretty soon."

Bridget was glad to know she wasn't the only one dealing with grown-up kids under her roof. "A talk about . . . ?"

"She's taking a summer class at the community college and bartending on the weekends, so she's trying. But it's getting complicated."

"Complicated how?"

Mark looked down at his shoes. "She brought a date home the other night, and the next morning he was in my kitchen, cooking pancakes." He looked pained. "I've got to set some rules. It's my house, you know?"

The sound of a door closing made them turn and look up at Will's porch. Emma was slipping out of the loft, carrying gladiator sandals in her left hand and a slouchy purse in her right. She turned, saw Bridget, and gave a shy little wave.

Bridget waved back. "Coffee?" she called up.

"Work," Emma said, pointing in the direction of town. "But thank you."

Bridget nodded and waited until the sound of Emma's car faded before she turned back to Mark, who was flapping his hand to swat away a cloud of gnats in front of his face; he looked like a conductor having a tantrum.

"You might want to think about doing some repairs out here," Mark said, "before things get any worse. For starters, I'd say replace the tennis court fence, and it looks like you might need a new roof over the porch there. And you should at least paint the outside trim where it's rotting. You've got one window there that's spoiled," he said, pointing in the direction of the breakfast room, where one of the windows had a milky film over it, "but you can probably wait on that."

"Anything else?" Bridget said wryly.

"Yes," he said. "You need to repave the worst parts of the driveway so people don't get a flat on the way up. And you should clean up the weeds obscuring the stone wall and, generally speaking, make the place less . . . run-down. Some of it's pretty urgent."

"I don't really notice this stuff," Bridget said.

"You'll notice wood rot as soon as it starts raining inside your house."

Bridget decided not to mention that her house had already sprung a leak or two. "If this were your place," she said, "what would you do first?"

"Let's take a peek inside, then we'll talk specifics."

Through a window on the back of the house, she could see Oscar wandering into the kitchen, wearing nothing but boxers.

"Do you mind waiting here a minute? I need to let my son know you're coming in."

Mark nodded. "I'll walk around the house and check the rest of the exterior."

"For what?"

"Visible damage."

The porch door opened and Oscar's dogs came bounding out, running up to greet them. Mark bent his knees and placed his hands over his crotch. He was obviously not a dog person. Hudson, scratching at the slider door upstairs, started barking from the loft.

Bridget walked over to the house and saw that Henry Higgins, who was spending almost all of his time now outdoors or in the barn, was leaving a dead mouse on the doorstep. She used a leaf to pick the mouse up by the tail and flung it into the brush. Henry looked insulted. She tried to pat him, saying, "Thanks anyway, pal," but he dodged her hand and ran off under the bushes.

Oscar was standing by the stairs, watching Mark, who was studying the gutters and muttering to himself. "Who's that?" he asked.

"A Realtor."

Bare-chested with bedhead and dark circles under his eyes, Oscar looked like hell. "Are you selling?"

"I'm only talking to him. The house is in worse shape than I realized."

He placed his hand on Bridget's shoulder as though he needed physical support. "I'm so hungover," he said.

"Again?"

"Couldn't you *describe* the upstairs to him? Or start in the guesthouse? I need a few minutes."

"Are you okay," she said, "apart from the hangover?"

"Matt keeps calling," he said.

"I bet he misses you," Bridget said, wishing she had some solid marital advice to give. Surely her decades-long friendship with Will had taught her something about commitment, respect, loyalty, and the importance of honest communication. As angry as she was at Matt, she hoped they could work out their problems. "Maybe he's sorry and wants you back."

"There's more to it than that."

"What?" she asked. "What's more to it?"

He moaned as he turned around, walking up the stairs slowly as though his back ached.

"Forget the Realtor," Bridget said. "I'll just show him downstairs."

"Thanks, Ma." He turned at the top of the stairs and closed his door.

Looking out the window, she could see Mark kicking at the broken flagstone on the pathway. She opened the door as he leaned over and started taking his shoes off.

"You can leave them on," Bridget told him. "We're not a shoes-off household."

"I stepped in dog feces," he said. Bear knocked into him as the dogs ran past and into the kitchen, hair flying, tags clinking against the metal water bowl. Eliza Doolittle hissed as they ran by.

Mark came in, and Bridget tried not to look at his big toe poking through his beige sock.

They walked through the downstairs, as Bridget pointed out the fireplace and the built-in bookcases in the living room on their way to the kitchen.

"Needs updating," Mark said, pointing at the crooked pot rack that hung directly beneath the loft. The pots and pans would always rattle slightly whenever Will moved around upstairs. Last night they'd been knocking against each other like cowbells; at least someone was having sex.

"And the master bedroom," said Bridget. "I have my own little porch. Perfect for a glass of wine at night."

"Mm-hmm," said Mark, with a tone that suggested he was unimpressed.

"We're skipping the upstairs," she said, without any explanation.

Leaving the dogs in the house, she and Mark walked out and across the field to the other side of the barn. Bridget knocked as she opened the door to the guesthouse. She saw wildflowers in a vase on the coffee table. Bridget smiled at the tidy living room, relieved that one of her kids was acting like an adult. Mark stepped out of his shoes again and entered the house at the exact moment that the bathroom door opened and out walked Kevin, wearing nothing but a towel around his waist.

Bridget stopped breathing and stared.

"Ooops, sorry," Kevin said, turning red and tightening the towel. "Oh, man."

Bridget couldn't speak. *Kevin?*

Mark seemed to be missing the awkwardness of the situation entirely. "Oh, hey, Kev, just the guy I wanted to see," Mark said, walking right up to him. "She's got some bats living in the eaves over the front door."

Kevin nodded.

"Naturally, I thought of you."

"You . . ." He looked at Bridget. ". . . need a bat house?"

"You built some over at the Clarks', right?" said Mark.

"Yeah, a couple of years back."

Mark turned back to Bridget. "You should get Kevin to put one or two out in the field, draw those bats out. You don't want them flying in the house, but it's illegal to kill them, as I'm sure you know."

Bridget had no intention of killing bats, but she couldn't find her voice to say so.

"I can do that," Kevin said, trying to look agreeable in spite of the situation.

"Good to see you, man," Mark said, smiling broadly. "Did *you* bring the sheep?"

"Yeah, doing what I can to get the field under control."

"Great, great." Mark must have seen the confusion on Bridget's face and said, "I've known Kevin since he was a kid." Mark looked at Kevin and smiled again. "So how you been? I heard you were back in town."

Bridget finally thought of the right thing to say: "Why don't we move along and give Kevin a chance to . . . put some clothes on."

"Sure," Mark said. "I get the general idea here. Your basic guest cottage. Hasn't been renovated. Looks like some water damage on the floorboards over there. How many bedrooms here?"

Kevin and Bridget looked at each other.

"One," they both said.

"You're living here now?" Mark asked. "And working on the place? That's a swell arrangement."

Kevin started to answer when Isabelle came to the doorway of the bedroom in a tiny silk bathrobe. "Morning," she said, walking into the room looking especially cheerful.

Mark introduced himself.

"Well, we better get going," Bridget said, looking up at the ceiling. "Lots to talk about. Shall we?"

"Is there coffee?" Isabelle asked.

"Not anymore," said Bridget. The coffee had gone cold hours before.

"Wow, I could have slept all day." She ran her fingers through her tangled hair.

Bridget forced a bright, completely fake smile. "All righty then," she said.

Mark caught up with her between the two houses, tripping in his loafers. Bridget turned to face him, trying to put the image of Kevin in a towel out of her mind. "Off the top of your head, Mark," Bridget said, "three things. Name three things I should do."

"You want to start with three?" Mark looked around. "Only three, huh? Then I'd say porch roof, driveway, tennis court. No, porch, kitchen remodel, exterior trim. Or porch, court, and, man, what about that barn?"

"What about it?"

"It's an eyesore. It looks like it's actually sinking into the ground. Does the field flood around it?"

"Not that I know of."

"Because it looks like you could have drainage issues." He shook his head at the barn. "When those sheep leave, they'll probably give you a one-star Yelp review."

Bridget was not amused. "They like it here."

"If this were my place," he said, "I'd tear that thing down and grass over it. You could double the size of your yard."

"No way," Bridget said. "It's got character, and it's very old."

"I can see that," Mark said and chuckled.

"I mean, it's historic. It's an eighteenth-century structure."

Mark looked worried. "It's not landmarked, is it?"

"Not yet." In fact, Bridget liked the idea so much, she'd taken Kevin up on his offer to look into it for her at town hall.

"Don't do it," said Mark. "Keep the bureaucrats out of it in case you change your mind or a future owner wants to tear it down."

"I don't want it torn down," Bridget said, appalled he would suggest such a thing. "Anyway," she said, "it sounds like you think there's a lot of other work I need to attend to first."

Mark slapped himself on the face, killing a mosquito and leaving a bloody streak across his cheek. "If this were my place, I'd start addressing the urgent maintenance issues before they lead to bigger problems, and I wouldn't limit myself to three. See that tree over there," he asked, pointing, "leaning toward the house? It's stone dead. You get a big storm, and that's falling over and going through the roof."

So far, Mark had not said one positive thing about the property. His endless list of problems was making Bridget want to go back to bed.

"You need names?" he asked. "I've got a great tree guy."

The one thing Bridget did not need was names. Marge had a whole book full of them. "That's okay, I got it."

"Kevin's great, by the way. He'll get this place fixed up for you, whether you sell or not. But imagine if you *did* sell." He let his voice go dreamy. "No more property taxes for a school system you're not using. No more problems with plumbing or electricity, no more trees falling down. No more grown kids thinking they can stay as long as they like."

"And no more family home," she said, hating the sound of it.

Mark was looking at the barn with an amused expression. "Funny," he said. "People have such a thing for old barns. When they're being put to good use, I can get on board, but when they're just sitting there like that, taking up space . . . Hey, have you ever heard of Peter Latham?"

Bridget shook her head.

"He has an alpaca farm on Spectacle Hill. He bought his place several years back for peanuts and did a major renovation of the barn on his property. He put in a gorgeous office space in the upstairs, installed heat and A/C, solar panels on the roof, and started his whole business right there."

Bridget looked at her wreck of a barn and felt like a failure. She could see Mark's point: it did look run-down, and not in a cute Batshit Barn sort of way. It looked shabby and old. It looked unloved.

"I'm surprised you don't know Peter," said Mark. "He's kind of a big deal in the county."

"I'm not very social here."

"He's got a cool coffee shop in town where he also sells clothing, all made from his own alpacas. His mission is to create a community hub where people gather and talk. Sort of like a town square."

Bridget wasn't convinced. "Isn't that a lot of pressure to put on his alpacas?"

"You should check it out." He nodded his head proudly, as though he himself were responsible for Peter Latham's success.

"I'd like to clean out my barn, spruce it up, and make it usable again. I just don't know where to start."

"Usable for what?" said Mark, making a face as he looked up at the broken shingles around the cupola.

"You know what?" Bridget said, feeling motivated. "I'll do it."

"You'll sell?"

"I'll work on the place this summer. I'll deal with as much as I can—the roof and the dead tree and the bats—and I'll make the place as nice as it was when I bought it."

"And then . . . you're selling?" he asked with a hopeful expression.

Bridget looked around, considering the question. "I'll let you know at the end of the summer."

W ill stretched his legs and stared at the peaked ceiling, his arms spread out across the mattress. He'd been up for an hour already, but he didn't want to get out of bed. In spite of the brutal heat that morning, all of which seemed to rise into the loft and settle there, Will was happy to be in his room. The light filtered through the shades that covered the sliding door, and he could see the outline of the mountain through the fabric. It was a beautiful, comfortable space, and Will always slept well in it. As sorry as he was about Bridget's relationship, a part of him was very glad that Sterling hadn't taken over his room, used his shower, his deck, his chair, all of which Will considered his own, even though none of it technically was.

Over the years, Bridget had given him presents, always making it seem like he was doing her a favor in accepting them. They kept up the charade of reverse gratitude, regardless of how ridiculous it was. There was, for example, the Danish-designed sofa in his apartment. She had special-ordered it from Design Within Reach, got a case of buyer's remorse, and begged him to take it off her hands, claiming her cats were going to claw up the fancy custom fabric and it couldn't be returned. He'd offered to pay for it, but she'd refused. Many of his belongings had come to him in similar ways. "I somehow ended up with *two* Nespresso machines," she once told him. "Can you take one off my hands?" The antique bar cart was an impulse buy, she'd said, and "completely wrong" for her apartment. And then there was the time she said, "I bought Oscar a Hugo Boss suit on a final sale, and it's too big for him. Would you mind trying it on?" Will's only suit at the time was threadbare, and this suit happened to be a perfect fit. Coincidence? Of course not. And yet she said "thank you" when he agreed to wear it.

He appreciated Bridget's generosity. In return, Will liked to think he was a good friend, a trustworthy music partner, and an outstanding houseguest. In one week, he'd failed on all three fronts. As a bad friend, he hadn't told her that Caroline quit. As a dishonest music partner, he had attempted to solve the problem without even consulting her first. And finally, having Emma sleep over the night before was a leap into inconsiderate houseguest behavior. Regarding that last mistake, he really couldn't help himself.

The Monday after their first date, he'd gone back to New York for the week, and as soon as he got to his apartment, with the sign still advertising Will's tenuous grip on his living situation, he found he couldn't stop thinking about Emma. He waited a few days, not wanting to seem overly eager, and then he sent her a text: *Glad we met. Hope to see you again sometime.*

His phone had pinged a few minutes later. *Thinking about you,* she wrote.

Only three little words, but he read them over several times. *Really?* he'd finally answered. A weak response, but she replied right away: *You coming this weekend?* He wanted to say yes, but he had lessons to make up from the week before and a gig that Saturday. Besides, he wasn't ready to face Bridget to tell her about the debacle with Caroline and the email he'd gotten back from Gavin.

He and Emma texted back and forth the whole week and into the next one, shamelessly flirting with each other. Then, at the end of the second week, he was standing on the street outside the Mannes School of Music, ready to teach a lesson, when he'd heard the ping. He opened her text to find she'd sent a picture of her breasts. It was the sexiest thing that had ever happened to him.

He called Bridget right away and told her he was coming up for the holiday weekend.

He'd arrived at Bridget's house late the night before, had a glass of wine with her and the kids, and headed up to the loft. He texted Emma to let her know he was back in town.

Come over, she wrote back.

It didn't seem right to abscond with Bridget's Volvo in the middle of the night.

No car, he wrote. *Tomorrow?*

There was a pause, and then she wrote, *On my way.*

Emma left early for work that morning, leaving Will to replay every moment of their night together over in his head, like a fantasy reel. She was stunning and fun. Had they made too much noise? And—much more pressing—how soon could he see her again?

Will felt pressure to go downstairs, but he was stalling; he dreaded the conversation he had to have with Bridget.

When he finally got out of bed and looked out the window, he saw her walking around outside with a man; it took a minute for Will to recognize the Realtor he'd met in the grocery store. He'd never even given Bridget the man's card, so he couldn't imagine why he'd shown up. Another mistake Will would need to apologize for.

He took a shower and went out with Hudson, looking for Bridget, who emerged from the barn, sweaty but smiling. "Hey!" she called out, walking over to where he was standing by the porch door. "I have to tell you my brilliant idea."

Feeling the intensity of the sun, Will wondered how they would all get through the hottest part of the day without air-conditioning. "What was that pushy Realtor doing here?"

"Mark? He said you told him about the house."

"I'm so sorry, Bridget. I didn't invite him over. I just took his card—"

Bridget waved off his concern and opened the porch door. "I told him I didn't know if I was selling, but he gave me a hideous list of problems I have to deal with so the place doesn't end up condemned. It would be nice to revive the barn."

"We could make a list," he said, wanting to be helpful and thinking that the barn was the least important problem. "The skylight's leaking in the entry, and the slider door to the loft isn't sliding anymore. It's gotten jammed or something."

They went into the house while she waved him off again. "Listen, I'm so glad you're here because I have this idea. Do you have Caroline Lee's number?"

Will's stomach dropped. "Why?"

"I want the trio to play at my dad's wedding, and I was wondering *which* piece would be most meaningful, and then I figured it out: My dad keeps talking about that retreat he went on and the piece he wrote there. So, I was thinking, what if you arrange it for piano trio?"

Will wished he hadn't waited so long to discuss the crisis he'd both caused and partially averted.

"Uch, I'm so thirsty," Bridget said, going into the kitchen, getting two glasses, and filling them with ice from the trays. "The piece is called *Synchronicity*. He'd be thrilled to hear us play it, don't you think?"

Will took a breath, held his hands together, and said, "Look, here's the thing about the trio—"

"I know I'm asking a lot," she said, "but you're so good at arranging, and it would be special to play a piece he wrote so long ago." She filled the glasses with water and handed him one. "I know you have doubts about Caroline, but this will get us going in a positive way."

Will, overcome by regret, held up a finger and tried again. "About the trio—"

"And I know how busy Caroline is," said Bridget. She drank half the glass of water. "But I think she'd be honored to play for my father."

How to break the news? he wondered.

"You won't believe this," Bridget said. She leaned in and whispered, "Kevin spent last night with Isabelle. *Kevin!* He came wandering out of her bathroom in a towel."

"You said she was spending a lot of time in the barn." Will was glad the topic had changed, giving him a respite.

"Kevin," she said again. "It was *awkward*, let me tell you."

"I'm sure she didn't mean to be disrespectful," he said, feeling guilty about his own sleepover with Emma.

"She's a grown woman, I know, but this place feels like a circus."

Behind Bridget, out the window, there was a flock of guinea hens pecking around in the grass, and Hudson stood at the window, watching them with his tail wagging.

"Why do you have hens now?" Will asked.

"Kevin brought them for tick control."

Farther out in the field, the sheep were hard at work getting the grass under control. Will liked the herd with their fat, stocky bodies and bleating tenor voices. But the growing menagerie did give Bridget's circus comment some validity, although "zoo" might have been a more fitting term.

She leaned over and whispered again, "I'm so upset about Oscar and Matt. They're really at an impasse."

Will wasn't a fan of marriage, but the possible breakup of Oscar and

Matt's was indeed a shock. "Can't they talk it out? Or go to therapy?" he said. "They need to have an honest conversation." The irony of his statement did not escape him.

Bridget frowned. "Matt's cheating, and he's lying about it, so I don't think there's much to talk about unless he comes clean. Matt isn't who we thought he was."

Will considered that and felt somehow it was a lazy explanation. "Speaking of honest conversations," he said, feeling the heat along with the guilt as he took a seat at the table, "I need to tell you something."

Bridget sat down next to him, a knowing smirk on her face. "If this is about Emma sleeping over, you don't have to—"

"I wasn't sure if you knew."

Bridget pointed to the pot rack.

"Sorry," he said. "I'd hoped we were subtler than that."

"No, I'm happy for you," said Bridget. "I just hope she likes New York."

Will had no idea if she did or didn't. "There's something else," he said. "It's about Caroline. She's . . . Did you hear that she walked offstage in the middle of a concert?"

Bridget appeared as stunned as he had been. "Is she okay?"

"She's going through something, according to Randall, and the thing is, I talked to her briefly, and I guess, apparently, I offended her, and she . . . dropped out." He paused, letting the terrible news sink in. When Bridget didn't react, he added, "She won't play with us."

Bridget seemed to have stopped breathing. "She *what*?"

"She quit."

"She can't quit. Randall won't let her. She committed—"

"It's going to be okay," he said.

"When did this happen?"

"About two weeks ago."

"*Two* weeks—?"

"I know I should have told you right away, but then I got this terrific idea, a way to fix it, and—"

"You got her back?"

Will started to answer, certain that Bridget would be happy once she heard him out, but she cut him off. "Because the thing is," she said, "I'm really going to be ready to get back to my life and to work after this summer, and I want Caroline."

"Well, Caroline's out," he said, "but Randall's still working with us because I replaced her."

"I don't understand," said Bridget, looking aghast. "Since when do you unilaterally choose musicians for us? Who'd you replace her with, without even asking me?"

The truth was he hadn't gotten very far with Gavin in the negotiation over specific concert dates, but he was hopeful that would happen soon. Once Bridget also reached out to him, he would surely agree to two if not three concerts. "I've attempted to reunite us with our old violinist."

"Who?" Bridget asked. "Jacques? Julian? Please don't say Martina."

Will smiled. "Gavin."

Bridget's eyes opened wide.

He put a hand on her shoulder, giving it an encouraging squeeze. "I wrote to him," he said, "to find out if he was interested. And I was shocked when he finally answered yesterday, saying he wants to come here to see us."

Bridget finally blinked and shook her head.

"Good fix, right?" he said, hoping for a sign of approval, of happiness even. "Bridget?"

"He's not coming *here* . . . ?" It was part question, part declaration. Where was the smile? Where was the *Wow*?

"I know this wasn't the plan, but sometimes plans get upended. If he's willing to play—"

"I know all about upended plans," she said, looking stricken, almost like she might cry. "Why didn't you talk to me first?"

"I didn't want to give you bad news until I had a solution. Wouldn't you do the same for me?"

She pointed her finger at him, saying, "You didn't want Caroline, from the very beginning." She didn't look mad exactly. Oddly enough, she looked frightened.

"Maybe I don't like her attitude," he said defensively, "but I didn't sabotage our collaboration on purpose. Caroline's under a lot of pressure, and she was probably hoping for a reason to quit, and she's using me as her excuse."

"Gavin's not coming here," she said, definitively, like there was nothing more to discuss.

Will was confused. *He* was the one who had problems with Gavin. "He said he was looking forward to getting together, to talk about it. He even asked for your email address."

"I'll call Caroline," she said, "and I'll get her back. You call Gavin and call it off."

"Randall says we're not to contact Caroline under any circumstances—"

"That's absurd."

"—and Gavin's better than she is anyway. I honestly thought you'd be pleased with me for bringing the arrogant prick back into the trio."

Bridget dropped her head in her hands. "Don't call him names."

Her reaction was so bizarre, all he could think was that the stress of having her kids home, of Sterling breaking up with her, of her father's marriage plans, was all getting to her. "I'll tell you what," he said, "why don't you go to Edward's, cool down in his air-conditioned palace, and think it over. I swear this will be a good thing. We'll play a few concerts with Gavin, get lots of amazing publicity, and be in a much better position to find someone permanent. And then Randall might sign us after all." As he made this speech, he knew he was right about all of it. "And I bet Gavin would *love* to play your father's piece with us at the wedding. They used to have a mutual-admiration thing between them."

Bridget used her T-shirt to wipe the sweat off her face. "Fine," she said.

"Yeah? You're on board?"

"I meant fine, I'll go cool off at my dad's. I'll be back later." She got her car keys and walked out of the house without another word. He was hurt she didn't invite him to come along.

He would make it up to her for screwing things up with Caroline. He would arrange the piece for her father for starters.

He considered what it would mean to play an original Edward Stratton composition for Edward Stratton himself. It had been years since Will had arranged a piece that would actually be played in public, much less a piece of music written by a famous living composer. He could feel the pressure already.

Will's phone pinged, and he saw that Emma had texted.

Buckle up, babe. I'm going to do things to you tonight you've never even heard of.

Will felt a jolt rush through him and gulped. *I'm in*, he answered. This woman was a completely thrilling, delicious surprise.

Will sat down on the floor with Hudson, forehead to furry forehead, looking him in the eye. Hudson was yet another gift from Bridget. They'd gone to a posh pet store in Chelsea, where Hudson was playing with his littermates, letting the others jump on him, revealing his tolerant, loving nature. Bridget bought both Hudson and Hadley as sixteenth-birthday gifts for the twins. Soon after, she called him, saying, "Too much dog! My cats are going nuts. It's the Montagues and the Capulets over here. What was I thinking? Help me out, and take Hudson off my hands? The kids will be heartbroken, but if he lives with you, he stays in the family." Bridget brought him over in a cab, along with a crate, a dog bed, toys, a harness and leash, poop bags, and a case of puppy food, and she insisted on paying for the first year of vet bills.

Bridget had done a lot for Will, and given the fight they were having, he wanted to do something nice for her. He got up and went to the bottom of the stairs. "Oscar?"

Oscar came out to the landing, looking downtrodden.

"Let's do your mom a favor and try to clean out the barn a little."

"It's so fucking hot," Oscar whined.

He was right. Will couldn't completely blame him for balking at the idea. "I think it may be cooler outside than it is in here."

"I'll be down in a bit," Oscar said. "I have to make a couple work calls first."

Will went outside and saw Kevin coming out to the field from the guesthouse. Kevin and Isabelle? They weren't an obvious match, but Will liked the idea. He hoped Oscar and Matt would find their way back to each other as well. The joy of a new romance made him want everyone in his life to be similarly swept away. Bridget above all. Who could he find for Bridget?

A thought flashed through his head as he remembered the old trio, the long rehearsals, and especially the camaraderie Bridget had with Gavin. She was the anchor, the link that held them together. Why, he wondered, was she so reluctant to see him again?

15

Gwen didn't need to go to Edward's house to have a luxury bathroom. Or Frette sheets on a king-size bed, a chef's kitchen, or a spectacular view. Gwen had all of those comforts in her very own Fifth Avenue apartment. Nevertheless, in the summertime, while her show, *Influence*, was between seasons and she was doing more research and less filming, she enjoyed getting into her Range Rover and making the two-plus-hour trip up the FDR, out of New York, past commercial strip malls, pretty farms, fancy prep schools, and even an abandoned psychiatric hospital to go to her dad's house. She couldn't come as often as she liked, but she loved to step away from the city. Her dad's house was the perfect place to read the galleys her producer gave her and study up on the talented people being invited on her program. She would return to the city feeling well rested but charged, fully prepped and ready to delve into the psyches of her subjects.

This weekend Gwen had made the trip to her dad's with a pile of work, almost all of which intrigued her. She had a book of light short stories to read, a series of dark art house films to watch, a modern jazz album to listen to, and a possibly frivolous self-help book to evaluate. The summers were the best time to do this kind of digging, and depending on how she felt about the various works and the artists who created them (whether they be poets, novelists, musicians, dancers, psychologists, or philosophers), she would discuss them with her producer, Lucy, deciding whether or not to invite them on the show. Gwen's job was heaven.

She preferred these recent summer visits to the ones she made when she was still married. Back then she would come to her father's house alone, missing her husband, Charles, who would claim he had too much work to do, or a conference to attend, or a last-minute crisis at the office, when in fact he'd had none of the above. Charles was an ass-grabbing, coke-snorting, ethics-deficient cheater, a man so low in morality that a twenty-two-year-old receptionist in his office was now suing him for sexual harassment. Gwen was glad her marriage to him had been severed almost a decade ago so this latest scandal had absolutely nothing to do with her, not emotionally and not financially.

Charles. She should have known better than to pick a man with the same exact name as the cheating husband in the musical her father adapted for Broadway. Her Charles had been far worse than the "careless husband" onstage. He was certainly more lecherous than the fictional Charles (played by a young John Cleese), who cheated on his wife (Madeline Kahn) *in her own house* as the audience laughed at her expense. Gwen was a child when she saw her dad's musical, but it had an impact. She remembered all too clearly when the wife, Lady Easy, wandered in on Charles as he slept beside another woman, and rather than let him have it, she covered him up with a blanket, worried that he might catch cold. Yeah, well, when Gwen caught *her* Charles with another woman in *her* house, she was no Lady Easy. She was Lady Your-Worst-Fucking-Nightmare. She snapped pictures, hired the most vicious divorce attorney in Manhattan, and dragged him to court to massacre him. If the game was to make him very, very sorry, she'd won.

—◆—

Now she lived alone and arranged her schedule exactly the way she wanted. She went off to her father's when time allowed, and she never had to worry what was happening between her expensive sheets while she was away. She would lock the door and leave, glad to know that no one, but no one, would be there in her absence.

Gwen spent this hot July morning in Connecticut on the phone in her room, trying to explain to her producer, Lucy, why she had no intention of interviewing that fucking Sterling character after she'd explicitly requested an interview with him a month ago.

"I thought you said you wanted him," said Lucy, sounding confused.

"But then I reread his books," Gwen said, although she hadn't. "His writing is so derivative, and I didn't respond to the themes of his most recent novel at all." The truth was, Gwen hadn't cracked the spine of his latest, nor would she. Once he'd dumped Bridget there was no way she'd give him a single second of her time and certainly not a millisecond of *air*time. "Honestly, Lucy," Gwen said, "and I hate to say it, but he's so overrated. I can't imagine what I would even talk to him about." And then she went in for the kill: "I've heard from a friend of a friend that he's *boring*."

Boring worked with Lucy. Boring meant low ratings. Lucy gave in, and they crossed him off the list.

After that victory, Gwen went downstairs to the kitchen, still wearing her pink-striped pajamas, to refill her coffee cup.

Marge was in the kitchen, and when Gwen told her about canceling Sterling, Marge pinched her cheek affectionately, saying, "Good girl."

It still felt nice getting Marge's approval.

"I hope I never wind up on your bad side," said Marge.

Edward barged into the kitchen, dressed to go riding, clearly agitated. "Where's Jackie?" he asked.

"Good morning," Gwen said pointedly.

He looked at her. "Ah, my apologies. Good morning." He turned to Marge. "Good morning. Will that suffice? Now, has anyone seen Jackie?"

"Jackie strapped on some very fast-looking red sneakers," said Marge, "and she took off like a gazelle. She may be halfway to Manhattan by now."

"I can't find my email anywhere in my computer," he said, "and I need to contact a colleague in China. When will she be back?"

"Relax," said Gwen, knowing it would be impossible for her to explain where email actually *was*. "I wouldn't work for you, even if you asked me to."

"Which is precisely why I would never ask. I'd rather remain on good terms," he said. "Now listen up: No one is to distract Jackie this week. No more long dinners at Bridget's or afternoons at the pool—"

"I don't know what you're talking about," said Marge with a sigh. "She doesn't even have a bathing suit."

"I need her to do her work, so I can focus on mine."

"Calm down," said Marge, turning back to the dishwasher. "You're going to give yourself a heart attack."

Gwen smiled. "What work, Dad? What are you up to?"

"I'm working on a new piece, and it took a dramatic turn today. When Jackie returns from wherever she's hiding," Edward said, "tell her to come to the library. And ask her to be quick about it." He left the room, riding crop in hand, and Marge rolled her eyes.

"A little *introspection*," she said after the door closed behind him. "Is that too much to ask?"

Gwen's phone buzzed. She had a message from Bridget:
SOS meet me at the pool don't tell anyone I'm here.

"Introspection," Gwen said, looking for an excuse to go, "is best practiced . . . outdoors."

Marge looked baffled. "Says who?"

Gwen remembered the self-help book Lucy gave her that was on her night table. "Says Juliette Stark. I'll be back." Gwen got to her feet.

"Who's Juliette Stark?" Marge called after her as Gwen abandoned her coffee and went out the kitchen door. Running in bare feet through the woods and down the pathway, feeling the intensity of the heat, she opened the gate in the white wooden fencing that encircled the pool.

There was Bridget, floating facedown in her bra and underwear. Gwen, unsurprised by her own heroism, dropped her phone in the grass and jumped in to rescue her sister. As soon as she hit the water, Bridget popped upright, just as Gwen grabbed her.

"What are you doing?" Bridget yelled.

"What? You . . . I thought you were dead."

"Why would I be dead?"

"Well, who swims like that? You looked unconscious."

They stared at each other, treading water.

"I'm trying to lower my body temperature," Bridget said. "Menopause and ninety-degree temperatures are killing me."

They swam to the shady side of the pool and put their arms over the edge.

"What happened?" Gwen asked, knowing there was more to it than hot flashes.

"I got in a fight with Will," said Bridget.

"Oh, please." If there was one thing Gwen believed in, it was in the unbreakable bond between her sister and Will. "You'll make up. What happened?"

"Caroline Lee bailed on us, and Will kept it from me. And then," she said, "he went *behind my back* and got a replacement for us. A replacement! Without even checking with me first. He goes and picks someone, just like that." Holding on the pool's edge, she leaned her head back and looked up at the sky, saying, "He's brought back Gavin."

Gwen gasped and slapped the water with her hand. "No!"

"Yes," said Bridget, wiping the pool water out of her eyes.

"What was he thinking?"

"That Gavin could rescue us from the mess we're in."

"If Gavin thinks he can waltz in here after all these years," said Gwen, "he can forget it. You and Will don't need *him*."

Bridget raised her shoulders. "It wouldn't have been such a terrible idea . . . if *someone* hadn't made me tell him the truth."

Gwen, justifying her stance once again, said slowly, "Just because he'd moved to Australia didn't give you the right to keep it from him."

"I disagree."

"Will hates him," Gwen said. "I can't believe he'd do this."

"Gavin's the best violinist we ever had, and Will knows it. Everyone knows it."

"Well, he can't show up in your life now." Gwen was running through options in her mind: there was certainly no grounds for a restraining order, but a harshly worded letter might make an impression. "What if he says something? What if he tells the kids?"

Bridget didn't answer. She pushed off the wall and floated on her back, her ratty sports bra exposed to the sun. "When you get back to New York," said Gwen, "I'm taking you lingerie shopping."

"I'm not in a Victoria's Secret chapter of my life," said Bridget loudly, water stopping her ears.

"*Victoria's Secret?* What are we, fifteen?"

Gwen swam over to the steps and climbed out of the pool, took off her dripping pajama bottoms, and draped them over a lounge chair. She wrapped a towel around her waist and sat back down at the pool's edge with her legs in the water, watching her sister float on the surface. She refused to feel guilty. It's true she was the one who made Bridget tell Gavin that he might be the father. It never occurred to her that Gavin wouldn't give a shit *in the slightest* that Bridget was pregnant. She'd loathed him ever since.

"I don't think Gavin will say anything about it," Bridget said, treading water in the middle of the pool. "It certainly isn't something he wants to bring up *now*."

Gwen considered that possibility, knowing how many people in midlife rethink their choices, question their past decisions, maybe even feel a need to right wrongs. Surely even her ex-husband had regrets.

"He can't possibly want this out in the open," Bridget said confidently. "The whole thing was an accident anyway."

"An accident?" said Gwen.

Bridget swam to the wall. "It certainly wasn't *on purpose*," she said.

Gwen gave her a withering look. "You knew exactly what you were doing that night."

"It just happened," Bridget said innocently. "Gavin and I were hanging out and drinking too much, and then we— It wasn't planned."

"Oh, come on." Gwen knew how smart her sister was, and she couldn't abide watching her act dumb. Gwen didn't resent Bridget for her beautiful twin children, especially since her sister had made the bold decision to prioritize having babies over finding a man to raise them with. But it still smarted when Bridget implied she was a victim of her own fertility, like the whole thing was some distorted, modern version of the Immaculate Conception. "You knew perfectly well that you were ovulating like a motherfucker that night. You adored Gavin's quirky personality, his looks, and his brain; you thought he had great genes. You liked him and the whole musical-prodigy horse he rode in on, and you figured his sperm was as good, if not better, than whatever you'd paid for. Be honest."

Bridget splashed water at Gwen. Gwen kicked water at Bridget.

"Can we stop rehashing the past and figure out what to do *now*?" Gwen said. "I mean, are you sure he'll pretend like nothing happened?"

Gwen watched as Bridget sank underwater and felt protective, like she might have to punch Gavin in the balls if she needed to.

Bridget came to the surface again, wiping the water from her eyes. "He called me back," she said.

"Who did?" It took Gwen a moment to understand. "Gavin? When?"

"A few weeks after I called him in Sydney to tell him. He felt bad about being so harsh, and he said he was sorry and asked what I needed him to do."

"Why didn't you tell me?"

Bridget looked ashamed. "Because I told him I didn't want anything from him, even if the kids were his. I said it wasn't his business, and I basically told him to . . . fuck off."

"*Bridget!*" Gwen was recasting Gavin in her mind, moving him off her shit list and into slightly more neutral territory. "He apologized? He wanted to find out?"

"I knew he wasn't anywhere *near* up to the challenge of being a parent," Bridget said defensively. "He was immature and selfish and focused on his career, he was living halfway around the world, and I didn't want him in my life like that."

"And he let it go? That was it?"

"I hurt him," said Bridget. "He said he'd wait to hear from me when I wanted to talk about it."

"And?"

"I never spoke to him again."

Gwen suddenly felt sorry for Gavin. Bridget had gone into motherhood with the intention of doing it on her own, and she hadn't been willing to make room for him. Everything would have been different if there'd been a man in the picture. Even her friendship with Will would have been rocked by having Gavin in her life.

Gwen was jealous of Will, only a little, and she knew it was petty. Nevertheless, it had meant a lot to her that Bridget had told her the secret about Gavin; she liked knowing something important about her sister that Will didn't.

"I've been very consistent," Bridget was saying. "I didn't want my kids to know then, and I don't want them to know now. What good would it do for them to find out that Gavin Glantz might be their father?"

Gwen caught sight of fast-moving red sneakers darting behind a tree. "Jackie?" she called.

"Shit," Bridget hissed, "did she hear me?"

Gwen got to her feet and threw a towel to Bridget at the edge of the pool, while Jackie, red-faced and panting, walked up to the fence.

"I wasn't spying," Jackie said.

"Of course not," said Gwen, opening the gate to the pool. "Why are you out running in this heat?"

"I needed to clear my head," Jackie said.

Bridget was wringing her hair out and hopping on one foot, head tilted sideways, getting the water out of her ear, while Jackie started to wobble and grabbed on to the white picket fence, her face turning gray. "You okay?" Gwen asked just as Jackie leaned over and crumpled on the ground.

Bridget sprang into action, helping get Jackie into the pool house, giving her a ginger ale from the well-stocked fridge, and making her lie down on the couch. "I don't mean to sound judgmental," she said, "but you have *got* to take better care of yourself."

"I'm sorry," said Jackie, sitting up.

Bridget, with her hair up in a towel, put on a bathrobe and handed another one to Gwen.

"It's too hot to be out running," Bridget said. "You could have passed out from dehydration."

"Or heat exhaustion," said Gwen, trying to care as much as Bridget seemed to.

"There's a perfectly good treadmill in the house," said Bridget.

"I'm just a little overheated." Jackie tried to sit up. "I need to get back."

"You're not going anywhere until you drink something," Bridget said. "How about cooling off in the pool?"

Gwen wanted to go back to the house. Bridget might have felt like playing mommy again to this grown girl, but Gwen had more important things to do.

"What's going on, Jackie?" Bridget asked. "Is my dad being too demanding?"

"It's fine," she said, shaking her head as though she were perfectly happy. "The composers are coming next month; they seem a little high-maintenance, but they've been nice on the phone. Especially the Greek one."

"And?"

"And . . . otherwise, all I'm doing is booking flights and hotels, camels and trains. I think what your dad needs is a travel agent."

Gwen turned to Bridget. "Camels?"

"I asked him last week," Bridget said, "and he said he's planning a little trip with Lottie after the wedding." She turned to Jackie. "I thought they were going to Athens."

"They're *starting* in Athens, but from there . . ." Jackie trailed off. "I'd rather he tell you."

"Come on, Jackie. Where are they going?" Bridget asked.

Jackie looked torn but finally said, "They're taking an extended trip. A long one, pretty much around the world."

"How long?" Gwen asked.

"Mr. Stratton says we're not to put 'an end date on adventure.'"

"I was wondering why Lottie said she needed so much time to prepare to come here," Bridget said. "She's probably packing everything she owns."

"You talked to her?" Gwen asked.

"This morning. She says Hans isn't happy about the marriage."

"Of course he's not," said Gwen, not that she was too happy about it either, "because he's a difficult person. People don't change." She remembered watching the World Cup final on television with him one summer when he and his parents were visiting New York. Hans was constantly boy-splaining each play, as though she didn't have eyeballs of her own to rely on.

"I have to go," said Jackie. "Mr. Stratton needs me to book a hotel in Beijing."

"You're feeling okay now?" Bridget asked as she placed her hand on Jackie's shoulder in that maternal way of hers. "Eat a banana when you get up to the house. You're not going to faint or anything?"

Jackie tightened her laces. "I'm better. I'll take a cold shower." Jackie smiled and walked away up the path.

"Hey," said Gwen, "did you hear the one about the octogenarian newlyweds who took a trip around the world? What could possibly go wrong?" But Gwen could tell Bridget wasn't thinking about their dad. She was staring at the screen of her cell phone, looking at it as if a naked picture of herself had just gone viral.

"What?" Gwen asked. "Everything okay?"

Bridget shook her head. "He wrote me," she said.

"Who?"

"Gavin."

She turned the phone so Gwen could see it.

———◆———

Bridget, the email said. *We need to talk.*

16

We need to talk. We need to talk? Why, Bridget wondered, had Gavin felt the need to send such a cryptic message? Bridget hadn't answered him all week. She let the email sit there in her in-box, tormenting her. She hadn't spoken to Will all week either; they'd texted instead, keeping to the topic of his arrival that evening so they could talk about Forsyth, now that Bridget had had a chance to process the loss of Caroline.

Hiding in her bathroom, using her hairbrush as a pretend phone, Bridget stood in front of her mirror and made a serious face. "Hello, Gavin," she said into the hairbrush. "We *don't* need to talk. And I'm calling to cancel our so-called 'reunion.'"

What d'you think you're doing? she might say to him. *Call Will back and tell him you're too good for us and you aren't coming.*

She liked the sound of that because it fit nicely into Will's low opinion of him.

She put down the brush and picked up her real phone, dialing the number Will had given her for Gavin's landline in Los Angeles. It rang and rang until a recorded voice, a woman's, soft and gentle like a yoga instructor's, invited her to leave a message at the beep. Bridget didn't.

In spite of her worry about Gavin, Bridget had not lost sight of the bigger problem: the Forsyth Trio was missing a violinist, a manager, and any sort of viable plan to move forward. They were, as her kids would say, completely fucked. Will was likely still clinging to the idea of Gavin stepping in, and, of course, it made sense, professionally speaking, but it wasn't an option.

Was Gwen right? Had she known what she was doing that night? She had watched, in awe actually, as Gavin transformed over the years from a dorky, immature freshman to a handsome, successful adult. Even the sound of his name had changed in her ear: he went from the awkward geek named Gavin to the talented virtuoso Gavin Glantz. His genes were the kind she would have paid good money for. In her defense, he'd never asked if she was on the pill, never volunteered to get a condom; his complete negligence joined forces with her very strong intentions, and the next thing she knew, she was pregnant. If it weren't for Gwen, Bridget would have swept the whole situation under the rug and walked over the lumps for the rest of her life.

The phone in her hand began to ring, and she saw Matt's face appear on her screen. Cute as he was, the sight of him made her furious, and she couldn't bring herself to take his call. What could she possibly have to say to him? Or him to her? *Sorry for breaking your son's heart?*

Too angry to hear an apology or an explanation or anything at all from Matt, she silenced her phone just as a loud, crashing sound came from outside in the yard. She went out and saw that, with the help of three other guys, Kevin had knocked down what remained of the broken tennis court fence.

The guinea hens were still pecking their way around the grass, eating all the ticks they could find, but the sheep were gone, having finished the initial work on the overgrown field. Kevin had finally been able to mow, shirtless, riding a John Deere. Isabelle's attraction to him made some sense, Bridget had to admit; he had a Chris Pratt look about him, and he was proving to be the kind of man you'd want with you during an apocalypse: steady, reliable, strong, and resourceful. Isabelle certainly did seem light of foot and energetic lately, helping out in the kitchen, offering to do the grocery shopping, and—most of all—trying to get Oscar back together with Matt.

"Don't you miss him?" Bridget had overheard Isabelle saying that morning. "I bet Matt misses you."

"He misses the dogs," Oscar had said sadly.

"Why won't you at least hear him out? You're being appallingly stubborn," said Isabelle, "and you'll be sorry one day when you're lying on your deathbed and you realize how much time you lost with him."

"Jeesh, morbid much?"

"People screw up," she said. "You could consider forgiving him. Or listening to him at least."

"No fucking way," said Oscar. "And how can I forgive him if he won't even admit he's done anything wrong?"

Bridget was in no mood to forgive Matt either, but what did she know about relationships? Maybe Oscar's problem, she thought, was that he had no role model for marriage. Bridget certainly wasn't one, nor was Will. Gwen had offered a counterexample, a reason to avoid marriage at all costs, along with grounds for suspecting the very worst in one's partner. Where could Oscar look to get good advice?

◆

The men were now dragging the fence posts away from the court. From the spot where Bridget was standing, she heard a car horn and turned to see Kevin's grandfather Walter pulling up the driveway in his pickup truck.

He walked stiffly over to her with one hand in his pocket and the other holding a folder. "I heard there's a lot going on over here." He looked out across the field at the tennis court, where his grandson was using pure force to pull chain link off of the cedar posts and pile them onto the bed of a truck. "What's the plan for the barn?" he said.

"I'm sprucing it up."

"Because once the nomination is approved, you'll have to get permission to make exterior changes."

"Nomination for what?"

"I'm on the board over at the historical preservation committee," he said. "All applications go through me via the town council, and Kevin mentioned you needed a form." He handed her several stapled sheets of paper. "We'll need you to fill this out, and the board members will come to do a site visit."

Bridget leafed through the pages of questions. "This is to get landmark status? Like a plaque?"

"It's the application to start the process."

"Thanks for bringing it over." She looked over the application, nodding. "I'll get this back to you."

"Just give it to Kevin. I hear he's spending a lot of time here. Funny that your kids came home after all, isn't it? Getting to know each other again."

"Getting to know each other" was one way of putting it. Bridget smiled. "He's a huge help," she said.

Walter gave her a salute. "Let me know when you're ready, and the board will schedule a meeting about the landmark."

As he walked off to his car, Bridget faced the barn with hands on her hips, appreciating the way the late-afternoon sun was shining on the rotting vertical boards on the west side. Kevin had replaced a few of them, but it looked like many more needed attention. Looking up higher, she saw that the windows were blackened with decades of filth.

And then she saw Oscar posing in the barn's open doorway, holding an industrial push broom upside down like a staff. He looked like one half of the couple in a much cuter *American Gothic*.

"Hey," he called, giving her a wave and then wiping his face on his shirt.

Bridget walked over to him, and as she went inside the barn, his dogs came over to say hello before flopping down again in a shady spot. "You know, I think that broom works better with the bristles on the floor."

"Ah," he said, turning it over, "no wonder it's been slow-going."

"Have you seen Henry around?" she said. "He's MIA."

"He'll come in when he gets hungry enough. I saw Eliza sleeping on the piano." He flipped the broom over and started sweeping again with fast, angry movements.

There was another broom leaning against the wall, and Bridget went to get it. She started in the entry to the barn, sending the dirt out the door. "I hear physical work can be therapeutic," she said after a few minutes.

"It's keeping my aggression at bay."

Bridget waited.

"Watch me, sweeping all thoughts of Congressman Oakley out of my head. Bye-bye, you gorgeous, tall, brilliant public official," he said, with a hard sweep of the broom.

Bridget copied him. "Why are we exorcising Jackson Oakley?"

"Because it's him," he said.

Bridget stopped sweeping. "What's him?"

Oscar didn't say anything.

"No! The congressman? That's who Matt—?" Bridget was shocked. "That's scandalous. Are you sure?"

"I'm sure."

"That's not only horrible," she said, "that's bad . . . workplace behavior." She watched as he swept another big plume of dust out the barn door.

"Did you know the washing machine's broken?" he said.

217

She had to hand it to him for a well-executed change of topic.

"It fills up with water," he said, "but then it just sits there."

"Hell's bells," said Bridget. "Jackson Oakley? Really?"

It was strange seeing Oscar looking like an adorable farmhand, messy hair and dirty jeans, a sad expression. She hated Matt for hurting him like this and patted herself on the back for refusing his call. She went back to sweeping the wood floors, just as angry now as he was. "Is anything *not* broken in this place?"

"Broken appliances, broken windows, broken hearts," said Oscar.

Bridget put her broom down. "Maybe dinner at the Castle will cheer you up. I need a shower before we go," she said. "You?"

Oscar looked down at his damp, stained clothes. "Matt once told me that Congressman Oakley is so perfect, he doesn't even sweat."

Bridget and Oscar were cleaned up and well dressed as they walked across the courtyard of Edward's house. The front door opened, and Nicholas Donahue stepped out into the light, walking toward them. Not wanting to make assumptions, Bridget introduced herself as he approached.

"We've met before," Nicholas said, shaking her hand and smiling warmly.

"I remember," said Bridget. "You and your wife were at that festival in Austria—"

"Ex-wife," said Nicholas quickly.

"Sorry," said Bridget. "I didn't know."

Nicholas waved off her apology. "Quite all right. Yes, I saw you in Salzburg when your trio performed an arrangement of Liszt's 'Carnaval de Pesth.'"

If Bridget herself had been asked what they'd played at that concert, she didn't think she'd recall. "Sharp memory."

He seemed to realize he was still holding her hand and let it go. "It was a memorable rendition."

She turned to Oscar. "Nicholas is writing a book on your grandfather," she said.

He and Oscar shook hands.

"Your mother is an exceptional musician," Nicholas said and then shook his head, embarrassed. "But then you know that, of course. Are you a musician as well?"

"God, no," said Oscar with a laugh. "My sister and I didn't inherit that gene."

"Will and I," said Bridget, "—you remember Will?—we tried for years to get the kids interested in classical music, but we couldn't get them to appreciate anything further back than the '60s."

"Also a worthy period," said Nicholas. "Bob Dylan, the Rolling Stones, Jimi Hendrix. Some of my favorite musicians."

Bridget was surprised; she'd have thought he'd be snobbier.

"You're not staying for dinner?" Oscar asked.

"I'd love to, really, but I'm expected in New York," said Nicholas. "My daughter's in town for work, and I couldn't miss a chance to see her when she's so nearby." He pointed to an old Subaru parked in the courtyard. "I'm on my way to take the train into Manhattan."

"You may run into Will at the station," said Bridget.

"Excellent. Well, I'll look for him. And should we miss each other, please send him my regards."

Nicholas gave them a polite nod and turned to leave. Before getting in his car, he called out, "I'll see you at the wedding, if not before," and waved good-bye.

"He reminds me of Colin Firth," said Bridget. "Nice man, isn't he?"

"Very," said Oscar, "and attractive if you're into that charming, dignified professor look."

They watched his car sputter down the driveway.

"You do this thing," Oscar said, "and I don't know if it's on purpose or if you're even aware of it, but you made him think you and Will are a couple."

"No, I didn't."

"Yes, you did," Oscar said, smiling. "The message you just sent is that you're completely unavailable, which is fine if that's what you want."

"Oh, please," Bridget said, "he wasn't interested in my . . . status anyway."

"If you say so," he said, turning to walk to the door.

They rang the bell, and Marge greeted them, saying, "Still no Matt?"

"He's in DC," said Oscar, walking in the entry and kicking off his shoes.

Marge considered this. "You want my opinion?" she asked.

"Not really," said Oscar.

"You're not a child anymore, and you can't run away from your problems." She gave her words a moment to sink in before reaching up to hug him. "You look hungry," she said.

"I'm starved," said Oscar, walking away to the dining room.

Marge studied Bridget, then took her hand and turned her around in a circle. "What a pretty rig," she said. "You never dress up here. What's gotten into you?"

Bridget appreciated the compliment; she'd gone to a lot of trouble, even shaving her legs so she could wear the navy blue wrap dress she'd worn in May to Sterling's book-release party.

Marge sniffed the air, saying, "I hope that's not our dinner burning. I'm trying out a new caterer who's auditioning to do the food for the wedding." She hurried off to the kitchen, as Gwen came down the stairs in jodhpurs, a tucked-in, crisp white shirt, and a tailored blazer. Jackie came down slowly behind her, gripping the banister as though her legs might not hold her. She had rethought her wardrobe since her first visit and was wearing cropped linen pants and a pair of indoor Allbirds like the ones Gwen always wore. She moaned slightly, waved to Bridget, and limped into the dining room.

"Whoops," said Gwen.

"What happened to her?"

"I introduced her to equestrian life today. We went on an easy little trail ride."

"For how long?"

"About four hours."

Bridget gave Gwen a look.

"What? She's a runner. I thought she could handle it."

They went into the dining room, where Edward had already taken his place in his armed chair at the mahogany table. Technically, he wasn't seated at the "head," as this table was round and so large it brought the court of King Arthur to mind. Gwen and Bridget sat on either side of Edward, while Jackie, Oscar, and Marge took the other three chairs. The table was perfect for entertaining groups of twelve or more, but with only six of them there, there was too much space between them, leaving everyone a little unmoored.

Looking around the candlelit room, Oscar said in a spooky voice, "Everyone join hands, so the séance can begin."

Edward, who looked like Cary Grant in his belted, navy blue smoking jacket, said, "I can offer something even more mystical than a meeting with the dead. If I can have everyone's attention." He leaned over an iPad that was next to his placemat, pressed a few buttons, and said, "Abracadabra." Handel came out of the speakers hidden somewhere in the room.

"Is that your handiwork?" Oscar asked Jackie.

She nodded.

"Jackie," said Edward, "is a technological wizard."

Jackie looked embarrassed. "No, it's just iTunes."

"Nonsense," said Edward, holding up the iPad. "What you've accomplished with this device is a miracle of science."

"Now, listen up," Marge said over the music, "we're eating buffet-style tonight because I didn't have a clear head count." She directed their attention to the platters that were lined up on the sideboard. "Now, come on, Jackie, help yourself. Is Isabelle coming?"

"She said she was," Bridget said, starting to reach for her phone.

Marge stopped her. "Don't nag her," she said. "She'll get here when she gets here."

Bridget put her phone away. "Dad," she said, "how're the plans for the wedding?"

"Fine," he said. "It's certainly a very busy summer for me."

Jackie hadn't gotten up yet, so Marge encouraged her, saying, "Don't be shy. Go ahead."

Jackie started to stand, winced, and then tried again.

"You okay?" Oscar asked.

"Just a little sore," she said, going stiffly to the buffet and returning with a modest serving of beef tenderloin and asparagus on a Wedgwood plate.

"There's plenty of everything," said Marge, getting up to adjust the dimmer on the chandelier.

"Good," said Oscar, "because I did hard-core manual labor today."

Marge served a plate for Edward and brought it to him as Bridget tapped him on the sleeve. "Lottie says you're inviting about a hundred and fifty people."

"Closer to two hundred," Edward said, waving his fork around, "give or take a dozen."

"God help us," Marge mumbled, sitting back down.

"How many people are staying here?" asked Gwen.

"I don't know," he said, "ten or twelve? Marge?"

Bridget counted the upstairs bedrooms in her head. "Where will they all sleep?" she asked.

"Marge can sort that out," Edward said, pouring himself a glass of wine and offering some to Bridget.

"With Gwen, Lottie, and Hans coming, and the composers in residence, we'll be full to bursting," said Marge.

"Oh, and I've decided," said Edward, "to invite all of my former retreat composers to the wedding. It's a chance for them to get to know one another and discuss their experiences writing music here."

"That's kind of complicated," said Gwen. "Why do you want such a big to-do?"

"Your wedding was big," said Edward.

"And look how that turned out," Gwen said grimly.

The doorbell rang. "I'll get it," said Marge, standing up again.

"Lottie wants a big affair," Edward said, "so that's what we're having. This discussion is closed."

At that proclamation, Oscar and Bridget got up to go to the buffet as Marge came back in the room with Isabelle and Kevin. Kevin stopped in the doorway to admire the coffered ceiling and wainscoting.

"Sorry we're late," said Isabelle. She kissed Edward's cheek and introduced him to Kevin.

"Beautiful house, sir," said Kevin, shaking his hand. "Very impressive woodwork." Kevin came over to Bridget, looking excited. "I met a guy today at the lumberyard who's an expert on old barns, and I thought maybe he should come see the place, if that's okay with you."

"Do I need an expert?" Bridget asked.

"Yes," said Marge, "you do."

"Guess what, everyone," Isabelle said loudly, "I got a job today." She sat down in Oscar's chair. "Starting tomorrow I'll be working at Latham's."

Bridget thought the name rang a bell.

"The alpaca place?" said Gwen.

Isabelle looked surprised. "You know it?"

"There was a write-up about the owner in the local paper," said Gwen. "He has a store in town with a coffee shop in it."

223

"I'm working in the café."

"My sister's *finally* a barista," Oscar said from the buffet. "Dreams really do come true."

"Shut up," she said.

Bridget started to say something about better uses of her MBA, but Gwen jumped in first. "Well done, Isabelle," she said. "Landing on your feet. And a small business might suit you better."

"I met the owner today," Isabelle said, "Peter Latham. He's all about reviving the feel of an old-fashioned general store. I think I can learn from him. He's—"

"Move it, sister," said Oscar, standing over Isabelle with his plate.

"Get your own chair," sniped Isabelle. "And get one for Kevin, too."

But at Marge's direction, Kevin was already moving two of the armless Chippendales from the side of the room to the table. Everyone except Edward adjusted.

Bridget sat down next to her father, saying, "Oscar and I saw Nicholas Donahue outside."

"He's an entertaining and intelligent scholar," said Edward. "Come to think of it, he asked about you today."

"Did he?" said Bridget.

"Told you," said Oscar.

"We were looking through family photographs," Edward said, "and he asked to take a picture of you home with him."

"That's creepy," said Gwen.

Edward scoffed. "For research purposes, I assure you. He's interested in all aspects of my life, especially my annual retreat."

"Does Lottie know the composers are coming?" Gwen asked.

"Of course," said Edward. "She loves the idea."

Gwen smiled. "Can we set one of them up with Bridget?"

"They're always too young," said Bridget, "and I don't want to date a musician anyway."

"Jackie outdid herself bringing me candidates," said Edward. "She gave me an outstanding list of qualified composers."

"I posted on Musical Chairs," Jackie said, shrugging off her efforts. "It was nothing really."

"What's Musical Chairs?" asked Bridget.

"A Listserv for instrumentalists, music teachers, anyone in the music industry."

Edward said proudly, "I chose a woman from Russia, a man from France, and another from Greece."

"What are their names?" Bridget asked.

"Sonya, Simon, and Stavros," said Edward.

"Okay," said Isabelle, "that's . . . *adorable*."

"What's adorable about it?" Edward said. "They're composers, not puppies."

"I'm picturing an East European pop band from the '80s," said Oscar.

Edward shook his head, exasperated with the lot of them.

"Tell us about the trip you're planning," said Gwen. "Your honeymoon."

Edward put his utensils down. "As of September," Edward said, "Lottie and I will be citizens of the world, traveling for the foreseeable future. We're going to visit every continent and go to every renowned symphony hall on our list. It's been a dream of mine to hear all the music there is to hear across all cultures on an extended trip. Lottie shares this passion, so we're going."

"No one travels for the 'foreseeable future,'" said Gwen, "unless they're living out of their car."

"That's awfully ambitious," said Bridget. "Is Lottie . . . fit enough for that level of tourism?"

"Of course she is," he said, "and Jackie's helping us put together a marvelous itinerary using her whip-smart computer skills."

"Oh, it's not a skill, really," said Jackie. "It's just the internet."

"Stop being so modest," said Edward.

"Where are you going," Gwen said, "specifically?"

"Everywhere we should and a few places we probably shouldn't," said Edward. "You only live once."

"I'd love to see your itinerary," said Bridget. If Hans disapproved of the wedding, she thought, he was going to hate the idea of this trip.

"Why?" said Edward. "For your approval?"

"Of course not," said Bridget, laughing at the notion that she would have any say over her father's plans. "I'm just curious."

"If I see North Korea on the list," said Gwen, "I might raise an objection."

"Nowhere is safe these days," said Edward, "and if I want to see Vahdat Hall before I die, then I'm bloody well going to Tehran, regardless of what the State Department has to say about it."

"Very funny," said Gwen, just as the doorbell rang again.

Marge started to get up, but Oscar stopped her. "I got it."

Isabelle turned to Gwen. "Have you heard of Juliette Stark? She's a psychologist who created this new lifestyle program."

"I have her book upstairs," said Gwen. "You can have it."

"What do you think of her?" said Isabelle.

Gwen looked skeptical. "Not really my cup of tea. She says we should approach self-improvement by adopting the habits of our pre-tech ancestors or something along those lines. Not very convincing."

"Are you going to interview her?" Isabelle asked.

"I don't think so. Her followers swear by her, but I can't buy into her beliefs, like the power of ancient grains. Farro, bulgur . . ."

Edward took another bite of his dinner and closed his eyes. "What is this, Marge? Rice?"

"Orzo," said Marge. "It's not an ancient grain."

"It's good," he said.

"Look who's here," said Oscar from the doorway.

They all looked up to see Emma entering the room in a gauzy

white sundress. Bridget looked past her, but Will wasn't there. His absence unsettled her.

"Who are you?" Edward asked her, brightening at the sight of this lovely woman.

Bridget got up to greet Emma and to introduce her to Edward. Emma presented him with an orchid in full bloom.

"Ahhh," said Edward, taking the celadon pot in one hand and Emma's hand in the other, "a model for Georgia O'Keeffe herself. What perfection."

Bridget hoped Emma knew he was talking about the orchid.

She tried to introduce Emma to Marge, but Marge brushed her off, saying, "We've known each other for years. Who do you think arranges our flowers every summer?"

"Will's on his way?" Bridget asked as Emma pulled a cropped cardigan out of her purse and slipped it on.

"I certainly hope so," said Emma, "or I'm going to feel like I've crashed your dinner party."

"Nonsense," said Edward. "We're glad to have you. Here," he said, patting the seat beside him, "take Bridget's place by me."

Bridget rolled her eyes, picked up her plate and napkin, and moved. Kevin helped carry two more chairs up to the table, and they all scooted around again to make room.

"Will's train was delayed," Emma said. She looked apologetically at Bridget. "He said he texted to let you know I was meeting him here."

Bridget got her phone from her dress pocket and saw Will's texts, along with another from her tenants in New York:

Bridget, Thank you for letting us try on your apartment. It happens we found a different situation that is better for us and much lower price. We leave by the end of the week. We send regrets that this was not working for us. We hope for no bad feelings.

Oh, there were bad feelings. Why on earth, Bridget wondered, had they hated her apartment so much? And what could they have found that was both better and cheaper?

"I heard about your good news," Emma was saying.

Bridget looked up from her phone. Good news would be welcome.

"Will told me you're having a reunion tour with your original violinist," she said. "I feel ashamed that I've never heard of him; Will says he's quite famous. Gavin somebody?"

"Who?" said Edward.

"What?" said Bridget.

"Gavin?" Gwen said.

Bridget felt ill.

"Are we talking about Gavin Glantz?" Edward asked. "He was in your Juilliard class, wasn't he, Bridget? And part of your trio as well."

"Briefly," said Bridget, and she finished her glass of wine in one swallow. "That's all ancient history."

"He's an outstanding soloist," Edward said to Emma, as if to impress her. "And as I recall, I helped get him a seat in the orchestra at the Sydney Opera House when he was quite young. He's had a solid career ever since."

Bridget turned to Edward and blinked. "What do you mean you helped get him a seat?"

"Years ago," Edward said casually. "Gavin was looking for other options, I recall. Why you and Will chose to stay in a trio for so many years, I'll never understand. An orchestra provides a much higher quality of life, stability, a steady salary, a true home."

"No," said Bridget, shaking her head, trying to make sense of his words. "Gavin wasn't looking for options. He got that offer out of the blue, I remember."

"It wasn't out of the blue," Edward insisted. "I pulled strings."

"Why?" Bridget asked, putting down her glass. "Why did you pull strings?"

"I don't remember the details now," said Edward, "but I vaguely recall . . . Will mentioning that Sydney was Gavin's ultimate goal, or am I mixing things up. Who went to Sydney?"

"Gavin," Bridget said.

"Then where's the confusion?"

"Will would never do that," said Bridget.

"He wouldn't ask me to help a friend?" asked Edward.

"He wouldn't sabotage our trio," said Bridget, wanting to believe that was true.

"We were at Tanglewood," said Edward, "and your trio performed. Gavin was especially good—"

"You're saying *Will* mentioned—"

"The life of a chamber musician is a constant struggle," Edward told Emma, "but the music can be sublime and much more intimate; a piano trio can be as impactful as a full orchestra."

"The food's great," Kevin said to Marge.

"Emma," said Marge, "you haven't even fixed yourself a plate."

"Listen to this," said Edward, scrolling down the screen of his iPad and finding a recording. "Thanks to Jackie, I present you with Mendelssohn's Piano Trio in D Minor, featuring the highly alliterative trio Gavin Glantz, Louis Lortie, and Mischa Maisky, who happens to have spent almost two years in a Russian work camp in the '70s before repatriating to Israel." He closed his eyes, and they all sat silently as the music began.

With everyone's attention on the piece and on Gavin's bright, vibrant playing, Bridget got up and slipped out of the room. The piece was thirty minutes long, and knowing Edward, they would have to sit there and listen to all four movements, Edward editorializing throughout.

Passing through the kitchen, Bridget waved to the caterer, who was arranging chocolates on a three-tiered stand, and went out the back door to the patio to clear her head. Her dearest friend had possibly done something inexcusable, exiling their colleague and greatest asset to the other side of the planet. And now, when she least wanted it, he was insisting on summoning Gavin back.

Bridget sat at the patio table and stared out into the darkness. Leave it to Edward Stratton to turn an ordinary dinner into something unforgettable, to be the puppet-master of ceremonies. Her father reveled in celebrations, speeches, tributes, and milestones. Pomp and circumstance. He gave a eulogy at her mother's funeral, a speech on the occasion of Gwen's divorce, and a toast at Oscar's wedding. He enjoyed Bridget's graduation more than she did. He casually asked her friends to join them for dinner after they'd received their diplomas; they were so honored to be invited that some even abandoned plans with their out-of-town parents just to spend an evening with him. In the middle of the dinner, he stood up, tapped the side of his wineglass with a spoon, and gave an epic toast that was mostly about him. He gestured dramatically with his right hand, while running his left through his thick, wild hair, much darker back then, and told a story about a time in the late '80s when he drank champagne with a young Renée Fleming in Budapest. He told them all about that memorable night, describing his encounter with a talented young Hungarian busker to whom he offered a place in his orchestra right there on the spot, and finishing with a story about a tarnished but ornate sterling silver Prussian teapot (from a former "baroness") that he exchanged for his Seiko watch (an airport purchase). He spoke for thirty straight minutes without notes, quoting Adorno in German, Eco in Italian, and Derrida in French, along with George Bernard Shaw, George Gershwin, and George Harrison, pausing now and then to connect with his audience. Bridget's friends stared in awe. Then he turned to Bridget and handed her a box, telling the assembled grads that he was honored to pass along the very Prussian teapot to his daughter. He instructed Bridget to look inside, where she found a check for an embarrassingly large sum of money. As she quickly folded the check and put it away, everyone clapped, although it was disorganized, offbeat clapping for a bunch of musicians. Bridget felt her face burn, knowing her friends were watching.

Bridget was proud of her father that night, but for him to make such an extravagant display in front of her friends who were all heading into the world with massive debt and modest earning potential, to set her apart from them in such a public way, was painful. She looked around the table that night, and at Will in particular, knowing that her relationship with them would be forever altered; they would never see her as one of them again. And to become one of them, with the last name of Stratton, had been difficult enough.

The sounds were different up on Edward's mountain, and Bridget closed her eyes to listen to the cacophony, unable to tell if the chirping, humming, and croaking were coming from beneath her or over her head. Even from here, over the ruckus of the bugs, she could still hear Gavin drawing the bow over the strings of his violin.

When they'd slept together, it was like they were finishing a wonderful conversation they'd started the day they met. She liked Gavin. She'd missed him when he was gone, though no one would have known it because she never talked about him again.

If he came back now, her life would get very messy, but without him, her trio would fall apart. Edward's words about being in an orchestra came back to her: a steady job, a true home. What a monumental change that would be from her life with Will, linking together performance dates, fighting for bookings and recognition, breaking in a new violinist every three to five years.

She heard a door close behind her and turned to see Jackie walking slowly out on the patio.

"Sorry to bug you," she said. "Marge said to tell you we're having dessert."

"What did Gwen do to you?" Bridget asked as Jackie gingerly lowered herself onto a chair.

"It was fun," said Jackie. "A little terrifying at first, but I'm glad I went. It was my first time on a horse."

"Can I ask you something, Jackie? What was the name of that site you mentioned earlier? The one that lists jobs for musicians."

"Musical Chairs," she said. "All the orchestras, festivals, and music schools in the world post opportunities on it, from Beijing to Saint Louis. It's a great resource."

"I didn't know something like that existed."

"You and Will could post for a violinist, next time you need one. He's here, by the way."

Bridget didn't want to face Will. She wasn't mad at him, not exactly. Her feelings were too complicated for a one-dimensional, simple emotion like anger. She needed to think through what they'd both done to push Gavin so far out of their circle.

"Will brought his dog with him," Jackie was saying, "and Mr. Stratton's not too happy about it."

Bridget faked a yawn. "I'm so exhausted," she said. "Can you let everyone know I've gone upstairs to lie down? Tell my kids they can go home without me."

"Sure," said Jackie.

"I'm fine," Bridget said, although Jackie hadn't asked.

They went in the house together, and Bridget slipped up the back staircase to avoid Will, went into Gwen's room, and crawled under the covers.

17

Will had never been to therapy. He wasn't averse, and there were various junctures in his life, like during the weeks before he married Molly, when he probably should have gone. But in most respects, Will considered himself a fairly well-adjusted man with no need to talk anything through.

But the morning after he'd shown up for the tail end of dinner at Edward's, Will was lying on the squishy floral sofa at Emma's house, hands clasped on his chest, staring at the low popcorn ceiling, feeling shitty about himself. While a part of him was glad to be there, in the sweet-smelling living room of a woman he liked very much, with Hudson on the floor beside him, the rest of him was in turmoil.

The parrot was squawking.

"I don't think Ronaldo likes me," Will said.

"I don't think Ronaldo is what's really bothering you," Emma said.

It was hard *not* to be bothered. Will and Emma were trying to have a conversation, but they were interrupted by cawing, whistling, and screeching, along with some choice words the bird would belt out: "hello," "uh-oh," and "cock," to name a few. ("It's short for cocktail," Emma had explained.)

In the midst of this background clamor, Will was attempting to discuss his guilty conscience, repent his past actions, and express how awful it felt to be at odds for the first time ever with Bridget. He was grateful not to be alone.

"To be clear," said Emma, sitting in a chair by his side, "she didn't seem *mad* exactly. More . . . shocked."

"She didn't even come back to the table," said Will, still unnerved from that slight. "She was avoiding me. Did she really use the word 'sabotage'?"

"Call her."

Will took a slow breath. "Thanks for letting me stay last night," he said.

"I like having you here, but my place is a pretty serious downgrade from what you're accustomed to. Bridget's house is gorgeous."

Emma lived in a drab, one-story shoebox near the center of town. She had decorated it with a Bohemian flair; batik fabric covered the wall beside him, and a red, beaded chandelier hung over his head. There were billowing curtains, wind chimes, and potted plants that draped and bloomed all over a small patio in terra-cotta pots, but all that decor was trying to give character to a home that lacked even a single remarkable architectural feature. "I'd rather be here with you," he said over the ruckus of Ronaldo squawking and Hudson growling. Will turned his head to look at the bird, an intense, muscular little critter, very masculine and proud of his plumage, or at least it seemed that way since he kept puffing his feathers up to show off. "I know I should call her, but I don't know what to say. I'm worried we won't recover from this."

Emma uncrossed her legs and leaned forward. "Can I ask you something?"

Will knew exactly what she was about to say, the same thing all the women he dated wanted to know. "Look," he said, sitting up,

"Bridget and I are just friends. I know it seems strange because we act like a couple, but the truth is we are and always have been friends and colleagues, and nothing more. There's no sexual tension, no secret attraction. I'd say Bridget's like a sister, but she's not because, unlike my family, I choose to have her in my life. I love her, yes, but it's a platonic friendship, always will be."

Emma took a moment, and then smiled. "Wow. No, I was just going to ask if you guys ever discussed quitting the trio."

"Cock," squawked Ronaldo.

Will squeezed his eyes shut. "Sorry," he said, "I guess I'm a little defensive."

"A *little*?" she asked. "Look, I assume if you and Bridget wanted to be together, you'd be together. Nothing's stopping you."

"Exactly," he said. He moved closer to her and saw that Ronaldo was glaring at him, hopping madly in his cage from one end of his bar to the other. Hudson whimpered and tried to hide his large body under the coffee table.

"Bridget's father," said Emma, "was telling me last night how hard life is for chamber musicians, as opposed to being in an orchestra, so I just wondered if you guys ever considered alternatives."

"I've never thought of quitting, but I've imagined having an easier, steadier life. A full-time teaching job maybe, settling down." And then, considering how he felt about her, he added, "Recently, I've even been thinking I'd like to be in a real relationship, spend more time with you."

"Uh-oh," said Ronaldo.

Will wanted to tell her how he felt about her in flowery, poetic language. What were the right words to use? "I know we only met a month ago," he started. Should he try an endearment? Which one? "Honey" sounded too 1950s domestic. "Darling" was 1920s corny. He decided to start instead with practical matters instead. "I'd like to stay with you all weekend, if that's okay with you."

Emma smiled. "*I* invited *you*, remember?"

"Of course," he said. And then he tried again. "I like you. And I was wondering if you'd . . . want to come to New York sometime?"

Will's building had sold, and all he knew about that was that the apartments on the top floors were being gutted and renovated. The noise from this project, a letter had informed him, would begin in the coming weeks, and he was to be assured that steps would be taken to mitigate any disturbance. He and Mitzy had discussed meeting with a lawyer to find out how high their rents could go, what their rights were, if any. He wanted Emma to come visit before the construction started, and before, God forbid, he was forced to move.

"I'd like to," she said, "but I've got the shop and Ronaldo."

"Right."

"Hello," said Ronaldo. "Good-bye."

Will got a sinking feeling, remembering what his cabdriver Frank always said about people who live in the country and their attachment to their communities. "Does that mean . . . Do you like New York?"

"Not especially," she said, as though she was saying she didn't care much for eggplant, "but it's a fun place to visit. I tried living there once, in my twenties; it didn't take."

Ronaldo squawked, and Hudson started barking from under the coffee table.

"Shhhhhh, Hudson, no," said Will.

Emma came over to the couch and sat next to him, draping her legs over his. She leaned in and kissed him. "Too bad. Only a month together. I guess it wasn't meant to be."

Will was used to deal-breakers, and while he knew that dating a woman who ran a business in the country, two hours away from where he lived and worked, certainly sounded like a deal-breaker, he wasn't worried, not even a little. There were longer long-distance relationships than this one.

"Oh well," she said, as if it would be nothing to end things between them right then and there, "sure was fun while it lasted." She smiled.

"It was all right," he said, shrugging, also pretending like he didn't care, like he wasn't willing to do pretty much anything to be with her.

She started to get up again, and he pulled her back down on the couch and kissed her. Ronaldo squawked loudly.

There was a knock on the door, and Emma got up, fixing her shirt and smoothing her hair. Hudson, almost knocking the coffee table over, followed her, as Will adjusted the crotch of his pants.

He heard mumbling, and then Emma came back in the room, smiling encouragingly. "Bridget's here," she said quietly. "She wants to know if you can come out and play."

"Now?" said Will, embarrassed by the weakness of his voice. "But . . ."

"Go," said Emma. She went over to a bookshelf and gave him a house key on a disco ball key chain. "In case I'm at work when you get back." She held his hands. "Say you're sorry, and don't get defensive. If you take a left and walk north for about a quarter mile, you'll see a dirt road on the right that goes along the Housatonic. It's beautiful down there, very few cars." She gave him Hudson's leash and a bottle of bug spray. "You'll need it."

She walked Will to the front door and gave him a little push. There was Bridget, standing in Emma's yard in running shorts and a T-shirt, her back to him. Oscar's lab, Hadley, was running around the yard with Hudson, both completely carefree, while Will's stomach was in knots. Bridget turned around, and from the look on her face, he could see how tense this interaction was going to be. "Take a walk with me?" she said with a forced smile.

"Yeah, sure," he said, trying to keep the tone light. "Where's Bear?"

"I couldn't handle that much dog," she said. "I'm sorry to take you away from Emma."

"No, I'm so glad you're here. I was going to call. I barely slept."

They walked in silence down the dirt road for a moment, with both Hadley and Hudson scrabbling at the ends of their leashes, delighted by the smells. Bridget turned toward him. "Is it true you exiled Gavin to the other side of the world?"

Will looked down, rubbing the back of his head. "Yes," he said plainly, wondering if he would lose her over a dumb mistake in the past, dumb but so very consequential.

She looked away. "Why?"

"Initially I said it as a joke."

"Since when do you make jokes with my father?"

"No, more like I was joking with myself. We were at Tanglewood, and we played for your dad. Gavin was being Gavin, an unbearable show-off, and he waved his bow so close to my face, he almost hit me with it."

"I remember," she said.

"And then afterwards your dad took us for a drink at the Red Lion—"

"In the bar downstairs, I remember—"

"And you and Gavin went off together, who knows where, and I—"

"What?" she said, stopping dead in her tracks. "What does that mean, 'who knows where'? What are you even—"

"Gavin was leering at you all night—"

"So?"

"I know it's irrational," Will said, feeling simultaneously ashamed and righteous, "but it was messing up our chemistry—"

"You're obsessed with 'chemistry.'" Bridget looked disgusted. "I could handle Gavin—"

"Between his insanely inflated ego and his mad crush on you—"

"Why would that even bother you?"

Will knew it would be difficult to explain his jealousy. He and

Bridget had always dated other people and talked about it openly. He never felt jealous. But for *Gavin* to think he had a chance with her, for them to look at each other in a way that sometimes felt surreptitious, private, like they were keeping something from him, hurt. He was too embarrassed to explain it, so he just said, "We were working together and investing ourselves in an enterprise that had real potential, and Gavin felt like a threat to that."

"So, you got rid of him?" They were standing in the middle of the road and had to step to the side, pulling the dogs toward them as a car slowly rumbled by.

"I was left at the bar talking to Edward," said Will, "who was going on and on about how fabulous Gavin was, how immensely talented. And my feelings were hurt, and I said, 'You think he's better than us, don't you?' And your father said, 'I do. Because he is.' So, I said, 'Well, I hope he achieves his biggest dream in life someday. He wants so much to be in the orchestra in—' And I thought, *China? Russia? The moon? To where would I banish Gavin if I had the power?* And I blurted out, '—Australia.' And then a few weeks later, Gavin announced that he got second chair in Sydney. I didn't know your dad would actually *do* anything. It was just a stupid thing to say."

"But you *did* want to get rid of him. And it's a fact: Forsyth was never as good again."

The weight of what he'd done settled over him. "I'm sorry. I was young and stupid, and threatened by him, and jealous, and I had every other unattractive quality you can think of. If I could take it back, I would." Hudson and Hadley were looking down the road, eager to press on. "What can I do?"

They began walking again in silence, kicking up dirt from the dry road. The Housatonic was on their right, and they turned onto the path. The mosquitoes and gnats began to swarm. "Bug spray," said Will.

They each unclasped the leashes, and the dogs took off into the woods. Bridget sprayed the back of her neck and her ankles and handed the bug spray to Will.

"I really am sorry," he said sincerely.

"It was a long time ago," she said.

"Does that mean you forgive me?"

"The thing is," she said, and then she let out a heavy, deep sigh, like she didn't want to go on. "This may sound nonsensical, but if you hadn't sent Gavin away, I might not have had Oscar and Isabelle."

Will didn't see the connection.

"I was with Gavin the night he got the offer," she said. "And I slept with him."

Will stopped walking. "You and *Gavin?*" He wanted to add, *I knew it!* but he kept himself from blurting it out, feeling more stung by the revelation than pleased for being right about it.

"It was only one night," she said. "And I understand your whole point about group dynamics, and I agree with you, but it didn't apply in this case because he told me he was leaving us."

"Eww," Will said flatly, hating the idea of them together, even now.

"Don't judge me," she said, taking his arm, making him walk again.

"Did you love him?"

Bridget didn't answer right away. "No, not like that. Even when I had the chance to bring him back, I got rid of him, too, just like you did."

"Wait," Will said, recalling that she'd brought Oscar and Isabelle into the discussion. "Is this . . . You're saying that Gavin's—?"

"I don't know."

"How can you not know?"

"I went to the doctor the next morning for my appointment to get inseminated."

Will was processing, more slowly probably than he should have.

"So, you *really* don't know? Why didn't you find out? Do a paternity test?"

"I called Gavin when I found out I was pregnant, and he made it clear he wanted nothing to do with them."

"He's known all this time?"

"Only that it's a possibility."

"What a dick," said Will. "And to think he missed out on . . . everything." Will was glad—and proud—he hadn't missed out, that he'd stepped into a role that perhaps should have been Gavin's.

"It's not his fault," she said. "He offered a few weeks later to find out and do the right thing, and I told him to stay away. And then I acted like the whole thing never happened." She looked at him, pleading, "I don't think he's their dad, though, do you? They have zero musical ability. Oscar's tone-deaf—"

"What do *they* think?"

Bridget didn't answer. She kicked a rock, hard, and it rolled off the path.

"You're telling me before you tell them?" Will said, feeling the responsibility of their friendship, wondering how he could help.

"I'm not proud of any of this," she said. Then she looked into the woods, saying, "Where are the dogs?"

Will whistled, and they turned at the sound of snapping twigs. "They'll be covered in ticks," he said as they came bursting out of the woods and back onto the path, their paws muddy.

As the four of them went farther along, the river widened and the water coursed around big, bleached rocks. Will put a hand on Bridget's shoulder. He hadn't seen Gavin in a long time, but he certainly didn't see any resemblance between him and the kids. The same coloring maybe, somewhat, but it wasn't an obvious match. None of Gavin's smirking arrogance or cocky affect.

"What I want you to know . . ." Bridget said, "the reason I came over this morning is to tell you that I only slept with Gavin because he quit Forsyth that night. And he only quit Forsyth because you gave him the reason to go. So it's possible, in a roundabout way, that your actions led to Oscar and Isabelle."

Will was taken aback. "Ah, are you thanking me?" he said.

"Sort of," she said with a smile.

"And if they're not his kids?"

She shrugged. "Gavin was going to leave us eventually anyway. He had his sights set on something more prestigious."

She slid her arm around his waist, and he put his over her shoulders, relieved to feel her close to him. He whistled again to the dogs, who came running toward them, Hudson carrying a tree branch in his mouth.

"I need your help," she said. "Gavin's coming here now and—"

"I'll cancel," Will said. "I'll tell him not to come. I never should have talked to him without telling you—"

"No, I should have dealt with this question a long time ago, and—to be honest—I feel like we both owe him an apology."

"He hasn't committed to any concert dates," said Will, "but he said he wants to come here and see us."

"Can you call him and ask him to the wedding and to play my dad's piece with us?"

Given all she'd just told him, he wasn't entirely sure this was a good idea.

"And will you arrange the piece for us?" she asked.

"Of course," he said, trying to mask his reservations. "I'll do it, but honestly, I don't think Edward wants *me* messing around with one of his compositions. If he's willing to have it arranged for piano trio, he'd rather do it himself."

"We're not telling him," she said. "I want it to be a surprise."

Edward had never struck Will as the kind of man who appreciated surprises.

"Then hire a real composer," he said, "one of the composers he has coming to the retreat. I'm not . . . worthy."

"You are." Bridget held on to his arm. "Please? A collaboration would be like an icebreaker, a way into the world's most awkward conversation ever. Gavin wrote saying he wants to talk, and somehow I don't think he meant that in a casual way."

Will didn't feel like this was a moment to argue with her. "I'll try," he said. "Get me a copy of the score."

Bridget stopped walking and covered her face. "How do I tell my kids about this? What am I going to say to them?"

"You say, *Isabelle, Oscar, it's possible that a wonderful old friend of mine, a brilliant musician and good person—*"

"Oh, come on, you hate him—"

"Have we not established that my judgment in my twenties was terrible? And we've all grown up since then, or I should hope so. You tell them, *He's possibly your father. Would you like to find out for sure?*"

"And when they say, *Why didn't you tell us?*"

"You say, *I should have. But he left the country for several years, and we lost touch. The door between us closed, and I didn't know how to reopen it.*"

Bridget nodded.

The path came to an end at an entry point to the Appalachian Trail. There were boulders by the river, and Bridget walked down the bank and sat down on one. Will chose his own flat rock next to hers, while Hudson lay in the mud, chewing on a stick and Hadley sat in the river, lapping up water.

"There's something else, Will," she said, looking as though she might cry. "After all these years, I think we have to consider letting Forsyth go."

Will felt a sharp pain in his chest. "I don't want to."

"I don't either. But here we are, and I think we should make a conscious decision to opt *in*. We have no manager, no violinist, so before we start all over again, we should decide: Is this really what we want, over everything else out there?"

Will held up a hand and started to tell her, *Yes, of course it is.*

"Don't answer now," she said before he could speak. "Let's take the rest of the summer to think about it, ask ourselves what we want moving forward, and then we'll see where we each stand." Bridget leaned across to his rock and took his hand.

Will didn't answer. A sadness swept over him, and then fear joined in. The idea of a career without Bridget was unthinkable, lonely. And then a tiny little sliver of excitement made itself known as well: What *were* the possibilities?

18

One day, thought Oscar, life is going along according to plan, and the next everything turns to complete shit. Waking up in Connecticut one morning, it occurred to him how nuts it was that instead of having breakfast with Matt in his own condo near Dupont Circle, Oscar was getting ready to take a fucking road trip with his mom.

When she said she was driving to New York for a night to check on her now-empty apartment, Oscar decided he would go along. He needed a change of scenery. He craved a break from the quiet, the fresh air, and the relentless green of Litchfield County, and there could be no greater change in scenery than that provided by Manhattan's gray sidewalks, smoggy air, and crowded subway cars. Oscar wanted to see faces he didn't recognize, people who didn't know him.

The night before they were leaving, he'd walked across the dark field to the guesthouse to hang out with Isabelle. Eliza was there keeping her company as well, and Oscar rubbed her chin as she slept soundly on an armchair, in spite of the fact that the Grateful

Dead was blasting from a portable speaker. Isabelle was standing on a ladder with a paint roller, having already covered two of the walls with a pale gray.

"Not bad," he said, turning down the music enough that she could hear him.

"Don't look too closely." She pointed to the ceiling, where she'd gotten dove-gray paint on the crown molding. Stepping off the ladder, she showed him her paint-spattered hands.

He smiled at her and quoted the song she was playing: "'Oh well, a touch of gray kinda suits you anyway.'" He never felt that urge to tease her about the stupid shit she did or said when they were alone. Those ribbings were more for the benefit of an audience.

"I know you don't want my advice," she said, "but I think you should skip New York, fly down to DC instead, and talk it out with Matt in person. This hiding out all summer is pointless."

"It's not that simple." Oscar was so sick of his family getting in his business.

"You think he cheated, and that's—"

"He did cheat."

"So you say, and that's upsetting," she said, "but you have to address it—"

"I don't want to talk about it."

"You're being so stubborn," she said.

"Are you done?"

"Fine." She found a rag and wiped her hands. "Sorry I'm not going with you guys tomorrow. I've got a shift at the store, and I don't want to ask for time off already."

Her new job was a bizarre fucking choice, but Oscar kept his mouth shut. He might be on a better career track, but his life was a way bigger mess than hers. He'd visited her at Latham's: a retail store that sold locally sourced, handcrafted alpaca sweaters and throw blankets. It had a coffee counter in the back with seating and free

Wi-Fi; Oscar was surprised to see how crowded the place was and how happy his sister looked, chatting up the shoppers.

"Can you take care of Hadley and Bear?" he asked.

"Sure, if you bring me back Kiehl's," she said, putting her paint-flecked hands together, begging.

"I don't even know where to find—"

"You can get it all over New York, like at Bloomie's. Please? My skin is shit these days. Look at this, do you think I've got some weird disease?" She rolled up her sleeve and showed him a bumpy rash on her arm.

"Poison ivy. You probably got it from Kevin."

"Very funny," she said.

He hadn't meant it as a joke. "Do you have a suitcase I can borrow?" he asked. "A small one?"

She went in her room and came back with a carry-on bag. "You better rest up," she said. "Alone with Mom in a car for two and a half hours? I hope you're in the mood to share."

"And what if I'm not?"

"Pretend you're asleep."

Oscar loved his mom, sure, but that didn't mean he found it easy to spend endless amounts of time with her. She had habits he'd forgotten about in his years away. She talked to herself when she washed the dishes. She laughed way too easily at his jokes, and even louder and harder when they weren't very funny. She literally didn't know how anything worked in terms of technology. Like anything. She'd peered over his shoulder at his laptop screen in the middle of an important Skype call, and when he shooed her away, she laughed and ruffled his hair, saying, "Silly, it's not like they can see me."

She used a roundabout and yet totally transparent method of

handing out criticism. "Now that's strong coffee," she would say whenever he was the one who made a pot. "Easy does it," when she thought he was drinking too much. "Are you getting sick?" when he slept in past ten.

But everything was relative, and compared to Matt's mother, his mom was a saint. Matt's mom was a terrible person in disguise as a put-upon victim. At the wedding she whispered bitchy comments to Matt about everything from Bridget's dress ("Black at a wedding? That's not very festive.") to the food ("My steak isn't cooked, look. Is yours raw, too?") to the tone of Oscar's grandfather's toast ("Bit of a blowhard, isn't he?"). Oscar held his tongue because it wasn't Matt's fault his mother was boorish and insulting. But it *was* weird that Matt never seemed bothered by it.

In comparison, Bridget was a rock star. It was true she asked too many questions, leaving him to wonder why the hell she gave a shit about the mundane details of his day. But at least it showed she cared. "What'd you eat for lunch?" she would ask. *Why the fuck do you wanna know?* he was tempted to respond. He wouldn't; he wasn't a teenager anymore, and he wasn't going to be an asshole for no reason.

Spending two hours in the passenger seat of the station wagon, the same blue Volvo he and Isabelle had ridden around in as kids, would be super uncomfortable in a flashback-to-middle-school kind of way. *Don't get snippy*, he told himself, *no matter how many questions she asks, no matter how slowly she drives.*

Strangely enough, as he and Bridget got in the car on the last Monday morning of July (ridiculously early, as she'd insisted on "pushing off" at six thirty) and buckled their seat belts, she was unusually quiet. They were heading down the driveway when she leaned forward over the steering wheel and sighed loudly, as though they were at the end of the trip, not the very beginning.

"You okay?" he asked.

"Yeah. But it's too bad Isabelle couldn't come."

Given that the three of them had spent more time together this summer than they had since high school, her desire for more family togetherness seemed greedy. "She has more important things to do, tending to the customers at Latham's, the much-needed, one-stop-shopping paradise for alpaca ponchos and caramel macchiatos."

"Hey," she said, ignoring his bitchy remark, "do you feel like driving?" She stopped the car and put it in park. "I mean, would you mind?"

Oscar was surprised by the request, feeling a shift of some kind between them. "Sure, no problem."

They unbuckled their seat belts and got out, each walking the half circle, Oscar around the back of the car and Bridget around the front, to switch seats.

Oscar knocked his knee getting back in and slid the seat back. His mom wasn't four feet tall, so why she drove with her seat practically under the dashboard was a mystery.

"Did you have breakfast?" she asked.

"Yeah."

"What'd you eat?"

Oscar adjusted the rearview mirror. "Fine, I lied, I didn't have breakfast."

"You're going to get hungry," she said in a singsong warning.

"I never eat in the morning."

He prepared himself for a lecture, but she didn't say anything more. She settled in and looked out the window. She was right, of course; he'd been driving only ten minutes when his stomach started grumbling.

His mom did not backseat drive. She did not turn on the CD player and sing Broadway show tunes, nor did she pry about his marital problems.

"At least you've got me," he said.

"What?"

"Isabelle isn't here, but at least you got my stellar company."

She reached over and patted his shoulder. "What are you going to do today?"

"See some friends," he said, meaning buy some pot, "have lunch with a colleague," meaning go on a job interview, and "eat sushi," meaning exactly that; Litchfield County was not known for its kamikaze rolls. The job interview was the main reason he'd come along, of course, but if he told his mom about it, she'd spend the rest of the drive questioning him. He wasn't up for an inquisition. "What about you?"

"Same," she said. "Errands, a meeting. Want to have dinner together tonight?"

He didn't. He'd had dinner with her about a thousand times this summer. But as he imagined her sitting home alone or eating at a restaurant by herself, he had a change of heart. "I'd love to."

Bridget turned on a classical CD. He didn't know what they were listening to, but it was familiar enough that he knew he *should* know. By the time he got onto the Saw Mill (at her suggestion, though the Hutch would have been faster), they had settled into a comfortable silence, leaving him to think about what the fuck he was going to do with his life.

Over the past few weeks, Oscar, sweating under the ceiling fan in the heat and humidity of his childhood bedroom, staring out his windows at the trees, had come to accept that he was, in fact, an overconfident, act-before-you-think, impulsive dick. But he also knew that his flaws were not what blew up his marriage. He would have to work on himself, sure, but Matt's actions were far more damaging than his own. And Oscar had sadly concluded that repairing the marriage would be impossible since Matt was irrationally angry and disgusted with him and yet wouldn't even admit that *he* was chiefly responsible for their relationship's demise. Oscar didn't think this was up for debate, given that Matt was the cheater and liar, lying being the more egregious of the two sins, in Oscar's opinion, although both really fucking hurt.

Was it ironic, he wondered, or just plain pathetic that in one month—on the brink of divorce—Oscar was going to have to attend his grandfather's wedding in the exact same spot where he and Matt had said their vows a year before? It was insensitive of his family, to say the least, and a hell of a lot to ask of him. No one seemed to have even considered how the upcoming event might make him feel.

As far as grooms went, Matt looked better in a tux than anyone Oscar had ever met, his grandfather included. Oscar would have to get hammered at the wedding to avoid thinking about Matt, the vows they'd made that day, and the fights that followed. How they went from being in love to being at odds, from talking about getting a surrogate and starting a family together to not talking to each other at all.

It had not been fun seeing his husband become somebody else's right-hand man so soon after the wedding, to have his place by Matt's side occupied not merely by some successful, good-looking guy, but by the man who was recently named DC's most eligible bachelor. Jackson was vice-chair of the Congressional Black Caucus, an outspoken environmentalist, a leading voice for social justice, and his name was frequently mentioned when pundits discussed future presidential contenders. And he was smart, charming, and handsome on top of all that. Oscar fucking hated him. Even his name: Jackson Oakley. What kind of a prick was born with a perfect name like that? (And meanwhile, he was stuck with *Oscar*, like Oscar the Grouch or Oscar the Wiener, as the elementary school kids cleverly called him.) For months Matt brushed off Oscar's worry, repeatedly denying that there was anything going on between him and his hot politician boss, in spite of all the late nights in the Rayburn office building, the overnight trips, and that way they had of looking at each other, like they were reading each other's fucking minds or something. The coded text messages—*Let's meet at the place for the thing*—and the less-coded ones—*In a word: wow. What would I do without you?*—started to drive Oscar mad. He had never thought of himself as a jealous person, but Jackson was impossible competition, what with his being absolutely perfect on paper and in real life. As the evidence piled up, Oscar began to think that Matt was gaslighting the shit out of him, and he hated it, hated being made to feel stupid. "It's all in your head," Matt would say. "You're acting crazy again."

Matt was supposedly working late one Friday night when Oscar got a notification from their bank that a charge for a $340 boutique hotel room had been approved. Oscar felt like he'd been punched in the gut, and to alleviate the pain, he drank one martini after another until Matt finally came home at four o'clock in the morning, acting as if nothing had happened.

When Oscar confronted him, showing him the notification on his screen, Matt came up with some bullshit story that the room was for Jackson's sister, who had come into town unexpectedly. Jackson would be reimbursing him, of course. "Let's not fight in the middle of the night, okay?" he said and kissed the top of Oscar's head, smiling like it was no big deal, before heading off to take a shower and go to bed. Oscar—thanks to what his mom referred to as his underdeveloped frontal lobe—Googled the congressman's office number, and left a drunk message, saying some bullshit he could barely remember. *Back the fuck off, home-wrecker*, maybe. Or *Get your own husband, you fuckin' assclown.* Something really childish. A threat or two, maybe. *I know where you live.*

An intern called the Capitol Police, and Matt almost lost his job.

Oscar was sorry for the message, but there was an emptiness to his apologies because he knew—*knew*—the sister story was crap, some lie they'd cooked up together while rolling around in the sheets at the George. As he told Matt, he was willing to discuss the affair, willing even to reconsider how they defined their marriage, set up parameters based on an honest conversation, just Dan Savage the hell out of their relationship. But how could they try to do that if Matt was still being a lying dirtbag?

"Red light," Bridget said.

Oscar pressed hard on the brakes. He'd forgotten about the Saw Mill's traffic lights that popped up out of nowhere.

"Sorry," he said.

"No biggie, piggy-wiggy."

God. Kill me. Whenever Bridget said stuff like that, Matt just beamed, saying how adorable she was. She was, sometimes. Anyway, it felt good to have been jolted out of his shame-and-anger spiral. "What's your plan today?" he said. Had he asked her that already? Had he even heard her answer?

"See what shape the apartment's in," she said. "And I have a meeting with a manager who might have some advice for me. Maybe take a walk in the park."

"Advice on what?"

"Will and I lost our violinist again."

Oscar knew what a drag this was for them. "Forever filling the empty chair," he said. "You guys must be so sick of it."

"We are," she said. "We might be done."

"Done?" he asked. "Done how?"

"I don't know," she said, as though she were actually trying to solve the problem right there in the car. "We might launch into something new. On our own. We haven't decided."

"Like a duo?"

"No, I mean on our own, like separately."

She said it brightly, with an excitement that both confused and relieved him. Her nonchalance about the fate of the trio, given that it had been around a lot longer than Oscar had, was unexpected. It was hard to imagine Bridget without Will as her partner, although it didn't really matter, he supposed, since Will's membership in the family was irrevocable. It was true what Matt said: Will was way better than any real father he could have had because there was none of the fucked-up competition or unreasonable expectations or hideous disappointment, all of which Matt had suffered in his relationship with his dad.

"What would you do instead?" he asked her.

"Strap my cello on my back and take a leap into . . . something."

A cello, Oscar thought, is no fucking parachute. Whether she'd meant this idea to sound terrifying or thrilling, he couldn't say. "What about Will?"

"Same."

"Strap his piano on his back?"

Cue: over-the-top laughter. "He might be getting a little old for his gig-to-gig, freelance lifestyle," she finally said.

"His new girlfriend's cool."

"Very," said Bridget. "Did you see her tattoo?"

Oscar pictured the white flowers and delicate green vine on Emma's upper arm and decided he might make another stop today: a tattoo parlor in the East Village. Maybe he could do something bold to show Matt how sad he was, how much he loved him. He spent the rest of the drive wondering what image would best express his feelings.

Manhattan, what a difference from the country. The traffic was grid-locked coming into the city, and they sat bumper to bumper on the Henry Hudson. They finally made it to the lot on Amsterdam and walked to their building on West 93rd Street. After saying hello to the doorman in the lobby, they took the quaint, rickety elevator up to the sixth floor and put their bags down in the hallway, while Bridget fumbled with her keys, dropping them once on the floor. Oscar picked them up for her and she tried again, this time turning the lock and pushing the door open.

The smell brought Oscar instantly back in time: coming home from soccer practice at Riverside Park in November, dropping his puffer coat on the floor, and going into the black-and-white-tiled kitchen, where either his mom or Marge would be getting dinner ready: spaghetti and meatballs, garlic bread, ice cream. Good memories and bad came flooding back, as they always did when he came home. Childhood was a bitch, under the best of circumstances.

"Are you kidding me?" Bridget was saying. "They didn't even have the decency to turn off the lights."

He walked back to his bedroom, which hadn't changed much since he'd left for college. His AP US History book was still on the shelf, a cheesy junior prom picture (with his friend Jessica Bollinger, who tried to make out with him that night until he finally outed himself to keep from hurting her feelings) was still tacked on the bulletin board, and a pair of old Adidas cleats were still in the closet. His electric guitar was in its stand, untouched ever since he grew out of his Green Day phase.

In front of the full-length mirror on the back of his door, he dressed in khaki pants and a button-down shirt, deciding to skip the tie. By the time he was ready to head out, his mom was in the kitchen, aggressively wiping down the kitchen counters. "Gross," she said. "They left food in the refrigerator."

"The place looks pretty cleaned up to me."

"I have this urge to remove every trace of them." She held up a block of cheese—"Dutch Gouda, can you believe it?"—and she threw it in the garbage can.

"Should we perform an exorcism?" he asked.

Disproportionate laughter again. "Are you leaving already?" she asked.

"We're only here for thirty-six hours," he said. "Gotta make the most out of it."

"Take their key," she said, handing him the key chain that was lying on a note the tenants had left. Bridget sat at the kitchen table to read it. "They *say* they washed the sheets before they left. Do we believe them?"

"Yes," Oscar said. "Otherwise we have to strip the beds and do it ourselves. I'll see you tonight. Text me where we're having dinner."

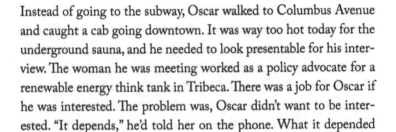

Instead of going to the subway, Oscar walked to Columbus Avenue and caught a cab going downtown. It was way too hot today for the underground sauna, and he needed to look presentable for his interview. The woman he was meeting worked as a policy advocate for a renewable energy think tank in Tribeca. There was a job for Oscar if he was interested. The problem was, Oscar didn't want to be interested. "It depends," he'd told her on the phone. What it depended on, he didn't say.

Oscar looked out the cab window, happy to be in New York but sad about the prospect of moving back to Manhattan with two big dogs and no Matt; what a depressing change of circumstances that would be. What choice would he have, though, if Matt didn't take him back? And if Matt chose Jackson, no way could he stay in DC then. It would break his heart.

19

Wearing the same navy wrap dress that she'd worn to her father's for dinner a few weeks earlier, Bridget stepped out of a cab in front of the Time Warner Center and walked to the Museum of Arts and Design. On the top floor there was a restaurant called, simply, Robert, known for its cocktails and impressive views over Columbus Circle and Central Park. She was early and asked the hostess to seat her at a table where she could see Randall as soon as he walked in; she didn't want to be taken by surprise.

From her spot by the window, she got her phone out and took a quick picture of the park, feeling like a tourist in her own hometown. She'd been to this restaurant with Sterling last spring to celebrate the release of his new novel. Come to think of it, most of what she and Sterling did together was celebrate Sterling or problem-solve for Sterling or strategize for Sterling. Having had several weeks to analyze the breakup, Bridget had decided that his most unattractive quality was self-absorption that came from a place of weakness. He had a wimpy, needy nature. As she sat there only two tables down from where they'd had dinner together, she wished she'd chosen a different restaurant for this meeting.

She ordered iced tea and sat tapping her freshly manicured nails on the side of the glass as she looked over the menu, trying to keep from fidgeting with her hair.

There was Randall, striding into the room in a light gray suit and tie, looking hurried and humorless. Bridget wondered, as he spotted her, marched over, and shook her hand brusquely, if arranging this lunch had been a mistake. He sat and immediately motioned for their waiter.

"Diet Coke with lime," he said. And then, to Bridget, "I don't have much time."

"Sorry this was so last-minute. I'm only in town for the day."

"I never heard back from Will about the concert dates," he said, getting right down to business, "so I assume a reunion with Gavin's not happening."

Hearing Gavin's name made Bridget's stomach turn. "We'll see him in August, but he hasn't agreed to any performances, so do whatever you have to do. And I'm sorry, by the way, for everything."

"I had a feeling Will was getting ahead of himself," he said, putting his napkin in his lap and picking up his menu. He looked annoyed. "It's unfortunate it didn't work out with Caroline, but I'm starting to think you guys may have dodged a bullet."

Bridget waited for an explanation of that cryptic remark, but he didn't go on. She admired his discretion and shrugged. "Let's consider it a blessing in disguise then." Sitting straight in her chair, elbows on the table, hands clasped in front of her, she said, "I was hoping we could talk about what's next, given that—"

"It's like I told you guys the first time," Randall said, closing his menu. "There's nothing I can do for you two without a star violinist. The Caroline thing was a fluke—"

"No," she said, stopping him, "I'm not asking you to work with us or manage us or anything. Actually, Will and I are considering the possibility of moving on—separately, I mean. Ending the Forsyth Trio, for a while at least. And I've never been on my own before, professionally. I was hoping to get your advice on this thing I found." She got her purse from the back of her chair and pulled out a piece of paper she'd printed at the apartment from the Musical Chairs site. "Not a *thing*, a listing. A job opportunity. An audition, actually." She unfolded it, smoothed it with her hand, and handed it to him.

She waited while he read it over.

"Cello number three, London Philharmonic." He looked up at her. "You're interested?"

Bridget couldn't bring herself to answer, so she nodded, shrugged, and shook her head all at once, as if to say, *Yeah, but no, who cares, fine, whatever.*

"Why are you telling me?"

She took a sip of her tea and cleared her throat. "I was wondering if you know what kind of person they'd be considering for this. Am I overqualified or totally underqualified? It's the London Philharmonic Orchestra, I know, but I graduated from Juilliard, and I've been playing chamber music for the past thirty years in a somewhat well-known trio. And it's not like I'm auditioning for first chair. But am I all wrong for this? Am I . . . too old?"

Randall seemed to relax for the first time since he'd sat down. He smiled. "No, you're not too old. But London? You want to move to London? Why?"

"It's just a fantasy," she said, putting her hands in her lap. "A chance to do something new. And it's not *that* far away. You hop on a plane, and you're back in New York in six hours."

"I could never leave the city," Randall said. "What about Will?"

"He'll do his thing."

He tilted his head. "I assumed you two were . . ."

"No, we're just friends. Always have been."

"Wow," he said. "You've lasted longer than most marriages I know."

That was certainly true. "We may stay together. But I was online, and this audition jumped out at me. I'm unattached, my kids are grown, and I've got a chance to do something new."

"What does your father think?"

"I haven't told anyone about this, but I think he'd like the idea of my moving to his hometown. Did you know he's getting married in a month?"

Randall looked stunned. "At his age? That's . . . impressive."

"You can come to the wedding, if you like," Bridget said. "Will and I will be playing one of my dad's pieces." She didn't mention Gavin; it was too hard to even say his name out loud. She put her elbows back on the table and got to the point. "Randall, I asked you here to get your brutally honest opinion—"

"Call me Randy."

"Randy," she said, preferring the more relaxed version of this man, "would I be a serious candidate for something like this, or will they reject me?"

"I'd say . . . you have a good shot. You'll probably be up against people who haven't had near the level of solo experience you've had. Want me to make a call?"

"What do you mean?"

"They might take you more seriously if you've got someone calling on your behalf." The brusque side of his personality made a sudden reappearance as he quickly added, "This wouldn't mean I'm representing you, I'd just do it as a favor."

"Thanks," Bridget said, "but I think I'll apply on my own and see what happens." She didn't want any strings pulled; if getting this job was meant to happen, it would happen.

Randy looked over the paper again. "I know I don't have to tell you this, but you'll have to be completely prepared for the audition;

if they invite you, they'll put you through a marathon. So get ready."

The sound of that warning gave Bridget a restlessness, an urge to practice. How could she best prepare? What schedule of rehearsing would she arrange the rest of her life around? Cello would come first; everything else would come after.

"And let me know how it goes," Randy said. He leaned back in his chair comfortably. "Hey, Bridget. What would you say if we treated the rest of this lunch as a date?"

Bridget ran her hand through her hair. "Like a *date* date?" She narrowed her eyes at him. "I thought you were in such a hurry."

"I thought you were after something I couldn't give you, so I was anticipating an unpleasant interaction." He smiled at her. "It's pretty cool you wanted my opinion."

"I figured you know more about the competition I'll be facing than anyone." She sat back as well, feeling like she could relax now, too, enjoying the feeling that came over her at this hint of romance.

"You're gutsy," he said.

Faint praise maybe, but she liked it. "Sure," she said, "I'll be your lunch date."

"Should we get a bottle of wine?"

Bridget had nowhere to be and a smart, well-respected, halfway decent-looking guy asking her to drink wine in the middle of the day. "Absolutely."

The next afternoon, Oscar offered to drive them back to Connecticut. Bridget, buckled in the passenger seat, could tell that the brief trip to the city had done her a world of good. She was feeling less distracted by her own problems and wanted to have a meaningful conversation on the road.

"What'd you do today?" she asked. He'd been out of the apartment already when she got up that morning, arriving back just before they'd agreed to leave. While she waited for him, Matt called her again, this time from a number that wasn't in her contacts. When she'd answered and realized it was him, she'd hung up without even letting him speak. Childish, maybe, but she was being protective of Oscar and didn't want to listen to Matt's excuses for his inexcusable behavior. But as she pressed the red button, she knew Isabelle wouldn't have approved of her cutting him off like that. Isabelle was still certain there was hope for the marriage.

He shrugged. "Not much."

"What'd you have for lunch?" she asked.

"Chipotle."

"Barbacoa or carnitas?"

"Steak."

Asking about food had been Bridget's way of launching into deeper conversations when Oscar was younger and didn't want to talk about something. Will called it her "lunch launch." She wasn't sure it worked anymore now that Oscar was an adult. She wished there was no need to ask him about his future, his marriage, his plans. When they got married, Bridget had hoped that any hard times Oscar had ever suffered, being picked on as a kid, coming out when he was in high school, dealing with his homophobic soccer teammates, were well behind him. She hated to think of his heart being broken, of him losing the love of his life, having been lucky enough to find him.

"Have you talked to Matt?" she asked.

"He left a few messages," he said flatly.

"Maybe," she said, "you two should talk about what comes next. Are you thinking couple's counseling or lawyers or what?"

"I don't know."

"Well, it's all very sad," she said.

"Sorry to disappoint you."

"It's not about *me*. I just never imagined Matt would be so duplicitous and disloyal."

"Have you ever seen Jackson?" Oscar said. "He's the perfect human specimen. He's a war hero, a lawyer, *and* a congressman. And he's gay. Why wouldn't Matt want to be with him?"

It sounded almost like a defense of Matt's behavior. "What about me and Will?" Bridget asked. "Will's handsome and accomplished and straight, and we're only friends. Why is it so hard for some people to have platonic relationships? And why do so many people think they don't even exist?"

Oscar drummed his fingers on the steering wheel.

Bridget wondered if she should be encouraging a reconciliation. "I don't know what you want, or what you're hoping will happen. But you love him and maybe you should do something bold." Knowing that Oscar's impulsivity sometimes got him into trouble, she added, "But not too bold."

"So, say, getting a tattoo of Matt's initials on my back, you're saying that would be a mistake?" he asked.

Bridget laughed hard at that; Oscar could be so funny. "Exactly. But maybe call him when we get home. You have to deal with your marriage eventually, one way or the other. You can't just walk away."

"Why not?"

She dropped her smile. "I've walked away from problems before, things I didn't want to face, and believe me, they come back to haunt you— Red light."

Oscar slammed on the brakes. They didn't talk much after that.

It was dark by the time they finally pulled up to the house. So dark that Bridget realized that the power was out. Isabelle and Kevin were sitting on the porch playing cards by candlelight.

"The electric company says there're no outages in the area," said Isabelle, "so it's something here at the house."

"The electrician's coming first thing in the morning," Kevin said.

Bridget had not completely loved being back in her New York apartment, and she felt funny being back at the house so soon, especially in a blackout. She felt in limbo, like she didn't quite belong anywhere.

She got her phone and turned on the flashlight. "I hope no one minds," she said, "but I think I'll turn in."

As she walked to her room in the dark, she heard Oscar say, "Guess who got weed?" and the three of them cheered.

Bridget woke up the next morning to find the power was back on. She went to the kitchen and felt a sudden urge to bake something, to have the whole house smell like butter and cinnamon. She looked in the fridge to see what she had to work with and found blueberries and eggs. Flour, baking powder, and sugar in the pantry. She turned on the oven, hoping she could finish a batch of muffins before the power went out again.

The house was getting a "heavy up" of the electrical panel that day (which meant the electrician had arrived at seven in the morning to start messing with the fuse box), and the skylights were being resealed (which meant a friend of Kevin's was up on her roof). And thanks to Kevin's barn expert, a slightly graying Yale-educated man named Elliot, she was having four windows torn out of the barn and replaced because, he'd pointed out, the frames had leaked for over a decade and rotted. While the muffins were baking, she went outside to take a look at the progress. As soon as she opened the door and stepped out into another hot, cloudless morning, she heard splashing and saw that Isabelle and Kevin were in bathing suits, wrestling on the floating dock in the middle of the pond. Isabelle was shrieking.

"I wouldn't do that," Bridget warned. "I've seen a snapping turtle in there, a big one."

"We're pulling out the sedge grass, trying to get it under control," Kevin called back, warding off Isabelle's attempts to grab his arms. "It can take over your whole pond." There was a pile of wet, soggy weeds on the dock with them, and Kevin pointed to show Bridget the edge of the pond, where more of the tall grass was growing. As soon as his back was turned, Isabelle pushed him in.

Kevin emerged from the water, shaking his wet hair out of his face, and pulled himself up onto the dock in one easy movement.

Isabelle was laughing, keenly aware that she was going to get pushed in next. "But the snapping turtle," Isabelle yelled as Kevin picked her up and held her over the water. He didn't drop her in, setting her back on her feet instead; Bridget found that act to be gentlemanly.

"Hey, Mom," Isabelle called out. "Did you see the huge package you got yesterday? It's in the living room."

Bridget went back inside and saw that Isabelle wasn't kidding. She pushed the enormous box into the hallway where she sat on the floor with a pair of scissors to open it. Inside were three fancier gift boxes, all embossed with the words "LODENFREY, Seit 1842." Before Bridget opened the first, she read the enclosed, handwritten note: *My dearest Bridget, Here is something special for you to wear to our Hochzeit. Looking forward to seeing you and your sister, to meeting your children, and to being part of Edward's life, forever. With love, Lottie.*

Bridget lifted the lid on the first of the three boxes and pulled back a layer of white paper. Under the tissue was a traditional German dirndl, much like the one Lottie had given her when she was a girl. This one was a beautiful dark gray, intricately embroidered and layered with a navy silk apron. There were fasteners across the bodice that were hand-sewn. The dress was gorgeous, yes. But it looked like a costume. She opened the next box, which contained the same dress but with a forest green apron. And on opening the third, Bridget could not contain her laughter. It held a pair of leather pants, like the kind men wore to the Oktoberfest. The whole family was going to attend Edward's wedding looking like the Von Trapp Family Singers.

Bridget picked up her phone and called Gwen in New York.

"Marge just told me you were here in the city yesterday," Gwen said. "You didn't even say hi?"

"I was barely there for a whole day," Bridget said. "Did you get a package from Lottie?"

"Oh, *that*," she said with disdain. "I'm not wearing it."

"I don't think we have a choice." Bridget remembered how insistent Lottie could be. "We'll hurt her feelings. She must have gone to a lot of trouble."

"I already bought a Carolina Herrera for you and an Elie Saab for me. If you'd let me know you were here, you could have come over to try it on."

Bridget was touched. "That was nice of you." On the outside of the shipping box, taped under a plastic seal, there was a customs form and the receipt. Bridget opened it and gasped. "Lottie spent a fortune on all of this."

"I'm still not wearing it."

"Oscar's vest alone cost eight hundred dollars. Or euros, I guess. The dresses were three thousand, not including the shirts."

"Still," said Gwen. "It's not happening."

"What color is your apron?"

"It comes with an *apron*?" Gwen asked, sounding appalled. "What am I, a hausfrau?" There was a pause. "Burgundy."

"We're wearing them," said Bridget. "It was a kind gesture. And we don't want to start this relationship with a family rift. Who cares what we look like?"

"*I* care," said Gwen. "We're adult women, not flower girls, and I find this very manipulative and controlling."

"She's a bride," said Bridget. "Brides are always manipulative and controlling."

"I wasn't," said Gwen.

"Yes, you were," said Bridget. "From the pale pink dyed shoes I had to wear to the headbands with bows, you were very . . . in charge."

"I was young, and that was the mid-'90s," said Gwen. "What's Lottie's excuse? That she's almost *in* her mid-nineties?" There was a long pause. "Actually," she said, apparently giving her dress another look, "they're very well tailored. I'll think about it, but I won't button the shirt all the way up to my throat."

"Of course not," said Bridget, holding the dress to her chest. "Aren't dirndls supposed to be sexy?"

"I'll call you back after I try it on," Gwen said and hung up the phone.

At the bottom of the stairs, Bridget yelled to Oscar.

"Yeah?" he said.

"Come down, I have to show you something."

The dogs arrived first, followed by Oscar in his boxers. He came into the living room, took one look at the suede pants draped over the couch, and started laughing. "What is that," he said, "my Halloween costume?"

"It's your groomsman outfit. No, Bear," she said sharply, pushing the dog away from the boxes before he could drool all over the silk.

Oscar was holding up the long socks that came with his outfit. "You have got to be fucking kidding me. Whose idea was this? I'm going to look like I've joined the Hitler Youth."

Bridget was afraid he was right. "I know you're a grown-up, and you can say no, but I think we should just be agreeable, regardless of how ridiculous we'll look."

Oscar studied the thick, heavy leather. "Holy shit, I'm trying it on." As he headed to the powder room, carrying the embroidered shirt, the leather knickers, the linen vest, and, yes, even the hat, he said, "Something smells good, like cookies."

He closed the door to the bathroom, and Bridget went to check on the muffins. They were puffed up but too pale, needing a few more minutes.

The dogs ran off and started barking in the entry. Bridget followed them and looked out the window to see a car coming up the driveway. *Never a moment's peace*, she thought. It was a Ford Expedition, shiny and black, with opaque windows.

The car stopped, and the driver, wearing a black suit, black tie, and sunglasses, got out and opened the door to the backseat.

Bridget instantly regretted her sloppy workout clothes when she saw Congressman Jackson Oakley step out of the car, followed by darling Matt.

Bridget ran to the bathroom door and said, over the loud yelping of the dogs, "It's Matt! He's here!"

Hadley and Bear expressed less alarm and more joy as soon as they recognized Matt. Bridget opened the front door and went outside to greet her son-in-law with a reserved hug, but the dogs, showing no restraint, knocked Matt over in their excitement. He sat on the ground, letting them jump and drool all over him. Jackson, his suit pressed, his little congressional pin shining from his blazer lapel, took a step out of the fray and watched from the sidelines. Bridget introduced herself to the congressman ("Welcome, please don't mind the guinea hens") and invited them in, apologizing for the cardboard boxes, one of which Eliza had now claimed for her own, while Congressman Oakley ("Please, call me Jackson") was complimenting Bridget on her property.

"It's beautiful up here," he said. "And that barn! I love old New England farms."

Bridget, amazed by the good timing of her desire to bake, took the hot muffins out of the oven and offered them one. "They may need to cool for a minute," she said.

Bridget poured them coffee, while Matt, who was antsier than usual, said, "Is Oscar even here?" He looked as though his parking meter were about to expire. How many times had Matt sat leisurely at Bridget's kitchen table in pajamas and bare feet, either on the phone with his mom or reading the *Washington Post*, helping himself to whatever he wanted in the kitchen? Seeing him there, formal and reserved, turning down a freshly baked muffin, was a hard transition for Bridget and made her think something terrible was about to happen.

"He needs to stop avoiding me."

Remembering that she herself had hung up on Matt only yesterday made Bridget blush.

"We came all the way here to tell him something," Matt said, "something very important."

That sounded ominous. She mustered a bitter smile and said, "I'll go see what's keeping him."

But before she could go, Oscar called out, "Whoa, I look fucking *awesome*!" He came into the kitchen yodeling loudly in his tight new lederhosen that stopped just below his knees, leather straps over his shoulders, a feather in his cap.

Matt burst out laughing before Oscar had time to look up from buttoning his vest. Oscar's smile dropped when he saw the two men, and he turned and glared at Bridget. "Thanks for the heads-up."

"I thought you heard me," she said with an apologetic lift of her shoulders.

Isabelle, wearing nothing but her wet bathing suit, rushed in, clearly excited to find Jackson Oakley hanging out in the kitchen, which made sense because who *didn't* want to meet the young freshman congressman from New York? She took one look at Oscar, and whispered, "Dude, what are you wearing?" as she dripped pond water on the floor.

Matt came over to hug Isabelle, not caring that she got his suit damp.

There they all stood in a circle around the perimeter of the kitchen, looking at each other.

Well, this is awkward, thought Bridget. "Does your driver want a cup of coffee?" she said. "Or a bathroom maybe?"

And then, with a strange *thunk*, the electricity went out. This sudden shift didn't have the dramatic effect it might have had after dark, but nevertheless, it felt like the house had died: the noisy buzz of the refrigerator stopped, the coffeemaker shut off, and the fan blades slowed to a halt, the air growing still.

"The electrician said this might happen," Bridget explained. "Whatever a 'heavy up' is," she said, "I'm getting one."

No one said anything.

Finally, Jackson cleared his throat and smiled at her. "Have you considered adding solar panels?" he asked. "There are a lot of incentives offered for residential installation, and they'll reduce your electric bills by up to eighty percent." His cropped, dark hair allowed his dreamy eyes and long lashes to get all the attention; Bridget could certainly understand why Oscar was jealous.

"Good idea," Bridget said, thinking it was, to be fair, a very good idea. "I'll look into it."

Oscar fidgeted uncomfortably. The only sound was that of creaky footsteps on the roof, where Kevin's friend was caulking the skylights.

Matt walked over to stand next to Jackson, across from Oscar and Isabelle, like they were on two sides of a tennis court, with Bridget somehow stuck in the middle, as the net referee. *Here we go*, she thought. But before Matt could say anything, Jackson took a step forward.

"I've come here today," he began, as if addressing the nation, "to set the record straight once and for all, and I'm hoping that by saying this in front of you, Oscar, as well as your family, and even your overgrown, slobbering dogs, that you'll listen once and for all and stop the nonsense." He took off his blazer, hung it over the back of a bar stool, and began cuffing his sleeves. "There is nothing, and I mean absolutely nothing, going on between Matt and me. He's told you that our relationship is strictly professional, and yet you insist on being jealous and suspicious, and frankly, you're acting delusional." Under his shirt, Jackson's muscles flexed attractively. "If you continue with this absurd drama, I'm going to do something evil, like put you on a TSA watch list, or sic the IRS on you, or report you to DHS as a member of a neo-Nazi hate group, which"—he held up his phone and snapped a quick picture—"I have a feeling they'll have no problem believing."

Bridget noticed that Matt was smiling.

"I'm joking, of course," said Jackson, "but not really. Now that hotel charge that caused you to lose whatever's left of your mind was, as Matt already told you, booked for my sister. I'd be happy to give her a call right now and put you on the phone with her if you require confirmation."

Oscar shook his head.

"The point is," Jackson continued, "I don't want to lose Matt; he's smart, we work very well together, and I trust him. I consider him a friend. But I'll tell you exactly what I said to him: you have to drop this jealous, immature, paranoid bullshit because I can't have rumors swirling around my office about fraternization between me and an employee. And I can't have Matt acting all lovesick and pitiful around me; it's annoying and unproductive."

Oscar bit his lip and nodded. Bridget nodded as well; there was no arguing with the congressman.

"Honestly, Oscar, I said you were being stubborn," Isabelle said. "I knew Matt wasn't lying."

Bridget hadn't known it. "I'm sorry I hung up on you," she said.

"It's okay," said Matt.

"Now, I'm going back to DC," Jackson said, "because I actually have more important things to do than to patch up my staff's love lives. So, work it out. Now. And, Matt, I'll expect to see you in a few days, back to your normal self."

Jackson looked around the kitchen, giving them each his most winning campaign smile. When he got to Oscar, he dropped the smile. "Oscar," he said sternly, "stop being a . . . What did he call me in that message he left?" he asked Matt.

"An assclown," said Matt.

"Right. Knock it off, assclown. Understood?" He gave Oscar a warning look with a wag of his finger and then clapped him hard on the shoulder. Draping his jacket over his forearm, he said, "You look fetching in this alpine-kink getup, by the way. I didn't know that was your thing.

"Bridget," he said, shaking her hand, "you have a beautiful home. You know, I met your father at the Kennedy Center not too long ago. He congratulated me for going into public service and said, 'Never forget why you're there. Always keep in mind: "Some work of noble note may yet be done."' He said it was from a Tennyson poem, so I went home and printed it out, and I keep it on the bulletin board in my office."

Bridget was so taken with the congressman that she insisted on wrapping up muffins for him and his driver and walking him out to his car. And before he drove away, she invited him to the wedding.

20

Happy and relieved to get back to his routine, Will returned to the city on Metro North after spending over two uninterrupted weeks in the country with Emma. He and Hudson got a cab at Grand Central and cruised downtown with little traffic to delay them. When he opened the door to his fourth-floor apartment, which seemed especially stuffy and dark, he immediately turned on the air-conditioning unit, threw out all the old food in the fridge, and took out the trash. Hudson, looking sluggish and depressed, fell asleep on the couch.

Will was happy to be spending the next week riding the subway uptown and downtown, teaching lessons, doing a commercial gig at a recording studio, and all the while considering the big question: Should he and Bridget continue with Forsyth or let it die?

His first morning back, he woke up to sunshine streaming in his window. Hudson stood over Will on the bed, wagging his tail. As Will quickly dressed for their morning walk, the sound of hammering in the apartment above him began, loud and jarring. With Hudson on his leash, they went down the stairs and out the door, taking in the smell of sun-warmed garbage as they walked down Barrow Street. Will tried to see his neighborhood through Emma's eyes: It was prettiest in summer, leafy and bright, but the contrast to the country was admittedly brutal. The air was stale, the sidewalks were filthy, and the noises were an assault on his ears. He picked up Hudson's poop and dropped the bag in a trash can on the corner, adding to the countless other shit bags already in there.

On the next block, they walked into their regular coffee shop, and Will was surprised to see a brand-new face at the counter, in place of his usual barista. "Hello," Will said.

The young man frowned and wiped his hands on his apron. "You can't bring a dog in here."

"I'm getting my order to go," Will said. "Medium coffee." He pulled the money out of his pocket.

"I can't serve you with a dog, but if you tie him up outside—"

"Look," Will said, as if he were explaining some very basic technique to a student, "I come here all the time, like almost every day, and I order the same thing—"

"I've never seen you before."

"I've been away."

"It's a health code thing. A city violation. No pets." He pointed to a sign in the window.

"I understand that," said Will, "but I'm not tying my dog outside where anyone could steal him. Now if we stop talking, I'll be out the door in the exact amount of time it takes you to pour a cup of coffee."

"Next," the pimply barista said to the woman now standing behind him.

"You're not going to serve me? Seriously?" Will asked.

"Seriously," he said.

Will left the shop in a foul mood. He and Hudson walked back down the street and climbed the dingy, narrow stairs to their apartment. While Will fumbled with his keys by the door, Mitzy stepped into the hallway, closing her door behind her.

"I thought I heard you earlier," she said, bending over slowly and giving Hudson a pat on the head.

Will felt guilty; he'd abandoned Mitzy this summer. "You're up early," he said. "Would you believe I got refused service at my regular coffee place? Because of Hudson! What's happening to our neighborhood?"

She pointed to the ceiling, where the hammering and drilling continued. "Someone's putting in hardwood floors upstairs, and tearing up the kitchen and bathrooms, and they start working every day at the crack of dawn. You're lucky you've been away so much. Are you having a good summer?"

"I have a girlfriend," he said proudly, wishing Emma were beside him to be introduced. "She lives in Connecticut."

"That's inconvenient. Couldn't you find someone closer to home?"

"Apparently not," he said. "Do you need me to pick up anything for you today? I'm going out later."

Mitzy cracked her door open and pointed, showing him that somebody was sleeping uncomfortably on her small couch. "Ellen's visiting. She's taking me to the eye doctor today."

Will had met Mitzy's daughter many times over the years when she'd taken the train down from Boston. "Are you getting new glasses?" he asked.

"I have cataracts," she said. "I'm having surgery next month, only the left eye for now. Tell me about the girl."

"I'll introduce you, if she visits," he said.

"If? Don't you mean when?"

"I hope so." The deal-breaker they'd joked about didn't *have* to be such a big problem, thought Will, as long as spending weekends together now and then was enough for them. "Let me know when you're having your cataracts removed. I'll be coming and going this summer, but if you tell me the date, I can plan around it and take you to the doctor."

Mitzy rubbed his arm. "It's all right. Ellen's coming to stay with me for the whole week of the surgery, but thank you."

"You know, if I'm away . . ." He didn't want to complete the thought but felt compelled to. "Ellen could stay in my apartment. Would that help?"

"Bless you, Will," Ellen called from the couch. "That would be amazing."

Will did not like the idea of having anyone, even a responsible adult like Ellen, in his apartment, but he also couldn't imagine her having to sleep on a hard Victorian sofa for a week.

"No problem," he called back. "I'll drop off a key."

"You're a saint," Ellen said. "My back says thank you."

Mitzy blew him a kiss and went back in her apartment, and Will went in his, turning on music, the same recording of the Mendelssohn piano trio that he'd heard at Edward's house, hoping it would distract from the construction noises upstairs. He made a pot of coffee and sat on the couch with his iPad. Checking his email, he saw that the brand lady Bridget hired in the spring had just sent them a new logo, and it was fantastic—so fantastic, in fact, that it made the idea of killing the trio ridiculous. She'd sent a few different color options, and Will flipped through them on his iPad, trying to decide which he liked best. He forwarded the files to Brendan so he could incorporate the logo into the website he was designing.

He had also received an email from Jackie with a PDF of *Synchronicity*. Turning off the music, he sat at his table with a few sheets of composition paper and a pencil, analyzing the piece and deciding that the soprano melody would work beautifully for violin. Of course, he thought bitterly, Gavin would be the one stepping in to play the best part.

They'd get some press playing with Gavin at the party, but Will was sorry he'd ever reopened the door to him; if he could ship Gavin off to Australia again, he thought he might do it. Then he chastised himself for being as insecure and envious as he had been when he was young.

Maybe the kids would like Gavin. Bridget had always liked him. If the whole family decided to welcome Gavin with open arms, would Will get pushed out of the circle?

His phone pinged, and he saw a message from Brendan: *Dude you're live.*

Will went to Forsyth3.com, ready to be wowed, and there it was: their new website. Brendan had put the logo on the home page, and the page design looked neat and professional, but other than that, the website fell short. It wasn't Brendan's fault. He couldn't do anything to fix the "About Us" page that had a big white space where Caroline's picture should have been. Nor was it his fault that the page labeled "Events" was completely blank. There was a "Gallery," but every photo featured a violinist from their past. There was nothing to indicate the trio's bright future or relevance to today's music scene, and the whole site felt disappointing. Will decided not to forward the link to Bridget.

The constant banging sounds from the construction over his head were unbearable. After gathering some paperwork (his birth certificate, Social Security card, and proof of residency), he left Hudson in the apartment and took the 1 train downtown to Rector Street to the DMV, where he took the written driver's test with no preparation; common sense prevailed, and he passed. He had only two steps left to complete the process of becoming a licensed driver: a five-hour course and a road test. The class he would take that week. The road test would have to be scheduled. If he wanted to spend more time with Emma in the country, he would need a license.

With his temporary learner's permit in his wallet, he took the subway home and sat down at his piano to work on the arrangement of Edward's piece, wondering why he was feeling so *blah*. He was home, back in the city where he belonged. He had interesting work to do. He was spending a summer day in his comfortable apartment with his beloved dog. He had lessons to teach that afternoon. The next day he was finally scheduled for the session at a recording studio to play piano for the heinous country song "About You and I." This was his life. So why did he feel lost and alone?

He got his phone and texted Emma: *Miss you, babe.*

Emma answered with a picture of her hand resting on her lovely stomach, fingertips just under the lacy waist of her thong. Beside her on the mattress, there was an empty space she was saving for him.

AUGUST

21

Returning to Juliette and Danny after a trip, violin case in one hand and suitcase in the other, always gave Gavin the feeling that everything was right in the world. He loved to take his key from his pocket, turn the lock on the door to his perfect bungalow, and breathe in the familiar smell of home. Danny would run to the door and hug his knees, and Juliette would tell him everything he'd missed while he was away. He loved his bed, his terrace, and his walk-in closet. The carpet in the bedroom, the marble in the kitchen. His wife and his son. Everything about his life with Juliette made him know where he belonged.

When he came home from Germany last month, however, he found himself rejected by the source of all that comfort. One night about a week after he arrived, Danny was tucked in bed, and he and Juliette went outside to sit on their terrace. He finally decided that now was the moment to tell her. He started at the beginning, went all the way through the saga with Bridget and their night of passion, and ended with his most recent communication with Will. When he was done, he realized that Juliette was glaring at him.

"Are you fucking kidding me?" she said. "Are you some kind of sadist? Why are you telling me this?"

Gavin was bewildered. "You said the truth should come out," he said, "and 'secrets damage the soul.' I thought you'd be proud of me for telling you."

She was sitting in a position that was completely closed off to him: arms folded, legs crossed, and eyes squinted. "Why *now*?" she asked. "You've kept this hidden for twenty-something years?"

"I think," he said, trying to understand himself, "that I wasn't able emotionally to process what happened. I wasn't ready to be a father, not until Danny came along. And now that I've heard from Will, and Bridget by extension, it's like my past and my present are on a collision course." He thought she would like a metaphor. "And I'd like the pending collision to be . . . unharmful to all involved."

"The hell are you talking about?"

He'd never seen her angry like this before. He found that her temper was—only a little and not in a disrespectful way—turning him on.

"What do they want from you?" she asked.

"They've asked me to perform with them a few times this fall," he said.

She got up and started pacing around the outdoor table, not an unfamiliar act in their household since Juliette believed that most meals should be eaten in motion. "You're not entering into *any* kind of arrangement with them," she said, "especially since we don't even know what she's after."

"I don't think she's *after* any—"

"She could sue you for past child support."

"This is Bridget *Stratton* we're talking about," said Gavin with a chuckle. "I hardly think she needs the money."

"You can't take this so lightly. Why didn't *she* get in touch with you? Why is she having Will be the messenger? It's all very shady. I think we should hire a lawyer."

Gavin had no intention of hiring a lawyer, and he told her so. Juliette accused him of being naive.

"There's more," he said.

Juliette sat back down again, humming to herself with her eyes closed.

"They've invited me to play a piece with them at Edward Stratton's wedding at the end of the summer. It's a piece written by Edward himself, arranged by Will for piano trio. I can see by the face that you're making now that you hate the idea, but this invitation is an honor."

"You're not going."

Gavin and Juliette were very much equal partners. So he simply looked at her and said, "Yes, love, I am going and already told Will I'd be there the day before to rehearse the piece."

"With Bridget?"

"Of course with Bridget."

They were equals, so Juliette stared back at him and said, "Then I'm coming, too. You are not having some fucked-up, complicated reunion—"

"Fine, come."

"Yeah, it's fine, you bet it's fine, because if you're going to see these people, then you're going to have your family present."

"Well," he said, "technically speaking, if the twins are my kids, they're also my family."

Juliette—and this was a first—stormed away into the house and slammed a door.

Gavin wanted to make it up to her, to apologize for having kept a secret (or maybe for having told her a secret—he couldn't tell which one had made her angrier), so as part of the trip east, he planned a romantic vacation for the two of them. Two weeks on Cape Cod, alone together, would be the perfect way to get in the right frame of mind before they went to Bridget's house to face the music, as it were. It would have been nice, he was sure of it. But Juliette insisted on adding to their itinerary a weeklong visit to an aunt in Rhode Island. And then she insisted they bring Danny along for the whole trip.

To travel with a young child is to experience hell on earth. Gavin and Juliette learned this the hard way. The flight from Los Angeles was a seven-hour battle of wrangling Danny into his seat and making him stay there for the duration of the bumpy flight. Picking up the rental car took almost an hour, and since Danny had barely eaten all day, Juliette broke her junk-food rule and got him a granola bar out of a vending machine. Danny threw it up all over the Avis parking lot.

The car was not the SUV Gavin had requested, but rather an economy-size hatchback. Gavin carefully stood his violin case on the floor of the backseat, padding it in such a way that it wouldn't tip over no matter what happened or how quickly he accelerated or braked. This was a good move, as it turned out, because the drive from Logan Airport to the Chatham Bars Inn on Cape Cod, which Gavin had imagined would be a short jaunt down the Massachusetts coast, was a clusterfuck of traffic jams, bathroom stops, crying, screaming, and one bout of diarrhea. The air conditioner stopped working about an hour in. As Juliette was jabbing at the climate-control buttons, sweat started to run down Gavin's back. By the time they were out of the worst of the Boston tunnels and bridges and lane closings, Danny started hollering. They pulled off the highway and picked up milk-shakes at Wendy's, the only thing they could find to calm him down. Ten minutes later, he was crying again.

"What *now*?" Gavin snapped.

"Don't ask me, ask him," said Juliette with a bitchy edge to her voice. "You undermine his autonomy when you act like he can't speak for himself."

"I can't comfort him and drive at the same time," said Gavin.

"Just admit it, you expect me to do *everything*." She turned around. "Danny, sweetie, are you too warm?"

"He'd better be on fire making noises like that. If you see a CVS, I'm stopping."

"What for?"

"Earplugs," said Gavin.

"Very funny."

Gavin wasn't joking. "I'm a musician, and he's doing actual damage to my ears."

"Oh, boo-hoo," said Juliette, miming a baby wiping her eyes.

Gavin heard a loud, violent thump in the backseat, a sound that in Gavin's mind sounded exactly like Danny's fat foot kicking the back of his Stradivarius case. "What was that?" He reached his hand behind him to make sure his violin was safe.

"Watch the road," Juliette yelled.

He heard the thump again and swerved off at an exit while simultaneously holding on to Danny's feet to keep them from kicking. He thought Juliette might do something to help, but she just sat there, looking out the window. He parked the car at a gas station and turned around in his seat to check on his violin, stretching Danny's right leg out to see how far it could reach. Juliette unclicked her seat belt, opened the car door in a huff, and stomped around to the driver side of the car. "Out," she said through the window. "You babysit your precious violin, and I'll drive."

"Good idea," he said, getting out of the car.

Danny was still sniveling in his booster.

Gavin walked around to the other side of the car, and before he got back in, he took his violin case and then sat in the passenger seat, hugging it to his chest.

Juliette pulled out of the parking lot and got back on the highway as Danny kicked the back of his seat, knocking Gavin's chin into the hard case.

"I don't see why Danny couldn't stay with your mother," Gavin whispered. "This is *so* not the trip I had in mind for us. Maybe we should go home."

"We can't," said Juliette, "because *somebody* knocked up his college sweetheart—"

"I told you, she wasn't my college sweetheart." He thought they'd been through this already. "I just really wanted her to be."

Juliette stepped down hard on the gas, and they sped along the highway at a nice clip. For a brief, lovely moment, the only sound was Danny singing a song to himself. It was sweet and quiet, a gentle cooing. Then, the moment Gavin started to relax and try to enjoy the ride, Danny lobbed his chocolate Frosty onto the dashboard. Gavin hugged his violin tighter.

Juliette turned on the wipers, which did a good job getting the smashed bugs off the outside of the windshield but did absolutely nothing for the milkshake running down the inside. Gavin looked for a napkin in the glove compartment, thinking that if he and Juliette were in a movie, they would find this situation funny; they would see the mess dripping and the wipers wiping and burst out laughing.

Neither of them laughed; Danny was wrecking everything.

———◆———

After four hours in the car, they reached their destination, an elegant resort on the beach. The bellhop carried their luggage to the room and demonstrated how to work the remote control for the television. Danny, who had never been allowed to watch TV, spotted a character on the screen named "SpongeBob" (who, Gavin came to learn, lives in a pineapple under the sea), and thus began a family fight that got so noisy, someone walking on the beach went to the front desk to report a domestic dispute.

Although he demanded food at all hours, Danny never wanted

what was offered. Gavin and Juliette took turns chasing him around restaurants, forcing him into high chairs, and apologizing to people at neighboring tables for his behavior. Other daily activities included making sure that Danny didn't fall down stairs, get sand in his eyes, poop in the swimming pool, or drown in the Atlantic. His bathing suit chafed his ass, his sunblock stung his face, and he lost his favorite beach toy in the surf. And just when Gavin thought things couldn't get any worse, Danny stopped sleeping.

Three days into the trip, and they hadn't had sex even one time, nor were they reading by the ocean or enjoying a romantic harbor cruise to watch the seals. Nor did they team up and deal with Danny together, bonding over a common enemy, which might have offered some consolation. Danny, who had been their joint cause, who had brought them so close together as a couple, set their nerves on edge and drove a wedge between them. They bickered constantly and over everything. Who was this woman with the scraggly eyebrows and the mean tone to her voice? Gavin wondered. He missed his wife, longed for their well-regulated life in LA, her hands on his face, a gesture that, for some reason, never failed to put him in the mood.

Through it all, he was consumed with thoughts of seeing Bridget, her children, and Will. Every time he took off his baseball cap and ran his hand over his head, hairs came loose in his fingers. He would shake his hand and watch the gray strands float to the ground.

In the late afternoon on the fifth long day of their trip, Juliette made a spa appointment for herself without so much as consulting Gavin, telling him he was "on duty" all afternoon while she got a massage and a facial. She did not suggest reciprocating the next day.

"What do I do with him all afternoon?"

"Figure it out," she said, putting on her sunglasses and walking out of the hotel room.

Gavin talked to the concierge, who came up with a swell idea: putt-putt golf. There was a course not too far from the resort that boasted waterfalls, caves, lighthouses, and pirate ships. Gavin was sure this outing was going to be a winner. He imagined coming back to the hotel and gloating about it to Juliette. He and Danny headed off happily in the car together in matching salmon-colored Bermuda shorts. Gavin hadn't realized, however, how difficult putt-putt would actually be for a little kid. Danny smacked the ball with his club over and over and over, missing the goddamned hole every time and then getting screaming mad about it. He was so slow, the players started to pile up behind them, and Danny refused to let Gavin cheat on his behalf. They finally gave up on the seventh hole and got ice cream.

Sitting at a picnic table with a soft-serve cone that was melting rapidly and dripping all over his shirt and shoes, Danny seemed happy for the first time all day. He was a cute kid when he wasn't howling. Gavin reached over and patted his son's head, just as Danny's soggy sugar cone squashed and crumbled in his little fist, sending his ice cream to the concrete patio.

Ten minutes later Gavin had calmed Danny down and was getting him into his car seat when his cell phone rang.

"Gavin, old friend," said a deep voice with an upper-crust British accent. "Nicholas Donahue here."

"Nicholas, hey, how's it going?" He had meant to call Nicholas early in the summer after he ran into Miriam, but he'd never gotten around to it.

"I heard you're on the East Coast. Edward Stratton tells me you're attending his wedding."

"That's right," Gavin said. "I'll be playing actually. But don't mention that to Edward. Apparently, it's supposed to be a surprise."

"How thrilling. Which piece?"

"It's called *Synchronicity*, one of his earliest compositions."

"I wonder if I can get my hands on a score," Nicholas said, more to himself, it seemed, than to Gavin. "I'll be going to the wedding as well. And I was calling to see if there's any chance you could stick around for a day or two after the big event and come by my cottage in the Berkshires? You'd be welcome to stay with me, of course. I've rented this place on a lake, you see, while I'm writing a book on Edward, and I'd love to get your insights if you'd be willing to make the trip."

Gavin liked this idea very much. Anything to get him out of this miserable family trip. Anything to get out of the weeklong visit with Juliette's aunt in Providence. "Actually," he said, "what if I visited the week *before* the event? Would that work?" Maybe, he thought optimistically, he could go by himself. Rent a second car for this last-minute, work-related excursion and meet back up with Juliette and Danny just before the wedding. "I'm on the Cape right now for a vacation."

"Perfect," Nicholas said. "Let me know."

"I have to check with my wife, Juliette. We're here with our son."

There was a lengthy pause that made Gavin wonder if Nicholas was hesitating over the idea of having them all show up.

"But I'd likely come alone."

"There's plenty of room here," Nicholas said graciously. "Honestly, I'm rattling around all by myself."

"I'll figure out the details, and I'll call you back tonight. Most likely, I'll be on my own."

"Lovely," said Nicholas cheerfully. "I'll be looking forward to it."

As Gavin drove back to the resort, Danny fell sound asleep, giving him a moment of peace. A few days with Nicholas, Gavin hoped, could provide all kinds of insight into Bridget's family and might even shed some light on why Gavin was being included in the wedding in such an important way. Had Bridget had a change of heart about him?

And how, he wondered, could he best broach the topic with Juliette?

22

August was hot and dry; the ponds were low, the grass was brown, and Bridget's yard did not have the youthful beauty of early summer. It looked tired.

Bridget, on the other hand, was invigorated. Isabelle must have noticed how much more time she was spending alone in the living room with her cello and was careful never to interrupt. Unfortunately, nothing could be done about the other distractions; Bridget just had to play through them. She had a team of people helping whip her once-neglected house into shape, and it was noisy all the time. Chain saws were chopping down trees and cutting off limbs, and hammers were pounding new raw shingles onto the porch roof. Elliot, who Kevin had failed to mention was an actual architect, had another set of workers in the barn who were painstakingly sanding down, bleaching, and sealing the old floorboards. Eventually, he told her, they would whitewash the walls, replace the hardware on all the windows, and paint the door a beautiful muted red. Elliot had brought over paint swatches, all of which looked identical to her, and he explained how each red complemented, in its own way, the style and age of the structure. They'd finally chosen one. Thank God, Bridget thought, they weren't in a hurry to get the project done.

It was already hot this early in the day, and from the spot where Bridget was sitting on the floor of the bedroom, she had a good view of the barn. Having practiced for three hours, she was now confronting a mountain of clothes she'd pulled out of her dresser drawers, systematically sorting them into piles: to keep, to trash, and to give away. It was the discovery of a *nursing* bra in the back of her top drawer that had launched this particular cleanup of her bedroom. She'd found old moth-eaten sweaters, dozens of single socks, ratty T-shirts the mice had chewed, and jeans that, sadly, no longer fit and didn't have any intention of doing so in the future.

As she went through the pile of clothes, she suddenly missed having Oscar's dogs around. Normally during an activity like this one, they would have barged clumsily into her room for a visit, curious to know what she was doing on the floor. Bear would have snuffled and drooled on the threadbare T-shirts, and Hadley would have wandered away with a lone ski sock in his mouth. Oscar and Matt were together in DC, which, she kept reminding herself, was a very, very, very good thing. But she felt, irrationally maybe, like she'd been cheated, that her summer with her son had been unfairly cut short by a whole month, even if it was for the best possible reason. Oscar had been gone for over a week, and Bridget was missing everything about him, from his shedding dogs to his cereal bowls on the kitchen counter to his bad jokes.

At least she still had Isabelle to keep her company—Isabelle, who was enjoying a home-improvement binge of her own, spending much of her time walking around the house with a gallon of shiny white trim paint and a brush, touching up all the door frames, chair rails, and crown molding. There were *Don't Touch!* signs taped to every window.

Once Bridget got to the bottom of her sort pile, she started to go through the clothes hanging in her closet. She found blazers from the '80s and overalls and denim skirts from the '90s. She had used this oversize closet as a dumping ground, accumulating stuff she should have gotten rid of in New York decades before. She took shirt after flannel shirt from their hangers, sundresses and tiered skirts, garments she would never wear anymore, and added them all to the growing pile for the charity clothing bin. By the time she was finished, there wasn't much left: some jeans and sweatshirts, a linen skirt, and a raincoat. Clothes she could fit into a single suitcase.

And there in the spacious closet, which she could now see needed a fresh coat of paint, hanging in all its embroidered glory, was the dress from Lottie. Isabelle had already tried on her dirndl, and it fit beautifully. She walked into the kitchen one morning, looking like a Bavarian milkmaid, and Kevin had lost his ability to speak at the sight of her. "Will you be my date at the wedding?" she'd asked him. Bridget smiled as Kevin opened his mouth, put his hand on his heart, and nodded.

Now it was Bridget's turn. Closing the door to her room, Bridget undressed, pulled the tissue from the sleeves of the blouse, and put it on first before stepping into the skirt and finally trying on the bodice, discovering right away, and quite miserably, that all the parts of the dress were a size too small. Her boobs spilled out of the blouse in a way that was sloppy rather than sexy, and the skirt squatted unflatteringly on her hips. The apron made her stomach look paunchy and the bodice was far too tight. *Shit*, Bridget thought. She could get it altered, she hoped—but where? She stared at her reflection, looking like she was backstage at a theater, playing dress-up in some skinny girl's costume.

Rather than take a brisk walk or do a set of sit-ups, both of which sounded like good ideas, Bridget hung the dress back up, put on loose jeans, and carried all the giveaway clothes out to her car.

Her confidence had taken a few hits recently. Bridget had enjoyed her lunch with Randall, but he hadn't bothered to contact her since then. Nor had he tried to kiss her when they'd said good-bye. Sure, she was living over two hours away, and yes, she'd told him she was thinking about moving to England, but they'd had a nice time together, hadn't they? And although she'd found the courage to submit her CV and application for the orchestra position in London, along with a cover letter that had struck just the right tone—amiable and professional—she hadn't heard anything back from them either, and it hurt her feelings. She worried they wouldn't even give her the chance to audition.

Early that afternoon, she went outside, stretching her back as she looked across the yard. There was no sign of Henry, who'd taken to disappearing for days at a time and wouldn't let Bridget near him anymore. In two short months, he'd gone feral, slinking away from anyone who approached, and Bridget had finally resorted to leaving food and water bowls in the garage to make sure he was eating. The idea of making him return to their cramped New York apartment was getting harder to imagine with each passing week. As she went looking for him—in the barn, in the garage, around the pond—she spotted him under a bush near the driveway, noticing with relief that his tick collar was still on. "Hi, Henry," she said, "good kitty." She held her hand out, fingers pinched together as though she were holding something enticing, a piece of turkey or a scrap of tuna. He took a step toward her, his whiskers twitching, but bolted away at the sound of Bridget's phone ringing in her pocket.

"You and Gwen were right," Jackie said before Bridget had even said hello. "They're *very* high-maintenance."

"Who?"

"The composers. The Russian woman is lactose-intolerant and gluten-free, and the Greek guy, who looks like a model, is allergic to down, and don't get me started on the French one, who already rearranged the furniture in his room and pretty much gave Marge a heart attack when he tried to move an antique dresser on his own. Mr. Stratton wants you to come for dinner."

Bridget gave up on Henry and walked out into the field. "You haven't exactly sold me on the idea of coming over."

Jackie paused and then said, "Did I mention the Greek composer is very handsome? And smart and funny. And the Russian one is . . ." Her voice trailed off, and Bridget heard Jackie sniffing.

"The Russian one's what? Are you okay?"

"Sorry, something smells bad. The Russian one is very weird."

Out of the corner of her eye, Bridget saw Henry dart from the row of bushes across to the barn, chasing a grasshopper or field mouse. "I shouldn't interfere on their first night," Bridget said. "Wouldn't my dad rather spend time with them alone, lecturing them on principles of Schenkerian analysis or something? Why would he want me around?"

"Because . . ." She paused and then whispered, "Mrs. Lang is here."

"Lottie! Since when?"

The idea that Lottie had kept her arrival a secret was odd and precisely the kind of thing Edward would do, demonstrating independence as if to prove a point.

"She got here an hour ago. She's like a movie star. She showed up with seven suitcases, a whole set of fancy Rimowa luggage." Jackie then whispered something completely incomprehensible.

"Say that again," said Bridget. "I can't hear you."

"Hang on," Jackie said. Bridget heard a door close, and then Jackie said in quiet voice, "She asked for her own bedroom."

"How proper," Bridget said. She looked up and saw Elliot coming out of the barn, wearing a pink button-down shirt tucked neatly into his jeans.

"Is that, you know, like, an old-age thing?" Jackie asked. "Also, her son has called her four times already."

"Why?"

"I don't know, but it sounded like she was fighting with him. Or maybe that's just how German sounds."

Elliot looked up and gave Bridget a wave. He had a kind, stubbly face that made her want to place her hand on his jaw. He was more attractive than Randall, but so soft-spoken, his voice made her sleepy. He was walking toward her now, pencil tucked behind one ear. "Hang on a sec, Jackie."

"Sorry," Elliot said as he approached. "We can talk later if you want."

"No, it's fine," said Bridget.

"I've been thinking about the best way to light the barn, aesthetically and practically, now that you've got power over there. But it depends somewhat on how you'll be using the space."

Bridget hadn't given that much thought. So far all she was trying to do was keep it from collapsing in on itself. "What are your thoughts?"

"I'm thinking rustic fixtures for the exterior of the barn," Elliot was saying, almost in a whisper, "and I happen to know a few shops that make really cool vintage ones. Sort of industrial chic."

"Nice," she said. "You want me to go look at them?"

"We could go together. Say, tomorrow? Or next week if that's better? No rush, of course."

Before Bridget could respond, she heard her name being called from far away, urgently, loudly. She remembered the phone in her hand and quickly put it to her ear. "Jackie, sorry. Elliot's here and—"

"Oh my God," Jackie said frantically. There was the sound of loud, high-pitched ringing in the background. "Marge, call 9-1-1!"

Bridget pressed the phone to her ear. "What? Is it my dad? Jackie!"

"It's the house," Jackie said and hung up the phone.

———◇———

The fire department sent two large trucks, one smaller one, an ambulance, and a police cruiser up the mountain to Edward's estate.

By the time Bridget arrived, Edward was in the driveway sitting up on a stretcher, with an oxygen mask over his face, and there was Lottie beside him, holding his hand as she leaned over to talk to him.

Bridget ran to them before even finding out what was happening, noticing with relief that Lottie seemed perfectly calm. Her linen pants looked like they were fresh off the rack, barely rumpled, although she had probably been wearing them since getting on the plane in Munich early that morning. Her hair was silver and perfectly in place, and she was wearing her signature bold red lipstick.

"What a welcome," said Bridget, hugging Lottie politely and kissing her dad on his sooty forehead. "Are you okay? What on earth happened?"

Lottie held Bridget's hands. "It vas a mishap," she said.

By the looks of things, "mishap" sounded like an absurd understatement. "Disaster" was more like it.

"How did the fire start?" asked Bridget.

"We haven't the faintest idea," said Lottie. "One moment we're having our coffee, I go off to unpack, and the next sing I know, fire everyvere." She raised her shoulders. "Vat can you do?"

"But I can't believe this," said Bridget. "And you just arrived. You should be resting after such a long trip, and instead . . ." Bridget gestured toward the flashing lights and the fire hoses.

"No, I never rest," said Lottie. "I don't believe in naps. And I hate to see everyone looking so glum. Here's the good news, darling, which I told your father: everysing can be fixed." She waved her hands as if performing a magic trick. "It only takes time and money, and the house vill be like new again." But she wasn't looking at the house at all; she was looking at Bridget, holding her hands up and out to her sides as if to inspect her. "You haven't changed a bit, do you know that? To me, you'll always be the eight-year-old girl in the Florence Eiseman dress, sitting on your father's lap. You look so like your mother, but I suppose you hear that all the time."

Bridget didn't hear that almost ever, not because it wasn't true but because her mother had been gone for so long, no one thought to draw the comparison.

There were shouts and the sound of a window breaking.

"So many memories of you. You vere such a dear little girl," Lottie said, ignoring the shattering glass. "I'm overjoyed to see you and to be here at last."

Bridget thought her attitude was remarkable.

As if reading Bridget's mind, Edward lowered the mask and said, "Isn't Lottie wonderful? I would be in despair if she weren't here."

Lottie smiled at him. "Leonardo da Vinci said, 'I love those who can smile in trouble,' so that's vat I try to do." Her phone rang, and she looked at the screen. "*Achhh*," she said, sounding like she was coughing up a hairball, "Hans, *noch einmal*— You remember Hans, *ja?*"

"How is he?"

"He vorries about me too much; it's getting on my nerves. He should spend more time sinking about his own problems." She gave Edward's hand a squeeze and walked off to take the call.

"What problems does Hans have?" Bridget asked her father.

"He's unhappy," Edward said with a cough.

"Are you okay?"

Edward nodded. "Go check on my scores and books."

Scores and books seemed the least of the problems, but Bridget nodded. "I'll be back."

The three composers were huddled together under a tree in the courtyard, watching the drama unfold. Bridget studied them, trying to determine which one of them had lit her father's house on fire.

298

Was it the stocky, dark-haired woman with wire-frame glasses, wearing a scarf around her neck in August, a sheath of papers under her arm? Or was it the tall, gorgeous, broad-shouldered boy, clutching his laptop to his barely buttoned linen shirt? Or could it have been the thin-lipped, dark-haired man in rubber sandals who was (aha!) smoking a cigarette with one hand and grasping at his thinning hair with the other? Bridget put her money on the smoker.

She went over to Jackie and Marge and whispered, "Did flip-flops over there light his curtains on fire?"

Marge, Bridget realized, was crying. Bridget put her arm around her.

"Edward's room got the worst of it," Marge said. "I put the composers in three rooms right above his, so who knows where it started. Thank God no one got hurt."

"How far did it spread?"

"We don't know," said Marge. "The alarm went off, and Jackie and I got everyone out. We all ran outside and waited for the trucks." Marge dabbed at her eyes with a dishcloth.

"I'm so glad you're okay," Bridget said, the thought flashing through her mind that someone could have actually died in this accident.

"Those firemen are brutes," said Jackie. "They're breaking the windows on purpose—"

"—and they're wearing their boots in the house," added Marge.

"At least they're here, getting the job done," Bridget said.

As if on cue, the firemen came sauntering out the front door, hoses trailing limply behind them. One of them, the last to emerge, was approaching them with muscular purpose, striding across the courtyard with his helmet straps loose and a heavy axe in his right hand. His chiseled superhero face was perfectly dappled in soot, and the only thing missing from this image was a golden retriever puppy tucked under his arm. Were his shoulders really that broad, or was it an illusion caused by his uniform? And what was it about the way his suspenders looped down next to his thighs that made him look so sexy, like the rest of his clothes might accidentally slide off?

Bridget, Jackie, and Marge all took a few steps toward him.

"We're done here," he said. He took off his helmet and ran his fingers through his lovely hair. Was it slightly gray, or was that ash? Both, she decided, as a plume of dust shimmered around his head like a halo. "You'll need the name of a good company that cleans up fire and water damage."

"How bad is it?" Bridget asked.

"You're lucky the fire was contained to the downstairs bedroom, hallway, and entry. I don't know for sure, but it looks like someone dropped a shirt or something over a halogen fixture."

He handed Bridget a swatch of burned material.

"Edward's cravat," sighed Marge.

"*Dad's?*" Bridget asked, but she knew the answer as soon as she saw the tiny scrap of blue-and-burgundy paisley fabric in the palm of her hand. It was Edward's. Edward's room. Edward's sconce. She apologized in her head to the thin-lipped smoker. "The rest of the house," Bridget said, "the library at the back, the bedrooms upstairs, everything else is okay? My father has music scores and books that are really valuable. And a piano . . ."

"So long as the items weren't downstairs on that side of the house"—and he pointed to Edward's wing—"they're likely fine. But not much in the master bedroom made it."

Bridget, with a lurching sickness, thought of the paintings. Her mother's paintings, the Turner and Gainsborough landscapes, were gone. That realization was especially painful, and Bridget realized she, too, was about to cry.

Her face must have shown her sense of loss because the fireman put his hand on her shoulder. "I know it's tough," he said, "but you got really lucky today. People over possessions, that's what I always say."

"Yes," said Bridget, trying to pull herself together. "Quite right."

He walked off to his truck, giving them a wink as he climbed in.

"I know he's got a point that we're all okay," said Jackie, "but if it was my nice house and all my fancy shit that got burned up, I'd lose my freaking mind."

———◇———

Bridget called Kevin as soon as the last fire truck headed down the mountain. He arrived within minutes with a group of guys who were now carrying an armoire and pedestal table, the only two pieces that survived with minimal damage, from the master bedroom into the living room, placing them on wood pallets to dry out, while Marge barked orders at them.

Finding a quiet place to talk wasn't easy, so Bridget went into the butler's pantry to call Gwen and tell her the news about the inferno and the arrival of Lottie and the three composers.

"*Thank God* everyone's okay," Gwen said for the third time.

"They're fine."

"And Lottie? What's she like? And don't be all diplomatic. I want the dirt."

Bridget was tempted to mention that Lottie was being irritatingly positive through this crisis but felt guilty saying something bitchy. She looked out to the back porch, where Lottie was pacing back and forth, gesturing as she talked into her phone. "Hans keeps calling and calling. I don't know what his problem is."

"Oh, brother. That seems so *Hans*, doesn't it? And I mean that in a bad way."

"It's like he doesn't trust us," Bridget said.

"Burning the house down probably didn't help our case. Is he going to sue us for negligence? Pain and suffering? I wouldn't put it past him."

Bridget decided not to mention the soaking-wet rugs and the burned antiques. And she couldn't bring herself to talk about the two paintings she loved, masterpieces, gone forever.

"You're sure that *Dad* started the fire?" Gwen asked. "He must be mortified to have done something so careless. How do we know it wasn't Lottie?"

"Lottie and Dad are sleeping in separate rooms."

There was a pause. "Why?"

"Who knows. Propriety? Romantic anticipation? Closet space? In any case, we've got all five bedrooms in use upstairs now. Dad had to move into Jackie's room, and Lottie's taken yours."

"*My* room?" she asked.

"Sorry."

Gwen sighed. "Sounds too chaotic. And what are we going to do about the elephant in the room?"

Bridget didn't know which elephant she was referring to. The paintings? The broken glass? Hans?

"Dad and Lottie obviously can't get married in a house that's half burned to the ground," Gwen said.

The wedding hadn't even entered Bridget's mind until then. "It only a quarter burned to the ground, but . . . I see your point."

They were quiet for a moment, Bridget wondering if they could move the whole event outdoors.

"There's an obvious solution," Gwen said.

"Find another venue. An inn?"

"An *inn*?" Gwen said, sounding appalled. "God, no, inns are so provincial. *You* host it."

Bridget started to laugh. "I hardly think my house is the kind of setting—"

"Not your house. Your barn. You fixed the roof already and got the floors refinished. You have that nice architect working on the walls and windows. It's a gorgeous place to have a wedding."

Bridget closed her eyes and tried to imagine Batshit Barn as a wedding venue. "Lottie would *not* want to get married in my barn." Looking out the window, Bridget could still see her talking on the phone.

"Don't be negative," Gwen said. "The barn is perfect. And it would go so well with those ridiculous dresses she sent us. I tried mine on, by the way, and I look very sexy, like Teri Garr in *Young Frankenstein*. 'Roll, roll, roll in zhe hay,'" she sang. "I can't think of a better place to wear a dress that shows *that* much cleavage—"

Bridget didn't feel like mentioning her own humiliating struggle with her dress, the hooks refusing to come within an inch of the eyes. "My barn's not ready—"

"Oh, come on. You've got three weeks: that's more than enough time to do some landscaping and lighting. Throw money at the problem. It'll be perfect. Marge already has a caterer and whatever else you need. It'll be a cinch."

Bridget had her doubts. "You haven't even seen the place. Can you come up?"

"The next few weeks are absolutely crazy for me," she said. "I'm interviewing Steve Martin."

Bridget barely even registered the impressive drop of another big name. "When you do come," she said, "you can stay in the loft at my house. It's too crowded over here."

"I don't want to displace Will," said Gwen.

"Will," Bridget said, feeling like so much between them was changing, "would be happy to stay with Emma when you're here."

"Lucky for me that Will fell in love with a local," said Gwen. "Synchronicity, am I right? Otherwise *I'd* be stuck in an inn."

Is he in love? Bridget wondered.

After they hung up, Bridget followed the sound of hammering into what was now the ruins of Edward's bedroom. She took in the sad sight, watching Kevin and his friends, who were nailing plywood over the broken window panes.

The rest of the house, oddly enough, was perfectly fine, and as she walked around, she thought that if it weren't for the smell of smoke in the air, she could have pretended nothing had happened.

The skittish composers (the Russian in a modest red polka dot one-piece and bathing cap, the Frenchman in tight belted swim trunks, and the Greek in a tiny royal blue Speedo) went to the pool. Bridget wondered what the musicians were talking to each other about as they paddled around. Would they divulge to people in the music world what had happened? Bridget could imagine the Russian woman gossiping at a cocktail party in a mean whisper: *One minute I'm working on my experimental opera, and next thing I know, my score almost went up in flames.* The Greek boy showing off to his peers with a judgmental tone: *If you ask me, the old man needs a babysitter.* And the Frenchman whining to his mentors with Sorbonnian privilege: *He could have killed me,* mon dieu! Was it too late to require them all to sign a nondisclosure agreement?

Edward, relieved that his library had been spared any damage, was there having coffee with Lottie and Marge.

"What happens now?" Jackie asked. She and Bridget were sitting on stools in the kitchen, eating Marge's chicken salad out of a Tupperware container. "Do you think the composers will decide to leave?" she said, sounding concerned.

Bridget looked up at her, wondering why that would be a bad thing.

"I mean, they just got here," Jackie said. "It would be a shame if they had to leave already. Mr. Stratton would be so disappointed."

The door swung open, and Marge came in, looking harried. "Edward wants to get a contractor in here right away."

"He can't," Bridget said. "Not with everyone staying here. Can you imagine how disruptive that would be?"

"They'll just have to endure a little background noise," Marge said. "I can imagine worse conditions."

Bridget thought the shock of the fire was keeping Marge from thinking clearly. "The floors need to be torn out, new drywall put in. Windows replaced. No one will be able to hear themselves think, much less write music. If he wants to fix everything, then he should cancel the retreat."

Marge scoffed. "He has no intention of canceling anything."

"I hope they stay," said Jackie. "Mr. Stratton could fix the house in the fall."

"Exactly," said Bridget. "What's the rush? Board up Edward's side of the house and put off the renovation until after the summer when everyone's left."

Marge was not amused. "I do not approve of postponing repairs," she said.

"I postponed repairs for twenty years," said Bridget, almost with a sense of pride. "The problems don't go anywhere, I can promise you that."

"I agree with Bridget," said Jackie. "Salvage the retreat."

"It's the Greek one, isn't it?" Marge asked her.

"Stavros?" said Jackie. "What about him?"

Marge, noticing their forks sticking out of the chicken salad container, brought them plates, napkins, and a proper spoon to serve themselves. "You're enamored."

"You can tell?" said Jackie. "Am I that obvious?"

Bridget smiled; Marge could be so perceptive.

"The urgency with which you swapped his down comforter with a synthetic-fill one was remarkable," said Marge, "and downright heroic."

"Well, I doubt any of the composers will stick around after this debacle," Bridget said.

Marge was still focused on Jackie. "In any case, we've got to put you somewhere tonight, and we're out of bedrooms."

"I could sleep in the pool house," Jackie suggested.

"You'd be scared to death out there," said Marge. "All those doors and windows facing the woods? No, you can stay with Bridget."

Bridget certainly wasn't expecting Marge to volunteer her house, but she didn't mind. "Sure," she said. "The upstairs is empty now that Oscar's gone."

"I don't want to impose," said Jackie. "How would I get back and forth—?"

"I'll arrange all that," said Marge. She straightened up suddenly. "And what about the wedding?" she said. "We've got a couple hundred people showing up here for a party in three weeks."

"We could have it outside," said Bridget.

"A tent's not elegant enough," said Marge. "High heels on grass? Bugs everywhere? And what if it rains? Absolutely not."

If that was her reaction to a tent, Bridget could only imagine her reaction to a Batshit Barn wedding.

"I can look into other venues in the area," said Jackie. "Country clubs or restaurants?"

"I think there are better options in the city," Marge said. "MoMA maybe. Or the Whitney."

"Isn't it too late for that?" Jackie asked. "Places like that will be booked already."

"Maybe Gwen knows someone who could help," said Marge. "I'll ask her."

"Actually," Bridget said casually, "Gwen was saying we should have the wedding . . . in the barn."

Marge looked confused. "What barn?" she said.

Bridget shrugged. "My barn?"

Marge suppressed a smile. "I don't want to hurt your feelings or anything, toots," she said, "but your place isn't— That wouldn't exactly be Edward's and Lottie's style. They want, you know, valet parking, champagne flutes in the foyer, not livestock wandering around."

"The sheep left ages ago. I have nice, newly finished floors, and I'm getting the walls whitewashed. I replaced all the broken windows and I even have electricity in there. And while it hasn't been tested yet, I don't think the roof leaks anymore."

Marge looked at her and then started to laugh.

"What?" said Bridget, feeling offended. "You haven't seen it."

"Edward and Lottie are expecting press," Jackie said, trying to make this point seem like a non sequitur. "I guess the *New York Times* is sending someone with a photographer."

"Look, I know my barn was a mess, but it's not anymore, and I don't know what other options we have." Bridget felt an inkling of excitement. "You've already got everything cued up, so send the caterer, the florist, and everyone else to my—"

"Emma's the florist," Marge said.

"Perfect," said Bridget, "she already knows where to find me. Send them all over to my place instead, and I'll make it work."

"Edward's going to say no," said Marge, shaking her head. "Lottie is most *certainly* going to say no. And I have serious doubts of my own."

"How can Lottie possibly object to a barn?" said Bridget with a laugh. "She's literally outfitting the whole family in costumes for a hoedown."

By the look on Jackie's and Marge's faces, Bridget could tell that Lottie was standing behind her. She was about to explain, apologize even, when Lottie smiled at her and said, "Exactly right, *Schatz*. The dirndl is traditional *Landhausmode*, inspired by country living. Now, vat is this you vere saying about a barn?"

Looking at Lottie all neat and tidy in her white ballet flats and smooth linen slacks, Bridget decided that Marge was probably right: Lottie would not appreciate what Batshit Barn had to offer.

That evening, Jackie arrived with her suitcase, apologizing for the intrusion and offering to help with anything in the house.

"It's great you're here," said Isabelle, who'd spent most of the afternoon with her head in a book. She was wearing jeans with an oversize flannel shirt that looked like it might belong to Kevin.

"No apologies," said Bridget. "Make yourself at home. We'll have dinner in about an hour."

"Kevin's coming, too," Isabelle said as she left with Jackie to get her settled in upstairs.

Bridget studied the contents of the fridge, which were abundant thanks to Isabelle and Kevin, who had made a trip to the farmers' market. She wished Will were there to cook with her; she missed him the whole time she was arranging cheeses and ham, a bowl of olives, and smoked salmon with little triangles of pumpernickel bread onto a board. She threw together a bowl of orecchiette with shrimp and pesto and made a salad with chopped tomatoes and arugula. She sliced up a baguette and put salted butter in a small stoneware crock. She opened the rosé and found a cold bottle of sparkling water. *Ta-da*, she thought, and then she set the table on the porch and lit the candles.

Jackie, Isabelle, and Kevin came in and saw the spread.

"Delicious," said Isabelle. "But what if moving forward, we change things up a bit. Try something completely different."

Rather than ask what Isabelle meant by that, Bridget got everyone seated and started passing the pasta and salad. Isabelle stood back up, as if to make a presentation.

"Please, Isabelle," said Bridget, "the pasta's getting cold."

"I'd like to introduce you all to *this*"—and she showed them the cover of a self-help book: *Ancient Practices, Modern Life*. It had a sunshine-yellow cover with a photo of a woman doing a pose of some kind, standing on one leg with her arms out in front of her, a bright red apple in the palm of her hand.

"I've decided," said Isabelle, "that for the rest of the summer, we should go on a health kick and follow the steps outlined in this book. It could be life-changing. All the alcohol we've been drinking will evaporate, the carbs and fat banished. Our brains will sharpen, and our bodies will say thank you. This book guarantees we'll notice a difference in wellness as early as the first week."

"Can we talk about this after dinner?" asked Bridget. She hated the word "wellness."

Isabelle sat down while maintaining her enthusiasm. "Sure. And we can start tomorrow, of course, after this awesome last supper of sorts. But I'm really excited about this program and think we should all get on board."

"What do we have to do?" asked Jackie, looking nervous.

"It's not a diet; it's a *lifestyle*," Isabelle explained, flipping through the book. "We drink yerba maté tea instead of coffee. We increase our movement and eat healthy, unprocessed foods, mostly nuts and berries, and for dinner we have salads made of raw vegetables and heirloom grains. There's a variation of yoga poses we'll practice every night before bed for strength and relaxation, and the television will never be turned on."

They all looked at each other.

"Starting tomorrow," Isabelle said again.

While Jackie, Bridget, and Kevin filled their plates, Isabelle read aloud from the preface of the book, which made claims about weight loss and brain function that sounded too good to be true. "You see," Isabelle said, "this book has the answer to all that ails us."

"And what if nothing's ailing me?" said Kevin, as earnest as a six-year-old asking for concrete details about the tooth fairy's job.

Bridget had a thing or two ailing her, so she listened while Isabelle told them about the author, Juliette Stark, a blond Californian with a PhD whose perfect skin in her picture on the cover revealed her good health and glowing happiness.

Isabelle went through the rules, which were insanely strict, saying the regimen was designed to boost metabolism and rid them of all manner of toxins. "We have to follow Juliette's program religiously, to the letter, or it doesn't work. It'll be so much more fun if we do this together."

Bridget was going to take a hard pass, and she was about to say so when Jackie said, "I could try. But do I have to give up tea at Mr. Stratton's?"

Isabelle flipped through the book. "You can't eat scones," she said, "or cookies, or anything with sugar, but tea's okay."

Jackie looked disappointed.

"I know how you feel," said Isabelle. "I won't be allowed to eat the muffins at the café where I work anymore. But it's a sacrifice I'm willing to make. What about you?" she asked Bridget. "Are you ready for a life-changing, mind-body makeover?"

It hadn't escaped Bridget's attention that summer would be coming to an end, and so far, she'd drunk gallons of rosé and eaten her weight in cheese, two things she would hate to give up. "Does it help with frayed nerves?" she asked.

"Mom," said Isabelle, "if you end up hosting the wedding, we'll all help get the barn ready."

The wedding wasn't the only thing making Bridget nervous. Waiting to hear back from the orchestra in London was painful. She almost wished she'd taken Randall up on his offer to make a call on her behalf, to give her some legitimacy.

"And anyway," Isabelle said, "Juliette Stark says"—and she read aloud—"'Expect to experience a significant reduction of stress levels.'"

"By eliminating all the foods I love to eat?" said Bridget.

"No, by walking, meditating, and doing humming exercises," Isabelle said. "She swears by them. Also we can't sit down when we eat."

"What do you mean?" said Jackie.

"We have to pace."

"And what's the science behind that?" Bridget asked, trying not to sound snarky.

Isabelle flipped the book open to the index and then found the answer in the text. "Juliette says, 'Sedentary eating leads to slower digestion, which leads to toxins lingering in your intestines and colon, which leads to cancer.' *Cancer!*"

"I don't think that's how . . . anything works," Bridget said.

"Whenever we want to eat something," Isabelle said, "we have to swing our arms and walk. We have to move whenever we're chewing, like we're nomads."

"Or cows," said Kevin, taking another serving of pasta.

"And another thing," said Isabelle, "Juliette says for the first week, we can't use cutlery. We eat everything with our hands."

"Like pizza?" Jackie asked hopefully.

"Only raw unprocessed foods. No meat, no sauces or dressings, and no dairy."

"This sounds too extreme," said Bridget, leaning back in her chair and feeling the waistband of her jeans digging into her stomach, "not to mention ridiculous."

"Juliette says there are all kinds of things that make us sick that we don't even know about. Even *secrets* can make us sick," said Isabelle, landing on a page. "Juliette says, 'Secrets damage the soul.' *What!* Do you think that's true?"

Yes, thought Bridget. That statement was, in fact, the first sensible thing Bridget had heard this Juliette person say. Maybe it was time to go on a health kick. Maybe she could get fit in the three weeks before the wedding. How else was she going to squeeze into that damn dirndl?

"Fine," said Bridget. "I'll do it."

23

Will's new hobby was categorizing every circumstance he encountered in a pro and con list in his head. As happy as he was to be in a relationship with Emma, he woke up one day at her house in the middle of August keenly aware that the con column of his life was growing uncomfortably long. He was, for example, having a tough time dealing with (1) the absence of a piano at Emma's house and (2) the presence of Ronaldo at same.

Summer was always disruptive to his schedule, but *never* had he rescheduled so many lessons or passed along so many studio gigs to friends, and as a result, he was almost (3) out of money. For the first time ever he was ashamed to admit he had (4) no retirement account. His chaotic and unpredictable life as a freelancer had always suited him because he was his own boss, making his own schedule, but at his age, with so little to show, he wondered if he could change course and find a real job.

That morning, he was sitting at Emma's kitchen table, finishing his arrangement of *Synchronicity*. This endeavor had turned out to be a challenge, and a very satisfying one. The piece, if he might say so himself, was turning out as well as the original. He hoped Edward would like it, but (5) what if he hated it?

Will needed to review his part of the piece, but without a piano, he was stuck. One look around Emma's little house, and it was obvious that there was no place he could ever put one. Not that he was planning on moving in with her, but—as he and Bridget had agreed—Will was giving his future his full attention and consideration. And in his pro column of his life, there was (1) Emma.

They'd rehashed their early marriages together, laughing at their youthful stupidity and confessing the things that shocked them most about their past behavior. For Will it was his unwillingness to back out of his engagement, even though he'd already decided to get a divorce. For Emma, it was her obsessive focus on the wedding band, the seating arrangements, and the venue, while giving very little thought to the man she'd chosen or the institution of marriage. "I became a florist in my twenties just so I could have some kind of deranged control over my centerpieces. I spent an absurd amount of money and never asked myself if what I wanted was a party or a husband. As it turned out, I'm a big fan of parties."

"And husbands?" Will asked.

"Not so much."

She was a woman after his own heart.

His coffee cup needed refilling, but to reach the kitchen, Will had to get past Ronaldo, who was now perched on the back of a wood chair, posing in a variety of threatening stances. To say they were coexisting badly would be an understatement. Will hated to admit it, but he was scared of the unpredictable, noisy bird, his sharp beak, his flappy wings, and his murderous, prehistoric-looking talons. It was impossible to concentrate with the incessant noises and imminent threat of attack. Will hugged the wall to keep as much distance as possible between him and the creature.

Checking the time, he closed the door to the kitchen, refilled his coffee, and called Rebecca Goodwin, head of the music department at the prestigious boarding school that was right down the street in town. Will gave her a summary of his background and explained that he was seeking a steadier teaching job, possibly in the area. After telling him a bit about the school, she informed him that there was nothing available for the coming academic year but gave him a few leads (other schools with fancy, romantic names like Hotchkiss and Choate Rosemary Hall, and even the conservatory at Bard College). In a moment of sheer opportunism, Will invited her to Edward Stratton's wedding so she could hear him play.

"Really?" said Rebecca, changing her tone. "Would it be all right if I bring my husband?"

Will didn't see why not. "Sure. Bridget Stratton and Gavin Glantz will be performing the piece with me."

There was a short pause. "You know, Will, it's possible something might open up here before the school year begins. You never know."

"Excellent," Will said. "There's a little confusion about the venue, but I'll get an invitation to you soon."

It hadn't occurred to him that the wedding could be an audition of sorts. After they hung up, Will made another call, having a similar conversation with the music chair at Bard. And then another with Hotchkiss. By the time he was done, he'd invited six more people.

He opened the back door to take Hudson out. It was a pleasure—one for the pro column—to take Hudson out into Emma's small yard in the morning, without even having to find the leash. It was so much easier than in New York, where he had to go down four flights of stairs, always remembering to bring a poop bag.

Hudson wandered around in the ground cover by the fence at the back of the yard, while Will sat in a wrought iron chair and enjoyed the sunshine. When they went back in the house, Will realized he'd left the back door open for no less than five minutes. For a heart-stopping moment, he thought Ronaldo might have escaped. He rushed back inside, relieved to see the kitchen door closed and Ronaldo perched in exactly the same place as before, displaying the same hostile body language.

"Phew," Will said to Hudson. "How would we have explained that?"

Ronaldo responded by sticking out his chest and flapping his wings aggressively at him.

"Dude, settle down," Will said. Keeping his eyes trained on Ronaldo, he sat on the floral couch and called Bridget.

"Hey."

"Hi," said Bridget.

"I need a piano and a printer and a favor."

"I need food," said Bridget, her voice faint. "Something really bad for me. Bacon and eggs. Are you back?"

"Yes. Let's go to the diner."

There was a long pause, and then Bridget sighed. "I can't."

"Why not?"

"Isabelle has me on a diet."

"What for?"

"Not a diet exactly. A whole— Never mind."

"Cock," squawked Ronaldo.

He could hear Bridget laughing. "I take it the bird hasn't warmed up to you."

"He keeps stabbing his beak in my direction, and he's got claws like . . . an evil antique bathtub."

"Do you need me to come rescue you?"

"Please. Do you think I can leave the beast loose in the house?"

"No," said Bridget.

Ronaldo flew across the room, swooping toward Will's head and then veering away. "How do I get him in his cage?"

"Maybe it's like dealing with a toddler."

"Meaning?"

"You remember, Will: be the boss, don't stoop to his level, but show kindness and understanding."

"Right," said Will. "I'm the boss."

"I'll be there in twenty minutes. Kindness and understanding," said Bridget. "And don't die."

Will hung up and looked at Ronaldo, who was on his special perch near his cage. As Will took one step toward him, Ronaldo spread his feathers out in all directions and then turned in a slow circle to show them off. "Yes, yes, you win," said Will. "You have a much better body, and Emma likes you more, okay? Now, can you stop being such a dick about it?"

Ronaldo screeched at him.

Kindness, Will thought. *Understanding.*

Will took a deep breath and approached Ronaldo again. Using a calm voice, higher than his usual pitch, he said, "Come on, now, there's room for both of us, don't you think? I mean, maybe not in this house, but in life?" He lowered himself onto the arm of the reading chair. Ronaldo eyed him skeptically.

Will held out his pointer finger. "You want scritches?" he asked, using the expression he'd heard Emma use. He gently touched Ronaldo, first on the side of his neck and then on his head, gently stroking his bright blue feathers while he whistled *Eine kleine Nachtmusik*.

Ronaldo bobbed his head and made a sound like a coo. Will put his hand out, and Ronaldo stepped onto it. Will didn't move, feeling the weight of him. "Hi," Will said, trying to mask his fear with a casual pose. They stayed there, Will too afraid to budge and Ronaldo watching him. After several minutes Will slowly stood up and held his hand out toward the cage. Ronaldo went inside all by himself, and Will closed the door gently behind him. "Thank you," Will said earnestly.

Ronaldo cawed back in a way that felt like a step backward, so

Will continued to whistle Mozart until he heard Bridget's car beep in the driveway. He picked up Emma's disco ball key chain and his backpack and went outside with Hudson, feeling mildly victorious. "The bird and I have bonded," he said, opening the back door for Hudson and helping him get his rear end into the car. He got in the passenger seat and put on his seat belt. "Finally. I think we really got somewhere today. I'm not saying we like each other or anything, but this was progress in our relationship."

It occurred to Will that his avian drama was a triviality compared to what Bridget had been dealing with. "How are your dad and Lottie doing?"

Bridget started to back out of the driveway. "Lottie seems to like my barn, so I'm proceeding as if I'm hosting."

"Will it be ready?"

"Ready enough." There was an angry, grumbling sound, loud enough that Will could hear it over the car engine. "I'm hungry," Bridget said, clutching her stomach.

"So eat something."

"No. It's my fifth day on the program, and the book says you adapt after six."

"You sound like you're in a cult."

"I'm so woozy." She ran her hand over her forehead.

"Wait," Will said. He got his learner's permit out of his wallet and showed it to her. "I'll drive. I need to practice for the road test anyway."

Bridget took the permit from him, smiled as she looked it over, and pushed him on his shoulder. "God, it's about time," she said, opening her car door.

They both got out of the car and walked past each other, Hudson watching them as they swapped places. Will adjusted his seat and mirror and pulled out onto the street, while Bridget buckled in and sat back, looking like she might pass out.

"Is the wedding guest list getting too long, or may I add a few names?" he asked.

"Who are you inviting?"

"I was thinking about our performance at the wedding. It could be . . . an audition of sorts, an opportunity. Since the press will be there, we could generate some good publicity for Forsyth, of course. But if we decide *not* to keep the trio, it could be a chance to have other people hear us play." The truth seemed like the only way to explain it. "I'm inviting people who might be in a position to hire me to teach."

"You already teach."

"To teach *here*."

Bridget didn't answer, so he glanced over at her to gauge her reaction. "I'm considering the idea of a quieter life in a less expensive place with steadier work," he said with his eyes back on the road. "A regular paycheck and benefits would be sensible at my age."

She nodded her head.

Will decided he might as well tell her the rest: "And I may have to give up my apartment, so a move is likely imminent anyway."

"Why?" Bridget said, sounding as horrified by the idea as he felt.

"I'm getting priced out once my lease expires. The building was sold."

"Good God, Will," she said. "That's horrible. Why didn't you tell me?"

"It's not something I've felt like talking about."

She turned in her seat to face him. "May I say something? Do you want my opinion?"

"I don't know," he said, slowing down at the only stoplight in town. "I mean, I do, of course, but maybe not quite yet."

"Fair enough."

"Do you want my opinion on anything you're thinking about?" he asked. "I'm happy to listen."

Bridget seemed to consider that for a moment, but then said, "Actually no. I'm not ready to share yet either."

"All right," he said. "Then we'll wait."

He took a left and drove through the town, past the bookstore, wine shop, and grocery store. It had only taken twenty years, but he liked this little town.

"Would you mind if Gwen stays in your loft during the wedding?" Bridget said. "I'm assuming you'll be at Emma's anyway."

"Of course," he said. "I can clear out some of my things while I'm here."

"No need to do that," Bridget said. "It's only for that weekend."

Pulling up the driveway, Will slowed down to maneuver over the big pothole and parked by the garage. As they got out of the car, he marveled at the amount of work being done. There were men operating machinery out on the tennis court and workers in, on, and around the whole property. Most surprisingly, the barn itself was looking so much better. Not like new, not perfect, but marvelous, like a dignified old man, much like Edward himself, well-groomed and ready for company.

"Well, who wouldn't want to have a wedding here?" Will said.

Bridget turned and smiled. "You think?"

"It's a transformation," he said. "It's a miracle actually. Even *I* would want to get married here." The project wasn't yet finished, but everything from the landscaping to the bright, clean new windows, to the red color of the barn door looked ready to be photographed. "So which one of these Herculean young men are you sleeping with?" Will asked, handing Bridget back her car keys.

"Not a single one," said Bridget, sounding a little defeated.

"It's not too late," Will said. "You still need to repave the driveway."

"You think the asphalt repairman is my guy?"

He shrugged. "It could happen."

"Elliot's not bad," she whispered, pointing across the field to a man holding a clipboard.

"Which one's Elliot?"

"The barn guru. I keep thinking he might ask me out, but he never does. He's not my type anyway probably; he's a little too timid for me."

"Maybe he's waiting until the job is done to make his big move."

Bridget elbowed him. "At least my Realtor calls me from time to time."

"Ew, Mark? No, he's so pushy," said Will. "Do I have veto power?"

"You don't need to veto; he's only interested in my house."

They went inside, and Hudson found his favorite spot on Bridget's couch as Will took his place at the piano.

Bridget sat next to him on the bench while he warmed up. "If it weren't for you, this piano would never get played," she said.

"Look," he said, "the ever-sticky key." And he showed her by pressing the A4 over and over.

"I rented a grand piano for the party," she said.

"Good, the piece deserves it."

"Can I see it?" she asked.

"Not yet." He wanted to show her the finished arrangement but wanted it to be perfect. He played an A-flat major scale, warming up his hands. "I hate to add pressure, but you're running out of time to tell the kids about Gavin."

"I want to tell them when they're together, so we'll have to wait until Oscar comes back."

"'We'?"

"Of course 'we.' I need your diplomacy and calm demeanor. Please?"

Will nodded casually, but inside he was cheering, honored to know his presence in such an important moment mattered to her.

321

"I'll leave you to it," Bridget said, standing up. "Elliot and I are driving stakes into the ground to mark the new walkway to the barn."

———◇———

After Bridget went outside, Will got the arrangement out of his backpack and went through it note by note, making minor corrections. The violin part was especially beautiful, and Gavin would swoop in to play it, knocking everyone's socks off. Will decided he would be gracious. He would shake Gavin's hand and tell him how well he played. Will hoped, childishly, that Gavin would say something complimentary in return. When he reached the end of the piece, he proofread it once more, until he was satisfied it was correct. He didn't want Gavin to call him out for an error in the score.

As excited as he was about the piece, every time he imagined actually playing it, he felt like something was off or out of place. It wasn't the setting; a country barn would be the perfect place for such lively and whimsical music. He tried to picture the scene: the guests sitting at large, round candlelit tables, Gavin and Bridget walking on the stage and taking their seats, Bridget watching him as he nodded for the piece to begin. Will wasn't one for public speaking, but if he were, he would say a few words before they started playing, something about *Synchronicity* and the experience of arranging it, the joyful feelings the piece evoked. The complexity and dynamism of the melody.

He imagined Edward standing up to applause. And then . . .

And then what? And then wouldn't it be wonderful to gesture to the piano bench, offering Edward his rightful place, having him play his own piece as only he could? Wasn't that the way it should be? Since when was the Maestro the type of man who would want to sit by passively, especially when the story being celebrated was his own? It was his wedding, after all, his celebration, his piece of music.

Will closed the piano and looked out at the barn, where Bridget was pounding a stake in the ground with a mallet. He knew what he needed to do: *Step aside*, he told himself, *and give Edward the floor.*

Bridget had never performed with her father before, and wouldn't that be touching for them both? Memorable, certainly. The performance was meant to be a surprise for Edward, but Will could imagine a delightful twist, turning the surprise around on itself, giving Bridget the gift of an experience that she would never forget.

He looked at the arrangement on the stand, realizing the implications of this scenario: he was about to wreck the whole idea of using the performance as an audition, both for him and for Forsyth. What kind of audition would it be if he didn't even play? And how would he feel walking away, leaving Gavin to play with Bridget? Was this a sacrifice worth making?

He decided for now to keep his brilliant idea to himself.

24

Nicholas Donahue didn't think he'd ever regretted anything in his life as much as he did inviting Gavin to visit him at his lake house retreat. What he'd imagined was old friends drinking whiskey on the porch, enjoying the peaceful sounds of the woods, swapping stories about Edward Stratton for the book he was writing, talking about music, and enjoying each other's company. What he got instead was something quite horrid indeed.

It was a shame, too, because he'd been looking forward to seeing Gavin. True, Nicholas had disliked him when they'd first met a decade or more ago and maybe even for a year after that. But having gotten to know him better, he found he liked him, in spite of his arrogance. Some people deserved to be arrogant, and Gavin, who was immensely talented, was one of them. Besides, what many people didn't know was that beneath all the bravado, there was the insecurity so often found in musical prodigies.

After almost three months of solitude, Nicholas was hungry for camaraderie. He wanted to talk to someone about his latest chapter and—equally importantly—be directed *away* from his work. One of the things he missed about Miriam was that she got him out of his head by discussing topics ripped from the pages of the *Mirror* or *Us Weekly*. Harry and Meghan (a Brit-Yankee union, much like their own) provided endless commentary and speculation, and he'd enjoyed listening to Miriam's opinions, even if he didn't have much to add to the conversation. He'd found it hard to be alone in the Oxford house, but coming here hadn't helped. He'd liked being married, being attached—but Miriam, as it turned out, wasn't a big fan of monogamy, something Nicholas rather valued in a wife.

He'd spent the long summer days in solitude going over the interviews he'd recorded with Edward, analyzing his scores, and then writing pages and pages of text in longhand, filling in the details of Edward's life story, later typing sections into his laptop.

When Gavin called to say his wife and child would, in fact, be coming along as well, Nicholas didn't mind. But what he hadn't expected was a weeklong nightmare of having to deal with their heinous behavior. From the moment they arrived, Nicholas's peaceful haven turned into a zoo. Danny, the demon spawn, threw his first tantrum as the family entered his home, screeching about a toy he'd misplaced somewhere during the brief stop they'd made to visit some aunt on the way.

Offering them refreshment after their long drive, Nicholas guided them into the kitchen, where Danny spotted a package of biscuits on Nicholas's kitchen counter and went haywire. As Danny began shrieking, Nicholas's eyebrows went up his forehead involuntarily. Juliette seemed to notice his reaction and began inventing all manner of excuses to explain the child's outrageous conduct, everything from fatigue to hunger to stress to car sickness to something she called "discovering his passions."

Nicholas was no stranger to child-rearing. He and Miriam had raised three children, none of whom had ever thrown a fit of this magnitude. As he watched Danny scream, Nicholas felt immensely happy that his kids were grown and settled in life. He did not envy Gavin having a toddler at this age.

"Here," Nicholas said, offering the biscuits; he'd give anything to stop the noise the child was making. "He's welcome to have as many as he likes."

"No!" Juliette barked as she looked through her large bag for a healthier alternative.

"I'm afraid Danny can't have gluten or processed sugar," Gavin said over the wailing, but then he looked at Juliette in a pleading way, adding, "unless you think he deserves a treat after the long drive."

Juliette shot him a look that said, *Oh, hell no.*

Danny, understanding that he would not, in fact, be given a cookie, spun around and struck Gavin in the balls, causing him to double over and his face to turn red. Nicholas patted him on the back as he coughed and clutched at the countertop.

Juliette sighed and said patiently, "Daddies aren't for hitting, darling."

In response, Danny threw himself on the floor and, from his new vantage point, kicked Juliette in the shins. "Mommies aren't for kicking, sweetheart," she said, holding her injured leg.

Nicholas asked if anyone needed an ice bag.

The next few days revolved around Danny's fits and fury and the family's constant needs. How could three people require so many towels? How could they have such a wide array of eating restrictions and allergies? They asked to use the washing machine (with different detergent, as the one he'd bought had additives, apparently, and fragrances that were unacceptable), and it had been chugging away night and day while they washed more clothes than Nicholas had owned in his entire life. Most annoying was that Nicholas couldn't find anything because Juliette "childproofed" the house without asking, which, he discovered, meant she'd hidden all of his things, from his Lamy pens, to his headphones, to his reading glasses.

When Nicholas went with them for a swim in the lake, a quiet, clear body of water with a white sand beach, Juliette brought along a swim noodle, which Danny used as a weapon, smacking them all on their heads over and over.

Fortunately, the visit with Gavin wasn't a total loss. The two friends found time, especially late in the evenings, to discuss various compositions, to talk about the musicians who influenced Edward's works and the works Edward influenced in turn, and even to gossip about people they knew in common. Above all they shared a few laughs, something Nicholas hadn't done enough of lately. Gavin had a penchant for salacious old stories involving syphilis, duels, and courtesans, so Nicholas shared as many raunchy tales of dead composers as he could think of. He wondered if maybe Gavin were someone he could confide in, someone with whom he could discuss Bridget, who had been on his mind so much these last few weeks, but whenever he'd had just enough whiskey to speak his mind, Juliette would interrupt.

The final night of his stay, Gavin was sitting with Nicholas on the porch while Juliette tried to put the monster to bed. Nicholas could hear Danny crying in the guest room while Juliette attempted to sing to him. She couldn't carry a tune.

Gavin had his hands clasped behind his head, elbows spread out to the sides, and he sighed. "This is quite a place," he said. "How on earth did you end up renting such a massive house just for yourself? Five bedrooms, is it?"

Nicholas looked around the modest porch. He hadn't thought the house was massive when he'd arrived. It was certainly smaller than his place in Oxford. But it was true that there were times that summer when the empty house had an echo, leaving him forlorn. Returning home wouldn't make things any better; he simply needed to adjust to life as a single man.

"Tell me about the piece you're playing for Edward," Nicholas said. "*Synchronicity*. Any thoughts on how it fits in his oeuvre?"

"It's light and jaunty," Gavin said, "and not nearly as complex as his later work. Will's doing an arrangement for piano trio, which will work well, maybe even better than the original instrumentation."

"The original Forsyth Trio. I know Bridget and Will, and I was wondering," Nicholas asked, feeling slightly emboldened, "are Bridget and Will together? I mean, I get the feeling they're a couple."

Gavin seemed surprised. "No, I don't think so," he said. "At least they weren't back in the day."

Nicholas thought that was spectacular news, if true.

Gavin dropped his arms and looked down at his hands. "The thing is we haven't really kept in touch. I'm nervous to see them after such a long time."

This statement was precisely the thing that most people didn't know about Gavin. Under the facade, there was a rather insecure, sensitive man.

"I'm sure they're looking forward to reconnecting with you. Playing in a trio together must have made you all very close."

"Yes," said Gavin, "that's true. And yet . . ."

Nicholas waited, certain that Gavin had more to say on the subject. But when he didn't continue, Nicholas filled the silence. "I don't know either of them well," he said. "I happen to find Bridget quite interesting." Nicholas thought Bridget was stunning. He'd admired her from afar ever since he'd met her in Salzburg and was delighted to have run into her, albeit briefly, in the car park at Edward's house with her personable, handsome son. She was an outstanding cellist, for one thing; beautiful, for another. Edward had shown him some pictures of her, some recent and some from her conservatory years. In many of the pictures, Will was lurking in the background or smiling in the foreground; they seemed inseparable. Nicholas had asked Edward if he could borrow a few of the photographs to have on hand while he was writing. In one, professionally taken by the look of it, Bridget was onstage playing, her long hair over her right shoulder, her knees out to the side, giving Nicholas the irrational, juvenile feeling that there was something sexual about the pose. He, of all people, knew better. "I'd like to know more about her."

"I wonder who's going to be there," Gavin said, tapping his foot on the floor. "Do you think this will be a small affair or . . . ?"

"I don't have any idea."

"Because if it's only family, it might get kind of awkward."

Nicholas said, "*I'm* invited, so it won't be only family."

"I'm only wondering how hard it will be to find time to talk." He leaned forward and lowered his voice. "We—Bridget and I, that is—have a bit of unfinished business to discuss."

Nicholas's interest was piqued, but Juliette barged onto the porch before Gavin could elaborate. She was holding a hardcover book to her chest, and she looked exhausted.

Gavin made room for her on the wicker couch, saying, "How's our little pain in the ass?"

Juliette gave him an angry look. "He's doing the best he can under arduous circumstances."

Nicholas found that comment rather insulting. He wanted to be sympathetic, remembering what it was like to travel with children, to *live* with children, but Danny was, in fact, a huge pain in the ass, and the circumstances weren't *arduous* in the least. "Kids," he said, trying to come across as both neutral and understanding.

"I didn't know how hard it would be to take a trip with him," she said. "He's usually manageable. I can't wait to go home."

"When will you be back in LA?" Nicholas asked.

"We'll go to New York tomorrow," said Gavin, "and then to Connecticut for the wedding. We'll be home the day after . . . unless we decide to stay a little longer, depending on—"

"We'll go home the day after the wedding," said Juliette firmly, "no matter what."

A heavy silence followed.

"Well," said Nicholas, "as I was saying, I'm excited to hear the trio play together and to get to know Bridget better."

"Why?" said Juliette. She had a way of looking at him that was almost confrontational, like it was her right to know things about him he didn't want to share.

"For my book on Edward. I want a better sense of the family dynamic, and she's the one who followed in his footsteps, becoming a musician." Nicholas hoped he hadn't let on that he was smitten. He kept his comments in the professional realm, saying, "Edward tells me Bridget and Will may be collaborating with someone new this fall. I checked their website, and the space for the violinist is blank." He held his hands up. "It's a mystery."

Gavin leaned forward. "They asked me to join them." Juliette shot him a hostile look. "But as my wife correctly pointed out, I'm too busy this fall."

"It would be a backwards career move," she said.

Gavin seemed to agree. "I don't know why they've kept the trio going this long."

Nicholas felt defensive of Bridget and Will, saying, "I've heard them play; they're both exceptionally talented."

"True," said Gavin, "but all the hustling we used to do, the constant traveling, never knowing how much money was coming in. I don't know how Bridget did it, especially with kids."

"*Pffft*," said Juliette. "I'm sure she had oodles of help. She probably never even had to see her kids if she didn't want to."

Nicholas thought that opinion was in poor taste and possibly unfounded. "You know her?" he asked.

AMY POEPPEL

"Everyone knows the Strattons have money," she said.

Nicholas decided he didn't like Juliette, not her disagreeable countenance, her tightly crossed arms and legs, or her nasally American voice.

"It's true that Bridget never had to worry about money like Will and I did," Gavin said. "Edward gave a speech when we graduated from Juilliard, and at the end, he handed her a check, and someone said they saw six figures on it."

"Really?" Nicholas took a legal pad and pencil from the coffee table to make a note to himself, sure that Gavin was mistaken about the graduation speech. "He spoke at Juilliard? I've never seen a transcript anywhere—"

"No, no," Gavin said. "It was at a private dinner, afterwards. He spoke to maybe six or seven of us. He presented Bridget with this old silver box or something, an antique that an aristocrat in Europe had given him, something to do with paying it forward."

"Edward's done a lot of that. The retreat he runs every summer has given many composers their start." Nicholas heard himself sigh. "How amazing to find love again at his age. It gives hope to the rest of us, I suppose, even an old divorcé like me. Good for him. He certainly deserves a new chapter."

"His final chapter, I guess," Juliette said.

Was that rude, Nicholas wondered, or just plain factual?

"Did you hear," said Nicholas, "that the wedding was moved to Bridget's house? To her barn, in fact."

"Excuse me?" said Juliette. "She lives in a *barn*?"

"Well," Nicholas said, "it seems there was a mishap of some kind at Edward's house. He called to cancel an appointment with me and mentioned there may be the necessity of a change in venue. Bridget's place is nearby, I take it. You might want to give her a call, or Will, to find out."

Juliette got to her feet, saying, "I'm going to bed." She turned to

Nicholas. "As thanks for hosting us," she said formally, "I'd like to give you a signed copy of my book. Perhaps you'll find it useful." She handed it to him.

The book, *Ancient Practices, Modern Life*, had a picture of her on the cover. She was standing on one foot and holding an apple in her hand. Nicholas realized how little he'd bothered to find out about her. Had he said a kind word since she'd arrived? Asked an interested question? "Thank you," he said. "I look forward to reading it."

"Don't *read* it," she said. "*Live* it. You'll see improvements in every single facet of your life, including your hopes for romance."

Nicholas had his doubts, but he opened the book and studied its table of contents.

Gavin got up and said good night, and he and Juliette left the porch together, Gavin looking at her with reverence and adoration, taking her hand and kissing her knuckles.

People so often seemed to find the right partner. It wasn't so much that there was a right person for everyone that intrigued Nicholas, but more that two people could meet by chance and be exactly what the other wanted and needed. What are the chances of that happening, really? He flipped through the pages of Juliette's book, thinking that if he was lucky enough to find love, he wouldn't squander it. He would find out what, if anything, he had to offer, and he would give it freely.

Nicholas decided to go to bed as well. After his high-maintenance guests finally departed the next morning, he would clean up after them and spend the whole afternoon reading and writing with music in the background, tea on his desk, and his books to keep him company.

He turned off all the lights, stepping on one of Danny's Legos as he walked through the living room. Tiptoeing past the guest room, he overheard Juliette and Gavin in the middle of an argument.

"Why did you say we would consider staying longer?" Juliette whispered angrily. "I want to go home. Just do what you came here to do, deal with Bridget, and then we'll put this whole matter behind us."

"Unless we can't," said Gavin. "It depends. If they're *mine*—"

"You can't go back in time," she said, "so staying longer would serve no purpose whatsoever. Why even play the stupid piece with them at all? Find out the truth and end this."

"I can't explain it," he said firmly, but not unkindly. "Whatever happens, I want to be friends with them again. The three of us are connected somehow. I don't want to *end* anything."

"I don't get it. What's the point of playing music with a pair of lesser musicians who you haven't seen in ages in some back-ass country *barn* . . . ?"

"Well," said Gavin with a laugh, "if Yo-Yo Ma can perform in a barn, then so can I."

"Yo-Yo?" she asked. "Who's that?"

Gavin didn't miss a beat. "A *very* famous cellist," he said.

Juliette made a sound of exasperation. "Oh, great," she said, "another cellist. Did you get her pregnant, too?"

Nicholas couldn't decide if that line was the funniest thing he'd ever heard or the most scandalous. *Pregnant?* He waited to hear more, but when neither of them spoke, he went to his room and closed the door.

Bridget, he thought, looking at the picture of her Edward had given him. She was exquisite, truly. He would be himself. He would hope to deserve her. He would muster up the courage to ask her to dance.

25

"Right here, under the big windows," Bridget told Lottie as they walked around the barn, "will be the dance floor. And over here will be the bar, where people can pick up a glass of champagne before dinner. I think that will work best for the flow of the room."

Lottie's face was missing its usual bright, engaged expression, and Bridget couldn't read her mood; her expression was part Valium, part Botox, part constipation. She was staring vaguely around the room with her bright red lips pursed together and her eyes slightly glazed. Whether she hated this idea or was completely preoccupied with something unpleasant was unclear.

"We already put lights in the trees on this side of the barn," said Bridget, "so when your guests look out the windows next week, they'll see the branches lit up."

"Bridget . . ."

Bridget waited, wondering if Lottie was about to criticize her wedding venue.

"You tried the dress I sent you for the *Hochzeit*?"

"Yes," said Bridget, remembering the strain of the blouse buttons, the futility of trying to get the skirt to close. "It's perfect." Bridget hadn't dared to try the dress on again, but she hoped that all the pacing and humming, meditating and eating nothing but nuts and vegetables was doing more than improve her brain function and attitude. Juliette Stark was right: over time, the hunger had vanished and was replaced with an odd sense of resignation. Bridget wasn't feeling the ecstatic waves of energy described in the book. Rather, she felt peacefully zoned out. Nothing bothered her. The London orchestra had never called. *Oh well.* Neither had Randall. *Whatever.* Elliot had not asked her out, Oscar had not returned for a visit, and Gavin had never followed up to explain what he meant by "We need to talk." *So what?* She wasn't anxious or upset about any of these issues. Bridget was giving in to the universe, not passively but with tranquil acceptance. She was floating above it all, unconcerned and unhurried. Whatever happened would happen.

The bride, on the other hand, who was wearing a knee-length white skirt and pretty white flats as though she were heading out for her bridal shower at Per Se, seemed troubled and was looking at her doubtfully. "I'm—how do you say—*überrascht?* Surprised but relieved, *ja?* You remember ven you were a *Mädchen?* I got you a dress that vas too big. I didn't vant to make the same mistake again."

She was surprised that Lottie even remembered. "I grew into it soon enough," Bridget said, unable to recall if she'd ever actually put on the dress again. "So what do you think?" Bridget asked, indicating the clean, empty space. "We're still adding finishing touches, more lighting, more landscaping—"

But Lottie was clearly feeling needled by something other than her wedding venue. "Hans, my son, is a difficult man, *weisst du?* I always vanted a girl. I envied your mother."

"She probably envied you," said Bridget, "for having a boy."

"I don't sink so," Lottie said. "Hans did not bring out envy in other parents. He was a sulky child, always scowling." Lottie walked slowly around the perimeter of the room. "I missed Sophia after she died. I should have done more for you. I should have asked if you girls needed anysing. I deeply regret it."

Bridget hadn't expected this kind of heart-to-heart when Lottie had asked to come over. "We were all right," she said. They weren't, of course. But she doubted hearing from Lottie would have helped lessen the pain much.

"You liked traveling so much ven you vere small. Do you still?"

"I love it," said Bridget, "although Will and I get tired when we're on the road."

"I am so looking forwards to September. Vat could be better than starting off on a big adventure?" Lottie was beginning to look more like herself again, smiling and posing as though Bridget had a camera pointed at her. "I only vish for Hans to have a distraction. A romance perhaps."

Bridget felt silly stating the obvious: "Hans is married."

"His wife left him recently, and they're divorcing. He's focusing all his frustrations about his life onto me. He's become quite bitter."

"Do you know what happened?"

"I know what he tells me," she said, "but how would a mother know the details of what goes on in her child's life? How he behaves in a relationship?"

Bridget nodded, understanding her predicament only too well.

"Hans works all the time and can't let go of his need for independence." She took a step toward Bridget. "Gwen was always so much like him. Am I right about that?"

Bridget smiled, knowing how much her sister would hate to hear her name and Hans's linked together. "I don't know."

"They hated each other so as children. I always thought it was because they are similar. They always vanted the same sing, the same toy or the same *Süssigkeiten*, and neither wanted to share with the other, not a wooden animal and certainly not a candy." Lottie perked up suddenly. "Do you sink Gwen could pick Hans up from JFK before she drives up next week?"

No, Bridget almost said. "I'll ask her. Send me his flight information."

Lottie turned and looked out the window as a hawk circled overhead. If Bridget concentrated, she could feel the slightest change of the seasons coming, the angle of the sun, the tired, muted green of the leaves, and a dry, earthy smell. "I know this barn isn't what you had in mind when my father proposed," Bridget said, sorry that she didn't feel more like the cheerleader Lottie seemed to need. "I know it's not especially elegant or glamorous, but I hope your wedding will be . . . memorable."

Lottie smiled, holding out her arms to indicate the room around her, the pickled floors, the beams and the rafters. "But Bridget, I love it so much. It's going to be *ausgezeichnet, ja?*"

Bridget didn't know what that word meant but could tell it was positive. She also didn't know if Lottie and her father would have two years together, or five, or ten, or maybe more, but she hoped that whatever time they had left on this earth, it would be—what had Lottie said?—"*Ausgezeichnet*," repeated Bridget, feeling the word getting mangled in her mouth. And then she noticed a lightness, a fleeting jolt of elation in her calmly beating heart.

The next morning, exactly one week before the big event, something in Bridget had shifted. She woke up early, realizing that her energy must have returned in her sleep, and she all but popped out of bed when she opened her eyes. She went to the kitchen to retrieve her cell phone, where, according to the rules of *Ancient Practices, Modern Life*, it had to stay overnight, every night, banned from the bedroom where it would interfere with sleep.

At the sound of the ringing doorbell, she went to let in a crew that had been sent by Marge, who apparently had little faith in Bridget's cleaning skills. Throughout the morning, the brand-new laundry machines ran incessantly, and soon there were fresh sheets on all the beds and towels in the bathrooms that smelled like lavender. The carpets were cleaned, the hardwood floors were buffed, and the windows were scrubbed inside and out.

At noon, Emma and Elliot came over to make a final wedding party to-do list. The temperature was a bit cooler even though the sun was bright.

"This is so exciting," Emma said. "You have to bear with me; a barn is my all-time favorite event venue."

"It's a blank slate, which I guess is good," said Bridget, walking around the cavernous space, "but it still feels sort of cold in here."

"We've gone all out on the flowers," Emma said. "Since the party's here instead of at your dad's, I decided to do something more rustic and unruly. Wildflowers in mason jars for the tables and birchbark vases for larger arrangements. I still think we could use some additional landscaping, say three dogwoods by the barn entrance? And I'm thinking we could install wooden window boxes along the first floor, with flowers and ivy draping down, like those glorious boxes you see in Austrian villages."

Elliot was excited that the work he'd done was being given a chance to shine. "We're going to string lights across all the beams," he said. "And then—if you like the idea—I'm thinking we could go find an oversize, campy, antique chandelier to hang from the rafters. It would give the barn a kind of shabby-chic elegance."

"Perfect," said Emma.

"I wonder," said Elliot, studying the entrance, "if Kevin should put up a temporary railing along the ramp for your geriatric guests. And if the electrician should come back to install more tree lighting so they can see the path clearly. It's a pretty uneven walk to get out here."

Bridget's mind felt sharp and full of inspiration. "I could call the tent company and have them cover the pathway and put down flooring to make it a nicer route to the party, especially if it rains."

Emma seemed to like the idea, but Elliot shook his head, looking outside at the cloudless blue sky. "That's going to be—what?—thirty yards to cover?" he said. "There's no rain in the forecast, so it's not necessary."

"But it would be so much more elegant," said Emma.

"And very expensive," said Elliot.

"But better for high heels and long dresses," she argued.

"I think it's worth it," said Bridget. "It'll be like our version of a red carpet."

While the two of them considered the idea, Bridget's phone rang, showing an international call on the screen. She excused herself, going outside the barn to the spot where the dogwoods could be planted.

"Bridget?" she heard. "Hans Lang here, Charlotte's son."

At the sound of his name, a clear memory of Hans popped into her head from their childhood: Gwen, who couldn't have been more than six or seven at the time, was sitting cross-legged on the floor of his room, watching him line up little animals—molded plastic? porcelain?—in a long row, toys he wouldn't let her play with. Bridget had been old enough that she didn't particularly care, but Gwen got so mad when he refused to let her touch them that she stomped on one of them, making him cry. Bridget vaguely remembered that the fight got physical.

"Hi," said Bridget, noticing as she looked across at the house that the gutters needed cleaning; there was a plant growing out of the one by the kitchen window. "We're excited for you to get here. I'm going to ask Gwen if she can drive you—"

"I'm sure you're both as upset about this insanity as I am."

Bridget looked out at the new fence that was currently being erected around the tennis court. She'd gone to a lot of trouble over the past two weeks to get everything finished, but she wouldn't go so far as to call it insanity. "Not at all, Hans. We're looking forward to the party."

He cleared his throat. "You're *happy* about this? I'm not. I'm not happy, especially that my mother is behaving like a rebellious teenager. And why is she still staying at that house? I'm worried about her safety."

"The damage wasn't *that* serious," Bridget said. "It's perfectly safe. You'll be staying there, too, I understand."

"Certainly not. I'm of the opinion," Hans said slowly, "that we need to rethink."

Bridget waited, and then asked, "Rethink what?"

"Rethink the wedding."

Bridget was stunned.

"It's happened too fast," he said.

"Meaning . . . ?"

"My father died less than a year ago, and I'm concerned about my mother, and about Edward, too, frankly. Aren't you?"

Bridget thought of the fall her dad took earlier that summer, the sight of him in a hospital gown. "Sometimes," she admitted.

"Lottie's been in good spirits since this . . . romance began, and we like Edward, of course. However, we feel it would be best . . ."

There was a pause, and Bridget took the opportunity to ask, "Who's 'we'? 'We' as in you and Lottie?"

He sighed. "Habit," he said. "I mean 'I.' *I* feel it would be best to slow this down."

Bridget felt a panic starting to rise. "Hans, the wedding's in one week. Couldn't you have brought this up before—?"

"I assumed you and your sister were going to put a stop to it, especially after your father started a fire in his own house. And I can't have my eighty-four-year-old mother traipsing off on some endless excursion with a man who has enough to worry about looking after himself. What if he lights their hotel room on fire in the middle of . . . Siberia?"

The arson comment was rude. But Bridget felt a needling of guilt. Had she and Gwen been overly cavalier about their father's plans? It hadn't occurred to her to put on the brakes, and Edward wouldn't allow her to even if it had. "My sister and I have talked to him about it," she said, "and Lottie, too, and they're looking forward to traveling. I hate to infantilize them by telling them what they can and can't do at their age," said Bridget. "They're adults."

"They're old," he said flatly. "I can't be expected to hire a helicopter to airlift my mother out of Mongolia or Montmartre when she falls and breaks a hip or your father when he has a heart attack. I have a demanding career, and I need to know my mother is okay and within reach should something happen. Your father is being foolish, and I won't have him drag my mother along on this absurd excursion."

Bridget was so accustomed to hearing people speak reverently of her father that this whole conversation was jarring. Lottie probably wouldn't appreciate her son's tone either. "I thought your mother was a cocaptain of this adventure. She was just telling me that traveling is her passion as well."

"They've gotten carried away, and I simply want to know that you view the situation as I do."

Bridget would have liked to have been on the same page with Hans, but she wasn't. And she didn't see what she could do about his concerns anyway. Edward and Lottie had money, free will, and use of their limbs and brains. How exactly were they to be stopped?

"Are you upset about the wedding or the trip?"

"Both," he said.

"What if we modified the trip?" said Bridget, feeling a need to compromise.

"At the moment, and I'm sorry to be rude, I don't trust your father in his own house, much less on such a voyage. I'll put it plainly," said

Hans, as if he hadn't already. Bridget imagined him sitting in an office, little porcelain animals lined up on his desk, not to be touched. "This wedding announcement came as a great shock to me. But because I know Edward and respect him, I'm willing to put on a good face and go along with the wedding. But the travel is not happening."

"Have you told your mother that?" she asked, remembering that Lottie had complained that Hans was "a difficult man."

"If they insist on taking this absurd trip, I won't come to the wedding."

Bridget was stunned. "You want Edward to choose between Lottie and the trip?" she said, appalled that he was willing to blow up the whole relationship. "Maybe there's a better way to handle this?"

Hans didn't answer.

Bridget tried to think of a way to appease him. "They could go on a cruise instead." Even as she said it, she knew Edward would despise the idea.

"Go on," said Hans.

"Well," she said, "what if they start in Athens as planned and then take a yacht out for a week or so around the Mediterranean? Not much could happen to them on a boat," said Bridget.

"I don't know," said Hans, probably recalling the numerous stories of tourists toppling overboard after too many daiquiris or getting violently ill from norovirus.

"I'll talk to them," Bridget said, dreading the conversation. "I'll get them to make adjustments so you won't have to worry so much."

Hans didn't answer.

"Please don't boycott your mother's wedding; none of us will be able to enjoy it if you're not there. In fact, your mom will probably cancel the whole thing, and she'll resent you for it. I'll get him to rein in the trip. Deal?"

Hans sighed. "I'll consider it."

"I think Gwen wants to meet your plane," Bridget said. "And

you're welcome to stay at my father's. They have the pool house ready for you."

"No, thank you," said Hans. "I'll go back to New York directly after the ceremony."

What a party pooper, thought Bridget. They hung up, and Bridget looked sadly at her barn, knowing her father would never give in to Hans's demands.

26

The Castle, which had always seemed so formidable and grand, looked sad and broken when Will pulled in the courtyard Sunday evening before the wedding. As he parked Emma's car, he saw the big pieces of ugly plywood covering up the broken mullioned windows on one side of the house, above which black smudges marked the stone where the fire had licked the walls. There was debris littering the ground and a small dumpster filled with the charred furniture and floorboards. A broken mirror stuck out of the top. In the other direction, he could plainly see the house's enduring beauty, the sun lighting the chimneys and turrets, the green lawns and terraces. *"Last night,"* thought Will, *"I dreamt I went to Manderley . . ."*

Will had been to the estate countless times with Bridget and the kids, to swim in the pool, have four-course dinners, browse the antique books in the library. Friendship with Bridget had given him access to all kinds of experiences he might not have otherwise had, being granted an audience with Sir Edward Stratton being one of them. Most people of modest means would feel out of place walking up to such a grand house, approaching this solid door, and

Will had never lost his sense of awe in all the years of coming here. He only hoped he might find Edward in a mood to listen and not to lecture.

Will rang the bell, and Jackie answered instead of Marge. The house was quiet with the exception of the intermittent sound of the piano; someone was playing quite well from behind the closed living room door, a beautiful piece Will didn't recognize. It was hard to make Edward's piano sound bad. Will had played his Bösendorfer a few times over the years, another example of an experience normal people would never get to have.

He put his hand on the chair rail to balance as he took off his shoes. "What's the mood around here today?" he asked.

"Hard to say," said Jackie. "Marge and Ms. Lang are finalizing the menu for the wedding dinner, and Mr. Stratton's been in the library for hours."

"And in there?"

"The French composer," said Jackie.

"How's this health-kick thing you're all doing?" he asked. "Sounds brutal."

"It's good," she said, glancing down at her feet.

"You can tell me the truth. What's the book called again? *Ancient* something?"

Jackie dropped her shoulders. "*Ancient Nonsense, Modern Bullshit.* I hate it, and I cheat *all the time*. I haven't gone a single day when I didn't break most of the rules. I even sleep with my phone."

"Scandalous."

"Yesterday I had a Snickers bar and coffee for breakfast."

Will mimed zipping his lips. "But are you otherwise enjoying yourself?" Unlike the evening he'd first met her, Jackie now had the air of a young woman at ease; she was standing casually, hands tucked in the back pockets of her jeans.

She looked around the foyer, which was mahogany-paneled on

one side and burned to a crisp on the other, a plastic sheet separating Edward's wing from the entry. "It took some getting used to," she said, "but . . . I spent an hour swimming last night with the brilliant, adorable Greek composer, and when I got back to Bridget's, someone—I don't even know who—had done all my laundry and left it perfectly folded on my clean bed. I got up early this morning just because I felt like taking a bubble bath in Isabelle's tub. Honestly," she said, "I don't know how I'll ever go back to my shitty, dull life after this summer."

"I know exactly how you feel." Will remembered how small his apartment felt after staying at Bridget's house the first time.

Jackie looked surprised. "But you're sort of a family member, aren't you? Or an honorary one?"

"Sure, but I'm from the impoverished side of the family. This kind of grandeur is foreign to me, too."

"I didn't know there was an impoverished side," Jackie said.

"I'm the only one on it, actually."

Jackie was looking at him as if she hadn't met him until now.

"I happen to be pretty broke at the moment," he said, "but I'll figure it out. I always do. If I want to pay my rent, I have to earn the money, one lesson, one gig, and one dollar at a time." Will had seven months left on his lease and had finally started searching online for apartments in Queens and Jersey City, but he was still hoping—irrationally—that if he wanted to stay, he could find a place in his own neighborhood. It would be smaller, of course, and crappier, which at his age seemed a cruel joke.

"If my mom can't pay *her* rent, she calls me to bail her out."

"Ah, touché," he said, tipping a pretend hat to her. "You bested me." She curtsied back.

"You and I may not come from money," he said, "but we're resourceful, self-reliant, and we have grit." He made fists and held them up, with a little shake, as a gesture of encouragement. "And I'm not going to deny there are advantages to being friends with people who happen to be completely loaded."

"I've taken up horseback riding," she said. "It's a short-lived hobby, since I'm not exactly in the market to buy a horse."

"Borrowing horses is always better. I hear they make terrible roommates."

Jackie smiled. "I rented a yellow strapless dress to wear to the wedding this weekend, and I'll feel like Cinderella when I mail it back Monday morning."

"I'll think of you when I'm returning my fancy tux. The one I wear for performances is too old and shabby for this event. Wish me luck," he said, pointing to the library. "I'm about to go out on a limb."

Jackie smiled, held up her fists, and shook them back at him.

Will knocked on the door to the library and cracked it open.

"Come in," Edward called. He was sitting in one of a pair of antique chairs, very close to the French doors that led to the living room. Will wondered if the composer, who was playing the piano so well in there, knew Edward was only a few feet away, able to hear every note he played. If so, was it making him self-conscious?

Edward had no book in his lap, no phone in his hand. He was sitting idly with an empty brandy snifter, facing the table that held his many awards and dozens of silver-framed photographs of famous opera singers, dancers, actors, and politicians posing with him.

Will approached him and shook his hand. Edward barely acknowledged his presence. He had a sour expression on his face and was dressed as if for a funeral in a navy suit, pressed white shirt, and dark tie.

"Thanks for seeing me," Will said. "I know you're probably very busy with wedding plans . . ."

Edward looked sullen as he set his glass down. "Did Bridget mention anything to you about her objections to my upcoming trip?"

Bridget had, in fact, told him everything there was to tell about it. "No," said Will, examining his hands. "What objections?"

The composer in the next room had paused, but he now played a few harsh atonal chords followed by a graceful, tonal melody.

"When you get to be my age, you'll understand," said Edward, "that it's a bloody slap in the face to be treated like a child."

"I'm sure she—"

"Do I look like a man who can't handle a little international travel?"

Will had clearly come on the wrong day. "No, sir."

"I've traveled more than anyone else in this family. I was in East Berlin in the '60s, Shanghai in the '70s, and Leningrad in the '80s. I've been to war zones. Don't tell me where I can and cannot go."

Edward had yet to invite Will to take a seat, but Will did anyway, sitting on the matching chair that was placed at an angle beside Edward's. Will turned his body to face him, while Edward stared straight ahead.

"Where are you going?" Will asked.

"If Bridget gets her way, I'm being wheeled with Lottie onto a padded yacht, lashed to the mast to keep me out of trouble, and fed baby food with a plastic spoon."

"I'm sure that's not what—"

"Hans, my future son-in-law, put a bee in Bridget's bonnet. He thinks I'm not to be trusted." In his dark suit, Edward looked responsible enough to run a nation, in spite of the embroidered slippers on his feet. "I thought Lottie and I would be good traveling companions, and a happy couple, but I wonder now what I've gotten myself into at this point in my life. Maybe I'm better off on my own."

Edward looked deadly serious. Will understood his doubts all too well, but hated to think of Edward canceling the wedding, of Lottie jilted. Of a big family rift.

"I've been fine by myself for forty blasted years," Edward said. "I finally enter into a relationship, and I'm suddenly on trial by a jury of our offspring. I won't stand for a loss of my independence."

Will had come prepared for a very different conversation. "I'm sure you don't mean that. You and Charlotte have so much to look forward to."

Edward turned his head and looked at him then, for the first time since Will had come in. "You stayed clear of marriage, though, didn't you?" His expression had changed, as if he saw Will as an ally. "After one bad experience, you avoided getting married all these years, so you must value your independence like I do. Well? Aren't you going to tell me to run for my life?"

Will shifted in his chair. "Being single has its advantages," he said. "Or I always thought so. And then one day the alternative presented itself in the form of an extraordinary woman who happens to be your wedding florist. Now I find myself rethinking my position on love and commitment and everything else. Bachelorhood is lonely, and the future will be very bleak if Emma isn't part of my life."

Edward made a sound of disgust that conveyed his opinion: Will was being useless.

"Why did you propose to Lottie?" Will asked.

"I've been asking myself that question. As Goethe said, 'Heart, my heart, what are you doing?' But I'm enamored, unable and unwilling to escape the 'magic spun with magic skill.' And I thought—" Edward's face grew dark again. "No one ever tried to limit me before Hans came along. To be questioned now by a man who barely knows me, to be doubted and disrespected by him, is infuriating," he said. "I don't appreciate being treated like a child. Lottie and I are fully capable of taking care of ourselves, and it's not as though I'm proposing a trek up Everest."

"What *are* you proposing?"

In the next room, the composer slammed his hands on the keys in rapid succession and in no particular rhythm, causing both Will and Edward to jump.

"A folly," said Edward. He placed his palms on his knees and stared straight ahead. "When the girls were small, we took them to London, where we saw George Bernard Shaw's *Pygmalion*. Bridget loved everything about that trip, the city, the museums, the show. I remember watching Peter O'Toole as Henry Higgins that night, a character who is delighted to take on a new project, and when someone implies it's a foolish undertaking, he says, 'What is life but a series of inspired follies? Never lose a chance: it doesn't come every day.' I don't want to lose this chance. Or, in the words of Lin-Manuel Miranda, 'I'm not throwing away my shot.' It's the last chance I'll have to delight in a bold action, to take on a folly that inspires me."

Will already knew the answer, but he asked again. "And what's the folly you're inspired to take on?"

Edward glared at him. "Our itinerary is no one's concern. I was willing to discuss the plans until I caught wind of this mutiny in my own family. All of a sudden, my travel is everybody's business, and Hans is acting as if he has veto power over me. He's sabotaging the wedding! It's blackmail. If we don't capitulate to his demands, he won't come. Lottie folded immediately, agreeing to cancel the whole trip. But not me. I won't negotiate with a terrorist."

"Terrorist?" asked Will. "Really?"

"Maybe Hans can boss Lottie around, but Bridget can't tell *me* what to do."

"In that respect," Will said sincerely, "I envy you. I'll never have children to boss me around. I'm sure it's frustrating, but you have to admit, it's kind of sweet."

Edward didn't respond. He crossed his arms and frowned.

After a moment of silence, Will said, "Are there compromises you'd be willing to make?"

"Why on earth," he bellowed, "should I compro—"

"Let's say you and Lottie go to the Athens Festival as planned. You attend the concert of Handel's mythological operas at Odeon of Herodes Atticus, stay at the King George—"

"I thought Bridget hadn't talked to you about any of this—"

"She may have told me a little. You can even stay long enough to see Robert Wilson's production of *Oedipus* at the Ancient Theater of Epidaurus. And after a pleasant stay in Athens, you treat yourselves to a cruise as suggested by your loving daughter, soak up the sun, stop off in Crete or Cyprus if you feel inclined, and then return to New York."

"What for?"

"Clean boxers."

Edward almost smiled.

"To visit your daughters, of course," Will said. "To introduce Lottie to your friends, take her to the Met. Hans will see that his beloved mother is alive and well, at which point she can call to tell him that you're both going to Munich for a visit, during which you can take off to Salzburg or Budapest or Prague or wherever you like. Why spook everybody by trying to break some kind of record? Ease them into it. That's my advice."

Will was surprised by his own boldness. His usual stance with Edward was to maintain a respectful distance and speak very little.

"Give in to their demands?" Edward said. "No. I won't set that precedent."

"You're not giving in; you're outsmarting them. You're letting them think they've put on the brakes when in fact you're still doing exactly what you wanted to do anyway, on a slightly modified schedule. Hans is just looking after his mother, which, in my opinion, says something positive about their family. Your girls are looking after you because they give a shit, excuse me. You can get rid of all this conflict with a little diplomacy." Edward seemed to consider this advice, as Will added, "And speaking of diplomacy, I have a request."

He hesitated, and then said, "I want you to know that what I'm proposing will ruin a big wedding surprise Bridget has for you."

"I detest surprises."

The composer in the next room had gone completely silent, as Will second-guessed his plan. At the reception, when Edward took his seat at the piano and Will stepped off the stage, where would he go? Would he stand alone, off to the side, like a wallflower? Would he sit with some of the music teachers he'd invited so he could watch their reactions to his arrangement? Would he take a seat beside Emma and hold her hand? This decision was about more than playing the piece at the wedding. It was about his future. He felt a lump in his throat.

Rather than say anything else, Will handed Edward the sheet music. Edward smiled when he saw the title and sat quietly, reviewing the piece and tapping his foot as he heard it in his mind. "I haven't seen this in ages. It's naive, isn't it? Unsophisticated."

"I love it. And it's perfect for such a happy occasion. I hope you like my arrangement because I can't really make changes at this point," Will said lightly, though he was, in fact, completely serious. "Bridget and Gavin already have their copies and are preparing to play it for you at the wedding, and I don't want to spring more on them than I already am: I want you to play it instead of me."

Edward looked up at him. "Play with Bridget?"

Will nodded. "During the reception." He thought to add, *If there's going to be a wedding*, but Edward didn't balk at the idea, so he let it go.

"You're giving up the chance to reunite as your original trio," Edward said, looking at him. "Is this because Gavin Glantz is your nemesis?"

"No," Will said. "Not anymore."

Edward looked over the music. "You've given him the best part in the piece."

"The melody you wrote is beautiful—"

"You once instrumentalized me to get Gavin out of your life," Edward said pointedly.

It wasn't a question, but Will answered. "Yes, it was wrong." It occurred to Will that this was by far the longest, most personal conversation they'd ever had. Why not make it the most honest as well? "I was jealous of him."

"He's undoubtedly very jealous of you," said Edward.

Will laughed. "No, never. Gavin was the star, the prodigy, the one the faculty and press doted on. He got all the prizes, the accolades. I've always been the hard worker who keeps his head down and plugs along. There's nothing to envy."

"Gavin has problems of his own," said Edward. He looked at Will with his eyebrows raised and said, "The director of the orchestra of the Sydney Opera House called me after Gavin started there, angry I'd recommended him. It was embarrassing."

"Angry?" said Will. "Why?"

"His attitude made his colleagues despise him from his first day, and he caused tension in the violin section and beyond. Gavin is the kind of man," Edward said, "who makes a hideous initial impression. He inspires hate at first sight, poor man. Many make up their minds right then and dislike him forever. A few, like my biographer, Nicholas Donahue, take the time to get to know him and find him worthy of their friendship."

This observation was true, and Will also knew which group he was squarely in.

"I assure you," Edward said, "it's not easy going through life, personally or professionally, when you put people off as soon as you meet them."

"But why would he be jealous of me?"

"Oh, come now, Will. You're engaging and likable, generous and professional. Enough said, I'm not here to flatter you. I'm sure Gavin felt like the third wheel in Forsyth, since you and Bridget were always so close."

Will got an odd sense of satisfaction hearing all this. "Bridget and I are a good team," he said.

"It's impressive what you two have done together all these years. You're both exceptionally good."

A compliment from Edward was rare indeed. "Thank you."

Edward looked down at the score in his hands. "Change is not failure."

Will didn't know if he was referring to the arrangement he'd written, his upcoming nuptials, or Will and Bridget's future. The composer in the living room began to play again, discordant and jarring chords that physically repulsed Will. Why people wrote music that was ugly on purpose was something Will would never understand.

"Change," Edward repeated, "is not failure." He turned to Will. "Let's kick that composer off my piano before he breaks it, shall we?"

Will got to his feet, resisting the temptation to offer Edward a hand to help him up, lest he seem patronizing. But he stood by closely, in case.

"Do me a favor," Edward said, handing him the music. "I'd like to hear you play the piece first. Then I'll give it a whirl."

27

One of Isabelle's biggest flaws, she'd be willing to admit, was that she was convinced she could straighten out everyone else's life while her own was—to the objective observer—a shit show.

"You should write an advice column," a college friend had once said. And it was true. She had excellent instincts, as her mother had always told her, about all things, from judging character to making critical life decisions. This summer she'd offered counsel to Oscar (on his marriage), Will (on his girlfriend), and her mom (on pretty much everything).

So how the hell did she, of all people, end up working as a part-time employee at a country coffee shop, living with her mom, and dating a guy who didn't have a college degree?

This was a gap summer, if ever there was such a thing. The one and only reboot she was allowing herself in life. She didn't regret her decision to quit her job and get the hell out of Hong Kong. The homesickness she'd felt there had been debilitating, and her job was purposeless and Sisyphean, work that did nothing whatsoever for the good of society. She'd been sure she was getting tumors behind her eyeballs from the computer screen and worried about the severity of her cramps every month and the new pinching pain in her lower back. She was too young to feel this old. She wanted to interact with people rather than data. Wanted to live her life rather than endure it. She wanted to be part of a community.

She wasn't feeling old now. Maybe Juliette Stark's book wasn't scientifically sound, maybe half of it was bullshit, but it made her feel good, made her think. Isabelle was going to keep following her plan, at least for the rest of the summer. That Kevin was willing to go along with it was adorable.

But there was so much more she needed to do. Fate had brought her home this summer. Being home meant she'd been there to help her mother through her breakup. She'd stopped her brother from fucking up his marriage. She was attending her grandfather's wedding. She'd met a truly great guy. She felt better in every respect, that was for sure. And the best part was that Juliette's program had given them a common cause, some family "team" spirit. There was more to do. Meanwhile, she was biding her time, walking around with a paint roller in her right hand and an heirloom carrot in her left, considering the most difficult question: What would she do once the summer was over?

———◇———

The day before the wedding was warm and muggy, and Isabelle and Kevin were up early, ready to take on the final wedding preparations. But before she'd even made a pot of matcha tea, she was summoned by her mother to the main house. When she walked in, Oscar, who had arrived the night before with Matt, was explaining to Will why they'd decided to leave Hadley and Bear in DC that weekend. "It's better not to mix big dogs and caterers. That's what Matt said anyway."

"Probably a smart idea," said Will. "Right, Bridget?"

"What?"

"Dogs and weddings," he said. "Could get messy. Did your father go along with the cruise idea?"

"A cruise?" Isabelle asked. "What about all the plans Jackie made?"

Bridget didn't answer, and Isabelle began to suspect that something was wrong. Jackie had rushed out of the house early that morning, saying Marge was in a panic and needed her. (Matt offered to give her a ride, and on their way out, Jackie tripped and dropped her bag, which contained, Isabelle couldn't help but see, a large, half-eaten bag of potato chips. Isabelle pretended not to notice the contraband.)

"What's going on?" Isabelle asked. From down the hall she could hear the low rumble of the washer and dryer. Her mom sat down awkwardly on the couch. She was wearing a beige linen dress Isabelle had never seen before and a lot of eye makeup and lip gloss, strange given that the only thing happening that day, other than cleaning the house and making sure the tables and chairs arrived and were set up properly, was a Forsyth Trio rehearsal. Will took a seat next to her. He was also looking spiffy in well-pressed thin cotton khakis and a loose white button-down.

Eliza rubbed up against Bridget's leg and jumped in her lap. Across from them, Isabelle sat next to Oscar; they looked at the grown-ups with matching puzzled expressions. Something was definitely up.

"Are you two going on safari?" Oscar asked. "I feel like I'm on the set of *Out of Africa*."

"Is there a photo shoot we don't know about?" said Isabelle.

"Don't tell me. You're getting a divorce," said Oscar. "Was it my fault?"

Bridget laughed, a little too loudly. Will put his hand on her knee.

"The only thing more bizarre," Oscar added, "would be if you announced you're getting married. I'll need therapy if that's where this is going."

"Nothing like that," Will said.

"It may be a little surprising, though," her mom said.

Something about this scene, the four of them sitting so formally, with her mother's Prussian silver teapot of organic chamomile and a plate of ginger snaps (from a recipe in *Ancient Practices, Modern Life*) on the table in front of them, made Isabelle feel like she was in a bedroom farce. She wished they all had British accents.

"It's slightly awkward and a tad overdue," said Bridget. She picked up her tea, and the cup rattled against the saucer.

Isabelle saw her glance at Will, who gave her an encouraging wink. *What the hell?*

"There's a musician," Bridget began, "a violinist named Gavin Glantz, who's coming to the house today to rehearse with us. He went to college with us . . ." She trailed off and looked at Will.

"He was in our original trio, and we were friends for a decade," Will said, "so, of course, we were all quite close, back in the day."

"Around the end of that particular era," Bridget said, as though beginning a grand lecture, "was when I decided I was ready to have kids. I . . . was very eager to get pregnant."

Isabelle waited, seeing that her mother had hit some kind of dead end.

"So eager, in fact," said Will, smiling, "that she once asked *me* to be the father."

Bridget turned and looked at Will. "No, I didn't."

Will said, quite earnestly, "You did. I don't know how serious you were, but you did ask. I was honored actually."

"I must have been joking," said Bridget.

"That's offensive," Will said. "And you didn't sound like you were joking. We were at your studio apartment, and you said, 'Would you consider . . .' and 'no strings attached.' Remember?"

She squinted, her eyes focused on some point on the wall behind Isabelle. "Wait," Bridget said, "I did, didn't I? We were eating takeout—"

"Dumplings."

"—after you got divorced. And what did you say?"

"We *both* said it would be too thorny," said Will.

Noël Coward, thought Isabelle, could spruce up this scene, get it stage-ready. All that was missing was the slamming of doors.

Oscar was looking slightly horrified. "Too much information, you guys," he said. "Can we get to the point? The wedding's in T minus twenty-eight hours, and Matt and I are in charge of picking up the alcohol."

Isabelle had often wondered if Bridget and Will had ever . . . A single night in all their years together? But she'd come to believe that no moment of passion had ever taken place. It's true they were physically comfortable with each other, often touching casually or even affectionately. But there was no spark between them, nothing complicated or charged.

"The point is," said Will, "your mom really wanted to get pregnant—"

"I had artificial insemination," Bridget said, "but . . . Gavin, this violinist I never talk about, was leaving the country, and we were out one night . . ."

"Wait," Isabelle said. She wanted to make things easier for her mom but wasn't sure where to begin. "You think our donor wasn't some anonymous man from a sperm bank?" Isabelle said. "You think he's a real person?"

Oscar bumped his shoulder against Isabelle's. "He's a real person in any case, Einstein," he said. "They don't make artificial sperm."

"I know that," said Isabelle, shoving him back.

"I went to a doctor to get inseminated," Bridget was saying, "just like I told you. But I also— It's remotely possible that I— Well, I was convinced that I might have trouble getting pregnant, so I may have been a bit cavalier . . ." It was obvious that for Bridget discussing a topic that included her sex life was mortifying.

"Your mom really wanted you guys," Will said, "so she was a real go-getter when the time came . . ."

"I wasn't *that* much of a go-getter—"

Eliza jumped off Bridget's lap, as if to say, *I'm a good girl, I am!* "So, you've been worrying about this?" Isabelle said. "All these years?"

"'Secrets damage the soul,'" Bridget said, quoting from the Juliette Stark book, and then she put her hands up, sort of like *whoops*, and forced a smile, baring her teeth. "I'm sorry I never said anything before. I lost track of Gavin because he moved out of the country and on with his life, but he's coming here today, and I realize how wrong it was to keep this from you."

"You guys looked so serious," said Oscar, sounding relieved. "I thought for sure one of you had cancer."

"You could do a paternity test," Bridget said. "And if it turned out that it was him, you'd know more about your family history and genes or . . ."

"He's not psychotic or anything? A serial killer?" Oscar asked.

Will and Bridget shook their heads.

"So he's a donor either way," said Oscar. "A donor you know versus one you don't."

Isabelle reached for her mother's hand across the tea set. "He's the one you don't know," she said.

"But it could have been Gavin," said Bridget. "That's my point."

"It's not Gavin," said Isabelle.

Bridget looked at her as though she were a professor of the dark arts. Isabelle always tried to be patient with her mother when it came to her lack of technological knowledge. It wasn't her fault she didn't grow up with the internet. And her mom had skills that Isabelle didn't have, after all, good penmanship, for example. Reading music. But, *my God*, had no one heard of genetic testing? "I spit in a tube," said Isabelle.

"How does that rule out Gavin?" Will asked.

"Because we got a match," Isabelle said, pointing from herself to Oscar. "I wanted to know about our genetic makeup, what diseases ran in our family—"

"You're such a hypochondriac," said Oscar. "And how is this a 'we' thing?"

"You were already in the database, so you must have done genetic testing before."

Oscar smiled the way he did now whenever Matt was part of the conversation. "Right, Matt got us kits once." They waited, and Oscar said casually, "We're thinking about surrogacy down the road."

"You should go on the website," Isabelle said. "We got an 'extremely high confidence' paternal match with a man with no genetic health risks, mostly northwestern European decent, Neanderthal ancestry, and six other offspring from donations he made in college for money. Very into outdoorsy life, hiking, and climbing. He's a business owner—"

"Why didn't you tell me any of this?" Bridget asked, her voice much higher than normal.

"Yeah," Oscar said, "why didn't you tell me?"

"I was going to," Isabelle said, "but you were both having crises in your love lives, and I didn't think it was the right time." Isabelle couldn't tell what they were thinking. "If I'd known you were stressing about this," she said to her mom, "I would have said something." She thought she should probably explain her abrupt departure from Hong Kong while she was at it. "I came here in part because I wanted to meet him." She felt her face go hot and swallowed. "It's Peter Latham."

"The llama guy?" Oscar asked.

"Alpaca," said Isabelle.

"Your boss?" asked Bridget. "Is that why you—?"

"Does he know?" asked Will.

She shook her head. "I was waiting to tell you all first."

"You're so weird," said Oscar. "You're stalking our baby daddy?"

"I'm not *stalking* him. I'm getting to know him."

"And?" said Bridget.

Isabelle had no idea where to begin. "He has an Instagram page devoted solely to his alpacas; it has over a hundred thousand followers."

Oscar rolled his eyes. "Apart from his social media presence?"

Isabelle felt somehow proud, excited to talk about him. "Peter has a terrific sense of humor, a conscience, a wonderful life, great teeth, and a full head of hair." She smiled. "I admire him."

It wouldn't be right to make the discovery all about herself, so she didn't explain that once she'd found the name of her biological father, she'd googled Peter, reading an article about how he'd left a big corporation and moved to the country, transforming his barn into his place of work. How he hired employees from his own rural Connecticut community, paying them a living wage. He created the life he wanted. Before even laying eyes on him, Peter had inspired her to quit her job, and she had no regrets about that. This summer—one spent observing how Peter Latham ran his company—had ended up being more satisfying and educational than any work she'd done before. And her personal time—spent with Kevin, a man who could not have had his boots planted more firmly on the ground—was better medicine than all the Xanax she'd ever taken. The summer had been a win.

"We could tell him together," she told Oscar, "maybe after the wedding."

"I still don't understand how any of this works," said Bridget.

"Can we discuss the miracles of DNA databases another time?" said Oscar, getting to his feet. "We've got two hundred people showing up here tomorrow, and Matt and I promised Kevin we'd help set up the sound system, and we still have to pick up the booze."

"You'll like him," said Isabelle. "And you might be interested to hear that he runs his entire business using renewable sources of energy." There were other interesting aspects about Peter she would share with Oscar later: He came to work every day with his two big golden retrievers. He'd followed Jerry Garcia on tour in the '80s. And he was ethical to his core.

Isabelle couldn't read her mother's expression.

Will apparently could. "This is wonderful news," he said. "Everything's in the open, Bridget. Gavin is just . . . good old Gavin, you know? Our old friend. Nothing more complicated than that."

Bridget seemed to be processing his words, and then she smiled, with what seemed like enormous relief.

28

Oscar went with Matt to the liquor store, and Isabelle left with Kevin to pick up speaker cables, followed by Will, who headed upstairs to the loft to make sure his room was cleaned up for Gwen.

Bridget was alone.

She hadn't known how she'd react if or when she found out who had fathered her amazing, beautiful children, but now that she had, she felt as though she'd set down an awkward, heavy burden she'd been lugging around, leaving her off balance but free. She was elated. Gavin, her long-ago friend, a man she'd been trying to erase, could take his place in her life history. She found herself excited to see him.

And how odd, she thought, to have one of the most important partnerships in her life be with a stranger she had never met before who was living only a few miles away. She found herself—just as Isabelle had—wanting to know more about Peter, wanting to thank him for her children.

For the first time in weeks, the house was quiet, and she felt a pang of loneliness.

It was hard not to notice how paired up everyone around her was.

Emma and Will were in love. Her father and Lottie were starting their life together. Matt and Oscar were reunited. Isabelle and Kevin were happy.

It was too quiet. It occurred to her that this was how it was going to be once the wedding was over. Her and her cats. What a sad transition from this to that, she thought. She wouldn't be able to bear it. Eventually they would all leave. What reason would she have to come back here?

The house looked perfect. Maybe now was the time to let it go. She could imagine Mark showing her property to prospective buyers: *You've heard of Edward Stratton, right? Famous composer and conductor? He got married in this very barn.* If the *New York Times* showed up and printed photos in the society pages, the price might go even higher.

Bridget got up and went to her room, closing the door behind her. Before she could even find Mark's number in her contacts, she saw she'd missed a call from an international number: a woman named Diane had left a voice mail, inviting her to audition for the London Philharmonic in two weeks: "Please confirm the appointment at your earliest convenience." Bridget checked the time, added five hours, and called her back immediately.

"Yes!" she told Diane. "Yes, I'll be there. Absolutely, I can find it, and thank you, thank you very much."

Diane gave her the details, telling her to be prepared to play from Elgar's *Enigma* Variations and the second movement of Shostakovich's Symphony no. 10. She would email the specific excerpts.

"I'm thrilled," said Bridget, "and so honored for the opportunity."

After they hung up the phone, Bridget jumped on her bed and screamed into her pillow.

As soon as she regained control of herself, she called the Realtor.

Bridget took a seat in the living room and began to tune her cello. What, she wondered, should she work on first? Her audition excerpts or the piece for the wedding? Her heart was beating quickly, and she knew it wasn't only the audition making her feel so invigorated. She was excited to see Gavin and even more excited for the three of them to play together again, like old times, only better, now that they'd all grown up a bit. The very idea made her smile and gave her confidence.

As she turned the pegs, she could feel her cello fighting to stay in tune in the humidity. She would take it to the shop where she'd bought it years ago and ask for the name of a top luthier in London to give it some TLC beyond what she could give it herself. She would take a walk in St. James's Park, followed by a visit to the National Gallery. Every time she pictured herself in London, with a regular job in an orchestra, walking into a proper rehearsal room with a conductor and concertmaster, going out for dinner with a flock of musicians, she felt a thrill. A rafter of musicians? A throng?

And how would she find herself in such a large group?

Out the living room window, Bridget saw a man walking toward the house. It wasn't Kevin or Elliot. Bridget squinted. It was Nicholas Donahue, coming toward her with a satchel over his shoulder, and in his arms was Henry, in a posture of complete relaxation.

She put her cello on its side and went out to meet them, noticing the bank of clouds that was moving in, a hint of cooler air.

"Where did you find him?" she asked, afraid to speak too loudly in case she scared Henry away.

Nicholas seemed surprised by the question. "Isn't he yours? Don't tell me I've picked up a stray."

"He's ours," she said, smiling at him and tentatively reaching out a hand to pat Henry's head, "but he's gone wild this summer." She leaned down and kissed Henry. "This is the closest I've been to him in weeks." This was the closest she'd been to any man in weeks, and she could feel Nicholas watching her.

"He came out of the shrubbery by the driveway when I parked," Nicholas said, "and started meowing right at me, as though he could tell I'm starved for conversation. It's lovely to see you."

Nicholas had had his hair cut short since the last time she'd seen him and was neatly dressed, as if for a party. Had he got the date wrong? "Thanks," she said and pointed toward the house. "I'm sure Will would love to say hello."

Nicholas's expression turned serious. "I'm sorry for dropping in on you and Will like this," he said. "Frightfully impolite of me. I know the wedding isn't until tomorrow—"

"No, it's fine—"

"—but Gavin was staying with me at a house I'm renting and said he has a rehearsal with you today to practice Edward's piece. I was hoping you might allow me to sit in, for research purposes. Mum's the word, of course; I understand it's a surprise."

It was good to hear Gavin's name and not recoil. "I didn't know you and Gavin were friends," she said.

Nicholas pulled Henry closer to his face and said, "Be very glad that the Glantz family isn't staying here with you. Danny the Horrible would pull your tail from sunup to sundown."

"Really?" asked Bridget, curious. "Does Gavin have a difficult child?"

"I hate to be judgmental," he said. "Gavin's a good friend, but he and his wife are demanding houseguests and the most tightly wound parents I've ever known."

Bridget laughed, trying to picture Gavin as a family man.

"I'm not saying I was a perfect father," Nicholas said. "I botched it up, certainly. But my kids are adults now, and I can't fathom it—taming a toddler at this point in my life? And Gavin's child is . . ." Nicholas made a face of complete exasperation.

"Raising kids wasn't easy," said Bridget. "I can't imagine doing it at my age either."

"The whole situation wore me out utterly. I'm exhausted. Do you know about his wife, Juliette? She's a psychologist and lifestyle expert, which is rather ironic given the dynamics of her own family. She gifted me a copy of her book before she left, but after what I witnessed, I'm not at all certain her advice should be followed. *Ancient Rhythms, Modern Love* or some blasted thing."

"No!" said Bridget. "You don't mean Juliette Stark?"

Nicholas looked alarmed, saying, "Oh dear, have I said the wrong thing? Is she a friend of yours? I'm terribly sorry—"

"*The* Juliette Stark?" After almost three weeks of following the rules of *Ancient Practices, Modern Life*, Bridget felt as though she and Juliette were friends. "She's married to *Gavin*?"

"You know her?"

Bridget couldn't wait to tell Isabelle that their guru was coming to the wedding. "My daughter made me start doing her program. I have to admit, I feel pretty good after a few weeks of ancient grains and humming."

"Well, you look marvelous, so perhaps Juliette knows what she's doing after all."

"Thank you," Bridget said.

They walked inside just as a light drizzle was starting to fall. Bridget asked about the book he was writing, and Nicholas did, in fact, seem starved for conversation; he was delighted to discuss his progress. "It's been so interesting to hear stories from your father. He told me how he met your mother."

"*Synchronicity*," said Bridget, as he followed her into the kitchen.

"My father talks a lot about timing and coincidence, even the role of fate. It's funny, I haven't found that fate played a particularly impactful role in my life."

"Fate didn't bring you and Will together?" he asked, putting Henry on the counter.

Bridget looked at him and smiled, embarrassed. "I meant romantically."

"So did I."

"No, Will and I aren't together," she said. "We're friends."

"That's . . . well, lovely," said Nicholas. "I mean, wonderful that you . . . How special to have a long-time friendship." Nicholas drummed his fingers on the kitchen island, and Bridget could feel his eyes following her as she opened a can of cat food.

"Look at this, Henry," she said. "Remember the perks of a civilized life?"

The doorbell rang for the first time in a decade, a loud but soothing chime.

"That sound!" she said, delighted to hear the bell working. "My daughter's boyfriend is a miracle worker. I'll be right back."

Bridget left him to go to the front door, which she opened to find the chiseled fireman she'd met at her father's house (posed in a wide stance, wearing his full uniform), flanked by Elliot on one side (in jeans with a tool belt slung low around his hips, holding a flat package) and Randall Bennett on the other (wearing aviator sunglasses with his navy suit, carrying a briefcase). Bridget felt like she was hosting an elementary school career day.

Trying to get the greetings right, she kissed the music manager on the cheek, shook hands with the fireman, smiled warmly at the architect, and invited them all in.

After introducing themselves to each other, they stood around the kitchen. Bridget faced the men, unsure where to begin. She decided to start with the visitor whose presence was the most baffling.

"Marge called me at the station," the fireman said, setting his helmet on the counter. "I think the fire at the house shook her up pretty bad, and she asked me to make sure your barn's up to safety standards for the party. She says you've got some bad wiring over here, something about you getting electrocuted recently?"

Marge knew perfectly well that Bridget had fixed all the wiring issues in the house and barn; this was a setup. "We did everything by the book," she said, "but you can certainly take a look."

"I'd be happy to do a quick inspection."

Elliot looked defensive, like he was being challenged to a duel. "The electrical's completely up to code. A licensed electrician did the installation and wired in new fire alarms, and we got permits for all the work." In a voice more confident than his usual soft-spoken one, he added, "We installed all the exterior lighting fixtures just this morning for the safety of the guests."

"Glad to hear it," said the fireman, sounding somehow patriotic. "Marge will be relieved."

Elliot handed Bridget the small package. "Here," he said. "A gift from the town hall."

Bridget opened the brown paper and pulled out a heavy plaque:

State Register of Historic Places, Recorded Property 1795

"I'm landmarked?" she said.

"It went through. Congratulations."

"So even if I sold the place," she said, "no one can tear the barn down now?"

Elliot looked vaguely wounded. "You're thinking of selling?" he asked.

Bridget wanted to say something reassuring, but she couldn't.

Instead she hugged the plaque to her chest, saying, "I only meant in theory." She held the plaque out, like a trophy, and slowly turned so they could all see it.

"Would you like a bit of trivia?" Nicholas said. "Beethoven wrote his Opus 1 that year: three piano trios."

"Really?" she said. This day, she decided, was turning out to be marvelous. "You know, I feel like celebrating. Does anyone want champagne?" She went to her refrigerator and pulled out a bottle. "Juliette Stark is going to have to forgive me," she said, handing the bottle to Nicholas and getting glasses from the cabinet. "I'm in an outstanding mood." She looked around the room, realizing the whole scene was starting to feel like she was starring in an episode of *The Dating Game*. Bridget couldn't share the main reason she was feeling so elated, so she said, "We'll drink to the return of my cat Henry."

Bachelor number three . . . "What brings you here, Randall?"

"Randy. I really enjoyed our lunch the other day. And I have fantastic news that I wanted to tell you in person."

"The other day? We had lunch over a *month* ago," Bridget said. She felt an irrational need to explain to bachelors one, two, and four: "Randy's my manager. Well, he's not *my* manager, but he's *a* manager."

"And we went out on a date—"

The cork popped loudly and spewed champagne on Nicholas's shoes.

"It wasn't a *date*," Bridget said to the other men. "It was a work lunch—"

"—that turned into a date."

"Only because we ordered wine," Bridget said, "and then I never heard from you again." As Nicholas wiped the floor, Bridget took the champagne and poured herself a glass.

"I've been thinking about you," said Randy, "and everything you said about the trio and your plans. And I thought to myself, *Bridget*

Stratton doesn't really want to leave her life in New York City. So, I got to work, and I managed to find you and Will a soloist. A star! He's a little green but very talented, and he wants to meet you. I set up a meeting in my office for next week."

Nicholas filled the glasses and handed one to Randy. "Is it anyone I know?"

"That depends," Randy said, looking smug. "Are you familiar with classical music?"

Bridget waited to see how Nicholas would respond. Humbly, as it turned out: "Somewhat," he said. He offered glasses to Elliot and to the fireman, who turned it down. He kept that glass for himself.

"Nicholas," Bridget said proudly, "is a musicologist, historian, writer, professor at Oxford, and—"

"Nicholas *Donahue*?" Randy said. "Ah, I didn't put it together. You're here for the wedding?"

"Among other reasons," said Nicholas. "Who's the violinist?"

"Xing Luo," Randy said. "He's excited about Forsyth. He's a marvelous player, was a child prodigy in Beijing."

"Will doesn't like prodigies," Bridget said, wondering if there was even a point to this conversation. What would Will say? Would he be interested? Part of her was hoping he would surprise her; the other part was hoping he wouldn't.

"He'll like Xing," said Randy firmly.

"We haven't made our decision yet," Bridget said. "We're still thinking—"

"If you get Xing, you won't have anything to think about," said Randy. "It's an honor he's even considering joining you."

Bridget found that comment insulting.

"Look," said Randall kindly, walking right up to her, "you've dedicated your whole career to the trio, so I wanted to give you and Will one last chance to save it. I figured you couldn't possibly be serious about wanting to move to *London*."

"London?" said Elliot.

"London!" said Nicholas.

Before Bridget could respond, she looked up and saw that Mark was walking into the kitchen. *Hello, bachelor number five.*

"I got your message," he said, breathless and eager, a manila folder in one hand and his phone in the other, "and I just happened to be in the neighborhood. Thought I'd drop by. Is this a bad time?"

This, thought Bridget as she sipped her champagne and looked at the men assembled in her kitchen, was really too much.

Mark and the fireman clearly knew each other; Mark clapped him on the back.

"The place looks fantastic," said Mark. "I sure as hell didn't think it was possible to get that barn looking so good."

"Thanks," said Elliot. "I was in charge of the renovation."

"Is it safe in there now?"

"I'll let you know once I inspect it," said the fireman.

"Between the settling, the holes in the roof, and the bats," said Mark with a laugh, "I thought for sure it should be condemned."

"It's perfectly safe," said Elliot curtly, "and watertight."

Mark smiled at Bridget. "Nice! You've gone way beyond curb appeal. We'll have this place sold before the leaves change."

Elliot looked disappointed, Nicholas looked intrigued, and Randall looked slightly bored.

"Wait." Bridget wanted to change the subject. "I have to talk to Will before I say another word about any of this."

"Talk to Will about what?" Will came into the kitchen carrying a large cardboard box that was overflowing with books and clothing. Looking both amused and bewildered, he said hello to each of the men in turn, shaking their hands as he went around the room. "Randall," he said, "what brings you here?" He saw the open champagne bottle and glasses. "What are we celebrating?"

"I've got great news," said Randall.

But Bridget was fixated on the carton Will had set down on the floor at her feet. "What's all that?" she asked. His toothbrush and razors were in a cup balanced on top, his T-shirts folded underneath. He'd packed his stuff. All of it.

Mark looked pleased and smiled at Will like they were old friends. "Packing already," Mark said. "You guys aren't kidding around. Let's get this place on the market."

"What?" Will looked at the box. "No, this is just—"

"What are you doing?" Bridget said, surprised at the urgency of her voice. The sight of the box made it painfully clear: Will was done with her house. He was done with her. "I can't believe you're leaving."

"What's wrong?" Will asked. The five men watched as Will walked over to her, saying, "Bridget, this doesn't mean anything. I'm not going anywhere. I'm just making room for Gwen."

"You *packed*," she said, wishing she weren't about to cry in front of all these people.

"I was being considerate."

Will was, in fact, exceedingly considerate, but Bridget knew there was more to it. "We need to talk," she said.

Nicholas turned to the other men, saying, "I, for one, would really like to see inside that spectacular old barn."

Elliot got up, offering to give everyone a tour. Randall, Mark, and the fireman followed him and Nicholas out, leaving Bridget and Will alone.

Will hugged her. "I didn't mean to upset you," he said. "I honestly thought I was being polite. Tell me what's going on."

"I'm scared we're losing each other."

"Never," he said. "Even if things change—"

"I got an audition," she said, "in London."

Will let her go, and she saw the look of astonishment on his face. "I guess we do need to talk," he said.

"But I can cancel it. Neither of us *has* to go anywhere." She took his hands. "Randall found a new violinist for the trio." She watched him, trying to gauge his reaction. "I told him we don't know what we're doing, but he already set up a meeting for next week, and we need to decide . . . We could get right back to our life in New York, rehearsing and touring all the time. Is that what you want? How would Emma fit in to all that?"

"I don't know," said Will.

"Because you love her, don't you?"

Will nodded.

"Do you know what you want?" she asked.

"Do you?"

"Do you?"

They looked at each other, neither wanting to speak first.

Bridget heard the sound of a man clearing his throat and looked behind her. There was Gavin Glantz standing in the doorway of her kitchen.

He was taller than Bridget remembered, older certainly, but then, so were they all. He had circles under his eyes and less hair than he had back in the day, but when he smiled, he looked exactly like the boy she'd met at Juilliard, the one with whom she'd shared a stage for years. They'd grown up together, traveled, laughed, and, yes, spent one remarkable night together. He waved at them, with a shy smile and funny little flip of his hand. She squeezed Will's, and they crossed the room together to greet their old friend.

29

"**M**an, I'm so glad you *finally* get it," Frank said.

It was the morning of the wedding, and Will was about to take his road test. He was driving Frank's car from Emma's house to the DMV in Fishkill across the New York State line, and for reasons Will couldn't understand himself, he had told Frank his tentative plans. Frank reached a hand over for a high five.

"I can't," said Will. "I need to keep my hands at ten and two. Besides, it's not settled or anything." He had the wipers going at a fast clip and wasn't appreciating the extra degree of difficulty the rain was providing for his driver's test.

"You're giving up that cesspool of a city you live in," Frank said, "after all these years."

"Maybe." Will checked his side mirror. "I'm thinking about it."

"Stop thinking so much."

Will didn't have a choice. There were practical matters to go along with the emotional ones, real problems to solve. Moving would cost money, and Will hadn't made enough that summer. He had no concrete prospects for a teaching job in Connecticut, and yet he was strongly considering leaving New York.

"And slow down," said Frank. "You're going five over the speed limit."

Will put his foot on the brake. His trip to the city the week before had cemented some realities in his mind: he didn't feel the same about being there anymore. The closest he could come to describe how he felt when he was in his own apartment was to say he was homesick.

Mitzy was leaving. He and Hudson had brought her dinner after she had her second cataract surgery, and she'd told him she was moving to Boston to live with her daughter; the news hit him hard.

"I'll miss you," he told her.

She'd patted Hudson on the head with her tiny, bony hand. "If I can't stay in my apartment, then I'd like to be closer to Ellen. I'll stay here until my lease runs out, so I'll have plenty of time to go through my things. After thirty-some-odd years in the same apartment, it's gonna be a big job." Ellen was coming to help her move. "She asked if she can sublet your apartment so she can be here— Only if you're going to be away with your new friend, of course."

This arrangement would buy him time while he considered his options. Knowing that Bridget was weighing the possibility of a much bigger move, all the way across the Atlantic, was giving him both comfort and distress.

In his jeans pocket, Will had a vintage blue Lucite ring he'd bought from an antique shop in Brooklyn a few days before. The blue matched Ronaldo's tail feathers, which Will thought was a nice touch.

When the road test was over, Will asked Frank to drop him at the nursery, where he found Emma sitting at the cash register, going through receipts. Will brushed the water off his hair, went around the counter, and kissed her before either one of them said anything.

"I feel like celebrating," he said.

"Aren't we doing that in about . . ." she said, checking the clock on the wall, "four hours?"

"Let's start early," he said, getting his wallet out. "Look who just passed his driver's test."

She laughed.

"No, really," he said. "I haven't been officially licensed since I was a teenager."

"You daredevil," she said. "I guess all you need now is a car."

Will hadn't forgotten that getting the license was only half the battle of becoming a driver.

"Is Bridget worried about the weather?" Emma asked. "One forecast said the rain would taper off by the afternoon, but another said the exact opposite." She sighed, putting the sales receipts in a folder as an employee walked by with a bag of fertilizer. "Predicting the future isn't easy."

At the word "future," Will reached in his pocket. "I brought you something." He pulled the ring out and instantly regretted that he was giving it to her at work—not romantic at all—and that it wasn't presented in a nice box. All he had was a limp, little drawstring cloth baggie. It looked pathetic and unworthy of her. She'd already looked down and seen it in his hand, saying, "What's that?"

He had not, he realized, thought this through. Should he open it himself or let her do it? He should open it, probably, and show it to her, while telling her what was on his mind. He handed the pouch to her instead and heard the words come out of his mouth: "It's just a little something I picked up for you."

Well, shit, aren't you a coward.

She opened the bag, saying, "Oooooh, pretty," and casually slipped the ring on her finger.

"You like it?"

"I love it. It's very *me*." She held her hand up and admired it. "Thank you."

"You're welcome."

"Should we go home and start getting ready? I need to be at Bridget's early enough to make sure all the arrangements are where—"

"Wait, back to the ring for a sec," Will said. "What if I didn't buy it on a whim?"

She pulled him toward her. "Are we going steady now?"

"I hope so," he said. "I mean, yes, actually. I was thinking . . . I was thinking I might want to move here. I was wondering how you'd feel about that."

If Emma had had an erection, Will was pretty sure he'd just watched her lose it. She pulled back from him, looking skeptical, squeamish even.

"Or not," he said, wishing he could take it back. "It was just an idea. Too soon?"

"You'd leave New York?" she said. "You love it there. You talk about it literally all the time."

"I think I love you more." Bridget often accused him of being repressed, but here he was, sharing his feelings and finding it extraordinarily easy to do so.

"Will." Emma leaned toward him and put her hands on his shoulders. "If there's one thing I've learned," she said, "it's that you can't plant something where it doesn't belong. You should never, for example, stick a Nordic spruce in the Australian bush."

"That sounds overtly sexual," Will said. "You're saying I can't adapt?"

"I'm saying I don't know if this is the right environment for you. What would you do here?"

"So little faith in me and my skills," he said with mock weariness. "I've got options here, a few actually, and, if I'm lucky, a steadier income and less scrabbling for work. I could teach at a school. And I can read books, take walks. Cook and meet people. Build a life . . ."

"What about your apartment? The perfect one-bedroom in the West Village that you said you'd never leave unless you were in a coffin?"

"I'm going to have to move soon anyway since my neighborhood has become upmarket and extortionate, and in the meantime, my neighbor's daughter wants to sublet it."

"So what are you proposing exactly?" she asked. She didn't seem appalled, just curious. "Are you asking to move in with me?"

Will was not asking that. It didn't seem feasible. Emma's place wasn't big enough for the two of them and their pets, and he didn't want to feel like he was invading what was really her space. "I could look for a place on my own for now, or, I was thinking, we could find a place together, if you want." Will had spent some time on Zillow already and was trying not to be discouraged by Litchfield prices, which weren't cheap either.

"I guess we could," she said, "when you're ready."

"When *you're* ready," he said, kissing her hand. "I'm ready now. I'm ready for the whole thing. I know it's only been a summer, but do you— Would you ever consider marrying me?"

Emma looked down at the ring, spinning it around her finger. Will had the feeling he'd gone too far now; he'd scared her off and wanted to backtrack. He wished he'd stuck to cohabitating and left the marriage talk for another day.

"Here's the thing, Will," she said. "It's not *completely* out of the question."

That sounded pretty bad, and yet he felt hopeful. "No?"

"There's a catch."

"I don't mind catches," said Will.

"You might mind this one."

Will waited, praying she wasn't going to say something about polyamory or cults or, worst of all, a desire to have children. "I won't do anything official," she said. "I won't sign papers or go to a church, wear a white dress or make vows in front of any sort of religious leader or civil employee. I hate any kind of legal registrations, documents, all that bullshit, with the exception of your new driver's license, of course. But if we could figure out what it means between us? And throw a little party to celebrate?" She looked at the ring and smiled. "Yeah. I'll 'marry' you."

She used air quotes on the word "marry," but Will kind of liked that. What they had was original, something unique between the two of them. It was even better, he decided, than getting married without air quotes.

Will's first call was, of course, to his best friend. Bridget paused long enough to take in all that his news entailed. And although she sounded happy for him, she was also totally distracted, which was understandable given that two hundred people were showing up at her house in a matter of hours, and the rain had been falling steadily with no indication of letting up.

"Can you guys come over?" she asked. "Like as soon as you can?"

They got dressed for the wedding and drove through a downpour to her house.

When they arrived, Bridget was standing near the doorway to the barn, dressed in what looked like a German farm girl costume, waving them in. Will, in his high-end rented tux, opened an umbrella and took Emma's arm while she lifted up the hem of her blue dress, and they walked across the driveway. He closed the umbrella once they reached the tented pathway, decorated beautifully with greenery and flowers, Emma's handiwork.

The barn was transformed. The walls were bright, despite the storm clouds; the chandeliers were sparkling, and dozens of elegantly set tables were arranged to leave enough room for dancing. Candles were waiting to be lit.

"You look amazing," said Emma, walking up to Bridget and admiring her dress, an outfit that was far from Bridget's normal style.

"The hills are alive," Bridget said. "Do you think Lottie is playing some kind of awful joke on me?"

"It's a little early for the Oktoberfest, isn't it?" said Will.

"Wait till you see Oscar." Bridget started to laugh, but then stopped, sucking in her breath. "I have to give credit to Gavin's wife for the fact that my dress fits. I couldn't have worn it if it weren't for her." She was happy, Will noted, flushed with excitement. "The flowers are so beautiful," she said. "I came out to admire them, but it started raining like hell, and I got trapped."

"Where is everybody?" Will asked.

"Getting beautiful," said Bridget. "Gwen's driving up with Hans; we've called a truce apparently, but he's still leaving tonight right after the party. He's no fun."

"The rest of us will make up for it."

"Do you need anything?" said Emma. "Put us to work."

Will looked around the room, seeing the stage Kevin had built for them, front and center, a stage he wouldn't be performing on. "How can we help?"

Bridget took Emma's hand and looked at the blue band on her finger. Then she led them over to the bar, handing them each a glass of champagne. "I want to congratulate you," she said. "How wonderful you found each other, and here of all places."

Lightning struck, followed by a rumble of thunder and a gust of wind.

"I can't believe this weather," said Emma. "After the driest summer on record, it rains today of all days."

"I'm not worried about the storm," said Bridget.

Will thought she should be. The power could go out. It had happened countless times before.

"But I do have a *really* big favor to ask." She was holding her breath, and Will couldn't tell if it was because her dress was too tight or something else. "I wanted to tell you before anyone else: I've decided that if they offer me the job in London, I'm taking it."

Will felt a jolt of pain in his chest, knowing how happy she'd be there, fitting right in to a life without him. "You'll get the spot," he said.

"That's the problem." Bridget looked concerned. "If I get it, I can't keep this house sitting here."

Will felt the air go out of the room; he was already losing one home he loved, and now he would lose another. He rued the day he'd ever met that pushy Realtor in the grocery store.

"It would be a huge favor to me," Bridget was saying, "if you two would move in here. I wondered if you might be willing to look after the place for a few years. You wouldn't pay rent, of course, because you'd be caretakers."

Will glanced over at Emma; she looked stunned.

"There's a catch," said Bridget. "A few actually."

"We don't mind catches," said Emma. "Do we, Will?"

"I'd like to leave the guesthouse open for the kids," Bridget said. "Gwen got Isabelle a job interview in New York, but I think she'll end up back here. I was thinking you could take over the main house. I can empty out my clothes and stuff out of my room and move it all up to the loft. You'd call Kevin if you have maintenance issues, and I'll pay for any repairs, of course."

Will tried to keep his composure. "This," he said to Bridget, with a straight face, "is a lot to ask."

"I know it is," she said, meeting his expression with a serious one of her own. "Take your time, think it over. You'd have to take care of the piano, which, as you know, needs a lot of attention."

"There's *nothing* to think over," Emma said.

"Are you sure?" Bridget asked. "Because there's more," she said. "I need someone to drive my old car around, to keep it going."

"I suppose I can do that," said Will.

"And Henry Higgins would like to stay here. How does Ronaldo feel about cats?"

"He *loves* cats," said Emma. "I don't think he's ever seen one before, but we'll make it work."

"A cat, too?" Will teased. As soon as he landed a job, he would buy Bridget that pricey bat weathervane he'd seen in the antique store at the beginning of the summer. Kevin and Elliot would install it on the cupola before Bridget returned for a visit. They would sit on the porch together; nothing would change. Not really.

"I think Hudson wouldn't mind living here," said Bridget.

"True," said Will. "I could speak to him about it."

Emma smacked him on the arm.

"So, what do you think? Is it a deal?" Bridget asked, pretending she really didn't know what their answer would be.

Will had never experienced such a rush of opposing feelings. He was the most fortunate man on earth, and yet his best friend was leaving him. Forsyth was over. This moment marked the end of an era.

"Yes?" said Bridget.

"Yes," he said, hugging her. "All right."

Lightning flashed again, thunder boomed, and then Will heard another sound, like wind filling the sail of a ship, and to their amazement, they watched as the long tent covering the walkway lifted off the ground and flew away.

30

M y dear friends, if you'll indulge me, may I have everyone's attention please . . . Yes? Outstanding.

Although the rain has indeed stopped, it appears we're marooned together for a few more hours until we find a way to get you all across the rather sizable moat that has formed around the barn. Unless you happen to have worn very tall galoshes or came attired in waders, you'll have a muddy go of it trying to reach your cars. Fortunately, there's plenty of champagne and a magnificent wedding cake we'll be serving soon, so we should all be quite comfortable to remain here on our island for as long as we wish. If anyone is in particular need of a rescue (or a loo), I've been told that Kevin, a strapping young lad, is constructing a makeshift ark, much like Noah himself, and will soon be able to ferry anyone across to dry land.

———————◇———————

Bertrand Russell said, "Man needs, for his happiness, not only the enjoyment of this or that, but hope, and enterprise, and change." The music we've just played for you is a piece I wrote over sixty years ago—*sixty*? I can hardly believe it—a piece that was arranged (brilliantly, I might add) by Will Harris, steadfast, loyal friend of the family. So, let's have a round of applause for Will, and for my daughter Bridget and their old friend Gavin Glantz for this wonderful new arrangement, or *rearrangement*, of a composition that will now and forever exemplify to me the recipe for happiness: hope, and enterprise, and change.

The composition—titled *Synchronicity*, although I never dreamed how perfectly apt that name would become—is an example of the way music has directed the course of my life. The piece was performed at Carnegie Hall as the culmination of a composers' retreat . . . at the exact same time, I might add, that the Summer Olympics were getting underway in Rome. As I entered the concert hall that night, so did a young woman named Sophia, who soon became my wife. But—what you may not know—is that on that very same night, a stormy August evening much like this one, I also met Charlotte (or Lottie, to those of us who know and love her), this wonderful woman sitting by my side tonight. She, too, attended that concert to hear a sublime waltz that her husband, Johannes, composed. A wonder, isn't it, that I happened to meet both of my wives at the premiere of *Synchronicity*, a concert that brought us together in a way that was, yes, serendipitous, but also perfectly timed; complicated and yet marvelous, much like life itself: marvelous and complicated.

Playing *Synchronicity* again all these years later, in its new iteration, and watching that little boy there—that's your son, Gavin, yes?—as he was dancing so happily to it, reminds me that life is a perfect combination of chance and choreography. Much like the baroque dances I had in mind when I wrote the piece. Imagine: a group of people come together and delight in the act of rearranging themselves into new configurations. One person turns, leaving a space, upsetting the arrangement, but the other dancers follow suit and they all align themselves anew. For a moment they are all in motion, shifting with a chassé or a crossover, until a new constellation forms, and then there's a moment of equilibrium . . . before it begins again. Friedrich Schiller described this movement as "sweet chaos" and "wild confusion," until, finally, he said, "disentangled glides the knot," giving way to order and merriment. When you engage in such a dance, you never lose sight of the purpose: "the enjoyment of this or that." With music as a guide for the synchronized movement of the group, knots untangle, and the dancers glide. Such is life.

Now, is everyone's glass full? Good. Because Seneca, the great Roman philosopher and dramatist, said, "The last drink delights the toper, the glass which souses him and puts the finishing touch on his drunkenness. Life is most delightful when it is on the downward slope."

Why, some of you are wondering, would anyone marry so late in life, on the "downward slope," as it were? I certainly didn't anticipate finding love again. There I was, enjoying life's party, but sitting out the dance. Lottie was doing the same, until we suddenly found ourselves swept up in a "sweet chaos" of our own, a "wild confusion," spurred on by the music of our common goals, our mutual affection, and a simple wish to stoke our vigor and passion again. I like to think Sophia and Johannes would be happy Lottie and I found our way to each other as the world around us shifted, and we formed our new constellation. Seneca also said, "I have lived! Every morning I arise, I receive a bonus." Lottie has brought me the bonus of a most astonishing, unanticipated second act, a new chapter I welcome with great excitement.

Who remembers Tennyson's poem "Ulysses"? When I was young, I thought that verse was expressing sentiments reserved for a hero. But as I approach ninety, I see that a "hungry heart" and a longing "not to yield" until the bitter end should be the attitude of any great man. Of any man at all, in fact—or of any *woman*, yes, Isabelle and Oscar. (My thoroughly modern grandchildren do their best to keep me from old-fashioned, sexist turns of phrase.) Of anyone *at all*, I mean to say. And although Lottie and I may be on the delightful downward slope of our life, we want "to strive, to seek, to find." To love and to live.

My summer did not begin in the manner of a hero or a great man. Oh, no. Simply put, I fell flat on my "bloomin' arse," was strapped to a gurney and rushed to hospital with all the ceremony of a cow being taken to slaughter. No, no, laugh away. I, too, find it amusing. After that mortification, as I was doing my damnedest to prove to everyone that I am of very sound mind and body, I somehow managed—and I still can't believe it myself—to light my own blasted house on fire. Unfortunate business, that. I got swept away by the fiery drama (no pun intended) of "Jupiter" from Holst's *Planets* and started the blaze with my own cravat. In my defense, the piece is spectacular. I insist that each and every one of you—especially the composers here—go home tonight and listen to it with the volume turned high. Just make sure you stay far enough away from any halogen light fixtures, that's my advice.

Isabelle, my granddaughter, asked me an unusual question a few weeks ago. She asked if I think secrets "damage the soul." I had to think about that, and I've got an answer now— I'm sorry? Ah, all right then, it seems we have the primary source of that theory right here in the room with us. Yes, well, I was about to say, I think there's some truth to it. Secrets can be bothersome things that needle and render one disquieted. So, on the topic of fires and secrets: I will tell one now in hopes of setting minds at ease, a secret that, like a phoenix, came out of the ashes of my brief stint as an arsonist. Two paintings that belonged to my late wife were incinerated in my bedroom. They were valuable, quite valuable, actually. And although my daughters were surely devastated to know these two masterpieces went up in flames, they were too kind to make me feel badly about destroying them. Well, now, with relief and pleasure I'll share a happy secret I just discovered: the paintings were reproductions, insured for only $500 apiece. Sophia, believing the Turner and Gainsborough belonged in the public view, swapped them out with reproductions—*I* never noticed the difference—and donated the originals to the National Gallery in London, where they await your visit.

Conveniently, Bridget is traveling to England in two weeks' time to audition for the London Philharmonic, and I couldn't be more confident that she'll earn a spot. My hometown, as she well knows, is a magical place. Samuel Johnson once said, "When a man is tired of London, he is tired of life." Bridget, dear, while you're in that magnificent city, relishing everything life in London has to offer, I would ask you to keep a close eye on my friend Nicholas—the scholar sitting over there, scribbling notes in his Moleskine, good man. He will be returning to Oxford soon to finish writing his biography of me . . . You are to make sure he writes *only* flattering things! Understood? Excellent.

Gwen— Ah, that reminds me, before I continue, let's all express our gratitude to Steep Canyon Rangers and, of course, Steve Martin, for treating us to the joyful bluegrass we heard through the worst part of the storm. Thank you so much, Gwen, for inviting them. And for delivering Hans safely to us. My daughter Gwen collects friends the way some people collect beautiful things. Bridget, on the other hand, is more like a curator. I like to think I am a bit of both. I love bringing new people into my life, and I treasure my old friends. Hans, you represent both. Your father and I had a friendship that was the longest and closest of my life. I will endeavor to be as good a friend to you as he was to me.

And where is Marge? I raise a glass to you as well, my friend. Whatever would I have done without dear Marge? She even got me to the church on time tonight "spruced up and lookin' in me prime," like old Alfred P. Doolittle.

I look around at the faces here, and I see connections everywhere. Friends connected to friends. Artists connected to artists, past and present. Our world seems much less vast and cold, much more like home, when we place all of humanity in varying constellations, connecting them to one another, moving them about, synchronizing them to dance the allemande in our minds. Maybe I'll write a new piece for that purpose.

I'm sure my tireless assistant, Jackie—who has had little time off this summer—would love to know why I still write music, study music, play and teach music. I'll tell you why, Jackie: because, as Tennyson said, "Death closes all: but something ere the end, some work of noble note, may yet be done."

"A Work of Noble Note." *That* will be the title of the next piece I write. No, it will be a coda!—a final chapter for *Synchronicity*. I'll write it for Bridget, Will, and Gavin, the original Forsyth Trio, and I will call on them to play it for us at our one-year anniversary party, right here next August, in this very barn with the moat around it, which we will either fill with alligators or use for punting. But not both. Agreed? Agreed? Agreed? Good, all three said yes. You witnessed that, right? And I expect you all to be here as well. Same time next year, in this grand old barn whose roof has held up miraculously in the deluge. Lottie and I will be here to welcome you all with open arms.

In the meantime, Lottie, let's begin this coda of our own, this next and, yes, final section of our dance. As Goethe said, *"Und lieben, Götter, welch ein Glück!"* "And to love, oh gods, oh, what a prize!"

Lottie, my dear, to love you is a most marvelous, unexpected prize. *Prost*, my darling.

Cheers, my friends. Cheers to you all.

It's time to dance!

I cannot rest from travel: I will drink
Life to the lees . . .

—Alfred, Lord Tennyson, "Ulysses"

CODA

September

Bridget stands in the terminal of John F. Kennedy Airport, staring up at the electronic board, looking for her British Airways flight to London. She finds it (after Lisbon, before Madrid) and goes to check her bags, draping her Burberry trench coat over her arm. The woman at the counter hands her two business class tickets for the flight.

She makes her way through security and is sitting on a bench, putting her shoes back on, when her phone rings.

"I think Eliza's depressed," Isabelle says. "She feels very sad without Henry, and I'm not sure she can handle the daily grind of the city anymore. Do you think she needs antidepressants?"

Bridget knows her daughter is more self-aware than she lets on. "Tell Eliza to give her choices serious consideration and remind her what she learned about herself this summer."

"I'm not used to being so alone anymore," Isabelle admits.

Me neither. Bridget sits up straight and puts her cello on her back. "Trust yourself. You have excellent instincts, and if you miss Kevin, call him and say so. What time's your interview?"

"Ten tomorrow morning. I appreciate Gwen for the contact, but I don't think I want to live in the city. And I like Kevin."

"You had a very happy summer with him."

"But was that real life?"

Bridget thinks she will remember this past summer as the most real her life has ever been. "Of course it was."

"Oscar and Matt and I are meeting in Connecticut this weekend. We're having lunch with Peter Latham."

Bridget is sorry to miss this occasion, but she also knows that on some level, it has nothing to do with her. "I can't wait to hear how it goes. What are you hoping will happen?"

"I'm hoping for the start of something. And I wouldn't mind a little advice. I want a life like his, satisfying work and a sense of community. Maybe I want a reason to live near Kevin. Oscar's so happy these days, I don't know that he wants or needs anything."

An image of Oscar and Matt dancing at the wedding comes into her mind; Bridget hopes the photographer got a good picture.

"Will you text me when you get to Heathrow?" says Isabelle.

"Of course, the second I land." The time difference will complicate things, but Bridget doesn't mention it. "I love you," she says.

"Love you, too, Mom."

After they hang up, Bridget walks in the direction of her gate. There, on the front table of Hudson News, is Sterling's book with a 50-percent-off sticker smack in the middle of its drab cover. Bridget feels sorry for him; his book looks sad and unloved.

A few steps to the left, she spots a familiar, bright yellow, cheerful cover. Juliette is in good company with the other celebrated self-help gurus, nutritionists, and psychologists. Bridget picks the book up, smiling at the picture, the image a stark contrast to the sight of Juliette and her son scarfing down a big slice of rich vanilla-cream wedding cake. Gavin was elated to learn that he wasn't the twins' father—*only because*, he was quick to explain, they'd found out that morning that Juliette was pregnant with their second child. "I'm getting too old for this parenting racket," he said, his face turning slightly red, and then he quickly added, "Not that your children would have needed anything from me at this point, but—"

"I know what you mean," Bridget had said.

"Congratulations," Will added, patting him on the back. Bridget had noticed Will was making an effort to be especially kind to Gavin.

The afternoon before the wedding, the Forsyth Trio rehearsed together, Bridget reveling in how familiar and yet fresh it felt. And then the next night, at the reception, as they were taking their places, Will surprised them both by bringing her father onto the stage, offering him the piano bench, and walking away. She'd never played with her father before and fought back tears as she trained her eyes on him, instead of on Will, waiting for him to inhale on the third beat, with a nod of his head, to mark the beginning.

Bridget walks to her gate with Juliette's book sticking out of her tote bag and sits down to make her last phone calls. She calls Oscar first, and then her father. She calls Marge and Jackie. And finally she calls Gwen, who has been impossible to reach since the wedding.

"I hate you for leaving," says Gwen, "but I'll fly over for your first concert. Just tell me when to be there."

"How's Hans?" Bridget asks.

"*Hans?* How would I know how Hans is?"

The pots and pans hanging directly under the loft had been clanging together the night of the wedding after the last guests had finally left. "If you don't want to tell me about your hot night with him, then don't," says Bridget. "But you're not fooling me. I'm just glad you got him to stay overnight."

"Fine, yes, I took one for the team. *Hans*. What a ridiculous name. You know how much I hate him," says Gwen. "I always have."

"Yes, you get very worked up whenever his name is mentioned."

"He's opinionated and obnoxious. And he's a workaholic. He's divorcing a terrible person."

"Sounds familiar. And?"

Gwen pauses. "We've got great chemistry," she says, "and I'm really ticked off about it."

When Gwen and Hans were dancing, Bridget saw Lottie and her dad smiling at them, whispering, conspiring. Had Lottie predicted this? she wondered. Standing in the barn's open doorway, the rainy night making wonderful drama behind her, Bridget watched the joyful scene unfold.

———◈———

Bridget hears her flight being called, sends kisses to Gwen, and boards the plane, putting her cello on the aisle seat beside her. Once she settles in, the flight attendant stops at her row.

"Would your instrument mind being upgraded to first class?"

"Excuse me?"

"There's a gentleman who says he knows you, and he'd like to switch seats with your cello." The flight attendant points up the aisle.

Unbuckling her seat belt, Bridget gets up, walking to the front of the plane.

Nicholas Donahue is sitting in 3A, a glass of champagne in his hand. "Hello," he says.

Bridget smiles. "Fancy seeing you here."

He stands and steps into the aisle, ducking his head to avoid the open overhead bin. "I saw you earlier at the gate and waved, but you were on the phone. I didn't want to interrupt."

"That's a pretty nice seat you've got," she says. "Why on earth would you downgrade?"

"I would consider it an improvement actually," he says. "I was hoping we could keep each other company. Unless you'd rather be alone."

Bridget tries not to be too obvious about how electrified she feels to be near him, but finds she's unable to control her smile.

"Hmmm," Bridget says. "Is this an interview? Are you going to make me talk about my father for seven hours?"

Nicholas holds up his hand to make a pledge. "I'll never mention his name, all the way to the UK. In fact, I'll probably sleep for a few hours. I have to catch a train to Oxford as soon as we land."

She feels shy but asks anyway, "What's the rush? You could spend the day in London with me. We could have dinner?"

"I don't know," he says. "You see, I heard recently, according to Samuel Johnson, life is very tired of London."

Bridget squints at him. "I'm pretty sure that's not what he said."

"When a man is tired of life, he's especially weary of London."

"Still wrong," she says with a shake of her head.

He pretends to concentrate. "'When a man is tired of London, he's tired of life.'"

Bridget snaps her fingers, saying with her best British accent, "By George, he's got it."

"Dinner would be smashing actually. I so enjoyed dancing with you, and if it's not painfully obvious," he says, shrugging helplessly, "I rather like you."

Bridget takes a moment to appreciate the word "smashing" used unironically in conversation.

A woman goes by them with a carry-on far too large to be the acceptable size, and they move to the side, pressed together until she passes them.

"How about we start our journey with a glass of champagne," he says. "And later, if you find me dull or irksome, you can take my seat here, and I'll keep your cello company for the rest of the flight."

"I don't find you irksome or dull," she says, her face feeling warm, "not at all."

They get Bridget's cello settled in its first class seat, and sit side by side a few rows behind it. By the time the plane is taxiing, their shoulders are touching as they talk, and he's smiling at her, as if she is the prize, the bonus the day has brought him.

Her phone pings with a message from Will: *Have a nice flight, friend. Your house is in good hands. We're in heaven. Love you.* He sends a picture of him beside Emma, holding up glasses of wine on the porch.

She sends a selfie back, Nicholas's temple pressed to hers. *Synchronicity!* she writes. *Love you, too.*

Before the plane takes off, Bridget tightens her seat belt and looks out the window, the words of her father's wedding toast, a recipe for happiness, filling her with optimism, driving her on. As the plane accelerates, she cherishes this moment in time, this threshold of an adventure, the start of something new.

On your mark, get set, go!

ACKNOWLEDGMENTS

I'm very grateful to Emily Bestler at Emily Bestler Books and to everyone at Atria/Simon and Schuster (especially Lara Jones and Megan Rudloff) for all the work they do to conjure a book into being. I had the world's best production and copy editors, Sonja Singleton and Mary Beth Constant, whose knowledge and attention to detail, musical, grammatical, and otherwise, amazed me. And thank you to Ella Laytham and James Iacobelli for creating a cover that captures the tone of the book so well. I feel so lucky and proud to be part of the EBB team. Thank you!

My agent Linda Chester is a champion. Thank you, Linda, along with Laurie Fox and Gary Jaffe, for your confidence in me, your friendship, and your support. I'm also so grateful to my fantastic publicist Kathleen Carter of Kathleen Carter Communications.

A million thanks to Anika Streitfeld for her patience (seriously, *endless* patience) and for her humor, high expectations, and brilliance. Working with her is a pleasure, and I appreciate everything she has taught me.

I have an incredibly funny, lively musical family. Sending love and gratitude to my husband, David, for surrounding me with classical music and for reading so many early drafts, traveling with me to new places, and keeping our (middle-aged) life fun and unpredictable. And sending love to my sons, Alex, Andrew, and Luke, for all the inspiration, comedy, and encouragement, with special thanks to Luke for his keen eyes and vast knowledge of classical music. My family and my family in-law are the best early readers, party throwers, audience members, book buyers, website designers, publicists, and cheerleaders ever—thanks to you all for your love and support, especially to my sisters, Wendy O'Sullivan and Laurie Mitchell, my brother-in-law Brent Woods, my nieces and nephews, and, of course, my father, Jere Mitchell.

For their expertise (in chamber music, parrot behavior, sperm donation, and barn restoration, in that order), I am so grateful to authors Marcia Butler, Kira Jane Buxton, Julie Clark, and Amanda Stauffer for answering my many questions. And I'm so indebted to all the wonderful fiction writers I've been fortunate enough to get to know and love in New York City and beyond, especially the partiers of the NY Writers Salon and the authors with whom I've and traveled and done events. You are endlessly understanding, generous, and entertaining and you always help me see the humor in this crazy life. Thank you, M. Elizabeth Lee, Suzanne Rindell, Caroline Leavitt, Marcy Dermansky, Elinor Lipman, Stephen McCauley, Fiona Davis, Lynda Cohen Loigman, Grant Ginder, Georgia Clark, Jenni Walsh, Lauren Willig, Jamie Brenner, Elyssa Friedland, Susie Orman Schnall, Rochelle Weinstein, Crystal King, Sara Goudarzi, Lisa Barr, Brian Platzer, Sara Goudarzi, Laura Catherine Brown, to name only a few.

Speaking of generosity, many thanks to April Benasich and Jamie Melcher for the many invitations to their home in Litchfield County, Connecticut; their beautiful property was always on my mind when I was writing scenes set in "the Castle."

My hilarious, lovely friends are always willing to share funny stories, work on plot holes, talk me down, and cheer me up. Hugs to Amy and Jonathan White, Hilton Als, Felice Kaufmann, Donna James, Jon Virden, Dawn Charles, and my beloved B-CC crowd, Liz and Matthew King, Liz Lee, Dacel Casey, the Gan clan, Candy and Mitchell Moss, Julie Kutner, Anna Salajegheh, Brett Burns, John Kim, Amy Weinberg and Norbert Hornstein, Ana Blohm and Keith Sigel, Lindsay Ratowsky, Theo Theoharis, Karina Schultz, Ashley Cooper Bianchi, Heidi Dolan, Maria White, and Tracy Tisler. I'm also very happy to have recently reconnected with so many class-mates from Kent ('84) and Hockaday ('83) who are just as wonderful as adults as they were when we were kids.

And I have to give a special thanks to Andrea Peskind-Katz (Great Thoughts, Great Readers) for her friendship, good advice, terrific sense of humor, and shared love of guac.

Many thanks to BookSparks for their marketing know-how and non-stop Instagram parties. And I'm so grateful to the librarians, book sellers, and online book enthusiasts/bloggers who put novels like mine in the hands of readers . . . from Interabang in TX to Warwick's in CA, from House of Books in CT to Pamela Klinger-Horn (Literature Lovers' Night Out/Excelsior Bay Books/Valley Book Sellers) in MN, from Book Culture and Shakespeare & Co in NYC to Belmont Books in MA, from Suzanne Weinstein Leopold to Ann-Marie Nieves, from Robin Kall Homonoff and Emily Homonoff to Lauren Margolin, from Cindy Burnett to Zibby Owens, along with Jamie Rosenblit, Kristy Barrett, Christina Powers, Kathy Lewison, Melissa Amster, Betsy Blumberg Maxwell, Cindy Roessel . . . There are far too many wonderful book people to list here, all of whom do such a wonderful service to authors and readers. Thank you!

And above all, thank you, readers.

And a special shout-out to Tucker, the lapdog next to my laptop, for being the best writing companion.

No comment on my cats.

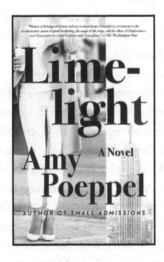